Praise for Barbara Kyle's Novels

"Riveting Tudor drama in the bestselling vein of Philippa Gregory."
—*USA Today* on *The Queen's Exiles*

"A bold and original take on the Tudors that dares to be different. Enjoy the adventure!"
—*New York Times* bestselling author Susanna Kearsley on *The Queen's Exiles*

"Barbara Kyle owes me two nights of sleep for writing such an enthralling book that I couldn't stop turning the pages until the final mesmerizing sentence. . . . The reader takes a galloping horseback ride through the feverishly patriotic and brutally violent spectacle of the Netherlands in 1572, only to slide breathlessly out of the saddle at the story's conclusion, craving the next installment of the riveting Thornleigh saga."
—Christine Trent on *The Queen's Exiles*

"This moving adventure pulses with Shakespearean passions: love and heartbreak, risk and valour, and loyalties challenged in a savage time. Fenella Doorn, savvy and brave, is an unforgettable heroine."
—Antoni Cimolino, Artistic Director of the Stratford Festival, on *The Queen's Exiles*

"Fact and fiction are expertly interwoven in this fast-paced saga . . . this story exudes authenticity."
—*Historical Novels Review* on *Blood Between Queens*

"Gifts the reader with an intimate look into the minds and hearts of the royal and great of Elizabeth's England. Again, Barbara Kyle reigns!"
—*New York Times* bestselling author Karen Harper on *Blood Between Queens*

"Starts strong and doesn't let up . . . Kyle's latest is extremely accessible for readers unfamiliar with the series, and the Scottish uprising, a little explored piece of Tudor history, enlivens a well-worn genre."
—*Publishers Weekly* on *The Queen's Gamble*

"Riveting, heady, glorious, inspired!"
—*New York Times* bestselling author Susan Wiggs on *The Queen's Lady*

"Weaves a fast-paced plot through some ⌷ English history. There is romance, adv⌷ science . . . what more could one want?"
—Judith Merkle on *The ⌷*

Books by Barbara Kyle

The Traitor's Daughter
The Queen's Exiles
Blood Between Queens
The Queen's Gamble
The Queen's Captive
The King's Daughter
The Queen's Lady

The
TRAITOR'S DAUGHTER

BARBARA KYLE

KENSINGTON BOOKS
www.kensingtonbooks.com

KENSINGTON BOOKS are published by

Kensington Publishing Corp.
119 West 40th Street
New York, NY 10018

All Kensington titles, imprints, and distributed lines are available at special quantity discounts for bulk purchases for sales promotion, premiums, fund-raising, educational, or institutional use.

Special book excerpts or customized printings can also be created to fit specific needs. For details, write or phone the office of the Kensington Sales Manager: Attn. Sales Department. Kensington Publishing Corp., 119 West 40th Street, New York, NY 10018. Phone: 1-800-221-2647.

Kensington and the K logo Reg. U.S. Pat. & TM Off.

eISBN-13: 978-1-61773-208-9
eISBN-10: 1-61773-208-7
First Kensington Electronic Edition: June 2015

ISBN-13: 978-0-7582-7326-0
ISBN-10: 0-7582-7326-6
First Kensington Trade Paperback Printing: June 2015

10 9 8 7 6 5 4 3 2 1

Printed in the United States of America

HISTORICAL PREFACE

In 1582, Elizabeth Tudor, age forty-nine, had ruled England for twenty-three years, and under her reign the country had enjoyed peace and increasing prosperity. But her throne, and her life, were under constant threat. Religion was the cause.

Elizabeth's first act as Queen in 1559 had been the Act of Supremacy, which, without violence to Catholics, had made the realm Protestant and confirmed the monarch's position as head of the English church. Elizabeth herself advocated religious tolerance, saying she had "no desire to make windows into men's souls," but she knew that strong leadership was needed to restrain the growing antagonism between Puritans and Catholics, and she hoped her religious settlement would unify them. It did not. Neither side was satisfied. The Puritans felt she had not taken England far enough away from "papist" customs, while Catholics considered her a heretic and found the concept of a woman as head of a church grotesque. They believed her Catholic cousin, Mary Stuart, Queen of Scotland, was the rightful claimant to the English throne, one who acknowledged the supreme authority of the pope.

In 1568 Mary was deposed in her own country and fled to England seeking Elizabeth's help, but Elizabeth, anxious that Catholics would rally around the Queen of Scots, put her under house arrest. Mary's supporters in England and abroad were outraged. Mary herself, though comfortably lodged in a series of castle suites, chafed at her captivity and secretly communicated with leaders who were eager to free her by insurrection or invasion—or both. In 1570 Pope Pius V issued an edict of excommunication against Elizabeth that called on Catholics throughout Christendom to rise up and depose her. This emboldened English Catholics in their opposition to the Church of England, and many refused to attend their parish churches. Known as "recusants" (from the Latin *recusare*, to refuse), these dissenters faced heavy fines.

In France, in August 1572, on the feast day of St. Bartholomew, the country's Catholic rulers instigated a savage attack on French Protestants, the Huguenots. In a convulsion of religious violence, over three thousand men and women were slaughtered in Paris by mobs of their Catholic neighbors. The carnage spread throughout France, claiming seventy thousand Huguenot lives. The St. Bartholomew's Day Massacre sent shock waves through England. The Protestant island nation, its population far smaller than that of powerful France, was galvanized by fear.

Elizabeth had at first been lenient with Catholic recusants. But in 1580 the threat to her became dire when Pope Gregory XIII, reinforcing the anathema against her, issued a declaration that it would be no sin to assassinate her. It was a clear license to kill. Assassination plots multiplied. Jesuit infiltrators from abroad fomented insurrection. Mary Stuart's supporters pledged to free her by force of arms. Elizabeth's government leaders discovered and thwarted the plots, but in their acute alarm they became more aggressive in rounding up agitators, real and perceived. Punishments became harsh: no longer mere fines, but imprisonment and, in some cases, death.

By 1582 England, feeling under siege, was in the grip of mind-darkening terror.

"It's all so familiar in our own deplorable time: torture . . . spies and counter-spies, the seminaries of mutually exclusive faiths, the cult of martyrdom, invasion and resistance movements . . . projects for exterminating the liberties of peoples . . . the implacable hates, the use of assassination, the division of families, the riving asunder of friends, and the conflict within the individual conscience itself, which tore men's hearts open."

—A. L. Rowse, *The England of Elizabeth*

❧ 1 ❧

The Prisoner

London: September 1582

Thornleigh House was dark as Kate Lyon closed the door of her bedchamber, careful to be quiet. Cloak in hand, she went quickly down the stairs. Dawn pearled the lancet window halfway down, the sky luminously gray, as gray as the River Thames that flowed past the mansion. Kate glanced out, frustrated that the orchard trees obscured her view of the riverside landing. She could only hope the wherryman was there waiting. She had ordered the wherry last night. At the bottom of the stairs she turned into the great hall as the bell of the nearby Savoy Chapel clanged the hour. Six o'clock. *Two hours to go*, Kate thought. Her journey east to London Bridge would be just two miles, but the flood tide at this hour would slow her so she had to leave plenty of time. Her destination was the Marshalsea prison. Her husband had been a prisoner there for six months. At eight this morning he would be released. Kate was determined to be there.

She whirled her cloak around her shoulders as she crossed the shadowed great hall. The deserted musicians' gallery that overlooked the hall was a black void. Even the tapestries Kate moved past were indistinct, the light too feeble yet to fire their gorgeous silk colors or to illuminate the gold-lettered spines of the books stacked on the dining table. The books were a new shipment from Paris that her grandmother had ordered. Old volumes—they smelled like dust. Having lived in Thornleigh House for six months Kate had become used to its two distinctive smells: old books and fresh roses, her grandmother's twin passions.

She rapped her knuckles lightly three times on the table as she passed, a small ritual developed in her visits here as a child. Always three taps. For luck? She was twenty-two now and did not believe in luck, but some childish habits never die. The Puritans would call it a pagan impulse close to blasphemy. But then Puritans could sniff blasphemy in a summer breeze.

"So you're going?" Her grandmother's voice startled her.

Lady Thornleigh stepped out from the shadows behind the stacked books. Though seventy-two the dowager baroness stood as straight as a sapling. The velvet robe of forest-green she had put on over her nightdress was tied at her narrow waist, and her silver hair, plaited for sleep, curved over her shoulder. Even in the dim light Kate felt her grandmother's dark eyes bore into her own. Kate had hoped to avoid this confrontation. Hoped their truce would hold. Straining for neutrality, she said, "You are up early, my lady."

"You don't have to do this." Her grandmother's voice was stern. A warning.

"Pardon me, but I do." Nothing would stop Kate from meeting Owen when he walked through the prison gates. Her grandmother, though, stood resolutely in her way. "Please let me pass."

"Do you know what you're doing? Don't you understand what your future will be? He will make you an outcast. From society. From our family."

"If I am cast out it is not his doing. Nor my wish." Owen had been arrested in a brewer's cellar for attending a secret Catholic mass—an unlawful act. In disgrace by association, Kate had been snubbed by friends she had known for years.

"But it will be your lot," her grandmother shot back. "Unless you stop."

"I pledged my future at the altar. How can I stop?"

"By removing yourself from his bed and board. By showing that you will have nothing more to do with him. You have been a bride for scarcely seven months, you did not know his true character when you took your marriage vow. Separate yourself from him now, Kate, and all the world will approve."

"All England, you mean." Protestant England. Everywhere else in Europe Catholicism reigned.

"It is the land you live in, child. Its laws must be obeyed."

If only you knew! Kate bit back the words. Secrecy was the life she had chosen now. *Bed and board,* she thought. Of the second, her husband had none. The crippling fine handed down with his imprisonment had forced them to sell his modest house on Monkwell Street by London Wall. Owen was homeless. Kate would have been, too, but for the charity of Lady Thornleigh. Kate's father, Baron Adam Thornleigh, had made it clear she was not welcome at his house.

She lifted her head high. There was no turning back. "I am no child, my lady. I married the man my husband is, and I love the man he is. My life is with him. Nothing you say, or all the world can say, will change my mind."

Lady Thornleigh's eyes narrowed in a challenge. "And you expect to come back here? With him? Expect me to keep a felon under my roof?"

"If you will let us bide until we can find lodging, yes. If not, we'll shift for ourselves."

"You'll shift . . . What impudence!" Her tone conveyed indignation, but Kate now saw something quite different creep over her grandmother's face: the ghost of a smile. "Ah, my dear," the lady went on, "you sound like my young self." She stepped close and enfolded Kate in her arms. "This house will always be open to you, and to your husband. I must say, I admire you."

Kate pulled back, astonished. "Admire?"

"I had to be sure you have the courage." Tenderly, she caressed Kate's cheek, a sad look in her eyes. "You are going to need it."

The mansion was Lady Thornleigh's town house, a home away from her country estate. Its cobbled courtyard faced the Strand while its rose-trellised rear garden and orchard sloped down to meet the Thames. Moving through the garden, Kate gathered her cloak about her, feeling the river's chill dampness on the breeze. At the water stairs she found the wherryman napping in his boat, arms folded. Impatient, she rapped on the stern.

He snuffled awake. Lumbering to his feet, he made an awkward bow in deference. "My lady."

She did not correct him. The grand surroundings and her fine clothes prompted him to call her that, but she was a lady no longer. Mere months ago she had been known as the daughter of a baron. Now she was the wife of a commoner, a felon. A Catholic.

"To Cock Alley Stairs," she directed him. About to step aboard, she took a last glance at the house. *Bless you, Grandmother,* she thought with a grateful smile. A candle flared to life in an upstairs window. A maid coming down to light the kitchen fires, no doubt. The workday was beginning.

"Mistress Lyon?" a high voice asked behind her.

Kate turned. "Yes? Who's there?"

A boy stepped forward. He looked about ten, dirty clothes, hair like a bird's nest. The faint dawn light made a white pallor of his face. He looked unsure, as though cowed by the grandeur of the place, but Kate detected a native boldness in his eyes.

The wherryman cleared his throat. "Sorry for the fright, my lady. The lad was sitting here when I come. Said he was waiting for daylight to go up to you at the house. I told him you was coming down."

The boy held out a sealed letter. "For you, m'lady." The letter was as dirt-smudged as its bearer. Kate hesitated. She was used to receiving covert messages, but from couriers she knew and trusted. Surely her instructions would not come by way of this young stranger? "From my master," the boy added.

She took the letter. "And who might that be?"

"Master Prowse."

She could think of no such person. "A master of chimney sweeps, is he?" she asked with a wry smile. Soot blackened the boy's hands.

He looked puzzled by her jest. "No, m'lady. Master of boys. Schoolmaster."

A memory flickered to life. "Bless my soul, not Master Tobias Prowse? Stooped old man with a wart this side of his nose?"

"Aye, m'lady. The same."

Prowse, the tutor who had taught her and her brother when they were children. It had been years since she'd seen the old man—a lifetime, it felt, given all that had shaken Kate's world since then, but in fact it was just thirteen years ago that she and Robert had sat in their father's study reciting Latin rhymes to Master Prowse. She'd been nine, Robert seven. Even at that age her brother had been more clever with the Latin than she was. A pang of regret squeezed her heart. She hadn't seen Robert in a decade. They had been so close when they were children, inseparable, especially in that frightening time after their traitorous mother had fled with them to Antwerp. Three years later their father had got Kate back, but could not get Robert, and since then their secretive mother had again moved on with the boy, their whereabouts now unknown. It weighted Kate with guilt that she had been the one who got out, leaving Robert to endure a hard exile with their embittered mother. She could never shake the feeling that she should have done more to try to save him.

She looked at the sealed letter. A good old soul, Master Prowse. Old in those long gone days, so he must be ancient now. But why would he be writing to her? Perhaps about Lady Thornleigh's book collection? Her grandmother had been quite public in seeking donated volumes for her ever-expanding library, which she intended to gift to Oxford University. Did old Prowse, feeling his end draw nigh, want to bequeath his humble collection to her? But that was fanciful thinking. More likely the poor man had fallen on hard times and was hoping for charity from Her Ladyship and felt Kate would be his link to her. Well, no doubt his letter would make all clear. She tucked it away in the pocket of her cloak. A petitioner, however deserving, could wait. Owen could not.

The candle in the upstairs window went out. No longer needed, for the pewter light of dawn was gathering strength. Kate dug into the purse at her waist for a coin for the boy. "Where have you come from?" she asked.

"Seaford, m'lady."

The Sussex coast. "That's a long way." She gave him a shilling. His eyes went huge at the overpayment. "How did you come? A farmer's cart?"

"Walked, m'lady."

Over sixty miles, and shod in rough clogs. He was no doubt hungry, too. "Knock at the kitchen door and ask them to give you breakfast. Tell them I said so." He brightened even more at that. She asked if he had a place to lay his head tonight.

He shrugged. "I can shift for m'self."

She had to smile at this echo of her own defiant pride. "I warrant you can." She told him he could sleep in the dovecote in the corner of the garden wall. "But stay clear of the steward," she warned. The man was a Puritan and known to whip vagrants.

The moment Kate was seated in the cushioned stern the wherryman pushed off. With the current against them, and the river breeze, too, he strained at his oars, and the bow bucked against the choppy waves. Kate's heartbeat quickened at the thought of seeing Owen, but beneath her excitement ran a ripple of uneasiness about the note she had received last night. Summoned to a meeting, both she and Owen. What could be so urgent that they would be sent for on the very day of his release? Kate doubted it was good news. Looking ahead at the waking city she felt a kinship with the struggling half light all around her, the night not quite yet vanquished by the sun.

Her spirits rallied in the bracing river air, and when the first beams of sun lit up London Bridge in the distance ahead her excitement rose, too. To have Owen with her again, a free man! Watching the buildings glide past she felt the great city cast its spell over her. The stately procession of riverside mansions stretched in both directions from the Savoy, their windows glinting in the rising sun. Ahead of her rose Somerset House, Arundel House, Leicester House; behind her Russell House, Durham House, York House, and the river's curve that led to the Queen's palace of Whitehall.

Across the Strand the leafy market of Covent Garden would already be bustling with people from nearby villages bringing their produce to sell. The mid-September bounty would be fragrant with fennel and fresh cresses, blackberries, quinces, and tangy damson plums. Watercraft of all shapes and sizes were busy on the river, some under sail, others under oars, some beating against the current, others gliding with it. At Paul's Wharf the first customers were calling, "Westward, ho!" beckoning wherrymen to carry them upriver—lawyers and clerks heading for Westminster, most likely. More wherries rocked alongside the Steelyard water stairs, ready to take shipping agents downriver to the Custom House quay. Kate's wherry passed a canopied tilt boat ferrying a pair of snoring, rumpled gentlemen, no doubt returning from an all-night carouse in Southwark. Fishing smacks trolled near a feeding bevy of swans. Through the still-distant arches of London Bridge Kate glimpsed lighters beetling from shore to unload cargo from ships moored in the Pool.

A peal of church bells rang the hour. Seven o'clock. She cocked an ear for the pattern: 1-3-2-5-4-6. When bell ringers rang a set of bells in a series of mathematical patterns they called it "change ringing," and the patterns had pleased Kate for as long as she could remember. Her tutors used to sigh at her slowness with languages—Latin and Italian had been a struggle for her—but with numbers she was always at ease. The clear, calm beauty of mathematics spoke to her as no human tongue ever did.

Passing Queenhithe wharf she smelled the yeasty aroma of baking bread. Also, a whiff of the stinking tannery effluent polluting the Fleet Ditch. Above it all drifted the smells of charcoal, sawdust, and fish. She imagined the city coming to life. Yawning apprentices opening shops along Cheapside, milkmaids ambling down Holborn Hill, servants hefting water pots from the big conduit in Fleet Street, fishwives setting up stalls at Billingsgate. Lawyers would be hustling through Temple Bar and merchants striding into the great gothic nave of St. Paul's to do business with colleagues. On the shore by the Three Cranes Stairs a couple of mudlarks, a boy and an older girl, were bent sorting their finds from the river's sludge, intent on their task before the tide rose farther. Kate could never behold the city without a rush of affection.

Its brash, brawling exuberance had always enthralled her, even as a child. She had been born the year after Queen Elizabeth's coronation and had spent her childhood here in the springtime of Elizabeth's reign. At nine Kate had been torn from England by her mother and her exile had lasted four years. Now, she loved her homeland fiercely, as only an exile can.

She caught the sweet scent of apples drifting from an orchard. Autumn was nearing, and the shortening of days. The harvest would soon be over. In manors throughout England bailiffs would be making out the accounts for the year. Here in London the law courts would mark the beginning of the Michaelmas term.

London Bridge loomed ahead, near enough now that its four-story shops and houses, crammed close together, blocked the sun. Kate looked up at windows where the last candles and lanterns were going out. A flock of sheep on the Southwark side bawled as the farmer waited for the drawbridge to be lifted. The gatehouses on either end of the bridge were closed every night. This was the city's only viaduct, so city-bound travelers who did not make it across in time had to spend the night in one of Southwark's unsavory inns. Southwark was Kate's destination.

The bawling of the sheep was drowned out by the din of water rushing between the bridge's twenty stone arches. There, each tide created a dangerous rapids. When watermen on the roiling water jetted between arches they called it "shooting the bridge." Kate remembered the thrill of it one brisk spring day when she was a child. Her father, a ship owner and an expert sailor all his life, had taken her and Robert in a boat from Paul's Stairs out to his ship moored off the customs house, and on their way they shot the bridge. Rollicking through the tunnelled arch like a cork in a whirlpool, Kate had squealed in delight, her father holding her hand and grinning, but little Robert sat gripping the gunwale, big-eyed, rigid with fear. He did look rather comical, and Kate and her father had shared a laugh. That carefree time seemed so long ago—before her father became Baron Thornleigh, and long before Kate could ever have imagined the chasm that separated them now. The chasm that had opened with her husband's arrest.

A ghastly sight jerked her out of her thoughts: the heads impaled on the bridge's gatepost. Traitors' heads.

Anger streaked through her, a sad fury that this normal bustle of daily life and commerce around her masked the deep anxiety of Londoners, of all the English people. A struggle for England's soul held the country in a death grip. It was a struggle that had turned friend against friend, parent against child, twisting her countrymen's honest passions into hatred and fear. The first blast had come from Rome with the pope's declaration that it would be no sin for any Catholic to kill Queen Elizabeth. Since then Her Majesty's government had kept up a relentless search for radicals. Assassination plots had been thwarted. Missionary priests preaching allegiance to the pope above the Queen had been captured and hanged. The government's position was rigid, implacable. To be a Catholic in England was to be a traitor.

Kate felt equally implacable as she gazed up at the grisly, withered heads. The blithe springtime of Elizabeth's reign was over.

Shifting her position on the seat, she heard the rustle of the paper in her cloak pocket. The letter from old Master Prowse. A voice from those happy long-gone days would cheer her, she thought. She pulled it out and opened it. It read:

Good Mistress Thornleigh,

So, he did not know she was married. He must have sent the letter to her father's house and there the boy had been redirected to Lady Thornleigh's. She read on:

> *After my right hearty commendations to you, I hope you will kindly remember your humble former tutor, for I flatter myself that in your father's house you and your young brother Master Robert did imbibe from me good learning to the credit of your duty and obedience, ever in the ways of God.*
>
> *A delicate matter concerning Master Robert prompts my pen. You will be astonished to hear that your*

*brother, having slipped the bonds that kept him so long
in foreign parts, has recently come among us again in
England. Yea, good mistress, he has been living nigh me
these ten months gone. He bides with a merchant named
Levett in the town of Lewes, not ten mile from my
house, and proud I am to say he calls me friend. You
will rejoice to hear that your brother is hale. He gets his
bread by dispensing physic to ailing folk, a vocation to
which he was called through his studies in Italy.*

Kate looked up with a gasp. Robert—back in England! A physician! She read on hungrily:

*However, for the security of himself and his well-
beloved relations in London, your brother judged it
right and prudent to return to the land of his birth
under a new name. He goes by plain Robert Parry and
no one hereabouts knows he is in fact the son of Baron
Thornleigh. The necessity of this pseudonym, it pains me
to say, is the evil reputation of your mother, yours and
his. Having opened his heart to me, he enjoined me
never to mention his return to his relations for fear that
a connection with him, tainted by his mother's infamy,
would be injurious to you and yours. As he told me, he
wants only to be left in peace to make his own way.*

*Therein lies my quandary. Your brother's injunction,
I fear, does no one good. This fine young gentleman
should not be estranged from the family he loves, cut off
from the largesse of his good and gracious father. Thus,
I have taken it upon myself, may God forgive and
preserve me, to acquaint you with your brother's plight,
for well I recall the love you bore him when you were
children, just as I recall your generous heart.*

*Do with this news what you will, good Mistress
Thornleigh. I trust it will gladden your heart to know
that your brother is home. I trust, too, that you will*

vouchsafe to speak of it to no one but those in whose
honesty you have steadfast confidence.
   And thus I commit you to God's good protection and
bid you farewell, from Seaford this VII of September,
    Your assured friend,
    Tobias Prowse

"Cock Alley Stairs, my lady," the wherryman announced.

Kate looked up. They were approaching the wave-splashed steps on the Southwark shore.

Southwark was the squalid side of the Thames, known for its unsavory haunts. The Marshalsea prison was minutes south of the river. Making her way along Bankside, Kate could not stop thinking of Robert. What joyful news! She longed to see him. Would she even recognize him? He'd been a child when they'd been separated and he was now a man of twenty! Curiosity burned in her to know about their mother, too. Where had the two of them lived all these years? *How* had they lived? She thanked God that Robert had broken away, had come home, and she was eager to assure him that he could rely on her for whatever help she could give. And yet, what help was that? She had no influence with their father. And a reunion with her might even *worsen* Robert's position. Should she simply let him be? Leave him "in peace" as he'd asked Master Prowse, to make his way alone? That felt heartless—and not at all what she wanted. But which course was better for *him?*

At St. Saviour's church she turned south onto the main street. It was strewn with refuse. She sidestepped a scummy heap of cabbage leaves and bones. A skinny dog trotted past her toward the bones. Alehouses, dilapidated inns, and brothels lined both sides. Stewhouses, Londoners called the brothels. The Bishop of Winchester, whose riverside palace was the grandest structure in Southwark, was responsible for maintaining law and order in the area, and because he licensed the prostitutes they were known as Winchester Geese. Kate glanced up at a weathered balcony where a woman in flimsy dress was brushing her hair with tired strokes, her eyes closed to enjoy the sun's warmth on her face. *A weary goose,* Kate thought with a twinge of sympathy as she walked on. A kite flapping its wings above the Tabard Inn descended into an elm tree and alighted on its nest of scavenged shreds of rags. A beast bellowed from the far eastern end of the street. The bear pits and bull pits there regularly drew afternoon crowds.

Kate knew the area. As children she and Robert had come with their father to the yearly Southwark Fair. Again, Robert and memories of those carefree days filled her thoughts. The fair had been such fun, a boisterous event attended by large crowds, both lowborn and high, who came to marvel at the tightrope acrobats and dancing monkeys, to eat and drink too much and, if they were not careful, to have their pockets picked. Now, a bulbous-nosed man lounging in a doorway leered at Kate as she passed. She picked up her pace. Thieves abounded here. Many ended up in one of Southwark's prisons: the Clink, King's Bench, the Borough Compter, the Marshalsea. Conditions in all were appalling, even for the wealthy who paid to live in the Masters section separated from those in the Commons, but Kate feared that the Marshalsea was the worst. Its inmates were entirely at the mercy of the Knight Marshal's deputy. While the master's side had forty to fifty private rooms for rent, Owen had had to endure the common side, nine small rooms into which over three hundred people were locked up from dusk until dawn. It made her shudder.

"Penny for the poor prisoners, my lady?" An earnestly smiling man in shabby clerical black held out his hand for an offering. All prisoners had to pay for their own food, so without charity the poorest often starved. Churchmen begged coins to buy them bread. This fellow, though, looked to Kate more pirate than prelate. The donations he weaseled would likely go to buy himself grog. She ignored him and carried on, but with a knot of dread tightening her stomach. She had paid the marshal's deputy every month to supply her husband with food, but had that food reached him?

She turned the corner at the Queen's Head Inn and the Marshalsea rose before her. Two long mismatched buildings, the gray stone walls slimed with black, the brick ones crumbling in places after more than a century of neglect. The arched double gates of wood were closed, and a small crowd of twenty or so men and women stood waiting for them to open. Kate had made it—the bell of St. Saviour's had not yet chimed eight. Though the gates were a solid barrier, a stench seeped out like swamp fog. A scabby-faced girl hawked rabbit pasties, to no takers. An elderly churchman, this one looking genuine, begged coins to buy food for destitute inmates. A solemn young man with a mustard-colored cap moved through the crowd offering willow crucifixes for a ha'penny. A couple of painted women lounged in the shadowed angle of the wall, awaiting trade. Kate looked up to an unglazed window above the gates. A wild-haired man glared out at the crowd from between iron bars. He spat. Kate looked away.

A clang behind the gates. A rattling and grating as one of the wooden doors was marched open from inside by a ragged worker. The people surged forward, most of them straight into the prison courtyard. Kate stood still, craning to see beyond the moving heads and backs. Then she saw him, Owen, a head taller than most of the other men. She gasped. How thin he was! And how dirty. And what had happened to his hair?

He saw her, and his deep-sunk eyes brightened. He strode to her, shouldering past the people streaming the opposite way. She ran to meet him.

They stopped, face-to-face, hers upturned to his, both of them gazing, the moment too charged for words. Kate was shocked by his hollow cheeks, hollowed eyes. His hair, once a rich black mass of lazy waves, was now so close-cropped it was as thin as a shadow on his skull, with erratic tufts, and nicks in the skin as though a drunken barber had wielded rusty shears. Black stubble bristled his chin, as ill-shaved as his head. His doublet of chestnut-colored wool was rumpled and grease-stained. A rip in his shirt's collar was so straight it could only have been cut with a blade. He stank.

Tears sprang to her eyes. "What have they done to you?"

He gave her a tight, forced smile. "A fine day, wife. Thank you for coming."

The words were oddly impassive. His voice strange. So was the look in his eyes, glassy yet intense.

No, she would not have this! She threw her arms around his

neck and went up on her toes and pressed her cheek to his. He held himself rigid. Would he not embrace her? Shocked, she pulled her head back. "Owen, are you ill?"

His glassy look dissolved in a faint film of tears. He gathered her in his arms and pulled her close. He held her so tightly she could scarcely breathe. "No," he murmured shakily. "Not ill."

She felt a tremor run through his body. She suddenly realized: the formal greeting, the rigid stance—it was to clamp his emotions inside, to forbid himself any show of weakness after his ordeal. Kate's tears spilled. From love, from pity. Then, quickly, before she could speak any more of her heart, she let him go. She must not undermine his effort. Must not unman him.

Swiping away her tears, she looked at his shorn scalp and forced a wry smile. "I cannot say I like this new fashion." She ran her hand over his head and shivered at the stubble sharp as pins.

He matched her half smile. "Less of a handhold for lice."

Warmth rushed through her at his jest. This was the Owen she knew and loved!

His eyes flicked to the young man selling the willow crucifixes a stone's throw away, then back to Kate, a clear warning. He said very quietly, eyes still fixed on her, "A disciple of Campion."

Edmund Campion, executed last year, the most famous of the priests secretly sent by the Jesuit order in Rome to preach defiance of the Queen. To Catholics, he was a martyr. To Protestants, a traitor. Kate understood what Owen was telling her. *We're being watched.*

"You?" she asked quietly. *He suspects you?*

He shook his head. "You."

She was not surprised. *Because of Father.* Yet still, it stung.

"Ah, wife," he said, his voice suddenly loud and sorrowful, loud enough for the spy to hear, "a prison is a grave for burying men alive. It is a little world of woe."

His theatrical words were deliberate, Kate knew—a poetic lament that might be expected from a playwright, for until a year ago that was how he had made his living, meager though it was. He could bewitch you with words. He had bewitched Kate from the moment she'd been introduced to him at the playhouse called the Theatre.

"And how are *you*, my love?" he asked. This time his simple sincerity rang through.

"Well. Very well."

"And your lady grandmother?"

"A rock." Her gratitude to her grandmother was heartfelt. The lady was an island of tolerance in a sea of mistrust. "You will be welcome in her house."

"We'll find our own house soon, I promise."

She smiled at him for that.

The bells of St. Saviour's chimed the hour. The young man selling crucifixes moved away. Kate watched him go. He was well beyond hearing them now, but still she lowered her voice to a mere whisper. "Owen, we are summoned."

It startled him. "Now?"

"Now."

He ran a grimy hand over his stubbled chin. "I need to wash. Shave."

"You need to *eat*." Fury at his mistreatment shot through her again. "They starved you!"

He shrugged. "No more than the others."

If only he had let her give that wretched deputy more silver! For another few pounds he would have had meat and drink fit for the Masters. But she knew why he had refused. He'd needed to bear the misery, because it was essential that the Catholic inmates accept him as a fellow sufferer. What those inmates did not know, and must never know, was the real reason he had agreed to suffer. In this battle for England, Owen had pledged himself to protect Her Majesty. And so had Kate.

"Come," she said, "I have a boat waiting."

He took her elbow. The squeeze he gave it told her how much he would rather be alone with her than hurrying to a meeting. But he said steadily, "Lead on."

❧ 2 ❧

Enemies of the Queen

Kate and Owen took the wherry. As they were rowed across the Thames they were so locked in looking at each other she scarcely noticed the river traffic. She had a hundred questions for him, but they could not talk openly in front of the wherryman. Nor could they touch the way they longed to. She felt Owen's hot impatience to be alone with her, and she could only tell him with her eyes: *Soon, my love.* She had made Matthew Buckland promise to assign him no more missions until absolutely necessary. A few weeks of peace and quiet would do her husband a world of good. Heaven knew he had earned it.

"God bless her!" the wherryman blurted. "Look, that's Her Majesty, yonder!" He nodded westward.

They looked upriver. The magnificent royal barge was unmistakable even at this distance. The crimson silk banners rippled in the breeze and sunlight gleamed off the dazzling gilt prow and the dozen pairs of oars arcing and dipping. Kate thought it looked like some golden insect gliding over the water. Small craft swarmed around it, with wherry passengers and fishermen alike eager to see Her Majesty up close. The barge was passing Blackfriars where people cheered from the riverbank. More people were rushing out of houses and shops all the way east to the Steelyard, the Baltic merchants' wharf where a loading crane was noisily at work. Someone there tooted a horn. Kate and Owen shared a smile. The people of England loved their queen and none were more effusive in their affection than Londoners. Cries of "God save Your Majesty!" always rang from the riverbank whenever her barge brought her from Whitehall to dine at some friend's riverside mansion, or merely to take the cool river air on a sultry summer night while her musicians serenaded her.

"It's early for her to be abroad," Kate said. Everyone with any connection to the court knew that the Queen did not enjoy rising early. On the morning of Kate's sixteenth birthday her father had presented her to Her Majesty, the start of a busy day for the sovereign, and on the way he had cautioned her that their royal hostess would not be at her best. *Downright grumpy,* he had said with a wink. It had made Kate nervous. But Elizabeth, in welcoming her to Whitehall Palace, had been gently cordial—for Father's sake, Kate had quickly realized. She had been in awe at the easy camaraderie between the two. "Your father is my well-beloved friend," Elizabeth had said with such quiet sincerity that Kate, making her curtsy, had swelled with pride.

"Even a queen must revel in the glory of this morning," Owen said. The warmth in his voice told Kate how thrilled he was to be free and with her again. He was looking at her, not the Queen. She grinned. A glorious morning indeed!

They alighted at the Old Swan Stairs in the lee of the bridge. Buildings crammed the riverside, houses cheek by jowl with businesses: a cooper's shed, a tavern, a chandlery, a brewery that belched steam from its boiling cauldrons. Seagulls wheeled and screeched. More wherries nudged the stone steps, depositing or taking on passengers at the busy landing, but many had come to the water's edge and peered upriver at the progress of the Queen. Neighbors chatted with neighbors, pointing at the royal barge. Women came out of doors wiping their hands on their aprons, eager to have a look. A couple of cooper's apprentices emerged, hammers still in hand. Three boys halted their makeshift game of football with a pig's bladder and one shinnied up a post for a better view. Shutters banged open. An old couple gazed out from a second-story window. Even the squeak and grind of the Steelyard loading crane went silent.

Owen and Kate, though, could not tarry. He took her hand with a gleam of impatience in his eyes that told her he was as eager as she was to get the meeting with Matthew over with. They headed north on Swan Alley, passing under laundry strung between houses. The breeze lifted the clothes, making shirts and hose seem to dance a jig. The moment they passed the eaves of the first houses he tugged her into a narrow lane. He backed her against a recessed doorway. "My Kate," he said, half moan, half sigh.

Their kiss was long and deep, fired by six months of pent-up yearning. Heat coursed through Kate from her lips to her toes. Any lingering worry that Owen's ordeal had damaged him dissolved in the loving crush of his arms. When he finally eased his embrace it was only to kiss her throat, murmuring, "I wanted to do that from the moment I saw you at the gate."

She let out a laugh of delight, still catching her breath from their kiss. "All wives should send their husbands to prison if such passion is their reward."

"Then all husbands would have to be married to you, for you alone can light this fire." He chuckled even as he frowned at his own words. "Now, that's a thought to drive a man mad!" He gazed at her and his tone became serious. "No, Kate, you are mine, all mine. And as soon as I get you alone at Her Ladyship's house, I'll—"

"Wash?"

He winced. "Do I stink so badly?"

"Most foully, my love." She wrapped her arms around him. "Foul or sweet, you are my heart's desire. Kiss me."

He obliged with fervor.

A scream from the riverbank broke their kiss. Curious, they stepped out of the lane and looked back down Swan Alley. People were shouting in alarm, running, pointing westward. Kate and Owen exchanged a glance. Was a thief on the loose? A man burst from a doorway at her elbow. Owen grabbed her to keep the man from knocking her down. "Watch where you tread!" Owen warned him, his voice a snarl, a sound Kate had never heard from him before. *He needed it in prison*, she thought with a shiver.

"What's amiss?" she asked the man, a baker by the look of his flour-dusted jerkin. He looked strangely distraught.

"Lord save us!" he cried. He jerked his thumb to the second story behind him. "I saw it from up there. Saw with my own eyes!"

"Saw what?"

"Her Majesty's been shot!"

Kate's heart thudded. She groped for Owen's hand. They shared a horrified glance. *Assassinated!* In her mind she saw the Queen lying on her gilded barge in a crimson pool of blood. They looked toward the river where the people's shouting had become louder, panicky.

The baker dashed toward the crowd and so did Kate and Owen. They found people crowded to the very edge of the water stairs, everyone shouting, gesturing, alarm on every face. A woman stood weeping, hands helplessly on her head. Men were running west on Waterman's Row.

"Is she dead?" the baker called out.

"Aye, murdered!" a woman wailed.

"No, but deathly wounded!" a man said. "She's taken a bullet in the head!"

"No, she's drowned!" someone cried. "Look!"

Utter confusion, Kate thought. She and Owen had pushed through the crowd to the water's edge, straining to see the royal barge. It had stopped and was slewed sideways in the water. Impossible to make out faces at this distance, but the hectic activity on it and on boats all around it was clear. Soldiers of the Palace Guard moved quickly along the barge's side decks. Its many oars were flailing in disorder. Dozens of small boats had swarmed closer and people on them stood shouting, wildly gesticulating, causing their craft to wallow dangerously. A man who'd fallen overboard splashed with piercing cries.

Everyone around Kate was shouting, some saying the Queen lay dead, some that she was bleeding from the head, some that the bullet had torn into her chest. *But how can they know?* she thought. The barge was too far away. *Panic is making them see things.* Panic thrashed inside her, too, and she struggled to subdue it. *Real information, that's what we need. From a trusted source.*

Owen demanded of the man next to him, "Where did the shot come from? The barge? A boat? The riverbank?"

The man threw up his arms in despair. "Who knows?"

"The Steelyard, looks like," a fat woman answered. "From my window I saw folk there scurrying about. It's the poxy foreigners. They've murdered Her Majesty!"

Owen turned to Kate. "Go back to Her Ladyship's. Stay there." He pushed back through the crowd.

She called after him, following him, "Where are you going?"

"After the villain." He was making for Waterman's Row, which led to the Steelyard. "Go back, Kate. Stay with Lady Thornleigh."

"No!" She caught up with him. "You can't do this."

"Yes, from the Steelyard he can't have got far."

"Don't! You'd be showing your true colors." *Showing you're loyal to the Queen*, she meant, but could not say that with so many people near. "Come with me to our friend." She hoped Matthew could tell them what was happening. "Owen, we might be needed now more than ever."

He stopped. She saw that her words had sunk in. He threw a tortured glance toward the Steelyard. "But if he escapes—"

"He may have already. Or he may have been captured. Either way, scores of men will be dealing with it, all of them closer than you to where it happened."

He looked at her, torn. She knew how hard this was for him—to abandon action, to simply wait. But he gave a tight nod. "You're right."

A woman dropped to her knees at the edge of the crowd, hands clasped in prayer as Kate and Owen hurried up Swan Street.

The alehouse was snugged into a recess of Little Elbow Lane. Its customary afternoon trade was a thin scatter of workingmen, but when Kate and Owen arrived it was well before noon and no one was there but the barkeep, Mistress Tern. She owned the place.

"Well, what news?" she demanded gruffly as she mopped the bar. She was a blowsy Cornishwoman with unkempt red hair and a short temper. When Kate and Owen had been here before she had never asked their business, just took their coins with a scowl. Owen called her the Red Cow. "They say Her Majesty's dead," she said. "Is it true?"

"We know no more than you do," Owen said.

"My man's run off to see for himself," she said, flapping her gray rag toward the door. "Ran out like a headless hen, the fool. I told him word will come raging in here soon enough." She resumed mopping the bar. "Your gentleman friend ain't come yet, if that's who you've come to see."

"Thank you," Kate said. "We'll wait."

They went up the stairs to the back room. It was small and dark, a scarred wooden table and three stools by the hearth its only furniture. Kate went to the window and closed the shutters. The window, unglazed, overlooked a smithy. When she'd been here before there had been a strong smell of charcoal. Not this morning. No clanging of the anvil, either. The whole city seemed quiet, as though holding its breath, waiting for the dreaded report of the Queen's death to be confirmed.

"He's late," Owen said, beginning to pace.

"Caught up in the panic?" Kate did not dare speak her fear: that Matthew and the Queen's councillors at Whitehall Palace lay dead, too. A unified assault.

Owen ran a hand over his stubbled head, looking shaken. "Christ, I wish we knew!"

A knock on the door. Owen wheeled around. Kate's eyes locked on the door. *Matthew?* "Yes?" Owen said.

Mistress Tern came in. "You'll be wantin' ale, I warrant." She stood with her hands on her hips as though in a challenge. "The world don't stop for one woman's passin'."

"No, we want nothing," Owen said harshly, then muttered under his breath, "Heartless cow," as he went back to pacing.

"Yes, ale, please, mistress," Kate said. "And have you some meat?"

"Aye, rabbit stew, made it m'self. Or there's cold pig's feet."

Kate ignored Owen's grimace. "We'll have the stew," she said. "Bread, too, if you have it." When they were alone again she said to him, "You need food."

"Hers will be a witch's brew." He stopped pacing, and his tone turned deadly serious. "Kate, if he's not coming we need to find out for ourselves."

"I know," she granted. "Eat. Then we'll decide."

She sat down on a stool by the cold hearth. Owen came to her and took her hand to give comfort, and to take it. They both held tight. Far-off church bells blithely clanged the hour. The ringers could not yet have heard the news. Part of Kate's brain registered the ring pattern: *3-1-2-1-3-2*. Her fear churned. *Queen Elizabeth, dead.* There could be no greater disaster. She imagined the horrifying future unfolding. Elizabeth was childless—had never married—and her undisputed successor was her cousin Mary Stuart, Queen of the Scots, in Kate's eyes the most dangerous woman in England. Elizabeth and her council considered Mary such a menace to Elizabeth they had kept her under house arrest for over a decade. Now, Mary would rejoice in ascending to the throne she had endlessly plotted to seize. But that would split England apart. Elizabeth had kept a firm hand on both radical religious factions, the Catholics and the Puritans, but without her steady authority they would leap at each other's throats. Throughout England Protestant nobles like Kate's father would oppose Mary and raise their retainers and tenants to fight, while the Catholic gentry and nobles would support her. There would be riots. Rebellion. Civil war. With the realm weakened, the mighty Philip of Spain would seize the opportunity to invade as he had always hungered to do. Mary would welcome his army. The pope would support him, too. In her mind Kate saw Spanish troop ships cutting through the narrow Channel . . . thousands of foreign soldiers roaring onto English shores . . . butchering villages on their march to London. England's green pastures would run red with blood. She saw loyal lords like her father leading out the ill-prepared city militias and being cut down . . . saw her father's head on a pike on London Bridge. . . .

The ale arrived, brought by a pale-faced girl who set the two tankards on the table. Owen ignored it. Kate paid the girl, who left. Kate sat down again, her mouth so dry with dread she could not even swallow.

Footsteps sounded outside. A heavy tread, coming up the stairs. Kate jumped up. Owen came to her side and put his arm around her shoulder, his every muscle tense as they both watched the door open.

Matthew Buckland walked in. He stopped, and looked at them glassily as though in shock. Kate's hand went to her mouth to block a gasp. *Her Majesty . . . dead?* Her heart was a stone in her throat.

Matthew lowered his gaze to the tankards on the table. He moved toward them like a sleepwalker. He lifted one and brought it to his lips. His hand was trembling and foam spilled, sliding down the tankard sides. He forced control over his arm and took a long, steadying draft of ale.

Kate thought in horror: *Dead!*

Matthew lowered the tankard and looked at her. His first words were surprisingly calm, his voice low. "She lives."

The gasp Kate had bottled up burst out in joy. She twisted to Owen. "She lives!"

He beamed in relief. "She lives!"

They sounded like two idiots. It made her laugh. Owen laughed, too. Even Matthew—careful, deliberate Matthew—grinned.

The door banged open farther and Mistress Tern marched in, a wooden bowl of stew in each hand, a spoon set in each bowl. Oblivious, she thumped the bowls down on the table. "Tuppence each." She looked up, her hand already outstretched. The three grinning faces finally registered on her. She frowned. "What's funny?"

"Mistress Tern," Kate said, "Her Majesty lives!"

The woman gaped. Tears suddenly brimmed in her eyes. Her face reddened with emotion. She flopped down on a stool, overcome. "God bless her!" she cried. Her tears spilled and she buried her face in her hands.

Owen let out a laugh of astonishment at her outburst. "Why,

Mistress Tern! A secret acolyte!" He threw Kate a look of delight at the paradox. He handed the blubbering Cornishwoman a tankard and said with a kindly chuckle, "Best calm yourself. You'll soon have a rush of customers pounding in to rejoice."

She gulped the ale, then wiped her eyes, sniffling. "Mayhap I'll stand 'em a round," she said cheerfully.

Owen laughed again. "Wonders never cease."

Kate's own mirth was quenched by burning curiosity. She said meaningfully to Matthew, "You are well met, sir."

Owen took the cue. "Go now, good Mistress Tern, and spread the joyful word." He helped her to her feet and showed her out.

"No charge for the vittles," she said, sniffling happily as she left. "Lord, what a day!"

Owen closed the door. The moment the three of them were alone Kate burst out to Matthew, "What happened?"

"It was a shot from the Joiners Hall. It missed Her Majesty, but wounded one of her oarsmen in the shoulder. She drew her handkerchief and bent to stanch his wound."

Kate imagined the frantic scene: Elizabeth pressing her handkerchief against the man's bloody shoulder, her men-at-arms urging her to take shelter, mayhem in the riverside garden of the joiners' livery company. "You were there?" she asked.

"No. I was on my way here from the Exchange when I heard the shouting. I ran along Thames Street with everyone else, to the Joiners Hall. Heard what happened from a Dowgate alderman. He *did* see it, then saw Her Majesty's barge turn back toward Whitehall. Her guards surrounded her by then, but she was waving at the people on shore to show she was unhurt."

Owen asked, "Have they caught the gunman?"

"Not yet."

"Escaped," Owen grunted. "Devil take him!"

"But the city gates have been closed."

"I doubt he'll get that far," Kate said, thinking of Londoners' love for the Queen.

Matthew said, "You may be right."

She nodded. "Someone will snatch him and hold him."

"No, I meant the contrary," Matthew told her, looking worried. "If he has accomplices, they will hide him."

Kate had not thought of that. She felt a fool. Matthew never underestimated the strength of England's adversaries. She told herself that she must not, either. Beyond her quiet world of decoding there were ferociously dedicated enemies at work. One slip by her, one misjudged word, and they could find her out, unmask her. Owen, too.

Matthew sat down on a stool as though glad to be off his feet. *Relief is exhausting,* Kate thought, feeling sapped herself, overwhelmed with happiness at the Queen's escape. She sat on the stool beside him. He gave her a small smile, complicit in their shared emotion. Then he looked up at Owen. "Welcome back, Master Lyon."

Owen made a gracious bow. "Your servant, sir."

"It is good to see you a free man. It will save me hearing your wife's pleas that I send you cartloads of beef, French wines, and a feather bed."

Kate had to smile. No doubt she *had* been a nuisance.

"The sight of her is all the sustenance I need," said Owen.

She tingled at his look. "Nevertheless," she said, "I'll fatten you up yet."

As if obeying a queen's command he bowed again, sat down beside her, pulled a bowl of stew toward him and dug out a spoonful and ate. His eyes widened in surprise. "Another revelation! The Red Cow can cook!"

It did Kate's heart good to hear him jest.

Munching, Owen asked Matthew, "Any idea who the villain might be?"

Matthew shook his head with his customary sober manner. He was thirty-one, older than Owen by just two years, but Kate felt the men could not be more different. Owen, dirty and thin from prison, his clothes begrimed, but his whole being exuding energy, an exuberant self-confidence that no adversity could extinguish. And those clever dark eyes that sent a thrill through her whenever his gaze touched her. Matthew, his fair short beard neatly barbered, his clothes immaculate as befitted the right-hand man of the Lord Secretary of the realm, but with a solemnity always lurking in his gray eyes. Matthew was only a little taller than Kate and slightly built. His stick-straight hair the color of sand was cut very short, as though to cause him the least bother, and lay flat and brushed forward like a monk's. His tidy beard almost covered the skin scarred by burns from a gunpowder blast. Kate understood it had happened when he'd volunteered to fight in the Netherlands with a private expeditionary force to support the Dutch rebels against their Spanish occupiers. That had been ten years ago, but the Dutch people still suffered under the boot of Spain. And Matthew still suffered from his freak wound, for the blast had damaged a tendon in his neck, leaving him unable to fully raise his head. It made him look at people from under lowered brows, as though watching them with suspicion. It had unnerved Kate when she had first met him two years ago at her father's house over an evening at the card table playing trumps. But after a pleasurable hour as his partner she'd got used to his odd posture. He had approached her as the other guests were leaving. "You excel at the game, Mistress Thornleigh," he had said earnestly, eyeing her under his brows.

"A favorite pastime in our family, sir," she said airily, and added with a smile, "My father says I was playing with cards before I could talk."

"They seem to speak to you. Numbers. Patterns."

Direct, persuasive, determined, he had drawn her into a discussion about the danger England faced from the pope's inflammatory pronouncement against the Queen in which he had urged Catholics to oppose her authority, a danger Kate agreed was only too clear. She had accepted Matthew's invitation to visit him at Whitehall the following day before she quite realized that she had been recruited. The first assignment he gave her had been to decode a Spanish merchant's letter on its way to the French ambassador in London, intercepted by one of the "watchers" employed by Sir Francis Walsingham, the Lord Secretary. Kate had discovered, with a stirring of pride, that she was swift at deciphering the code. She had been decoding letters for Matthew ever since. He had others doing this work, too; men who were part of Walsingham's web. The original letters were always sent back on to their intended course so that neither the sender nor recipient knew they had been read by English eyes. So far, the letters Kate had worked on contained nothing actionable, but Matthew had assured her that every piece of information helped Walsingham build dossiers on England's enemies. A quiet man, Matthew watched more than he spoke. Kate trusted him completely.

"I need your report," he said now to Owen.

Owen drew his dagger, lifted his foot, and with the tip of the blade pried open the heel of his boot. From inside the heel he withdrew a square of paper folded several times. Opening it, he handed it over. "The names you wanted, all there."

Kate gathered it was a list of Catholics Owen had befriended in the Marshalsea. His arrest had been contrived for this reason, to gather information about the international Catholic network. Matthew flattened the list on the table as he perused it and Kate could see that Owen had written notes beside each name, no doubt concerning the threat he felt the individual posed to England, or, in some cases, the likelihood of their being turned to the government's side. Such turncoats were rare, but valuable. Throughout the realm Walsingham's web hummed with the murmurs of countless minor informants. Beyond England, too. Walsingham's spies prowled city streets and wharfs in Spain, France, and the Netherlands so that he could, as he put it, feel the pulse on the other side.

Matthew took his time studying the list. Methodical as always, Kate thought; it was his legal training. Owen had gone back to spooning up stew. He caught Kate's eye as he ate and they shared a happy smile. Now that he had done his duty he could take a rest. *When I get him back to Thornleigh House*, she thought, *I'll have the kitchen prepare his favorite dishes*. She was excited about having him all to herself. Excited imagining their lovemaking.

"This is good, Lyon," Matthew said as he finished his perusal, drawing Kate's attention back to the present. He dug into his doublet and pulled out a purse and handed it to Owen, the coins softly jingling.

Owen took the payment with a gallant bow of his head, then tucked the purse into his own doublet.

"Any here we need to watch especially?" Matthew asked, looking back at the list. "Calkins, for example?"

"Him, yes. And John Wye. The rest are tame enough."

"Or wear masks of tameness," Matthew suggested, though without malice.

"That's not all," Owen went on. He shoved aside his empty bowl. "Something big may be brewing. I heard talk of an invasion, financed by Spain and the pope, led by Westmorland."

His words made Kate shiver. England's worst nightmare: invasion by a Catholic alliance. It was all too possible the Earl of Westmorland was involved, a man exalted among the English Catholic exiles living abroad. Thirteen years ago he had fomented an uprising in England's north. It failed and he fled. Kate had met him once, in Antwerp, when she was a child. A scowling, driven man, always stirring the resentful passions of fellow exiles like Kate's mother. "Westmorland will never give up," she warned Matthew now. "Not until his head is on the block."

Matthew, unperturbed, folded the list and tucked it into his pocket. "Rumors of invasion are as constant as English rain."

Kate knew his calm exterior masked a deep concern. The exiles' goal was well-known: to depose Elizabeth, free Mary Stuart from house arrest in Sheffield, and set her on England's throne. Every plot the exiles hatched with their foreign supporters aimed for this objective.

"This time," Owen said, "they may have local help in high places."

Matthew frowned. This was serious: traitors at home. "Names?"

Owen shook his head. "They're careful. No names spoken. But I believe the man at the top may be Northumberland."

Matthew's wince betrayed how grave he felt this was. Henry Percy, the Earl of Northumberland, hailed from an ancient family notoriously loyal to the Catholic faith, though he made a show of conforming to the law that had made the realm Protestant. Was he preparing a treasonous move? Kate wondered. He was a powerful lord who could rely on the allegiance of hundreds of influential men, each with scores of supporters of their own, some believers in the Catholic cause, some merely gambling to be on the invaders' side when they installed Mary as England's new monarch.

"This time the rumor may have teeth," Matthew grimly confirmed. "Other sources have reported it, too. From Spain."

Owen went on. "I got friendly in the Marshalsea with a kinsman of Northumberland, name of Doncaster. He was bragging about the invasion. He's close to the family at Petworth."

Petworth House, Kate thought. The Earl's stronghold in Sussex, where he now lived.

"We know about Doncaster," Matthew said. "A cousin of Northumberland's wife. Arrested for shouting tavern insults about Her Majesty. I judged him a lackbrain, harmless. Am I wrong?"

"No, you're right, he's a fool. But he's close to the earl, so I recommend you keep a watch on him."

Matthew looked him in the eye. "It's Northumberland we need to watch. I want you to do it, Lyon. From inside."

"Inside Petworth?" Kate said in alarm. "Matthew, no! He just spent six months in the hell of the Marshalsea. He needs to rest, build his strength. You *promised* him a rest."

Matthew gave her a sad smile. "Kate, the enemy sleeps not."

"And how do I gain entry?" Owen asked, incredulous. "March in and tell His Lordship I have orders to spy on him?"

"His secretary died last week. The post is vacant."

"Ah," Owen murmured, the light dawning. "You want me to apply for it." He gave Matthew a flinty look. "Double the purse."

"Done."

"But why *you?*" Kate protested. "Matthew, don't you already have someone there?" He had spies in many great men's houses.

"I did. A porter. But we've just learned he's working both sides. I'm arranging now to have him dealt with. That leaves no one at Petworth."

"But surely you can find someone else!" she insisted.

"No one with your husband's bona fides. His Oxford education. His Catholic cover. His friendship with Doncaster. He's perfect."

"It's true, Kate. Someone has to watch Northumberland and I might be able to get that secretarial position."

Where you could be found out and killed, she almost blurted. But she bit back the words. She glared at Matthew. Curse him!

Owen squared his shoulders, signaling to Matthew that the thing was settled. "Get Doncaster released. He'll vouch for me to Northumberland."

"Good, I'll arrange his release today. Connect with him immediately. How soon can you leave for Petworth?"

Owen turned to Kate, the look in his eyes telling her: *I'm sorry, I wanted us to be alone, too.* "Wednesday," he answered. Kate muffled a groan. The day after tomorrow! But what could she do? Matthew wanted him to take this mission and Owen would not shirk. She knew how much he wanted the gold. He took her hand. "We'll still be together. If I get the job I'll bring my wife."

She mustered a smile. True, they would be together, though perhaps among the enemy. She could be useful, keep an eye out for any danger that might threaten him.

"No, I'm sorry. That's impossible," Matthew said. "Kate stays."

Her dismay leapt. "What?"

"I cannot send intercepted letters to you at Petworth, Kate. Too dangerous. You can see that."

"Let others decode them," she said. "You have able men throughout London."

"Several have decamped. Fled. Because . . ." He hesitated. Got to his feet and went to the shuttered window, where he stopped, his eyes on the shutter barrier, unseeing. His unsettled state, so unlike him, unnerved Kate. He turned back to them. "I'm afraid I have some bad news. Roger Griffith is dead."

They both stared at him, appalled. Kate had never met Griffith, but she knew he was Matthew's most valuable agent, a double agent, the link between the French ambassador in London and Mary Stuart. The ambassador, Michel de Castelnau, received letters for Mary from her supporters in France, Spain, and Rome. Castelnau gave the packets of letters to Griffith, whom he trusted as one of Mary's loyal supporters. Griffith couriered the letters north to Sheffield Manor, where Mary was in custody, but first he brought them to Matthew, whose band of decipherers copied and decoded them. Griffith then delivered the letters to Mary's agent in Sheffield, who smuggled them in to her. It had taken Matthew months to get Griffith in place. Now, this indispensable courier was dead.

Matthew went on grimly, "He was killed in a street brawl. Two days ago, on Ludgate Hill. Seems he and his cousin left the Belle Sauvage Inn and three of the owner's men came after them. The cousin gave me the details from his sickbed, where he lies with a broken arm and broken ribs. The men from the inn stopped them in the street with angry words, saying Griffith left without paying for their ale. Griffith insisted he *had* paid. Insults flew. Then blows. Two of the inn men set upon the cousin. Griffith drew his dagger. The third man pulled a knife. Griffith's throat was slit." Matthew shook his head. "The three from the inn have disappeared."

"Christ," Owen growled. "To die for a reckoning over ale."

A chill fingered its way up Kate's spine. "Or *was* it over ale?" she asked Matthew. His pale face told her there was something darker to this story.

"Ah, you have guessed it, Kate," he said. "We fear the brawl was staged."

Owen stiffened in alarm. "You mean . . ."

"Yes. Mary's people. I think they'd unmasked Griffith."

"And staged this to finish him . . . without tipping their hand to us." Owen whistled in reluctant admiration. "Crafty."

"We'll keep the search on for the murderers, but . . ." He spread his hands in a gesture that said how impossible he believed it to be.

"So, what now?" Owen asked. "Have you got someone to take Griffith's place?"

"Two candidates. Good men. But it took months to get Griffith in. God knows how long it will take to place a new man. If I'm right that Griffith's cover was blown, Castelnau and his people will be on their guard."

"But they have to move those letters somehow. It's essential to Mary's cause that she corresponds with her supporters, and Castelnau knows it. And *we* need to keep reading what passes between them. Her Majesty's life—the life of the realm—depends on it."

"You don't need to tell me that," Matthew growled.

Owen said no more, accepting the rebuke. He turned away, running his hand over his stubbled head in exasperation. Matthew frowned at the floor as though to regain his sober composure. Kate watched them both, but her mind had skidded elsewhere. Her skin prickled at the thought that had gripped her.

"I can do it," she said.

The men turned to her. Matthew looked puzzled. "Pardon? Do what?"

"I can be the new courier."

They both gaped at her.

"No, I'm not mad." Though she hardly knew where her voice had come from to volunteer. She had to clear her throat before she found the control to speak again. "You spoke of bona fides, Matthew. Well, mine are impressive enough to convince even Mary Stuart herself. For one thing, my mother is a known traitor. For another, I lived among the exiles for years. And if those credentials are not enough, my husband is a felon convicted for the very thing they hold most dear, the Catholic faith."

They continued to stare at her, amazed, and she felt a nip of fear. Never had she imagined doing anything so dangerous.

Owen broke the silence. "No, absolutely not," he said, his eyes flashing. "Don't even *think* of doing such a thing."

Matthew held up a hand to forestall him. He was regarding Kate with keen interest. "It is something to consider."

"No, not for a moment, Buckland. Think! If Mary's people should suspect her—" He didn't finish. He didn't need to. Not with the image of Griffith's slit throat hovering in all their minds.

"England is in mortal peril," Matthew said to Owen. "You saw today how Her Majesty's enemies get closer to her with every attempt. We all must do what we can to stop them."

"Kate is already doing more than enough. She's your best decoder."

"She may do more. Kate, you are indeed an ideal candidate." Matthew spoke as though discovering an extraordinary truth he should have seen before. "Trusted by our people because you're

Lord Thornleigh's daughter. Trusted by the Catholics because you're Lyon's wife."

"Exactly," Owen said, a threat in his voice. "She's *my* wife."

Matthew looked at him. "You don't know how strong she is."

"I know it better than anyone. That's no reason to place her in peril."

They both looked to her for her answer. Matthew's gray eyes bored into her from under his brow. Owen said, "Kate, you do not have to do this."

Fear seeped into her as she recalled Matthew's words: *The enemy sleeps not.* But she felt a tremor of determination, a sense that now *she* was the one who could not shirk. "I believe I do."

Owen said in dismay, "It's too dangerous, I tell you. How could we even get you in place? You have no connection to their world."

"Actually, I do. Marie de Castelnau."

Matthew exclaimed, another discovery, "Of course!"

Kate saw Owen's alarm. But he knew she was right. The French ambassador's wife was her friend.

3

The Good Doctor

In the south of England, ten miles from the sea, the River Ouse cut a gap in the chalk hills known as the South Downs. The town of Lewes nestled here under the great amphitheater of the hills. On a high point overlooking the river the Saxons had built a rudimentary castle as a defensive stronghold. After the Norman invasion William the Conqueror rewarded his brother-in-law, the first Earl of Surrey, with a swathe of land along the river from the coast to the Surrey boundary, and the earl built Lewes Castle on the Saxon site. For five hundred years the castle's twin towers and forbidding barbican had looked down on this town in which, during the reign of the Catholic Queen Mary, seventeen Protestants had been burned at the stake in front of the Star Inn. When Mary died her half sister Elizabeth became queen and made Protestantism the religion of England, but the Catholic faith had by no means died out. It had gone underground.

The High Street of Lewes occupied the west bank of the Ouse, climbing steeply up from the bridge, and where it intersected with St. Nicholas Lane stood a fine oak-framed house, its gardens facing the Downs. This was the home of Gilbert Levett, a cloth merchant, and his wife, Agnes, and their thirteen-year-old daughter, Judith.

For ten months a young man had been living with the Levetts

as their guest. He had come to them on a chill, wet night, the last day of October, showing Levett a letter of recommendation with a signature that moved the merchant to welcome this stranger into his family. The signature was that of Charles Paget, an exiled English nobleman known to be a champion of Mary Stuart, the deposed Queen of Scotland. Gilbert and Agnes Levett cherished the old church they had been brought up in and they hoped for a day when Mary, a pious Catholic, would become Queen of England, for they knew she would return the realm to the eternal truths and mystical beauties of Catholicism—return England to God. They had heard whisperings among their secret Catholic friends that influential exiles like Charles Paget were making plans to bring Mary to the throne by force of arms. Gilbert and Agnes wondered if the stranger who had come to them might be part of this grand scheme. If so, they felt privileged to give him the refuge he required. He had told them no details and they had asked for none. For his safety and their own, silence was essential.

The young man alone knew how truly dangerous his position was. The name he had given his hosts was Robert Parry, for he did not dare divulge his true identity. He was Robert Thornleigh, son of the traitor Frances Thornleigh. Raised by her among the exiles in the Low Countries, he would be under immediate suspicion if the English authorities knew who he was; they were vigilant in watching for Catholic infiltrators. In Dieppe harbor he had paid a handsome sum to the shipmaster of an English bark, a small ship out of Seaford on the coast of Sussex, for passage on the bark's return from delivering a cargo of hides to Dieppe. Using some of Robert's money the shipmaster had paid off the Seaford harbor official whose job it was to check arriving ships and their passengers. The payment had bought the harbor official's silence. Waiting until dark, Robert had been rowed ashore at nearby Newhaven. He made his way alone on foot to Lewes. At four in the morning he had reached the safe house of Gilbert and Agnes Levett.

The ten months since then had been sufficient for Robert to quietly establish himself in Lewes, the first stage of his mission. The Levetts had told their neighbors he was the friend of a merchant colleague's son. Robert had come prepared. At the University of Padua he had studied medicine—physic, it was called in England—and he was now well-known amongst the neighbors in Lewes as a young physician skilled beyond his years, clever at treating their agues, fluxes, and various persistent maladies.

Robert felt confident that the authorities did not know he was secretly back in England, but soon, if the plan he had set in motion succeeded, one of the most prominent among those authorities *would* know: his own father, Baron Adam Thornleigh. Robert had not seen his father in ten years, but he had come to loathe everything he stood for as a friend and defender of the heretic Queen Elizabeth. That revulsion had fueled Robert as he'd bided his time in Lewes under the cover of dispensing physic.

"Has the wild pansy calmed her cough?" Robert asked the Levetts.

He was sitting knee to knee with their daughter Judith at the girl's bedchamber window, examining her sputum, which she had spit into a glass. Her parents stood beside Robert, anxiously watching. Pallid-faced, the girl sat slumped in her chair, exhausted from another night's attack of asthma. The sun was up, but she still wore her night clothes. Her sleep had been so racked, she said, she had left her bed at dawn because being near the window gave her some comfort.

"The pansy did some good at first," Agnes answered hesitantly, hands clasped at her waist in concern. Robert heard in her voice her real meaning: *None at all.* She was being polite. Trusting his skill, she did not want to gainsay him. "But oh, Master Parry, at midnight her wheezing was so bad I feared she'd never catch her breath. Terrible to watch. Terrible!"

"It always strikes her worst at night," Gilbert said.

Robert glanced up at the couple's worried faces. Judith was their only daughter. Their four grown sons had homes and families of their own. Judith was the last chick in their nest.

Judith coughed. Her parents tensed. "It's like my chest clenches up like a fist," the girl said weakly.

So much for the wild pansy, Robert thought. Heartsease, people called the herb. Such a sweetly English name. So much about the English countryside moved him strangely. Brussels, Paris, Rome—

for thirteen years these great cities had shaped him, taught him, succoured him. Urban Europe was his home. Yet now that he had returned to the land of his birth the sights and sounds and smells of his English childhood induced in him a primal upwelling of emotion. *Home.* If the grand plan in which he had come to play a part succeeded, England would be his home for good.

The Enterprise of England—that was King Philip's name for the invasion plan. How Robert itched to see it triumph! He had chafed during the months spent impotently watching from this backwater as several of his brethren in religion, Jesuits sent by Rome, had been imprisoned and hanged. But he hoped to emerge soon from his self-imposed exile in Lewes. His plan depended on his sister. Kate would have received the letter by now, signed by their old tutor, Master Prowse. That had been Robert's first move. This morning he had awoken with a ripple of queasy excitement, knowing his next move had to be today. A visit to Prowse in Seaford.

He opened the satchel at his feet between him and Judith. "Try this," he said, drawing out a linen pouch tied with twine. "Butcher's broom and balsam of Peru." The first ingredient the Levetts would be familiar with; the herb grew in southern England's gentle clime. The second was more exotic: the scorched bark of a tree in the New World. "Mix it with treacle or honey and boil it to a syrup. It will help clear her chest of phlegm." But will do nothing to stop the attacks, he thought. What was at the root of them? Asthma had been written about for centuries, but its cause was still unknown. Fragments from his textbooks flitted through his mind. Greek: *asthma*, meaning a short breath, a panting. Latin: *asma*. He remembered the Levetts saying Judith's attacks had started when she was ten. But why?

"I'll have the kitchen start right away," said Agnes, bustling out with the pouch. Gilbert moved to Judith, offering her a cup of water, murmuring words of comfort.

Robert regarded the multipaned window beside the girl. She said she felt a little better when seated here. Why? She had not opened a pane, so outside air was not the reason. Did the garden view calm her mind and therefore her chest? Or was it sitting upright that helped, while lying in bed brought on the attacks? He looked across at the rumpled bed. Gilbert Levett was well-off and had furnished his daughter's bedchamber with a carved oak bedstead, velvet curtains of buttercup yellow, and fine Holland linens. *Always worst at night,* Gilbert had said. That had to signify somehow, Robert thought.

He stood and went to the bed. The rumpled, cream-colored sheet had an embroidered hem. He fingered the delicate pink embroidery, pondering. He picked up one of the pillows and absently plumped it back into shape as a memory surfaced: fitful sleep when he was six on a scratchy straw mattress in the rude Irish inn where his mother had first fled with him and Kate. Then another memory, when he was perhaps eleven, of lounging in luxurious bedsheets in the Brussels mansion of the Duchess of Feria, his mother's friend. He set down Judith's pillow, and a feather's sharp tip, protruding, pricked his thumb. He drew the small feather out through the linen weave and examined it. Feathers. Latin: *plumis.* Another memory surfaced: Giordano, a fellow student in Padua who said he never slept with pillows because they gave him a crick in his neck and a stuffy nose.

He turned to Gilbert Levett. "Has she always slept here?"

The merchant looked up from his murmured talk with his daughter. "Pardon?" The question seemed to puzzle him.

"Has this always been her bed?"

"Oh. Yes. Well, since she left the nursery."

That would have been when she was four or five, Robert thought. "And has she always had these pillows?"

"Pillows? Yes, I believe so."

"No," Judith said, her voice still weak. "Remember, Father? You gave them to me as a Christmas gift."

"When was that?" Robert asked.

Father and daughter looked at each other, puzzling to recall. She said, "It was the Christmas the river froze so early, remember?"

"Ah, that's right. Fine goose down. A delivery from Brighton."

Judith said to Robert, "I must have been ten."

Ten. When her asthma attacks had begun. Robert picked up one of the pillows. "Judith, sleep without the pillows tonight."

"Why?"

"Just try it."

Seaford, one of the Cinque Ports, lay ten miles from Lewes. Above its tidal mudflats and salt marshes the white cliffs of the South Downs faced out to sea. The clean, crisp September weather should have made Robert's ride there on his host's borrowed gelding a pleasure, but he took no joy in the pitiless task that lay before him. Would he be able to go through with it? Did he have the strength of will? He thought of his mother, of her unflinching determination in spite of everything she had suffered—or perhaps because of it. Her resolve spurred his courage. He had to prove himself worthy.

In the clear morning light he could see the massive cliff of Seaford Head long before he reached the seaside town. Terns swooped around the cliff. Seagulls screeched. He reached the humble cottage that lay halfway up the slope above the shingle beach and dismounted. The wind that bent the marran grasses had the faintest knife-edge of winter in it. Robert's face felt sticky from the sea salt carried on the breeze. On the beach below he could make out the red berries, called bittersweet, that grew low to the ground as protection from the coast's strong winds. The berries, he knew, were poisonous.

He turned to the cottage door. Behind him his horse munched the grass. He knocked.

Inside, a dog barked. The door opened and from the interior gloom a frail-looking man with tufts of white hair peered at Robert. He held a knobbly cane. "Yes, sir?"

"Master Tobias Prowse?"

"Yes, I am he." Behind him the dog, a shaggy gray wolfhound, barked in nervous warning. "Hush, Smoke," the old man ordered. Then kindly to Robert, "Can I help you, sir?"

"Good Master Prowse, I am come to pay my respects."

"Indeed?" Prowse looked vaguely surprised, but the cheerful expression on his face spoke of eagerness to be enlightened. "Do come in, sir." He beckoned Robert across the threshold.

Robert had to duck his head under the low doorway. The dog bounded to him. Robert stiffened. He didn't trust dogs.

"Oh, Smoke will never harm you," Prowse said, gesturing with his cane as he closed the door. "He's almost as old as I am. A cast-off from my lord's hunting pack years ago. A hound with a broken leg was not welcome there." The animal, its rear leg slightly crooked, contented itself with sniffing the stranger's boots. Robert relaxed. He scanned the dimly lit room. A floor of beaten earth. A narrow stone hearth where a low peat fire smoldered. A schoolroom desk messy with books and papers. On one wall, in pride of place, a bookcase crammed with volumes. Robert felt a tingle of surprise at recognizing several books' spines. Tomes that Prowse had used to instruct him and Kate.

"Have we a mutual friend, sir?" the old man inquired. A natural enough question following Robert's claim of paying his respects.

Robert turned to him and smiled. "I see you do not remember me."

"Remember?" Prowse squinted at him. "Forgive me, but I do not. Are we acquainted?"

"You taught me and my sister, Katherine, when we were children. I am Robert Thornleigh."

A bolt of surprise straightened the old man's posture. "Bless my soul. Not young Master Robert? You quite surprise me, sir. Why, it must be fifteen years!"

"Thirteen, to be exact. That's when you last corrected our Latin scribblings. Kate and I went to Flanders after that."

A polite silence. The old man surely knew that Robert's mother had fled with the two children. News of treason travels fast, especially such a spectacular attempt against the Queen's life all those years ago by Robert's late uncle, his mother's brother. *If only they'd succeeded,* he thought. He changed the topic. "Glad I am to see you so hale, Master Prowse. The years have been kind to you."

"Yes, God keeps me in health. My wife He took to her rest last year. I grieve her still, but I want for nothing. Tell me, how fares your good father? Goodness, I should say His Lordship, for he is Baron Thornleigh now."

"He is indeed. We lost my grandfather that same year my sister and I left England."

"God rest his soul," Prowse said gently. "Well, well, thirteen years." He thought a moment, then went on with pedantic exactitude, "If I am not mistaken that was the year the Scottish Queen Mary came into Her Majesty's realm. What a to-do was there. As it happens, I went on to tutor the grandson of her friend, the Countess of Arundel."

A warmth leapt in Robert's chest at hearing Mary's name. Mary, that angel among women! He would never forget the first time he saw the portrait of her at Charles Paget's house in Paris. Her shining eyes. Her alabaster skin. When she had taken up her birthright as Scotland's queen at eighteen many had called her the most beautiful woman in Europe. But she had lost her kingdom to her half brother's army and had fled to England, trusting that her royal cousin, Elizabeth, would protect her. Instead, Elizabeth put her under house arrest. For thirteen years no one had seen Mary but her jailers. Robert had never seen her in the flesh, but to him she was beyond beautiful. She was celestial. He was sworn to free her. That was the mission he'd been sent here to do. Then, backed by a Spanish army, Mary would take her rightful place as queen of England.

"Well, well, my dear young fellow," Prowse was saying, looking him over. Respectfully, he corrected himself. "Forgive me. Master Robert."

Respect, Robert thought with bitterness. He had, in fact, no position at all in society. His father had got the queen to annul his marriage to Robert's mother, and Robert he disinherited. The news had reached them in Brussels, shattering them. *The vile insult to Mother. And my inheritance, lost.*

Well, he had come back to right those wrongs, and more. But had the first step succeeded, the letter to Kate? He tried to imagine her reading it. Did she suspect that Prowse had not written it? She was clever. But Robert had worked hard in composing the wording to sound old-fashioned and authentic. Kate was clever, but she was also trusting. *She loves me. She will have believed it.*

Prowse lifted the cane he held. "You have found me about to take the air with Smoke. He loves a romp this time of day. But here, let me put my stick by and welcome you to take your rest." He snugged it into the corner beside the door. A walking stick, Robert realized, not a cane. "Come, sit you down and tell me what brings you to my door."

Robert hesitated. He would rather not deal with the old man in this cramped room. The familiar old volumes put him on edge, for they reminded him of Kate. A memory flashed of the two of them grinning over the Latin rhyme they had composed together, an exercise set by Master Prowse. They hadn't let their tutor hear the naughty words of substitution they had giggled over when his back was turned. *Kate*, he thought with a twinge. *Such a merry playmate.* It gave him a pang like a shard in his chest. With these books so near he could not do what he had come to do. It was as if Kate were watching him. She must never know what had brought him here.

"Do not let me keep you from taking the air with your hound, Master Prowse," he said. "It would be my pleasure to accompany you." He picked up the old man's walking stick and offered it to him. "Shall we walk and talk?"

Prowse looked pleased. "To be sure, sir. The very thing. I would enjoy hearing the news from Flanders."

They set out up the track toward the top of Seaford Head. The dog romped ahead, now bounding after a bird, now sniffing a shrub, now gamboling around the old man in wide, restless circles. Prowse moved with surprising briskness for one who looked so frail. The only sign of his age was a slight shallowness of breath from the climb. Robert's breathing was shallow, too, but not from exertion. His heart thumped as they crested the cliff. He stopped, and looked out at the sea. Prowse stopped as well, taking in an expansive breath of contentment as he beheld the view he clearly loved. The narrow beach lay far below. Waves rolled in with a booming, monotonous cadence. Seagulls swooped and screamed. The dog, accepting the halt, sat on his haunches beside the old man, panting, and looked out, too, watching the birds.

Prowse pointed with his stick to a small boat bobbing on the sea. "Cormorants."

Robert, his thoughts churning, made a pretense of scanning the sky for the birds.

Prowse chuckled. "Not the avian kind, sir. The human kind. The people hereabouts have been dubbed 'cormorants' because of their enthusiasm for looting ships wrecked in the bay. Residents have even been said to place false harbor firelights on these cliffs to cause ships to run aground. I've never witnessed it myself, but true it is that my neighbors grimly exploit their rights to flotsam and jetsam, for whenever a ship is grounded here the cormorants strip it of its cargo." He shrugged and gave Robert a philosophical smile. "I leave it to God to judge the actions of needy folk."

To avoid the old man's eyes, Robert lengthened his gaze across the water. He could not do what he'd come to do while he felt those gentle eyes on him. "Look," he said, pointing at the wavering horizon. "The air is so clear you can make out the coast of France."

"A mirage only, sir," Prowse said, turning his head to look. He spoke as one who knew this landscape well and added pedantically, "*Videre sicut nos videmus.*"

Robert knew the Latin: *We see what we want to see.* He took a final look at the horizon. There lay France, and his mother, and their community of English exiles led by Westmorland. His mother's determination was no mirage. The exiles' grand plan was no mirage. The invasion fleet, when it sailed, would be no mirage.

"My boot is caked with dog muck," he said, frowning at his foot. "Let me have your stick, Master Prowse. I'll knock this mess off."

Prowse handed him the stick with a chuckle. "I told you Smoke needed his airing."

Robert made a show of using its tip to scrape the sole of his boot. The moment he felt Prowse turn away again to look out at the sea Robert raised the stick high. The blow to the old man's head cracked the still air. How thin the skull! Robert held his breath as his tutor staggered. He dropped the weapon and caught Prowse as if to steady him. Prowse's eyes rolled. He was too dazed to stand. Robert half-dragged, half-marched him to the cliff edge. One push. A bag of bones, frail after all. Not even a sound as he plunged.

Robert forced his thoughts to Kate as he hurried back down the hill's track. *Take the bait, dear sister. Let today's work not be in vain.*

Seagulls swooped and screamed behind him. And another sound that seemed to pursue him. A dog, circling in agitated confusion on the cliff's edge, crying.

❧ 4 ❧

Blood Ties

Thames Street was abuzz. Everyone Kate passed was talking about the Queen's brush with death on the river a mere two hours ago. News of her survival had swooped through the city like a shorebird on the wing. Men and women had hastened from the narrow streets and lanes into broad Thames Street to gather in clusters, and their keyed-up chatter sounded to Kate like the clamor of starlings. Their excitement was palpable. It was as though Londoners felt that they, too, had just escaped death and were now reveling at being alive.

Kate felt abuzz herself from the emotions that had tumbled through her all morning. Astonishment at Prowse's letter about Robert . . . the thrill of Owen's kisses . . . horror about the assassin . . . joy at hearing the queen was unhurt . . . dismay at Owen's new mission. He would be leaving for Petworth in a day, two at most. They'd scarcely had three weeks as man and wife before his arrest and the thought of being separated again wrenched her heart. What a bittersweet homecoming!

But overpowering all this was her somersaulting doubt about her *own* mission—one she could now scarcely believe she had volunteered for. *Am I mad?* Until today, her work for Matthew had been confined to decoding in safe anonymity. If she were to become the new courier between the French ambassador and Mary

Stuart she would be perilously visible. *I'll be riding into the jaws of danger.* And that was only the *final* danger. First, she would have to convince Ambassador Castelnau and Mary's people of her dependability, a fearsome challenge. They had found out Roger Griffith's double game and murdered him. In her mind she saw Griffith sprawled on the muddy cobbles at Ludgate Hill, eyes staring as his life's blood gushed from his slit throat. He had been cunning, experienced in subterfuge, vigilant about his adversaries, knowledgeable of their ways. *If Griffith could not survive them, how can I?*

"Rosemary and bay! Rosemary and bay!" a woman cried, hoisting her basket of herbs to show passersby. Another called, "Buy my pudding pies!" The street was alive with vendors hawking their wares, making the most of the sudden increase in potential customers. Housewives, servants, gentlemen, shopkeepers—all were cheerfully chattering, common folk and gentlefolk alike enjoying the festive mood.

In gaps between houses Kate saw sunlight silvering the river and caught the fishy reek of the mudflats as she approached the Old Swan Stairs. There she would take a wherry back to her grandmother's house and wait for Owen. He had left the alehouse before her, gone to buy a horse for his journey to Sussex.

"There's no need to buy one," Kate had told him. "Take a mount from my grandmother's stables. I told you, she has accepted you."

"For your sake," he had said pointedly.

"It's the same thing."

"No, Kate, it's not. You are her kin. I am charity. And I will not beg." He patted his doublet where the purse of gold from Matthew lay inside and said with a wry smile, "I'll visit a bathhouse and barber, too, and a tailor. When Her Ladyship sets eyes on me I shall be presentable, if not transformed."

He had said the last words lightly, with a twinkle in his eye and an actor's flourish of his hand, but Kate knew the truth: Owen hated being without money. Playwriting had hardly paid him enough to maintain his modest house on Monkwell Street, even when he had let out rooms to lodgers. The house was gone now, sold to pay the huge recusancy fine at his arrest. All that, of course— the arrest and fine, the house sale, his incarceration—had been to build the cover for him that he and Matthew had devised, but even when Matthew reimbursed him for the fine he would still be far from well-off. As the fourth son of a Bristol magistrate he'd been given only enough funds to pay for his Oxford education, not to set him up in life.

Kate thought of the first time she had seen him, during the applause for a performance of his play *The Prosperous Apprentice* at a playhouse called The Theatre just outside London's wall. She had come with her cousin Nicolas Valverde, who had acquaintances in this exotic theater world. From their gallery seats Nicolas had pointed out to her the playwright below chatting with friends among the groundlings. Kate's eyes had taken their fill of the dashing, lanky form and the devil-may-care smile, the tousled black hair and self-assured swagger, but she had also noted his plain serge doublet worn almost threadbare at the elbows and the boots so worn the leather was cracked. The thought had sprung upon her that Owen Lyon was exactly the kind of clever but impoverished young man Matthew had asked her to be on the lookout for: well-educated, open to adventure, and able to move easily between social levels. A playwright, she reasoned, would have a foot in two worlds, the highborn one of his theater company's patron, the Earl of Leicester, and the shadowy world of actors, masterless men who had empty pockets, but plenty of energy, wit, and verve. Daring to take a risk, she had asked Nicolas to introduce her. And in that moment of meeting, when Owen Lyon's smiling eyes had fallen on her, she had known the heart-stopping truth of what poets call love at first sight. He had felt it, too, he told her later—a lightning bolt to his heart, he'd said. Kate's gamble had borne thrilling fruit. She had not only recruited him for the Crown; six months later she had married him.

But she had not anticipated the fire of ambition she had ignited in him alongside his fire for her. In those six months Matthew had sent him on an intelligence mission to Paris, where Owen had contacts among lawyers at the English embassy, friends from his Oxford days. He had thrown himself into cultivating acquaintances with French officials and reporting any information that concerned threats to England, and had quickly become one of Matthew's most valuable agents. But he wanted more than the occasional purse of coins Matthew paid him. He hungered for advancement, the kind that the Lord Secretary Sir Francis Walsingham could give him, recommended by Matthew. The kind that brought rich posts at court and eventually the security of rent-generating land, putting him on a footing almost equal to Kate, daughter of a baron. He told her this on their wedding day, assuring her that he would not be satisfied until he could provide the manner of life she had enjoyed in her father's house. "I want it for you," he had said. "For us. For our children." Kate herself would have been content to stay away from the competitive arena of court-climbing, but she was no fool. Having sparked ambition in her husband she saw that his inferior status would eat at him, and bitterness like that could erode even the happiest marriage.

Owen's parting words to her as he'd left the alehouse had been most sober. "When we're back at Her Ladyship's house we'll talk, you and I. About telling Matthew you have changed your mind. You leapt at the chance to help Her Majesty, I understand that. You have a generous heart, Kate, and I bless you for it. But this danger is not for you. Not while I have breath to prevent you and protect you." He had kissed her again, ardently. And then he was gone.

Passing Fishmongers Hall she realized she was obsessively fingering the row of buttons on her cloak. An unconscious habit that surfaced when she was anxious. The smooth, small buttons slipping over her fingertips felt comforting. *Like rosary beads,* she thought with a prickle of alarm, and instantly dropped her hands to her sides. Her father had brought her up in the English church, a Protestant, but when her mother tore Kate and her brother from England and settled them in Brussels she had immediately sent them for instruction in the Catholic catechism. Kate's mother had been about to place her in a convent when her father tracked them down and forcibly took Kate back to England. In Kate's mind, Catholic ritual was now fused to the image of her traitorous mother.

Enough disturbing thoughts, she told herself. They led to nothing good. She set her mind to the huge task ahead: how to become the new courier. Owen would not dissuade her. He was worried about her safety and she loved him for that, but she now knew that her mind was made up. The decision was sealed by the excited mood of the people in the street who so loved their monarch. It matched her own admiration for this queen who had been kind to her. Her Majesty had escaped a bullet today, but Catholic radicals would continue to try to murder her. They just kept coming. One day one of them might succeed. And if the rumors Owen had reported were true the would-be assassins might be the vanguard of an invading army. England would not win such a contest. Then, the victors would exact vengeance on people like Matthew and Owen and Kate. Nooses would snap their necks.

No, nothing would dissuade her. Not even Owen.

But now, how to proceed? Matthew had suggested she visit Ambassador de Castelnau using her acquaintance with his wife and make her case to him as a good Catholic who could no longer abide Mary's imprisonment, and present herself as ready and willing to act in Mary's interests. But, thinking it through as she walked along Thames Street, she rejected so direct an approach. It could look suspect, especially so soon after Griffith's death. No, her best entry into Castelnau's confidence was probably a more subtle route. She had first met Marie de Castelnau at a banquet Kate's father had hosted three years ago. Marie was Kate's age, four decades younger than her sixty-two-year-old husband. They had quickly become friends. It had been months since Kate had seen Marie, who had gone into her confinement with her third child, but Kate had sent her a note of congratulations at the baby's birth. Those good wishes had been sincere. *Now,* she thought with some discomfort, *I'll have to dissemble.* She decided that from her grandmother's house she would write Marie a note saying she would love to call and see the baby. But the real object of her visit would be the ambassador.

She was about to turn down the lane to the Old Swan Stairs when a commotion to the west made her stop. Near the mouth of London Bridge people were running toward the bridge. She heard shouting. A blue-smocked apprentice bolted out of a doorway across from her, caught her eye, then hurried toward the uproar.

"What's happening?" she called after him.

He didn't stop, just called over his shoulder, "The villain who tried to kill the Queen! He's running for Southwark!"

Kate's heart jumped. Could they catch the man? If he reached the other side of the bridge he might lose his pursuers among Southwark's warren of alehouse lanes and alleys. A new energy surged through her. This gunman must not escape! If he was part of a cabal his information could be crucial. She found herself running toward the crowd.

When she reached the bridge its entrance was crammed with shouting people. Beyond their backs and heads she saw several horsemen armed with swords holding the crowd back. Halfway across the bridge a half-dozen more horsemen had taken up positions to block the way to Southwark. Between the two groups of mounted men the bridge had been cleared of foot traffic except for a lone young man. Slight, fair haired, well dressed, he stood half-crouched, panting, eyeing his pursuers with a wild look like a hunted animal. He brandished a pistol. Kate took in all this even as her heart raced in surprise at seeing the badges the horsemen wore on their sleeves: a thornbush. The Thornleigh emblem. These were her father's men. She spotted their swarthy leader, Captain Lundy.

She craned to see if her father was with them, but the crowd blocked her view. People leaned out from windows in the houses four stories high that lined the bridge, the buildings so tightly packed they blocked the sun. A handcart and a mule-drawn wagon stood abandoned by their drivers, who had crammed themselves into doorways. The mule cast confused eyes on the tense scene and brayed. Someone had left a packhorse mare hastily tethered to a post. It shuffled nervously.

Kate needed to get closer for a clear look at the gunman. She squeezed between the backs of people and the doorways, edging forward until she was a long stone's throw from the cornered man. The tethered mare was to her right. Looking across its withers she saw her father. He sat astride his bay stallion, unmoving, his sword drawn, eyes fixed on his quarry. The three of them formed a triangle: Lord Thornleigh at the west side of the bridge, Kate at the east, the hunted man halfway to Southwark, his way barred by her father's mounted men. He was trapped. But he held his pistol rigid to fend off attack, jerking it erratically back and forth between the horsemen at the bridge's London end and those at the Southwark end.

The mare tethered beside Kate danced nervously in place, swinging its rump around, again blocking her view. Cursing in frustration, Kate moved the few steps to the back of the mule-drawn wagon. Its load of firewood and bundled faggots was low enough to see over.

Her father raised his sword in a gesture of authority, its tip to the sky, like a priest raising a crucifix. "I arrest you," he commanded in a clear, calm voice, "in the name of Elizabeth, by the Grace of God queen of England and Ireland, defender of the faith. Lower your weapon."

"A pox on your hellcat queen! A Jezebel!"

An angry roar rose from the crowd.

The gunman suddenly swung his pistol at the Southwark-side horsemen and shouted, "Move, you filthy heretics!" He aimed, his hand steady now, at the mounted man in the center, Captain Lundy. The crowd gasped.

Lundy and his horsemen did not move. But none of them had firearms, only swords.

"Surrender to Her Majesty," Thornleigh commanded again, "for I swear you shall not pass."

The gunman swung his weapon straight toward Thornleigh. Kate gasped. Her father did not flinch. The man took steady aim.

Lundy kicked his mount and bounded forward, sword raised high as though to cut the felon down. The gunman saw him coming and cringed.

"Stop!" Thornleigh bellowed. "I want him alive!"

Lundy, obeying, hauled on his reins. With a scowl he turned his mount in a tight circle that brought him back to his original position.

The gunman straightened, saved.

"Shoot any of my men, though," Thornleigh growled, positioning his sword at a threatening slant, "and your head will leave your shoulders the next minute. Lower your weapon, I say. You shall not pass."

A wild look swept the man's face. It seemed to Kate more like delirium than despair. He spoke in a strangled voice, but his eyes were shining. "Nor shall *you* pass, my lord. I'll send your stinking soul to hell!" He aimed the pistol at him with arm outstretched and cried, "And God will enfold me to His breast!"

Kate's breath stopped. The gun barrel was pointing straight at her father's head. He stiffened, but only to straighten himself in dignity for death. The horrified onlookers made not a sound.

Kate lunged for the nearest bundle of faggots and yanked out a stick. She whipped the mare's reins from the post and with the stick she stabbed its rump. The mare bounded forward in terror and skittered toward the gunman. Lurching, he fumbled the pistol. It fell and clattered at his feet.

In an instant Captain Lundy galloped to him, snatched his collar, and twisted him around like a weather vane as Lundy turned his horse and halted.

Cheers rang out from the crowd.

Thornleigh stared at Kate in surprise. She looked quickly from him to the prisoner to make sure he had not retrieved his pistol. Her father blinked as though recalled to the business at hand. He trotted his mount to Lundy, who still had hold of the disarmed prisoner, and gave him orders to escort the captive to the sheriff of London. Lundy gestured to his men and six horsemen fell in to surround the prisoner.

People swarmed Thornleigh, cheering him and calling his name. A girl fainted. A woman dashed out of a goldsmith's shop calling, "My lord!" and offered him up a goblet of wine. He barely acknowledged the cheers, looking almost angry as his dark eyes turned back to Kate. This time she did not look away. He waved aside the wine and turned to one of his lieutenants. "Harper, move these people on."

"Aye, my lord."

The lieutenant barked at the crowd, and Thornleigh coaxed his stallion through them toward Kate. People were already dispersing. The owner of the wagon of firewood climbed aboard and

called to his mule with a snap of the reins. The wagon creaked into
motion. On the Southwark side a farmer with a small flock of sheep
held up by the crisis now drove his flock across. The business of
the bridge resumed.

Thornleigh reached his daughter, his expression still stormy.
"Kate."

"Father."

"How come you to be here?" The steeliness in his voice sounded
like suspicion. His eyes flicked to the departing prisoner, then
back to her in clear mistrust.

Kate realized how bad it looked, that she had turned up in the
very spot the gunman had bolted to in the hope of escape. *He
thinks I might be implicated.* Resentment swelled in her. *How can
he trust me so little?* "I heard the commotion," she answered
steadily. "I came, like all these people, to see what was amiss."

"Came from where?"

"Chaloner's. On an errand for my lady grandmother." The
bookbinder's shop on Thames Street was well-known. Kate had in
fact taken Chaloner an order only yesterday. The lie, she hoped,
would serve.

The hard expression on her father's face melted, and a sad smile
took its place. "She tells me you have been a great help in organizing her library."

"It is my pleasure to help her, sir. She has been kind to me."

Their eyes locked. Kate knew how unforgiving her words
sounded. She had not intended such a blatant accusation. Or had
she? His stand in barring her and Owen from his house was an
open wound that stung. Yet in her deepest heart she did not blame
him. He knew nothing about her secret work, nor Owen's. To him
her husband was a convicted Catholic and therefore a threat to
Elizabeth. And no man was more loyal to Elizabeth than he was.
How could Kate not admire that? Keeping her secret from her father was the hardest thing she had ever done.

Sheep bawled as they passed. Thornleigh swung down from his
mount and drew the stallion out of the sheep's path. Here, under
the painted sign of a glover's shop, he and Kate were clear of the
traffic of carts and people on foot. She watched him as he adjusted

the reins in his gauntleted hands. She had always thought of her father as a handsome, hardy man and he was still as fit as a man half his age, but it struck her now that his cares had taken their toll. His dark hair was swept back from his forehead the way he'd worn it for as long as she could remember, but the silver streaks at his temples had widened to swathes and the laugh lines around his eyes had deepened and lost their mirth.

He looked at her. "Thank you," he said awkwardly. "I believe you saved my life." He was clearly flustered, as though realizing how absurd his previous moment of suspicion had been.

She said quietly, "As you once saved mine." She remembered the searing heat of the Brussels house burning around her, the flames, her terror, then her father suddenly lifting her in his arms and rushing her to safety. All her love for him forged in those child-hood days came welling up again.

"A father's duty," he replied. In another man's mouth the words might have sounded cold. Duty, not love? But Kate recognized that warm timbre in his voice. He could no more hide his affection for her than he could take up arms against his queen. She heard something more, too. His anguish at how he'd had to leave his other child behind. Robert. Kate felt the same anguish every time she remembered the smoke and flames separating her from her terrified little brother.

The news burst back into her mind: Robert was back in England. She wanted to tell her father. Wanted to give him that comfort. But Master Prowse's letter had made it clear that her brother was living under another name and wanted none of his family to know he was back. Certainly, he would be suspect if his true identity became known. *But not by me!* she thought with a fierce rush of sympathy. How brave of Robert to break free of their mother and return to make a new life! She longed to visit him, embrace him, offer her support—even, perhaps, persuade him to contact their father in the hope of a reconciliation, but for now she had to honor his wish and keep it to herself. It deepened her misery at the strained relationship with her father. *I am as shut out from Father's life as if iron bars stood between us.* She felt a prisoner of her secrets.

"I must go," he said, looking in the direction his men had taken the captive. "Must see Martin. I want to be there for the interrogation."

Sir Richard Martin, the sheriff of London. He would take custody of the gunman. "Who is he?" she asked. "The prisoner."

He looked at her, this time without a flicker of suspicion. She blessed him for that. "We don't know yet."

"Was he acting alone?"

"Don't know that, either. Which is why I want to hear him interrogated."

And tortured if he does not talk, Kate thought. The Queen's men were not gentle. She wanted to ask more about the gunman— Where had he been flushed out? Was her father sure no accomplices had fled the scene?—and she was trying to think how to pose these questions to sound like an ordinary citizen. He'd said he had to go, but had made no move to leave.

"Kate," he said, anxiety clouding his face. "Is it not today that he'll be released? Your—" He took a breath as though to gird himself to utter the word. "Your husband."

So, he'd been counting the days as she had! But with the opposite agenda. A knot tightened in her stomach. She dreaded rehashing their quarrel. But there was no hiding the facts. "He was. This morning."

Hope sparked in his eyes. "You did not go? You have not seen him?"

"Yes, I met him. But he had business to attend to. I will join him at my lady grandmother's house."

He gripped her elbow and said with sudden fervor. "Don't. I beg you. Don't."

Wincing, she slid her arm from his hand. It was not his grip that caused her pain, it was hearing his entreaty again. Since Owen's arrest she and her father had battled this out, over and over, until the chasm between them had become too wide to close.

"Kate, come home. I have missed you."

She looked away. The affection in his voice caused her agony. She said, with all the control she could muster, "I cannot."

"You can, and you should. If not for my sake, for your stepmother's. She misses you, too. She is still not well, you know. The best medicine for Fenella would be to have you home."

That was cruel! Her spirited stepmother had always been her friend. And Kate's heart had bled at the news of her latest miscarriage. Her father's second marriage was barren. "Please, tell her she is in my prayers."

"Tell her yourself," he urged. "Your place is with us. Come home."

"A wife's place is with her husband."

"Not when the husband is a criminal. Possibly a traitor."

"He is not a—"

"You don't know *what* he is. You married him in haste. You did not know his true character, nor what he might be mixed up in."

Grandmother said the same thing, Kate thought. She burned to tell him how wrong he was, how Owen was risking his life to protect the Queen and the realm. *It is you who do not know him!* But she could say none of this. She was sworn to secrecy.

Her pained silence seemed to encourage her father. "But now you've had time to think," he said, his hope clear. "Six months. And in that time what has *he* done? Consorted with the most militant, most remorseless Catholics in the Marshalsea."

"You have spies there?" She was shocked despite herself. She should have known.

"Listen to me, Kate. Sever yourself from him. Right now. No one will blame you. You will not be the first wife to leave a criminal spouse."

"Hear *me*, sir. I will never desert my husband." She checked her anger, and softened her voice. "Surely you can understand that, you who are so devoted to your wife. You would never desert *her*."

He looked taken aback, then scowled. She realized in horror the meaning he had taken from her words: that he had deserted his first wife, Kate's mother, and divorced her. Nothing could have been further from Kate's mind, but there was no going back—so she plunged ahead. "Father, I *do* know the man I married. He is a good man and I love him. Please, in the name of love, won't you open your house to him, and open your heart?"

But his face had closed like a door. "I have been patient. When you married a common actor—"

"Playwright."

"When you married him," he went on implacably, "I was willing to help him for your sake. I was about to gift him with a manor to set him up. But then he showed how beneath my trust he is. Caught red-handed at a secret mass. And now, consorting with radical Catholics. I ask you one last time. Will you come to your senses and leave this man?"

"Father—"

He raised his hands to forestall her reply. "Do not answer until you know the consequences. You are childless so far, and that is a blessing. But if you return to this man's bed, everything between us changes. I cannot—I will not—bequeath my fortune to the spawn of a Catholic felon."

She stared at him, incredulous. This was so vile, so utterly beneath him. Anger made her lash out. "Ah yes, your preferred solution, cutting out family. You divorced my mother and disowned my brother, and now you threaten me? At this rate, sir," she snapped, "beware you don't end your days alone."

Steel flashed in his eyes. He quickly controlled his fury, but it rang out in his cold, steady command. "Sever yourself from your husband and come home, or from this moment you are dead to me."

Sunset was a wash of harvest gold burnishing the rooftops and church towers of London when Robert reached Lincoln's Inn Fields outside the city walls. Two of these fields—Cup Field and Purse Field—had been a playground for students from nearby Lincoln's Inn for over a hundred years. They had once been leased as pasturage by the Ship Inn on Fleet Street, but had reverted to the Crown in the time of Queen Elizabeth's father, Henry VIII, when their owners' estates had been seized.

The third field—Ficket's Field—lay to the south. Too close to London's constables and bailiffs for Robert to feel comfortable as he tethered his horse to an elm behind the Plough Inn, but Walter Townsend had named this as the meeting place. Townsend could not easily venture farther south than London from his home in

East Anglia with his landholder father, Sir Thomas. Each of the six young men Robert was in contact with were keeping their heads down for now. That would all change, he thought eagerly, on the day they were called to action. The liberation of England. Then, Robert would lead this cohort of the faithful to ride north on their sacred mission. They would free the celestial Mary from Sheffield while King Philip's troops charged ashore, and Mary would claim her rightful place as England's monarch.

But that action lay frustratingly far in the future. Robert knew he had to focus on the here and now as he swung his booted foot over the stable's waist-high stone wall in an undignified sprawl of his legs, then clomped through horse shit in the stable yard. Water gurgled from a pipe in the shed to his left, no doubt the alewife's brewery. Starlings foraging in the field rose like a spray of black spindrift. Someone among the cottages across the field was noisily sawing wood.

Inside the stable he found Townsend pacing in the dim light between horse stalls. Nags' stalls, rather. The dilapidated stable was filthy, its matted straw rank with the stink of horse piss that left a sharpness at the back of Robert's throat. It intensified the bitter taste that had stuck there since he'd watched old Prowse plunge over the cliff this morning. That sight, he feared, would long haunt him.

"What's this about a botched attack on Elizabeth?" he said. A brusque greeting—but the news had troubled him on his ride from Seaford. This attempted assassination would result in tightened security around Elizabeth, and no doubt around Mary, too.

"You heard?" Townsend was of an age with Robert, just turned twenty. He was a strapping fellow, though a hint of baby fat still pudged his cheeks. His affable face was clouded with worry.

"At a tavern on the road," Robert replied. "A wine merchant from London was regaling the locals. He said it was a man with a pistol. Missed his mark, more's the pity. Who is he?"

"No one knows. Leastways, no one I talked to. I knocked on our alderman's door to ask, but his wife said he was none the wiser and had rushed off to ask the sheriff. All I heard was that Baron

Thornleigh's troop nabbed the fellow on the bridge as he made a run for Southwark."

Robert stiffened at hearing his father's name. Townsend did not know he was Lord Thornleigh's son. They had met for the first time only last month. "Nabbed just the one?"

"So far. They'll be doing a house-to-house search, though. God knows whom they'll charge, if only for show."

Robert knew that danger was real—a vengeful sweep of suspects. Hotheads like this gunman caused more trouble than they were worth. "Some fool acting on his own," he said with contempt.

"Righteous, though," Townsend offered. "Maybe one of the Jesuits."

Robert only grunted. Even priests could be fools. "We'll need to take into account the added security when we make our plans with the others. Now," he said, clapping his hands with vigor to change the subject, "did you arrange for the warehouse?" Robert had not yet met the five other young men who had pledged themselves to save Mary, but he had corresponded with them all. Paget had appointed him as their leader and Robert was eager to establish his authority immediately. He was also itching to see his personal plan bear fruit. This skulking around London was dangerous. He needed a safe haven, one that would advance his cause, and for this he had pinned his hopes on his sister taking the bait of the letter. If she didn't, Prowse's death had been in vain— and that was a burden of guilt Robert hated to carry. Kate *had* to respond. She would then be the conduit to his real target: their father.

"Robert," Townsend said, his voice tight with what sounded like fear, "we have to postpone the meeting."

"What? Why?"

"Roger Griffith is dead. A brawl on Ludgate Hill."

Robert blew out his cheeks in commiseration. "That's a blow." Griffith was another man he hadn't met, but knew by reputation, a diligent agent for Mary's interests. Bad luck that some personal conflict had turned lethal. "Well, Castelnau will find another courier. It needn't affect us." He had not received from Paget any change in his instructions.

Townsend shook his head. "You don't understand. We killed him."

"We?"

"Someone sent by Queen Mary's people." Townsend lowered his voice and fear crept back into it. "Turns out Griffith was working for Matthew Buckland. So, for Walsingham."

That hit Robert like a punch. "Dear God." He'd had no idea.

Townsend nodded morosely. "The ambassador told Feron and Feron told me."

Laurent Feron. Ambassador Castelnau's clerk. Robert balled his fists in fury. "Griffith," he growled, appalled by the man's betrayal. "The double-dealing bastard."

"That's why we have to lie low. Walsingham may be getting close."

"What evidence do you have of that?"

"Not evidence, exactly. But it stands to reason. Since they were running Griffith, who can say how much he told them?"

Robert thought about that. So perhaps postponing was the wise thing. But wise men could talk themselves in circles and never move forward. That could mean abandoning Mary to imprisonment for more weeks, months, maybe years. Robert hated it. Besides, what would he tell Paget in his next report? That the grand plan had to be aborted because he was nervous? "Townsend," he said, "if we quake and quail every time the enemy makes a move we might as well join their foul heretic church here and now. Shuffle like sheep to their communion table and swear allegiance to their Jezebel. Is that what you want?"

"Of course not."

"Then we need to move fast. I want to meet the others day after tomorrow."

"But that's a whole week before we planned."

"I'm *changing* the plan. Send word. The warehouse. Thursday."

❧ 5 ❧

Chaucer by Moonlight

Kate slipped out of the bedchamber with her candle, leaving Owen sinking into sleep after their lovemaking. Padding barefoot along the corridor she glanced over her shoulder at the wing where her grandmother's bedchamber lay. Not a sound from there. *Unlike the lovemaking,* she thought with an abashed smile. It had been animated, to say the least—she'd half feared they had woken the house. Happily tingling from it, she went quietly down the stairs.

The great hall was awash in white light from the huge full moon. A harvest moon. Upstairs, Owen had closed the shutters on it as he'd said again that she must tell Matthew she could not take the mission. Kate had not wanted that discussion. She had wanted Owen. It was she who had cut through his words and pulled him to the bed. Her hungry untying of his shirt strings had silenced him. Their lovemaking had been sudden, rushed, frantic. Kisses that almost cut her lips. Her chemise torn at the neckline. His urgent need, ramming into her. Her need for him, clawing his back.

She reached the parlor off the great hall. As she came in, her grandmother's gray cat, Erasmus, jerked his head up from his cushion on the window seat. This parlor was Lady Thornleigh's library, the crammed bookshelves rising almost to the ceiling along three walls. Moonlight through the oriel window silvered the books' spines. The soaring window and its window seat wide as a man dwarfed Erasmus. Kate went to him and scratched behind his ear and he leaned into her in bliss, then settled back on his cushion, purring. She set down her candle on the desk in front of the window. The night was warm—she had slipped on just a light silk dressing gown over her chemise—and with one arm she lifted the heavy fall of her hair to let the air cool the back of her neck, still damp from lovemaking.

She could not fall asleep. Her mind was too alive. Owen. Father. Robert. The men of her family seemed to surround her. In the silence she heard their voices. Owen insisting that she stay out of danger. Her father demanding her obedience. Her brother needing her help, though he had not asked for it. Robert's tone was hard to imagine. She still heard him as a giggling boy—"Kate! I took Master Prowse's quill. Don't tell!"—but he was now a man. What did he sound like these days?

She sat down at the desk and blew out the candle. The moon over her shoulder cast light enough, glimmering off the room's pantheon of books on philosophy, astronomy, mathematics, history, geography, exploration, agriculture, gardening. Many were in Latin, others in Italian, Spanish, French, and English. On the desk lay five green leather-bound ledgers, a silver ink pot, a quill pen, and five stacks of books, each several volumes high, her grandmother's most recent acquisitions. The ledgers catalogued the collection. It was an ongoing project, one that Kate had initiated. It had kept her gratefully occupied during the lonely months without Owen. Her secret decrypting work for Matthew she did upstairs in the privacy of her chamber. Down here, amongst her grandmother, the chamberlain, steward, footmen and maids, she showed her public face.

She lifted a book off the top of one stack, its brown leather binding spotted with age, then drew toward her the ledger farthest to her right and opened it to the page of creamy vellum where she had last left off. This ledger catalogued works by English writers. She flipped open the inkwell, took up her quill, dipped it, and wrote the date. Then: *The Canterbury Tales. Author, Geoffrey Chaucer. Publisher, William Caxton. Date of printing, 1483.* She paused and laid a hand respectfully on the old volume of Chaucer's beloved work. Next year would be its centennial. Lady Thornleigh particularly cherished her books by English authors, including her one-time guardian, Sir Thomas More, in whose household she had grown up.

Kate bent to her writing. So intent was her concentration she did not hear the footsteps until they reached the desk. She looked up in surprise. Owen.

He came to her side. He was barefoot and his shirt, pulled on in haste, hung loose over his breeches. With its lacings untied, the shirt exposed his chest almost to his navel, and the white scar tissue from a knife stab at his rib gleamed in the moonlight. Owen's life in the theater had not been all poetry and applause. He looked at her with concern. "Forgive me," he said.

"For what?"

He fingered the neckline of her chemise where he had slightly torn it. "I was too rough."

"You were not, my love," she assured him. She slipped her hand around his fingers at her neck. "These months without you, that was the rough."

He let out a small breath of relief. He bent and kissed the back of her hand as though in thanks. Glancing at the walls of books, then at the volume of *The Canterbury Tales* in front of her, he said with gentle warmth, "What is better than wisdom? Woman. And what is better than a good woman? Nothing."

She smiled. The words were Chaucer's. She countered slyly with another Chaucer quote:

> "Yet do not miss the moral, my good men.
> For Saint Paul says that all that's written well
> Is written down some useful truth to tell."

He chuckled. Sitting down on the edge of the desk, he shoved aside the volume, his expression turning sober. "But we must talk, Kate. Books will give no refuge from the storm you have volunteered to venture into. The times are full of murder, and our enemies ruthless."

"I know."

"Do you? I think not, or you would not have offered your life to Matthew."

"Offered my . . . ? Heavens, I do not intend to sacrifice myself."

"But that is what's at stake. It's why I cannot let you do this."

She slid her hand free of his. "Matthew thinks it's a fine idea. And he knows the stakes better than anyone."

"Matthew is blind when it comes to you. He sees you as a goddess, invincible as Athena."

She sputtered a laugh, the thought so absurd. "I beg your pardon?"

"He's in love with you, poor fellow. You didn't know?"

She blinked at him. She had *not* known.

Owen took her hand again, and in one smooth motion raised her to her feet and pulled her close so she stood between his legs, where he sat. He gazed up at her face and clasped her hand to his chest. She resisted, her free hand pressing his shoulder with just enough force to show her reluctance to be mastered by his magnetism. "What man could not love you?" he said. "But none but I knows the treasure you are. A treasure I will guard with my life."

"And what of *your* life? You risk it in going into the Earl of Northumberland's stronghold."

"That's different."

"Because you're a man?"

"Of course. Besides, I may not manage to get inside."

"You'll find a way."

She said it with fond admiration, but in her heart she hated to think of him going into the camp of a likely enemy, and all alone. She stroked his cheek with the back of her finger. He had arrived at the house clean-shaven and smelling of sweet almond oil. The barber had also cropped the erratic tufts of hair that had proclaimed his prisoner status. With his finely bristled skull he now looked like a soldier of ancient Rome. She bent her head and kissed him.

He broke it off. "Kate, you cannot keep avoiding this subject by seducing me."

He knew her so well! She took a step back from him and turned to the window. *He's right*, she thought. *Tell him the truth.*

She sat stiffly on the cushioned window seat. Erasmus jerked up his head. Kate raised a hand to stroke his fur, but he leapt to the floor as if he sensed danger and streaked away. Kate raised her eyes to Owen. "Something happened today. When I saw my father."

"Something about the gunman?" She had told Owen as soon as he'd arrived that she had seen her father arrest the would-be assassin.

"No. Something Father said."

That surprised him. "You spoke?" She had said nothing about their conversation.

"He asked me to come home. To leave you and come home. I said I would not, of course, and I . . . well, I insulted him." She scarcely knew how those harsh words to her father had come out of her mouth.

Owen left the desk and came and sat beside her on the window seat. "It's been hard for you, I know," he said kindly. "The breach with him."

"It's worse than that. He gave me an ultimatum. He said that unless I left you he would disinherit me."

Owen scowled. "That's plain cruel. He has no right."

"He has the power."

"Kate, we don't need him. I'm going to make good, I promise you. Walsingham himself has all but guaranteed me the post of customs chief in Ipswich."

"You don't understand. I *do* need him. He's my father and I need to know that one day, when this dark time is past, he will see that I've been on his side—the Queen's side—all along. And that you have, too. I need him to know I did everything I possibly could."

"You already are. You're the best decrypting agent Matthew has."

"Bah," she said dismissively. "Much of it I could have done as a child." She quoted the Bible: "The last will be first and the first will be last."

"Pardon?"

"*A* is *z* and *b* is *y,* et cetera. Child's play."

"Come, come, you crack far more intricate codes than that. Codes that have baffled the best."

"Don't you see? I want to do *more.*"

"But *this?* A double game is the most dangerous work there is."

"But yields the most valuable intelligence. Without Mary's letters that Griffith brought us we would never have known the extent of her scheming with King Philip. And with the exiles, those traitors from hell."

The vehemence of her last words took him aback. Kate always found it hard to control her bitterness about her mother.

"Kate, no one censures you for your mother's sins. You do not have to atone."

She did not want to speak of her mother. Or to waste another thought on her. "I've told you my reason. When the day comes that I can tell my father the truth about us I want to have done everything I can for the Queen. For England. If I don't . . . well, I may be telling him only as Spanish soldiers prod us all to the gallows."

Owen searched her eyes, a sad look in his. "Your mind is made up, isn't it?"

"Yes. I've already taken the first step. I've written to Marie de Castelnau asking to come and see her baby."

He said with gloomy admiration, "Ah. That's clever."

"My love, don't worry. I assure you, no one is better fit for this mission than I am."

He nodded, reluctantly agreeing. "Because you're a woman."

"Of course." It echoed what he had said about being a man, and she could not resist adding with a sly smile, "Besides, I may not manage to get inside."

He, too, heard his echo and smiled at her wit. Kate saw that he had accepted the plan, however unwillingly. Now that they were agreed, she felt a rush of excitement. In convincing Owen she had convinced herself. She *could* do this!

He said, "I won't be that far away in Sussex. If you need me, send word to the Angel Inn in Petworth. I'll come to your side the same day."

"I shall."

"Promise."

"I promise."

He raised both hands and gently smoothed her hair back from her face. "Dear God, I may not see you again for—"

"Shh," she said, laying her finger on his mouth. She did not want to think of that yet. Another separation. More lonely nights.

"Yes," he whispered. "We have tonight."

He lightly kissed her neck. She bent back her head to let his kisses brush her throat. He slipped her robe and chemise off her shoulder and ran his lips over her collarbone. She shivered with pleasure. His mouth found hers. She smiled under his kiss. "Who's the seducer now?"

He chuckled, then murmured, "The one who loves you more than life."

Their lovemaking this time was slow and languid, beginning with smiles and whispers, then quieting into a silent searching of palms and fingertips, of lips and tongues. It built to an exquisite ache, then an even more exquisite release. When finished, they lay on the broad window seat locked in each other's arms. The moon had trailed to the window edge, casting them in half shadow as if to give them privacy. The cat hopped up beside Kate's bare ankle, startling her with a tickle of his tail. He settled into a ball in the crook of her knee, purring so loudly it made her laugh.

Owen laughed, too, as he unwrapped his leg from Kate's. "Erasmus, when I am with my lady three is one too many."

Kate sat up, her legs bare to the thigh as she swung them over the window seat edge and tugged her chemise and robe back into place. Straightening his own clothes, Owen leaned against the casement, gazing at her in the white moonlight. "By God, but you are lovely. An alabaster Venus, warm with life."

Erasmus stretched languorously, yawning, his long body taking up all the space between them. They shared another smile. "Reclaiming his territory," Owen said. He winked at Kate. "As I've reclaimed mine." He got to his feet and held out his hand to her. "Come, my love. Sleep. We are both going to need it."

She rose and slipped her arms around his waist, her body still tingling from their passion, and pressed her cheek against his neck. She did not want to leave this nook of moonlight and love. Did not want to break the spell. He held her close, and she was filled with a sweet gratitude for him. He understood how much the Queen meant to her. And how much her father's esteem meant, though he had turned his face against her. But that would change if she held fast to what she believed. Owen understood that as well. This bond between them, a bond of absolute trust, made her want to share more. She was bursting to tell him the news that had brightened her morning.

"Owen, Robert is back in England."

"Who?"

She pulled back, but kept her arms around his waist. "My brother. It's a secret, though, and you must tell no one. I got a letter from our old tutor. He says Robert is living in Lewes. He's a physician. Imagine, Robert caring for the ill! When I last saw him he was a frightened little boy. It's such wonderful news."

Owen frowned. "A secret, you say?"

"Yes. He and Master Prowse, that's the tutor, have become friends, and he explained that Robert has taken another name. Robert doesn't want anyone to know his true identity."

"I can understand why."

"Our mother. I know." Her bitterness welled up again. "Her children cannot escape her taint."

"Not both children."

"You said no one censures me for her crime, and surely the same holds for my brother."

"You have not been raised by her," he said darkly. "He has."

His implication shocked her. She let go of him and took a step back, forcing him to release her. "I know Robert. Know his heart. He was once the only friend I had. I will vouch for him to anyone who doubts him, even to the Queen herself."

His frown deepened. "Why did this tutor contact you?"

"He thought it only right that someone in Robert's family should know. Robert actually told him not to. I hate that he feels he has to go to such lengths to distance himself from our mother."

"Maybe he's not."

"Not what?"

"Distanced from her."

The statement fell between them like a tree. Ice touched the back of Kate's neck. A moment ago she had delighted in the afterglow of making love, but now his accusation had chilled that. "You don't know what you're talking about."

"Kate, think. He has been raised among England's enemies. He should be brought in for questioning. Interrogated."

She felt a stab of fear for her brother, as if she had betrayed him. How she wished she had kept this to herself! A fierce desire to protect him surged through her. "Robert is an innocent in these battles. He only recently reached manhood yet clearly he has cut all ties with our mother and that took courage. I am going to see him as soon as I can to offer my support."

"Don't. You need to stay well away from him until he can be questioned."

She bristled. For the second time today a man was issuing her a command.

Owen groaned. "Oh God, let's not quarrel, Kate. Not tonight. Your brother may be the soul of goodness and charity for all I know. If I am too cautious about your safety and conjure danger where there is none, forgive me. Heaven knows we have enough *real* dangers to occupy us."

With thankfulness, her anger drained. Owen was her rock, her love. To wrangle with him was churlish. "True. Let all my troublesome relatives keep their distance from us this night," she said, hooking her arm in his. "And let us, my love, to bed."

But as they left the library she cautioned herself that her brother was someone she would not mention to Owen again.

❧ 6 ❧

The Ambassador

"How delightful, *chérie!*" Marie de Castelnau spread wide the jade taffeta wrapping and lifted out the baby's gift Kate had brought. It was a teething coral, the coral's spines buffed down to smooth knobs, mounted on a curving silver handle fashioned like a dolphin. It also served as a rattle. Marie shook it, making its tumbling stone granules whisper a soft *swoosh*. "Ha! *Merveilleux!*" Her laughter was clear and high, like a cluster of silver bells. She was a pretty woman of twenty-two, her birthday and Kate's just seventeen days apart. She beamed at the baby in his cradle. "My little angel will soon need it, as you can see."

Kate did indeed—and *felt* it. With his slippery gums the baby was gnawing her knuckle like a starved creature, his tiny hands clamped on her wrist. She laughed, too. "What an appetite!" She jested, "Do you not feed the poor babe?"

"Oh, his appetite is prodigious. I pity the wet nurse when my angel *does* grow teeth."

They left the baby happily gumming his new rattle, and withdrew to the parlor. The London residence of the French ambassador was a spacious old house on Salisbury Court just south of Fleet Street and near enough to Ludgate to the east that Kate could hear, through an open window, faint voices and the clatter of wagon wheels as traffic moved in and out of the city. The house was an active place of business. Kate had passed through the great hall where merchants and lawyers milled with the ambassador's clerks and secretaries and then a maid had ushered her upstairs to the family's private apartments. The two ladies sipped spiced wine in the parlor fragrant with vases of blowsy, late-summer roses. Kate kept their cheerful conversation on topics Marie enjoyed: her children, her planned visit home to her parents in Rouen, the baby gifts sent by other friends and well-wishers.

"From the Countess of Leicester," Marie said, displaying a bolt of exquisite ivory silk on the low table before them. "For a christening gown."

"It's lovely. Have you seen the countess lately?" Kate knew how Marie, the heiress of a family of French royal secretaries, loved to gossip about courtiers nearest Queen Elizabeth.

"We dined with her and Leicester last week," Marie said with satisfaction. "August was the first time she has lived openly as his wife, you know." The secret marriage of Robert Dudley, Earl of Leicester, to the Queen's cousin Lettice Knollys four years ago had been the talk of London when the secret came out. The Queen had been furious, for Leicester, a very handsome man and a friend of hers since childhood, was one of her favorites. She had raised him to great heights and many had thought she would one day make him her husband. So irate had she been at his marriage she had banished his new wife from court, and for three years Lettice had lived quietly with her relatives in Oxfordshire. But for the birth of her son she had finally moved into Leicester House, the Earl's palatial mansion on the Strand. Young, beautiful, married to one of the most influential men in England, and now the mother of his heir, Lettice had reached a pinnacle of female status outside of being royal. Kate's sympathy was with Elizabeth. Now forty-nine, she had apparently decided to remain single, and would surely remain childless.

"Leicester especially invited my husband," Marie went on with pride. "His wife has all his affection, and he introduces her only to those to whom he wishes to show a particular mark of attention."

Kate tried to think of some morsel to add to the gossip, but her mind had already slipped ahead to the purpose of her visit. She had come prepared.

"Marie, could I ask a favor? I would be grateful for a few minutes of conversation with Monsieur de Castelnau. I hate to disturb him on an obviously busy morning, but it is for my husband's sake."

Marie reached out to touch Kate's arm with concern. "My poor *chérie*." They had carefully avoided speaking of Owen's time in prison, but Kate knew that Marie detested England's laws against Catholics. A devout Catholic herself, she and her husband enjoyed special privileges due to his position; they were allowed to hold mass within the embassy for their family and servants. She had named her young daughter Catherine-Marie in honor of two pious French queens, Catherine de Medici, the present French king's mother, and Mary Stuart, who had once been the queen consort of a previous French king. "Of course," Marie assured Kate. "If there is anything my husband can do for Monsieur Lyon I am sure he will be pleased to do so." She added a gentle but firm warning: "Within reason."

"I understand." Kate knew that no ambassador could flout the laws of his host country, or even its social mores, without stirring up the host government's fury. And Owen Lyon, the convict, was officially suspect. "I would only ask him to consider recommending my husband as a tutor, discreetly, to some of his merchant friends. Nothing more."

Clearly relieved, Marie patted Kate's hand and rose to go to her husband. "It is an excellent time of day to ask, *chérie*. He is always in a good mood after his breakfast."

With a whisper of her satin gown she was gone.

Kate sat waiting. She felt nervous, and very alone. Owen was on his way to Petworth in Sussex. Mounted on his new horse, a handsome silver chestnut with a blaze down its chestnut nose, he had trotted out through the gates of Lady Thornleigh's courtyard before dawn, leaving Kate in bed with his last kiss on her lips. After their moonlit moment in her grandmother's library they had had just one day together, and Owen had spent much of it visiting the man he had befriended in prison, a kinsman of Northumberland, hoping he would vouch for him to the earl. Matthew had arranged the man's release for this very purpose. Meanwhile, Kate had visited Matthew at his house on St. Peter's Hill neighboring Paul's Wharf to further her own purpose.

Surprisingly quickly—before Kate even felt ready—she was ushered by a clerk into the ambassador's downstairs study. She found him standing at his desk with his back to her, bent over some papers. She heard the scribbling of his pen. A couple of clerks or secretaries moved in and out of the room with dossiers, scrolls, messages. Kate waited, her mouth so dry with nervousness she longed for a sip from the decanter of wine on Castelnau's sideboard. Never would she have imagined when she'd spoken briefly with him at that banquet her father had hosted four years ago that one day she would come to him in this capacity. But she had been well briefed by Matthew. Michel de Castelnau, Sieur de la Mauvissière, was a former soldier and a seasoned diplomat with a reputation for tact and moderation. He had been France's ambassador to London for seven years and had once used his influence to promote a marriage between Elizabeth and the French Duke of Alençon, hoping to strengthen the ties between the two countries. Elizabeth had at first actively encouraged the negotiations, but eventually declined.

He turned and smiled. "Ah, Mistress Lyon, what a pleasure. You have gladdened my wife with your thoughtful gift to our son."

"A sweet babe, sir. He is fortunate in his gentle mother. And, if I may say, sir, he has your eyes."

"Ha. I hope that attribute of this rough face is all he will be saddled with," he said with wry good humor. "He would have been wiser to inherit all from my wife." He was sixty-two and there was no denying the bluff aspect of his craggy features. His thinning hair of crinkly brown curls lay like a threadbare cap. But his good humor spoke of a man whose life was rich and full. He put down his pen and motioned to a chair for Kate to sit.

She was too keyed up to sit. Besides, she had an intuition that her chance of success would be better if she remained upright in the role of petitioner. Her marriage to a lowly playwright had severely reduced her status; if she were not Marie's friend, and a baron's daughter, Castelnau might not have agreed to see her. "Thank you, sir," she said, declining the invitation to sit, "but I will not take up any more of your valuable time than necessary."

He glanced at a clerk who was carrying in a gift box fancifully wrapped in gold satin and tied with a silver cord. "From Lord Burghley, sir, for your son," the clerk said. Castelnau motioned for him to put the gift on the desk, then turned back to Kate. "Now, what's this Marie says about your husband? Master Lyon has concluded his term in the Marshalsea, I understand. I hope he is well despite his ordeal?"

"Yes, sir, he is again a free man, and he is well, thank you for your kind concern. As he said to me, it would have taken more than six months of cold gruel to break his convictions."

The ambassador flicked a glance at the departing clerk, then a look of mild warning at Kate. It was not wise to speak in public, even lightly, of flouting the law. But she saw a hint of approval in his eyes.

She had bet on this approval; Castelnau was as devoutly Catholic as his wife. But would he take the colossal next step? She, of course, could not let on that she knew his embassy was the depot for letters between Mary Stuart and her powerful friends abroad, nor could she betray any knowledge of Griffith having been the courier. She could only hope that he needed a replacement for Griffith urgently enough for her ploy to work.

Only one way to find out.

"Sir, I have to come to ask, most humbly, if you would vouch for my husband."

"Yes, a tutoring position, Marie said. There are one or two gentlemen of my acquaintance who might—"

"No, it is not about tutoring I have come." She glanced over her shoulder. No clerks were in sight, but for how long? She turned back to him and said quickly, quietly, "I seek a recommendation for myself."

He looked puzzled. "I don't understand. For what purpose? Recommend you to whom?"

"To Her Majesty Queen Mary."

Surprise stiffened his back. The good humor in his eyes died and dismay flooded in. "Madam, I must warn you—"

"Hear me, sir, I beg you." She moved quickly to the door and closed it. "I intend to ride to Sheffield and deliver to Queen Mary a letter offering my husband's services in her great cause. I see you are amazed, sir, and well you might be, knowing my father's position. But I was a loyal daughter of the church in Spain's city of Brussels before my father carried me away, and I am now a wife. At my husband's arrest my father, as you must know, turned his face from me. But I care not, for my husband's abiding faith has reawakened mine. We are devoted to the cause of Queen Mary and—"

"Stop." He held up his hands to forestall her. He looked shocked. "You are too forward, madam! I cannot help you. And I will not hear another word. My position—"

"We crave only to bring England back to God," she barreled on. "In prison my husband heard rumors that Englishmen loyal to the one true Church are preparing to rescue Queen Mary from her bondage. He wants to ride with them. If you will but put your name to my letter to her, sir, assuring her of my faith, and of my husband's desire to—"

"Stop, I tell you," he said harshly. "Enough." He made to move past her toward the door.

She stepped into his path to block him. The desperation she put into her voice was only partly counterfeit. "There is no other way now for me and my husband. He is an outcast in his own land thanks to the heretic queen. And do not doubt my commitment, sir. Look." She lifted the gold chain around her neck on which hung a locket, the kind used for carrying a beloved's lock of hair. She snapped it open to reveal a pale blue wax disc with the imprint of the Lamb of God over the crossed keys symbol of the papacy. "Yes," she whispered, "an Agnus Dei." These medallions blessed by the pope were exceedingly precious to Catholics. And exceedingly dangerous. Possession of an Agnus Dei was a violation of English law. Kate had got this one yesterday from Matthew. It had been stripped from a Jesuit priest who'd recently infiltrated from Rome and had been arrested.

Castelnau looked horrified. "You could be thrown in prison for having this."

"No, sir, it protects me. God protects me, and my husband. As no one else will in this cursed queen's land. I am taking this precious object to Queen Mary as proof of our devotion."

"I will hear no more." He strode past her and opened the door. "Giles!" he called.

Kate's heart was pounding. She had to convince him. "I am going to Sheffield, sir, with or without your assistance. My aunt and uncle live in the north and my ruse is to travel to visit them, but the destination of my letter will be Sheffield Manor, where Mary is held. I want your endorsement to prove myself to her, but believe me, sir, I have credence enough in myself. Everyone knows of my late uncle's attempt, with my mother's help, to remove Elizabeth. My faith, sir, is in my blood."

He looked at her with what seemed like pity. "You are a foolish woman. And your task is impossible."

"No, sir, it is not! My husband heard from some of the faithful in prison that Mary receives letters smuggled in to her. I will go to Sheffield and find who does this. They will help me."

"Do not, madam. You will surely be arrested." He scowled. "Be thankful I do not call for a constable myself." He called again, "Giles!" and almost instantly a clerk rushed forward. "Escort Mistress Lyon to the street," said Castelnau. "Her visit to my wife is done."

You fool! Kate furiously berated herself as she tramped north on Salisbury Court. *Too forward,* Castelnau had called her, and he was right! She had blundered like an idiot with him by blurting about Mary Stuart. How had she ever expected a veteran campaigner like Castelnau to tumble to her plan? She had thought to spark the idea in his mind that she would be the ideal replacement for his man Griffith—*Matthew's* man Griffith. Had been so sure that by telling him she was hell-bent on going to Sheffield he would come up with the idea himself of using her as the courier. Instead, he had thrown up a wall of caution against her. He would not taint himself by associating with such a hotheaded, reckless, presumptuous woman. All she had accomplished was to make him totally mistrust her. *Fool!*

A wagon rattled past her mere inches from her toes. She halted in surprise and looked up to see she had reached busy Fleet Street. Stonecutters' hammers clanged to the east where they were rebuilding the stone tower of the Fleet Conduit. It was now topped by a new St. Christopher with stone angels ranged around the bottom. Maidservants and boy water-carriers moved to and from the fountain hefting their jugs of water. Kate turned and started the opposite way, toward the Fleet Ditch. It stank of the effluent from the leather tanneries who used it as a sewer, polluting the brisk autumn air. The Fleet prison lay just a hundred yards north, so some of the stink probably came from there. On the other side of the short bridge across the Fleet Ditch the street went up Ludgate Hill, then on through Ludgate. Just this side of the bridge was the Belle Sauvage Tavern. There, Kate remembered, Griffith had drunk his last tankard of ale. They had killed him on the hill.

She had taken only a few strides when a man came up from behind her and fell into step with her by her side, so startlingly close she thought he might be a pickpocket. She quickened her pace. He did as well, then took hold of her elbow.

"Let go," she snapped. She tried to shrug him off, but he held her elbow firmly, his fingers digging into her through her sleeve. He was heavyset, with a wrestler's beefiness, far bigger than Kate. She was about to kick his shin, when another man coming from behind suddenly flanked her other side and pressed so close to her she was crammed between them. This one was no taller than she was, and skinny, but as grim faced as the wrestler as the two of them marched her on.

"What are you doing? Let me be!"

Neither man responded. They looked straight ahead as they walked. Then they slowed and she could do nothing else but slow with them, then stop. They turned her, all three of them wheeling as one. Unable to struggle free, Kate was frightened now. "I'll scream for a bailiff," she said, trying to resist.

"Don't," the skinny one said. She felt a sharp pressure at her side. A knife. He held it at her ribcage, its tip dulled only by the folds of her cloak.

"This way," he said. Kate heard the French accent—*thees* way. Fear shot through her. *Castelnau sent them.* The beefy one jerked her to start her moving again.

"Where are you taking me?"

No response. She became stiff with dread. *Castelnau found out about me. Now his men are going to kill me. Like they killed Griffith.*

They marched her north on Shoe Lane. The narrow, winding way was puddled and Kate's foot slid on a patch of mud, but the wrestler held her elbow so tightly she kept her footing. The pressure of the knife point at her side did not relent. She frantically stared at the few men and women they passed, willing someone to make eye contact and see her terror and stop these men. But people were few, and the shops—a pewterer, a catchpenny printer, a cobbler—showed no signs of life in the dim recesses beyond their mean windows. A scatter of men shouted at an open-air cockpit, oblivious as the Frenchmen marched Kate on. They reached the tenements of Oldborne House, where a ragged beggar held up his hand and croaked a plea to tell the lady's fortune.

"Let me go and I'll pay you well," she told the Frenchmen. "This ring is worth—"

They halted her, stopping her words. They had come to a door. The skinny one opened it and the wrestler shoved Kate in. It opened onto a staircase, dark and smelling of something acrid that caused a faint burning at the back of Kate's throat. The smell was somehow familiar. The worn wooden steps creaked as she went up, the men behind her, the knife now prodding her back. The air became heavy and humid when she reached the top stair, where she came to another door.

"Open it," the skinny one said with a prod of his knife. She opened the door and the wrestler nudged her forward. She stepped into a large room suddenly bright with sunlight from a dormer window. Three women were at work at tubs, scrubbing clothes on washboards. Their sleeves were rolled up, their faces pink and damp. Steam rose from a cauldron suspended over the fire in the hearth. Kate now recognized the acrid smell—the lye used in soap. This establishment was a laundry.

The washwomen idly glanced her way as the Frenchmen marched her through the room. The women seemed uninterested and turned back to their work.

Kate and her captors reached a doorway. The skinny one opened it. He pushed Kate in. It was a storeroom, with wicker baskets and a heap of linen sheets that gave off a rank odor of sweat. A small, high window cast a pale light. She heard the men retreat and she whirled around, about to try to run out the open door. But Ambassador Castelnau walked in. He closed the door behind him. His face bore none of his former bonhomie. His look now was watchful, yet searching, like a card player gauging the hand of his opponent.

"Our conversation was too brief, Mistress Lyon. There are questions I need answers to. First, where is your husband?"

Her heart was banging painfully. Was this questioning a prelude to her death? She thought of the gunman, the would-be assassin, perhaps at this moment being interrogated by men of the royal council with their agonizing methods, and her fear made her tremble. She sensed that her only hope with Castelnau lay in answering with the truth. "He has gone to Sussex, sir. To Petworth. He hopes to get a position as secretary to my lord Northumberland. I told you, as a marked man he must make his way as best he can."

He considered this for a moment. "Second, have you told your father you intend to visit your relations in the north?"

"My father does not speak to me, sir. He has banished me and my husband from his house. My lady grandmother, Lady Thornleigh, has taken us in and I intend to tell her that my destination in the north is my aunt's house."

He studied her for a moment. His face was unreadable. Then: "Third, and most important, would you be willing to take Queen Mary another letter along with your own?"

Kate's heart jumped. She forced her face to betray no hint of the thrill that coursed through her. She feigned surprise at the request. "Another, sir?"

At her apparent hesitation he said, "Benign, I assure you. From a well-wisher abroad."

"Ah, I see. Then yes, indeed, sir. I am most willing to do anything to bring comfort to Queen Mary."

He held out his hand. "Give me your Agnus Dei."

That startled her, but she did as he asked, lifting the chain with its locket over her head and handing it to him.

"Now, your signet ring," he said.

With a chill of understanding she tugged off her ring. The signet, a thornbush, was her family's emblem. Linked together, the two items marked her as a heretic criminal.

"Good," Castelnau said, pocketing both. "Now we are each other's keepers. Wait to hear from me." He turned to go, then stopped and turned back. His eyes bored into hers. "One last thing, mistress. Never, *ever* come to my house again."

❧ 7 ❧

Through the Enemy's Gates

"He is exacting, Lyon, I warn you," said Arthur Doncaster. "Especially about the men he allows near him. He has already rejected three supplicants for the post you seek."

Owen nodded. He took his traveling companion's counsel seriously. It confirmed his conviction that gaining access to the Earl of Northumberland would not be easy. Doncaster, the earl's kinsman, would know.

They had slowed their horses to a walk. Doncaster looked weary from their day's ride from London. A flabby minor aristocrat in his mid-thirties, he was unused to physical hardship, and the two months he had spent in prison with Owen had been hard on him. He had not been talkative on their journey, but his energy seemed to have risen now that they were approaching Petworth House. Owen could see the flag on its stone tower rippling in the noonday breeze. He still wasn't sure exactly how Doncaster was related to the earl—a cousin's cousin on the distaff side, apparently—but it hardly mattered. Doncaster had an open invitation to this Sussex stronghold of his illustrious kinsman and that was passport enough for Owen. He was Doncaster's new friend.

"Then I must strive to impress," Owen replied. "What exactly is he looking for in a secretary?"

"Hmm, I would say a man devout, loyal, courteous, and brave."

"A paragon, by God! You make me quail, sir. I would not cast myself in the role of *a very perfect gentle knight*." He had to smile, for in quoting Chaucer he felt he was back again with Kate in the moonlight. Yet these expectations of the earl were no jesting matter if they prevented his employment. "I had hoped he might be satisfied with a creature of mere honest learning."

"He is a great man," Doncaster said soberly, "known for alms-giving and piety. A valiant soldier, too. In the war with Scotland twenty years ago he distinguished himself commanding his troop at the siege of Leith. The defeated French commander even asked permission, in a compliment to my lord's valor, to surrender his sword to him rather than to the commander-in-chief, Lord Grey."

Owen quipped to lighten his worry, "Then I take it he would not approve of my daily debauches?"

Doncaster smiled. "Not until we secure you the post."

"As you think we shall?"

"Oh, most assuredly. His Lordship values my opinion. And you know in what high regard you stand with me."

Owen had earned the high regard. In the Marshalsea he had shared with Doncaster the food Kate had bought from the marshal's deputy. Doncaster was such a weakling he would not have been able to defend his prison ration against the pack. Befriending him had been Owen's bid to increase his standing with all the Catholic inmates, for all were aware of Doncaster's connection to the earl. The friendship had served them both: Doncaster had retained his flab, and Owen was riding into Petworth. Yet food wasn't the only debt his companion owed Owen, if only he knew. At Owen's word, Matthew had ordered Doncaster's early release.

"Now," Doncaster asked, "do you write in Chancery hand or Italian hand?"

"Both," Owen assured him.

"Ah, that is good. His Lordship admires Italian hand. In fact, he admires all things Italian."

Owen mused on that. From what he'd heard elsewhere he would not have supposed the earl to value such refinements. In the brief time he'd had since taking this assignment he had learned all he could about the man he hoped to work for. Henry

Percy, eighth earl of Northumberland, was fifty years old and had come into his title after his elder brother, the seventh earl, had led a rebel army of several thousand Catholic supporters in a northern uprising against the Queen and was executed ten years ago. A year later, not long after Mary Stuart was taken into the Queen's custody, the new earl showed how much he was his brother's heir in allegiance by opening a clandestine correspondence with the Scottish bishop of Ross, one of Mary's agents in France, and in those letters Northumberland had offered to help Mary escape. But Elizabeth's agents had discovered his intentions and arrested him. After eighteen months in the Tower he was charged with treason. He threw himself on Elizabeth's mercy. She relented, perhaps because executing such a powerful peer would have incensed his supporters, influential landowners she could not afford to antagonize. Northumberland had been fined four thousand pounds and ordered to confine himself to his properties in Sussex.

Was he now conspiring against Her Majesty again? Plotting with foreign powers to assist their invasion? That's what Owen had to find out. Though Doncaster had murmured with approval about a possible future with Mary Stuart as Queen of England, Owen doubted he knew any details about the part his great kinsman might play in securing that future. Doncaster was an amateur academic, not a man of action. Sent as an adolescent to the English college in Douai in the Low Countries, he had entered its seminary run by exiled English Catholics, but had rejected the priesthood, saying the celibate life was not for him. He now lived in London among his books and canaries, contented in a liaison with his housekeeper, and grateful that his indolent life was supported by a stipend from the earl.

The clanging of hammers made Owen look toward the tower ahead.

"His Lordship is abuilding," said Doncaster. "He means to make the old house grand."

Old indeed, Owen thought, eyeing the place—a medieval compound, more castle than house. A moat. High stone walls enclosing the compound. Inside it, a square stone tower that rose six stories. A timber-framed gatehouse whose raised portcullis led arrivals through the gatehouse as if through a tunnel into the courtyard. Blocks of living quarters with steeply peaked roofs that, with the tower, were all that was visible above the encircling walls. On the eastern side lay a pond. Behind all of this stretched the earl's forest. Petworth House was an ancient stronghold which the great Northumbrian family of Percy had owned for over four hundred years, ever since Queen Adeliza, widow of Henry I, gave it to her brother as a wedding gift when he'd married Agnes Percy.

Wedding gift, Owen thought, and again he saw Kate in her dress of cornflower blue the day they'd pledged their vows in quiet St. Olav's church on Silver Street. A simple dress, yet Kate so radiant she would have put a fairy queen to shame. Her dark hair bright with bluebells. Her dark eyes aglow. *For me.* The thought never failed to stir him—that this marvelous woman was his. But always, on the heels of that thrill, came the hard reminder that he had taken her away from her life of ease and plenty. That was clear from the very day of their wedding. No lavish ceremony, as was her due as daughter of a baron. Her father had attended, for he loved Kate, and had been scrupulously polite, standing as a witness with his wife, but Owen had seen in Lord Thornleigh's stern gaze how poor a showing he expected of the hard-up playwright who was now his son-in-law. Owen had made a silent promise alongside his spoken vows. He would win preferment at court somehow and give Kate the life she deserved.

Where was she now? Had she made contact with Ambassador Castelnau? It made him sick to think of her being sent into harm's way. Damn Matthew for letting her do this! Owen wished he'd had more time to advise her, warn her of the traps and pitfalls for a double spy. But he had to push that worry to the back of his mind. Kate was clever. *And my mission is here,* he told himself. He had to accept that Kate was on her own.

He was aware of a low rumbling. It sent a vibration up from the ground, making his horse skittish. He turned in the saddle. A body of cantering horsemen was cresting the rise on the road behind him. They spilled over the crest and he saw there were at least twenty, maybe thirty, pounding on straight for him and Doncaster.

"Are we under attack?" he asked. A jest—but seeing the on-coming horde lifted the hairs on his forearms.

Doncaster was anxiously urging his mount to the side of the road. "Move, Lyon. They won't stop."

Owen spurred his horse, bounding to join Doncaster on the grassy verge. "Who are they?"

Doncaster didn't speak as the horde thundered past them. Men with mud-caked boots and sweat-grimed faces and blood-streaked jerkins. They were laughing. One tooted a horn in a sound like a fart. More hoots of laughter. They had bloodshot eyes, and a few grinning fellows were riding loose as scarecrows. Owen had en-joyed enough carouses to know what made them so merry. Drunk. A pack of braying dogs tore along in their wake.

Doncaster wiped flecks of mud from his cheek as the pounding of hooves diminished. He spat out a gob of dusty phlegm. "My lord's hunting party."

The earl! Owen stood in his stirrups, craning to see the lead horseman, but the pack was too far past now, riding straight for Petworth House. In moments the tunnel through the gatehouse had swallowed them, dogs and all. He turned back to see the rear guard come on: over a dozen servants on foot, three leading pack-horses slung with deer carcasses, and another horse slung with par-tridge and grouse. The servants, muddy and blood-speckled, trudged quickly as though anxious to attend their masters or suffer for lagging behind.

"Come on," said Doncaster, clucking his mount back onto the road. "I'll introduce you."

They trotted ahead of the servants and reached the gatehouse.

The courtyard was a clamor of dismounting hunters and tired, flubbering horses. Of creaking leather and jangling harnesses. Of tramping feet as grooms rushed to take the men's mounts and ser-vants hurried from the house. Of yapping dogs running in excited circles.

Owen and Doncaster skirted the wall, keeping out of the way as Owen asked, "Which is His Lordship?"

"There." Doncaster nodded to a tall, lean man striding away

from his horse followed by two servants from the house whom he barely glanced at as he tossed his sweat-stiff gauntlets to one and took a goblet offered by the other. He stopped long enough to quaff down the refreshment, probably ale. Owen studied him. So this was the Earl of Northumberland. Ruddy face glistening with sweat. Sharp cheekbones, hooded eyes, bony hands. Short russet beard scraggly with twisting hairs, and a russet moustache, out-grown like two drooping wings. His fawn-colored velvet doublet was daubed with the blood of his prey.

Northumberland wiped drops of ale from his moustache with the look of a man well satisfied. He belched. Then he strode to the middle of the throng, his eyes on the gatehouse, where the servants were straggling in with the packhorses. Half a dozen panting dogs wove circles around him. He stopped, fists on hips, and bellowed, "Where's my buck?"

"Here, my lord!" called a servant. He rushed forward leading a trotting packhorse so the big deer carcass on the horse's back jerked as if still in its death throes. The body was intact, unlike the other two carcasses, which had been field dressed, their organs removed. Owen understood now why the hunters had been in a hurry to get this buck here: if not gutted within an hour or two after death, the meat would taste too gamey.

Servants from the house had carried out a rough wooden table, and now three brawny lackeys carried the buck to the table and slung it down. The body, as huge as a steer, landed with a thud on its back, its antlered head hanging off the table's edge, its tongue lolling. Two lackeys held the buck's hind legs splayed open. Northumberland drew his long dagger and strode to the table, brandishing the blade in a show: the conqueror. His men chuckled.

With a steady hand he slit the buck's belly. He was skilled at this, Owen noted, cutting only through skin and a thin layer of muscle, not near the entrails—a nick in the bladder or intestine would allow urine or feces to taint the meat. He cut around the anus so it was free and could be removed, then severed the windpipe. He nodded to his lackeys, who then let the animal loll onto its side to let the organs spill out. Northumberland cut away the diaphragm and stomach and severed the center of the ribs. He reached up inside with his bare hands. A dozen dogs circled, yelping, frantic at the scent. He lifted out a fistful of gore and held it high. His hunting fellows grinned. Owen saw what Northumberland held: the buck's heart. He slapped it down on the table and with his blade chopped it into four sections. These he tossed into the air for the dogs. They leapt in a frenzy of barking. The bloody chunks landed in the dirt, and the jaws of four victors snapped up the prizes and gobbled them.

Northumberland laughed. An elderly servant shambled forward and handed him a linen towel, which he used to wipe the gore off his dagger. He sheathed the blade, and as he wiped blood off his hands his eyes ranged over his chattering hunting companions who encircled him. Looking past them, his gaze landed on Doncaster at the wall. "Arthur!" he shouted good-humoredly. "God's teeth, man, when did you creep in?"

Doncaster beamed and blushed. He bowed and called back, flustered, "Good my lord, you passed us on the road not five minutes ago."

"I did?" Northumberland snorted a laugh. "Didn't even see you. So they let you out, eh? A free man?"

"Indeed, my lord, and right glad I am to join your noble self." As he spoke he hastened forward. Owen judged it politic to follow.

Seeing his kinsman bow as he came, Northumberland's eyes seemed to glint with mischief. He whipped out his dagger again. Turning to the buck he grabbed one of its rear legs, lifted it, and hacked off the testicles. Arm outstretched, he offered them to Doncaster. "For you, Arthur. An inspiration to grow some."

The earl's men hooted with laughter. Doncaster halted, appalled.

Northumberland grinned at his own jest. "No? Not to your taste? Well, my dogs will enjoy the treat." He tossed the testicles, and the dogs leapt for them.

Doncaster, seeing the merriment at his expense, laughed uneasily, frantic for Northumberland's approval. Owen found it pitiful. And felt a lash of caution. Apparently his prison mate, far from being favored by the earl as he'd claimed, engendered his scorn. Owen recognized the type: the powerful man who enjoys belittling a weakling. *Can I use that?* he wondered. *Make him think I'm someone he can domineer?*

"Come, let's in to dinner," Northumberland called, expansively beckoning his entourage. "I'm so famished I could eat this buck raw."

The hunting party trooped toward the house. A cart clattered up to load the kill. The servant who drove it was a wiry fellow, about thirty, with an unruly thatch of bright red hair. Owen took note. He fit the description of the man Matthew had told him to be on the lookout for. Matthew had employed him as a watcher until he discovered the fellow was doing the same for Northumberland, playing both sides. The servants managing the pack-horses began unloading the deer carcasses and dead fowl onto the cart.

"Who's this?" Northumberland pointed his dagger at Owen, his question at Doncaster.

"Ah yes, this is Master Lyon, my lord. He comes to offer his services, to take the place of Ewing."

Northumberland frowned at the newcomer. "You want to be my secretary?"

Owen winced inside. Curse Doncaster for blurting this! The timing was all wrong. *His forwardness could get me thrown out.* "Pardon my friend's eagerness, your lordship," he answered. "I will be glad to approach you later to—"

"Can you read and write?"

Owen blinked, the question so absurd. "Most assuredly, my lord."

"Then why put it off?" He sheathed his dagger, his eyes on it as he said, "Arthur vouches for you, I gather?" It seemed a habit of his to ignore the person he was speaking to.

"I do," Doncaster put in respectfully. "Master Lyon was a fellow sufferer of the Marshalsea's vileness. I believe he saved my life."

Northumberland grunted. "For what it's worth." He slapped dried mud off his sleeve, saying, "Lyon, eh? What were you in for?"

"Attending a mass, your lordship. I have, of course, repented." He injected sarcasm into the mock-pious second statement, to let the earl know he felt precisely the opposite.

Northumberland's sharp features betrayed neither approval nor censure. He looked to his friends, who were already across the courtyard and moving inside. "Well, come along then." He added, with barely a glance at Doncaster, "Eat, Arthur. You know you want to. Then this fellow can write a letter or two for me. I'll soon know if he passes muster." He strode toward the house.

Owen was so startled he didn't move. Was he hired? He looked at Doncaster, who shrugged, equally surprised. Owen almost laughed. *That was easy.* He slapped Doncaster on the shoulder, grinning as he thought: *Blessed be the meek.* "Thank you, my friend."

They followed the earl inside. The great hall rang with the voices of thirty hungry, thirsty men settling down on benches at two long tables that abutted the ends of the lord's table, where Northumberland thudded down into a chair. The three tables formed a squared horseshoe and inside it maidservants hustled with bowls of water for the hunters to wash their hands and towels to dry them. Other servants carried in platters of food. At the smells of roasted boar, leek-festooned capons, and succulent quails Owen's stomach grumbled. He hadn't realized he was so hungry. Now, where to sit? The men ranged along the tables were the earl's retainers, certainly a few lordlings among them, their status above his. Did etiquette allow him to sit with his friend? Doncaster, as a family relation, would be admitted somewhere close to the earl. No, better not press my luck, Owen decided. He would sit with household officers, the steward and chamberlain. He was about to ask Doncaster to point them out when Northumberland bellowed from the head table, "Arthur! Here!" He swept his arm in a gesture to join him. "And bring the scribe."

"Thank you, my lord," Doncaster called back, smiling and bowing. He beckoned Owen, who followed. The two reached Northumberland's side. Space on the bench was made for them by two adolescents whose favored place beside Northumberland, and whose sharp features so like his, told Owen they were his sons. To the right of the earl's chair was another chair, but empty. There were only two chairs; benches for everyone else.

The earl was quaffing back another tankard of ale. Finishing, he wiped his moustache with a damask napkin and looked at Doncaster, then Owen. "Tell me about the Marshalsea. Did you be-friend anyone else?" The glint in his hooded eyes made Owen feel sure there was an agenda the earl was keeping to himself. Was he in contact with radical Jesuit priests who'd been arrested? Might he even know something about the gunman who'd so recently tried to kill the Queen?

"Oh, the place is the foulest cesspit, my lord," Doncaster said with a shudder. "The stench! The savage fellows! I do not think I could have borne another week." He launched into a litany of the prison's miseries, even as he took a roasted quail from the platter being passed and eagerly cut into it. Northumberland frowned at Doncaster's complaints. *He wants different information*, Owen thought. *Or am I imagining that? Keep a clear head*, he told himself.

Doncaster droned on. The earl sawed at a slab of boar. The two teen boys whispered to each other. The other men chattered and ate. Owen was about to take a bite of capon when his eyes were drawn to a movement at the far end of the hall, a staircase where a woman was coming down the steps. A lady. She looked in her mid-thirties. Slender, upright, she moved with self-assured poise, her dress of fine rose-colored wool, her blond hair tucked behind her headdress: a band of seed pearls with a fall of rose-tinted linen. She crossed the hall, servants bowing to her as she came. *The earl's wife?* Owen wondered. When she reached the earl's side a serving man pulled out the empty chair and she settled into it. *Yes*, thought Owen, *the countess.*

"A good day, Catherine," her husband said, chewing. "A fine buck, two does, and a mess of birds."

"I'll send a haunch of venison to my sister," she said, dipping her hands into the silver bowl of water a serving maid offered her. "Nan, tell cook to have it dressed."

"Yes, my lady."

"And bring me a small partridge leg."

"Yes, my lady."

The countess dried her hands on a napkin and languidly scanned the other platters of food as though wondering if any might tempt her. She seemed uninterested in the throng of men.

"Here's Arthur, come from London," Northumberland told her.

She gave Doncaster a nod, indifferent though not unfriendly. "Welcome, Arthur."

"Thank you, my lady."

"He's brought this young buck to take over for Ewing."

The countess's green eyes shifted to Owen. He gave her a respectful bow of the head. "Your ladyship."

"Don't I know you?" She frowned as though struggling to remember. "There's something about your face. . . ." Then, suddenly stiffening: "I *do* know you." She said it like an accusation.

Owen felt a prick of alarm. "My lady?"

"It was in London just before Lent. I saw you at the playhouse. The one they call the Theatre."

He relaxed. "You may have indeed, your ladyship," he said smoothly.

"He's a playwright," Doncaster put in, munching. "That's why I thought he'd be a good secretary. Clever with writing, you know."

She ignored him. "Henry, do you know who this man is?"

"A player, it seems," Northumberland said, disinterested. "And a jailbird," he added in a more pointed tone, as though he'd decided the fact might be useful.

"He is Baron Thornleigh's son-in-law," she declared. "The Viscountess Montague pointed him out at the playhouse."

Northumberland turned to Owen, frowning now. Suspicion glinted in his eyes. "You're married to Thornleigh's daughter?"

"I am, my lord. But the baron has closed his doors to me."

Doncaster made an effort to back his friend. "Little wonder, since his daughter married a common player. But that is hardly a crime."

Damning me with faint praise, Owen thought uneasily. "Not for that, my lord," he said to Northumberland. "It was because he mistrusts my faith. The faith for which I was imprisoned."

The earl and his wife stared at him. To speak of religion in front of so many people was dangerous, but Owen knew it was his best defense. Several of the men sitting nearest had clearly heard the countess's accusation. All these retainers the earl would trust— they were his friends, some were kinsmen, and most were probably secret Catholics themselves. Servants, however, were susceptible to bribes. The earl and his wife carried on in low tones.

"Do not listen to him, Henry," she insisted quietly. "Thornleigh is one of the Queen's closest councillors and this man is one of his family. Do not trust him."

"Well, I see that *you* do not."

"Send him away. You can find a secretary anywhere."

"No. I'll keep him."

Relief coursed through Owen. "Thank you, my lord," he said. "I assure you, I will pledge my heart and soul to your best interests."

"Keep you in my lockup, I meant," Northumberland growled. He stood and shouted, "Hastings!" He looked around. "Where's the marshal?"

"Here, my lord," came the answer behind him.

Owen twisted around on the bench. A bear of a man was coming for him. Before he could get to his feet the man grabbed him.

"Clap him in irons, Hastings," Northumberland said. "I'll come and question him."

Owen's heart kicked. He might rot for months in the lockup, no way out, no way to alert Matthew. "My lord," he said, "I swear you have no reason to doubt me. I have come to you because I am a poor man shunned for my faith and in need of a position, that is all."

"Or a spy," the countess hissed.

"Not so, my lady!" he protested. But Hastings, the marshal, hauled him off the bench. "My lord, question me here and now. You will find me true."

"You're right, I *will* find the truth," Northumberland said, sitting down again to his meal. "It'll come screaming out of you when you're swinging by your ankles."

"My lord, this man is a guest!" Doncaster cried in horror. "He has come as my friend!"

"Arthur, you always were a fool. Take him away, Hastings."

Owen dug in his heels in desperation. "Wait!" He had one last chance. "Her Ladyship speaks of spies. For a spy, my lord, look to your own household."

Northumberland was sawing again at his slice of boar as everyone watched. "I do. Any here, man or woman, knows a disloyal word would cost them their tongue."

The marshal was dragging Owen toward a side door. "Then there's one in your courtyard who should be mute!" Owen cried. "I know him for a spy."

Northumberland glared at him, but his curiosity was evident. He held up his hand to halt Hastings. The marshal stopped, but still held Owen tightly.

"Name," Northumberland demanded.

"I do not know his name, my lord." Matthew's watchers used aliases. He preferred not to know their names. "He is a porter here. My age. Hair red like a fox. I saw him outside with the cart loading your kill."

"Why, that's Rankin," someone said.

Northumberland looked taken aback. The porter was his own spy. He regularly sent him to London to haunt the taverns around Whitehall where clerks of the royal council took refreshment—clerks with information about their masters. But the porter was also secretly in Matthew's employ. Matthew had recently discovered the man's double-dealing.

"Bah," the countess scoffed. "Next he'll be accusing the milkmaids."

Northumberland ignored her. "How do you know my porter?"

"From London, my lord. I have seen him going into Baron Thornleigh's house. Twice. Both times he came out pocketing something. Looked like a purse of coins."

"You saw this yourself?"

"Yes."

"How?" He narrowed his eyes. "You said Thornleigh's doors were closed to you."

Owen felt the whole gathering watching him as if he were on trial for his life. He knew he was. "Before those doors closed, my lord. Before I was imprisoned for my faith."

Northumberland considered this. He turned to a nearby retainer, a thick fellow with a mutilated ear that was ragged and red as raw meat. "Bring Rankin in."

The man nodded to his seatmate and the two of them tramped out. Northumberland motioned the marshal to bring Owen back. This time the marshal took him around the end of the lower table and pushed him forward to stand before the earl as if before a judge. Northumberland sat down again, the table between them, and shoved plates out of his way. Owen watched him, feeling the countess's stern eyes on him.

Doncaster padded around to join Owen in a show of solidarity. "This is good," he whispered in Owen's ear. "He can't abide a spy."

The porter, Rankin, was led into the hall. The two retainers took him to where Owen stood: accuser and accused. Rankin looked wary, cagey, like a fox indeed. His clothes were streaked with the blood of the deer carcasses he'd been loading.

Northumberland blasted him with questions. Rankin's answers were swift and direct. Had he met with Thornleigh? Of course not. Met with some agent of Thornleigh's? No. Had he ever been to Thornleigh's house? Never. It went on for a few minutes, Northumberland never letting up, Rankin stoutly defending himself.

Owen's hope was slipping away. When it seemed that Northumberland was coming to the end of his questions Owen knew he had to make his last move—and then pray.

He murmured urgently to Doncaster, "Tell him to search his belongings."

"Ah!" Doncaster whispered back with zeal, then he parroted loudly to Northumberland, "My lord, you must search the man's belongings!"

Rankin flinched. His composure evaporated. He suddenly looked shifty-eyed, frightened. A fresh keenness came over Northumberland, like a hunter who smells the quarry's fear. "Where do you abide, Rankin?"

The porter swallowed.

"Above the stable," said the man with the mutilated ear. "That's his roost."

"Go," Northumberland ordered him. "Search."

The two hastened out again. Rankin stared at the floor. Men murmured, a couple waging bets. Owen heard them, and sweat chilled the back of his neck. Would this ploy save him? Or would he soon be swinging by his ankles?

It didn't take long. The two retainers ran back in. The disfigured one held a fat purse of maroon leather. The other held a paper folded like a letter.

"Here," Northumberland ordered, thumping the flat of his hand on the table. The men set the purse and the paper in front of him. He yanked open the purse's drawstring and upended it. Silver coins spilled out. A loud murmur went up from the men. "He wouldn't earn that in ten years," someone said.

Northumberland silently read the letter. He looked up at Rankin with a look of shock, almost of hurt. "Sell tales about me to the Lord Secretary's clerk, would you? And what next? Murder me in my bed?"

Rankin blanched. He sputtered words of denial, but Northumberland cut him off, saying, "You stink of stag gore, Rankin. A good wash is what you need."

They took him outside. The earl stood and insisted that his guests follow him and his wife to the tower. The party trooped across the courtyard, Owen alongside Doncaster. Up the tower's five stone flights of steps they went. At the top, the party fanned out along the flat roof used for centuries as a fighting platform from which archers had fended off the enemy. In silence they looked over the stone wall and across the meadow that slanted down to the pond, watching three figures: the marshal and the man with the mangled ear who were hauling the squirming, screaming porter. They dragged him to the pond's edge, thick with reeds. Holding him, both men waded in up to their knees. Rankin's screams stopped as they thrust his head into the water and held it under. His arms thrashed. Then feebly flopped. Then went still.

Owen felt his gorge rise in shock. *They've killed him.* And revulsion at his own complicity. *I killed him.*

Northumberland turned to him. The countess's stern green eyes were on Owen, too. Northumberland beckoned a retainer. "The lockup for this fellow. I have some questions yet."

ॐ 8 ॐ

The Meeting

Kate left the table in the common room of the Star Inn in Lewes as the breakfast dishes were being cleared. Impatient, she took up watch at the window that looked out on the High Street. She had arrived yesterday evening with a servant her grandmother had insisted accompany her, a sturdy fellow named Soames, and first thing this morning she had sent him to call at the home of merchant Gilbert Levett to speak to his guest, Master Robert Parry—her brother, though no one knew it. She had sent Robert a message and was waiting now for Soames to bring his answer.

The other guests who had breakfasted had gone to the stables to continue their journeying and she was alone with the landlord. A lumbering, shaggy-haired fellow, he was instructing a glazier replacing a broken windowpane, and Kate had to move to one side to keep her eye on the morning traffic outside. She was so nervous she had scarcely tasted a bite of her porridge. In coming to Lewes she was blatantly disregarding Robert's instruction to old Master Prowse to keep his whereabouts secret and let him live "in peace." She was also breaking Prowse's trust in her. But she had to see Robert. The awful sense that she had abandoned him as a child had haunted her for so many years, and she felt that her festering sore of guilt might heal if she could help him now get resettled here at home. The question was, would he agree to see her?

Tap, tap . . . tap, tap. The glazier's soft mallet knocked the new pane in place. Kate counted the taps—always sets of four—even as she kept her eyes on the street for Soames. *Tap, tap . . . tap, tap.*

"Pardon the bother, mistress," said the landlord, indicating the glazier, "but best have the window snugged up this morning." His voice was a deep bass, oddly mellifluous as if it had lazily rumbled around inside his large body. He put her in mind of shaggy Swedish oxen. "Looks like rain a-coming," he warned.

"Oh?" she said vaguely. The sky was robin's egg blue, untroubled by a single cloud. The morning was summer warm. "Surely not."

"I was born and bred on the Downs, mistress, and I can always smell rain. Not this morning. Afternoon, more like. We'll have a wet eventide."

Kate didn't relish riding back to London in rain, but she would have to be on the road with Soames this afternoon if she was to make it back the next day. She had to be there to await Ambassador Castelnau's signal. He had told her he would not make contact until at least Thursday, which had given her just enough time to come here to see Robert. She had told her grandmother she was making a charitable visit to her ailing former tutor in Seaford. Not too big a lie, since Master Prowse had indeed written to her and Seaford was only ten miles from Lewes.

Owen was at Petworth, not that far away, either. Thirty miles northwest. Was he already busy this morning seeing to Northumberland's correspondence? She had no doubt that by now he would have managed to infiltrate the earl's household, but his cleverness didn't lessen his danger. She longed to be with him. If she left now she could reach Petworth by supper. Impossible, of course, for a welter of reasons, none of which she could make public. What a web of secrets she had spun in her service for the Queen! Resentment jabbed her at what her life had become. If only she could live as normal people lived. Imagine—to cheerfully accompany your husband to his new post. Have a friendly chat with your father.

Seek recipe advice from your mother. Share family news with your brother. But she had married a spy, her father had banished her, her mother was a traitor, and her brother was pretending to be someone else. This family was far from normal.

"Now, don't you let my talk of rain worry you, mistress," the landlord said. "If the roads turn to bogs you're more than welcome to stay another night. Keep that pleasant room you're in, and I'll have Margery stew you a fine coney with sweet summer squash and raisins. That'll set you up. You'll sleep like a babe and be off the next day under clear skies."

She had to smile. With the other travelers gone on she was now the only paying guest and no doubt the landlord hoped the threat of rain would make her stay. His ploy, far from irritating her, lifted her spirits. He personified the England that she and Owen and Matthew were on guard to preserve: a people clear-eyed, crafty if need be, and good-natured withal. She almost could have hugged him. "You are kind, Master Sims, and I am sure the rabbit would be delicious, but I really must be on my way today."

He held up his hands in a gesture that said, *As you wish.*

A man behind her cleared his throat. "Mistress Lyon."

She turned to see Soames. His broad, peasant face was unreadable. "Yes?" she said, a flutter in her stomach. "Will he see me?"

"He was not there, mistress."

Her hope plunged. Had Prowse been wrong? Was Robert not in Lewes after all? "Is he not biding with Master Levett?"

"He is, yes. But Mistress Levett said he is out visiting a sick man."

Ah! "Did she say where?"

"Yes, mistress."

Soames was a good soul, but not as quick as Kate could wish. "*Where*, Soames?"

"Friar's Walk. At the house across from the cobbler."

"That'll be old Henry Hewson," said the landlord helpfully. "Lost his footing coming out of church and gouged his shin on the step."

"Can you direct me to Friar's Walk?" Kate asked him. "Is it far?"

"Just a pebble's throw, mistress. Not much farther than I throw

Jock Dobson when he's in his cups." He stretched out his arm, pointing past the glazier. "Make a right turning outside my door and take the High Street to All Saints. There, another right turning puts you in Friar's Walk."

"Thank you." Buoyed by knowing Robert was so near, she felt she could not wait. She told Soames she would go alone. *I need no protection from my brother,* she thought, though she could not say so.

She made her way along High Street, passing a group gathered around a farrier's old dray horse that had collapsed. Despite the warm air she felt a chill tighten her skin. Nerves, of course. It had been ten years since she'd seen Robert, but the image of their parting was burned into her brain. The awful fire, Father carrying her to safety, Mother's hired man dragging Robert the opposite way. Then, a decade of silence, of not knowing if he was alive or dead. Her guilt welled up again. *Father chose me.* She and Robert had once been so close, but could he ever forgive her for being the chosen child?

All Saints was easy to spot with its square Saxon tower. At the end of the churchyard wall she turned onto Friar's Walk, a leafy lane, the trees an autumn palette of amber and ochre and gold. The brittle fallen leaves rustled under her footsteps.

Ahead, the sign of the cobbler hung over the street, its painted black boot glinting in the sunshine. Directly across the narrow lane was a timber-framed house separated from its two larger neighbors by hedges and beech trees alive with birdsong. Its front door was protected by a little round-arched roof supported by posts, beside which a mullioned window jutted. Through the window's thick green glass Kate could make out someone moving. Two people? The sun's glare on the glass made the figures indistinct. Was one of them Robert? Someone plodding past her blocked her view for a moment, a rag-and-bone man pushing his cart that rattled on the cobbles. *Clackety, clackety, clackety.*

She took a deep breath and crossed the street. At the door she raised her hand to knock. But another glance at the window made her stop, her fist in midair. From here, in the shade under the arch, the two figures were clear: a frail old man sitting on a stool, his skinny leg outstretched with his hose rolled down, and a young man on his knees, winding a bandage around the invalid's calf. This had to be Robert, so gently tending his patient!

She took a stiff step away, her back to the wall so he would not see her. *He will not be so gentle with me.* After all, she must be the last person he would want to see. She imagined his accusing stare: *Why did you leave me behind?*

What to do? An impulse seized her to turn around and ride back to London and let Robert be. That's what he wanted. That's what he had asked for. She yearned to see him, to win his forgiveness, but that suddenly seemed a horribly selfish whim. *I want absolution. He wants peace.* The two could not be reconciled.

A dog trotted by. The church bell clanged. The rag-and-bone man and his cart disappeared down a lane. *Clackety, clackety, clackety.*

Kate made up her mind, unbearable though her decision was. *Let him be.*

She was stepping away to return to the inn when the door opened. She whirled around.

He stood before her. Tall. Gangly. A physician's black bag in his hand.

Later, she would remember this moment as one in which time seemed to stop. The house, the street, the city—the whole world faded away. She was aware of nothing but the wide-eyed man looking back at her—a man she did not know, but in whose face hid the ghost of a boy she had never forgotten. *Brother.*

He had frozen as though caught in a spell. He stared at her—a woman he did not know, but Kate knew in a heartbeat he was seeing the girl he had never forgotten. *Sister.* Emotions chased across his face. Shock? Disbelief? Anger? She could not read him as she once could.

She finally found her voice, but it was no more than a whisper. "Robin." Her childhood name for him. Saying it, her throat tightened with a hot threat of tears.

Abruptly, his face changed. A shadow darkened his eyes. The bony ridge of his brows tensed. "Pardon me," he said, head down, and brushed past her as though past a stranger.

She came after him. "Robin!"

He stopped and twisted back, alarmed at her raised voice. Kate winced, knowing she should not have said his name in public.

"Madam," he said, "you have mistaken me for someone else." He looked both ways to see if anyone had heard.

She saw his chin jut in and out, in and out—a small movement, but one she knew so well. He had always had this tic, even as a small child. Whenever he was nervous, back and forth his chin would go. The nuns had slapped him to break him of it. Kate would hold his hand with fierce protectiveness as he'd tried not to cry.

"No mistake," she whispered. "It's Kate."

"I know no one by that name. Now please, forgive me, I am in a hurry."

"Stop. Please. You know me. As I know you. I'm here because of Master Prowse. He told me where to find you."

His face changed again as suddenly as before, his mask crumbling. At this claim of hers he could no longer maintain the pretense. His voice when it came was faint and shaky. She could barely hear it. "This is not . . . what I wanted . . ."

His struggle broke her heart. "Please," she begged. "Just let me look at you."

They stared at each other. She searched for signs of the boy she remembered. It was as though an artist, taking the soft face of the child, had enlarged and hardened it with cartilage and bone. His hazel eyes held a childish openness, but the bony eyebrow ridge was a man's. His skin was smooth, but not like a boy's for it had been shaved of beard. His mouth still boyishly quirked to one side, but the narrow lips had the determination of a man. But all the foreignness about him dissolved when he touched her face in wonder, saying, "Kate . . . dear Kate . . ."

Joy coursed through her! She raised her arms to embrace him.

He flinched. "Not here."

She froze. "No, of course. I'm sorry."

"Come, walk with me."

He took her elbow and guided her. She scarcely saw her surroundings as they walked—a blur of houses, shops, people. A hundred questions tumbled in her mind as Robert marched her on in silence. Clearly, he wanted first to get away from the eyes of the town. The street they were on sloped down to the river.

"This is not what I wanted," he said again, speaking quietly though no one they passed was close enough to hear. "Curse the old man!" His voice rose despite his caution. "I made him promise to tell no one!"

"I know. He told me that, too. Please don't blame him. He thought he was doing the right thing."

"Well, he was wrong! Your connection with me can only hurt you. Kate, I wanted to spare you."

"I know. I understand. But you must forgive Master Prowse. He did not act from malice."

He looked flustered, though not appeased. "My own fault. I trusted him to keep things to himself. I should never have visited him."

"I'm glad you did. So glad!"

"No, it was a blunder. But oh, Kate, I so wanted some link to our old life. Just to feel again a touch of the way we were before—"

He did not finish, but she knew what he'd left unsaid: *Before Mother betrayed her country and took us away.* That rocked her. And the tender yearning in his voice moved her.

They had reached the bridge at the center of town and now crossed over the River Ouse, a slender waterway to the sea. They turned onto a grassy path that skirted the river. No one was on it except a stooped woman cutting bulrushes and, up ahead, a couple of children fishing. On the water two small fishing boats passed each other, moving in opposite directions. The breeze nudged the riverbank's tall grasses against Kate's knee. Now that she and Robert were alone she didn't know where to begin. The same confusion seemed to inhibit him.

"Robin, where have you been all these years?" she finally said. "We never heard a word."

"No. Because of—"

"Mother? She wouldn't let you write to us?"

He looked pained. "Please understand. I was a child."

She understood very well. Mother would have exacted a harsh price for disobedience. Kate's heart ached for him.

"Once I was old enough to know," he went on, "it seemed pointless, because by then I thought I would never come home. I was *made* to believe that."

Kate could well imagine. "Where is she now?"

"Brussels. Still lives with the Duchess of Feria."

The luxurious house on Balienplein Place, a leafy square lined with the mansions of the rich. Kate had once lived there, too. The widowed duchess, an Englishwoman who had married a Spanish duke, was Mother's old friend.

"They made me a frightened fool," he said, jabbing back into place an errant lock of his hair, "she and the Duchess. I lived nervous as a cat."

There was a jerkiness to his movements. It struck Kate that what had seemed jarring in his appearance was not just that he had matured, but that as an adult he seemed so familiar. The sharp features, the angular body. She was looking at a male version of their mother.

"So you've lived in Brussels all this time?"

"No. Well, at first, yes. Then I left to study medicine. The University of Padua."

"And became a physician." She smiled at him with enormous admiration. "I think it's wonderful." Because he helped the sick, but also because his studies had taken him far away from Mother.

He smiled back. The first smile she had seen from him, a tentative one, but it warmed her. "And you?" he asked as though suddenly eager to know now that the door between them had been opened. "Where are you living now?"

"In London."

His smile broadened. "Are you going to tell me you're a married lady with four children?"

How much did she dare confide? He was her brother, her blood, the sweet friend of her childhood, and she wanted to tell him everything, to open her heart. But she knew she must tell him as little as possible. "I am married, yes, but no children. Our wedding was just eight months ago."

He glanced at her waist and quipped, "Nine is all you need."

That made her smile, and a bubble of happiness rose in her. They were jesting almost like the old days. "His name is Owen Lyon and he's a playwright and I know you will love him when you meet him."

He gave her a look of astonishment. "Married into the theater! And I must call you *Mistress Lyon!*" He said it with as much affection as surprise. But then his face clouded. "And Father?" he asked.

She heard the brittleness in his voice. Had he not forgiven Father for leaving him behind? "He is well. He remarried. You remember Mistress Fenella?"

"She with the Dutch rebel friends?" He sounded amazed. "He *married* her?"

"Yes. They have been wed these ten years and are very happy. And she has been wondrous kind to me."

He stopped. They were completely alone on the path now, the sounds of the town behind them faint. "Kate," he said very seriously, "you must not tell him about me."

She hesitated. Her very purpose in coming here was to persuade him to seek a reconciliation with their father. It was only right. But her own position in the family was so precarious. "The truth is, Father does not approve of my husband." Impossible to leap into an explanation that Owen had been imprisoned, and why. This was not the time. "As a playwright he is beneath me, Father feels. So Father and I . . . well, we are not on speaking terms. I hope he will come round eventually—I believe he shall— but for now Owen and I are living with Grandmother."

This seemed to disturb him. "You do not see Father?"

"No. He is . . . angry with me. But, Robin, you can change that."

"I? How?"

"Give me leave to tell him you have come back."

He jabbed at his hair again in frustration. "Oh, Lord, this is not what I wanted. I am tainted, Kate. Because of Mother. You know that. Tainted by association. The one thing I did *not* want was to taint you, too, and yes, even Father. So no, you must not tell him.

You must let me carry on as I am, keeping my head down, making my own way, separate from you both. Don't you see? It's best for your sake, too."

"But that's so wrong! Living with people who are not your family? Pretending to be someone you are not? Who are these people, the Levetts?"

"He's a merchant, a colleague of a man in Padua whose son is a friend of mine. When I said I wanted to go to England they offered to contact Master Levett. He and his wife kindly took me in. But I will eventually find a place of my own."

"With what? Have you any money?"

"Not much."

And Father is a wealthy man, she thought. *A man with no heir.* It stung her to remember the ultimatum he had threatened on London Bridge: *Leave your husband or be disinherited.* Well, she had made her decision and would live with it. One day Father would know the truth about her and would soften. Meanwhile, her brother was an innocent in this. *He should not have to suffer for our sins.* "Robin, you cannot sustain this life. Hiding. Friendless. You need to be with your own people. You need to come home."

Exasperated, he started walking again. Kate kept at his side. They were in a wide-open space now, a plain that stretched out, peaceful and serene, all the way to the looming chalk cliffs. Cows grazed in the water meadows. The breeze undulated through the tall grasses flecked with wildflowers, the golds and purples of autumn, and there was a fragrance of lavender. But Kate could see that, farther ahead, the river widened. It was a tidal waterway where seaweed would be exposed at low tide and the air would have a salty marine tang.

"I would have been fine," Robert said, "if Prowse had not told you."

"But he did, and now I know and there's no going back."

"Maybe there is. You could leave me, right here, right now. Let me make my own way. Go back to London and forget about me."

This sent a lash of guilt through her. *Father chose me. Left you.* "No," she said firmly. "We did that once before. This time, you shall not be left behind."

He stopped again and gave her a heartrending look. "Kate, you cannot know how hard it was to live away from England all those years. Away from everything dear." He looked at the plain of swaying grasses. "From all of this. From *you*. I so longed to come home. I *needed* to come home."

"And now you have. That took great courage. Come back to *us* now, too. Let me tell Father."

He looked anguished, torn. Was she bending him? Would one more push win him? "Do it for me, Robin. As a great favor. Because if I bring Father this news he might soften toward *me*."

His face creased with indecision. But Kate saw the flicker of hope in his eyes. "I so want to, Kate—"

"Then do!"

"But . . . won't he hate me?" he stammered. "For all the years I spent with Mother?"

"Nonsense. No one blames you for that." A shard of memory cut through her thoughts. Owen telling her to beware of her brother. Her angry retort: *No one censures me for my mother's crime. Surely the same holds for Robert.* But Owen had not been convinced. *You have not been raised by her,* he'd said. *Your brother has.* But Kate knew now she was right. By coming home Robert had cut all ties with their mother. He was to be commended, not condemned.

"Then it's settled," she said with firmness. "I will tell Father you're here."

He said nothing, but the ghost of a smile tugged his mouth.

It made her so happy, she coaxed, "In law, you know, silence implies consent."

A smile broke across his face, lighting his eyes. "Dear Kate." He enfolded her in a warm embrace. Hugging him, she felt too much to speak. She choked back happy tears, and pulled away just as a sound reached them, a rumbling, far off to the west. They both looked to the western sky. Darkness, like a bruise, was creeping over the horizon.

"Rain coming," Robert muttered.

The landlord was right, Kate thought with a shiver. Well, if she must ride in a downpour so be it. She should cover half the distance to London by nightfall. An inn for the night, with dry clothes and a warm bed. Then, London the next day.

She looked at her brother, glad of this day's work. But concern nibbled a corner of her mind. She could not protect him from everything. If Robert's return troubled Owen, it would trouble the Queen's councillors even more.

"I spoke lightly of the law just now," she said, "but I must warn you, there may be legal pitfalls for you yet. You have spent your youth with a known traitor."

"But you said—"

"Don't worry. Father, I feel sure, will not impugn your motives. But he is Her Majesty's loyal councillor and his service to her rules his life. He will consider it his duty to alert his fellow councillors of your return. So be prepared. They will want to question you."

"Interrogation?" There was brittleness again in his voice. "It does not surprise me. Though I have tried to live here quietly, and bring no attention to myself, part of me always thought the day might come when I'd be taken to task."

"You shall have stout voices speaking on your behalf. Master Levett for one, an upstanding citizen I do not doubt. Your patients, too. And don't forget old Master Prowse. He will sing your praises loud and long."

"Prowse?" He gave her a stricken look. "Good Lord, Kate, I haven't told you. The shock of seeing you knocked it clear out of my head."

"Told me what?"

"The good old man is dead. He was walking his dog on the sea cliff and fell, they say. His body was found on the beach."

Rain pounded the south of England for two days, borne on a chill north wind. The Sussex fields were drenched sponges, the roads and lanes a mire of mud. Broken branches littered the city streets. Ficket's Field outside London wall was as sodden as a marsh.

Robert was half mud himself as he tied his wet horse to a dripping tree, straddled the waist-high stone wall behind the Plough

Inn, hopped down, and squelched through the stable yard muck. He had left Lewes just an hour after he and Kate had parted, but the sorry state of the roads had made slow going, and he hadn't got halfway to London when night fell and the darkness and rain made it impossible to go on. He'd set out before dawn from the wayside inn, but it still took all day to get here. So when he opened the stable door he was relieved to see he was not too late. Walter Townsend was waiting.

"Thank God," Townsend said. "I was about to give up on you."

"Filthy riding," Robert said, closing the door.

"I know. I was afraid my horse would snap a bone. What's happened? Urgent, your note said."

Robert held up his hands in a gesture that said: *Wait.* He shivered, for he was soaked to the skin. He rubbed his hands, stiff from the cold and his exhausting ride. The stink of the decrepit stable hit him as it had before. Spending the night here was not a pleasant prospect, bedding down in straw mildewed from horse piss. But even that could not dim his excitement. Kate's response had been all that he'd dared to hope for, and more.

"Well?" Townsend looked worried. *As usual,* Robert thought. "I can't stay, Parry, I must get back."

Parry. Robert allowed himself a smile, thinking that soon he'd be able to buck this pseudonym he'd been saddled with. He could leave the shadows of anonymity and step out into the public light. It made him feel slightly giddy. He grinned at Townsend. "Good news. I have reason to believe that soon I'll be welcomed into the house of a prominent lord here in London. Permanently. It will be the ideal position from which to operate."

"A member of our cause?"

"No. Of the enemy."

Townsend gave a low whistle of admiration. "And a lord withal! Who is it?"

"I cannot say. Not until it's sure. But that," he added slyly, "will not be the *only* happy disclosure." The public light would reveal him to the world as the only son of Baron Thornleigh. Robert was so pleased he could have danced a jig. Once he was back in the bosom of his family, who would suspect his actions? No one. His father was the Queen's loyal and trusted friend.

But his satisfaction was marred by a cold current running beneath. He had used Kate. Lied to her. Lured her to him and then manipulated her. She was no fool, but their bond was so strong, forged so tightly during their childhood suffering, it would never occur to her to mistrust him. Dear Kate. Like him, she was now an outcast. That news had surprised him. When he had lived in Paris he'd had good intelligence about his father through the exiles' networks run by Westmorland and Charles Paget, so he'd known of his father's remarriage—his response to Kate about that had been feigned—but since coming back to England the information he'd received had been piecemeal. He had not known about Kate's marriage to a playwright, nor of the rupture between her and their father. Perhaps Paget considered such domestic details unimportant. When she'd told him of the rupture he'd had a moment of panic, for he had been counting on her good offices. But then she had begged him to let her effect a reconciliation for both their sakes, and he was satisfied. He felt certain she would achieve it. He had only to wait.

But now, waiting, the fact that he had used Kate caused him pain.

He shook off that gloomy thought. The cause was worth it. The celestial Mary was worth it—worth all the pain, and more.

"Once I'm settled in this lord's house, Townsend, I'll have extraordinary access. To his correspondence, and to overhearing his talk with fellow lords. From this safe place—a hiding place in plain view—I'll contact Northumberland at Petworth. It's time to consolidate all the elements of our mission. That's why I needed to see you. You must call the other five to a meeting. Is the warehouse still safe?"

"Yes."

"Can you get them to come next Tuesday?"

"I think so. Same time?"

"Yes. Nine in the morning." He grinned. By next Tuesday

evening he could be sitting in his father's parlor, chatting with his father's wife.

A horse snorted and stamped in its stall. There was a thud on the roof. Robert tensed, his eyes on the ceiling's rough beams. Townsend looked up, too. Someone up there?

"A branch hit the roof, I imagine," said Townsend. "The wind."

Robert relaxed.

"I have news, too," said Townsend. "Word is that Ambassador Castelnau may have found a new courier."

"Who?"

He shrugged. "We don't know. But I heard it from Feron."

The ambassador's clerk. Feron was rarely wrong. "He doesn't know who it is?"

"No. Just said his master is preparing a packet of letters from Paris and Rome just as he used to do for Griffith."

Letters to Mary in Sheffield. From her most stalwart agents and supporters abroad.

"Well, if it's true we'll know soon enough." Robert's contact in Sheffield would alert him. "Go now," he told Townsend. "Tell our five friends." Smiling, he slapped the anxious fellow's shoulder. "And be ready to hear on Tuesday of my great step up in the world."

Three days later, in Lewes, Robert was in his bedchamber at Master Levett's house after breakfast, packing his bag to revisit his patient on Friar's Walk. He was sorting through his vials of salves, the glasses clinking like chimes, when he heard a sound outside that made him wonder if the thunder and rain were returning. Fanciful thinking. Bright sun shone outside his window. The sound was riders, he realized: horses' hooves. Minutes later there was a loud knock on the front door. Levett and his wife and daughter had gone to Hastings for a niece's wedding. The maid would inform the caller they were out.

Robert settled the last vial into the bag, then closed its clasp, ready to go. He was opening his door when the maid came hurrying up the stairs, wide-eyed with wonder. "Master Parry," she said. "A gentleman to see you."

The girl's astonishment . . . the horsemen. Could the caller be Father? Excitement leapt in him. *Stay calm*, he reminded himself. *Act contrite*. He set down his bag and went downstairs.

At the door stood a well-dressed, beefy man of about forty. One of Father's retainers?

"Master Robert Parry?"

"Yes?"

"I am Sir Thomas Heneage. You are to appear before a commission of the privy council of Her Majesty Elizabeth, by the Grace of God Queen of England and Ireland, defender of the faith. Come with me."

Beyond Heneage a body of men-at-arms in steel breastplates and helmets had their eyes on Robert. He counted eight, plus Heneage. And a horse with no rider, brought for him. Blood pumped loudly inside his ears. He had expected to be questioned, but had imagined it happening quietly, privately, orchestrated by his father in the security of his father's house. Not this. Had he been mistaken about Kate? Had she found out about him? Betrayed him?

He was alone. Impossible to run. Impossible to get word to Levett, or to Townsend.

He went outside peaceably. He mounted the horse, his skin clammy as the men-at-arms surrounded him. Heneage took the lead. They turned away from the merchant's house, and with their horses at a brisk walk were soon on the road to London. No one spoke.

Robert felt as if he were going to his execution.

❧ 9 ❧

Interrogation

The London home of Adam, Lord Thornleigh, was a three-story residence on Bishopsgate Street. An orchard grew within its expansive walled gardens. Across from its front lay the busy Merchant Taylors Hall. Its west windows were within hailing distance of the Royal Exchange, the hub of the city's commercial life. Its owner should have been a happy man.

But Adam Thornleigh had never felt more disturbed as he climbed the stairs to the bedchambers, his two greyhounds padding at his heels. Kate's news three days ago had astounded him: Robert back in England. At first, joy had coursed through him. *My son!* But his daughter's next words had crushed his joy. *He is living under another name,* she'd said. *He does not want to be found.* Why? What was Robert hiding? Instantly, Adam had feared the answer. His son had grown up among traitors, raised by his traitorous mother. Was he a traitor, too?

There was no keeping this secret. To do so might endanger the realm. Though profoundly conflicted, he had sent word to Lord Burghley. The next day Robert was arrested in Lewes. Today, at Whitehall, members of the privy council would interrogate him. Adam, a councillor himself, had told them he would be there.

Questions tormented him as he went up the stairs. *What dark-*

ness will they uncover? What treacherous whirlpool has the boy's mother set swirling? One thought was torture: *Will I see my son hang?*

He turned at the landing to carry on up to see his wife. He had left her sleeping. The dogs, sensing his destination, romped ahead. Adam went slowly, feeling all of his fifty-three years. Morning sunshine flooded the window at his back, but he felt none of its warmth, felt instead like a helmsman in a midnight gale steering between rock reefs. No, worse—this sense of danger beyond his control was utterly foreign to him. On his ships he had faced many perils, from the fury of nature to the fury of Spanish fighters, but even when battling a storm or slashing the foe on his blood-slick deck he had harbored hope, however faint, of eventual mastery. On land he *was* master, the lord of five great manors in Kent, Essex, and Somerset where hundreds in village and field were his to command, and the owner of two magnificent houses in city and country. But now, preparing to leave for Robert's interrogation, he felt only a sickening impotence. Of his children he no longer had mastery. His son and daughter had spun out of his control.

He opened the bedchamber door and the dogs romped in. Fear cut through him when he saw Fenella standing at the desk, bent over. "What is it?" he said, coming to her. "Pain again?"

She turned in surprise, straightening, a paper in her hand. "I thought you'd gone."

"What's wrong?"

"Nothing. I'm fine."

His heart settled. "Then get back into bed." He took her arm and guided her. "You shouldn't be on your feet."

"I just wanted this letter. Sir Humphrey needs an answer."

"Do that from bed. Call for the maid when you need something."

"Get help to cross the room? Adam, I'm not a hundred years old."

"No, you are a youthful sprite who could skip about singing, but please humor me and rest. Just a few more days, the doctor said. Then you'll be back in fighting trim."

He plumped her pillows. She got into bed, but did not lie down. The two dogs joined him, looking up at Fenella as if wanting to help her, too. She sat back against the headboard and Adam snugged the blanket up to her waist. At forty-one Fenella was no sprite. He wanted none. Her beauty was as timeless as a mermaid's song and never failed to lure him. Her auburn hair, glinting red in the sunlight. Her green eyes, ever smiling. Her Scottish spirit, part fire, and her body, of the earth. Her constancy like the sea. He loved her, body and soul.

"Adam," she said gently, "you must go. They'll be starting soon."

"I know. I just came to tell you I'm on my way." But he sat down on the edge of the bed, his hand on her knee. The two dogs sat by his feet, one on each side.

She covered his hand with hers. "I know it's going to be hard."

"To learn that my son is plotting treason?" he said grimly. He could imagine nothing harder. He looked into her eyes. *Except losing you.*

Loss, he thought with a pain at his heart. Fenella had lost the baby six days ago. Her third miscarriage. Adam knew the dark well of emptiness she felt. His own was deep enough. It felt like the loss was somehow his fault. He seemed unable to keep his children. Kate had renounced his protection by holding to her misguided marriage. That had hurt. Robert had been lost to him ten years ago in Brussels. When Adam had arrived back in England with Kate, Elizabeth had ordered him to disinherit his son. It had almost killed him to do it, but she had made it a command, simultaneously annulling his marriage to Frances. She had wanted no traitoress's son to inherit a barony in her realm. All he had left was Fenella. Everything in him wanted to stay here with her, not go to Whitehall and hear the awful truth. It would be like losing Robert all over again.

"He's likely not doing any such thing," she replied to his mention of treason. "You're imagining the worst. Why shouldn't we believe what he told Kate? *She* obviously does."

"Those two were always close. Two peas in a pod. Kate would defend Robert even if she found him plunging a knife in Elizabeth's heart."

He winced at his own words. He had meant only a barb of black humor, but he saw nothing mirthful in Kate's choice of allegiance: her Catholic husband over her father and her queen. And the image he had conjured of Robert standing over a dead Elizabeth made him almost queasy.

To banish the image he poked at the letter Fenella had set amid a scatter of papers on his side of the bed: letters, receipts, a ledger book. On the night table beside her lay an ink pot and pen. "Don't work too long at this," he said. "You need to rest."

"Sir Humphrey is not resting." She nodded at the letter. "He wants another thirty pounds for sailcloth and twelve more for cordage."

Fenella knew ships. She had owned a profitable enterprise salvaging vessels on the island of Sark when Adam had limped into her bay in a shot-up carrack eleven years ago. A decade before that, during England's fight against the French in Scotland, she had helped him escape hanging in Edinburgh. Adam owed her his life. Now, she was managing his investment in Sir Humphrey Gilbert's planned voyage to colonize Newfoundland. Gilbert was in a hurry. Four years ago the Queen had granted him a six-year exploration license and now time was running out to exercise it. The prospective colonists were well-to-do Catholic investors squeezed by England's recusancy fines and lured by the nine million acres Gilbert intended to parcel out. He would lead the expedition of five vessels. Sir Walter Ralegh, one of the Queen's new favorites, would captain his own ship, *Bark Ralegh*. Gilbert's plan appealed to both Adam and Fenella. Adam was all for shipping offshore these troublesome people who would not give their full allegiance to Elizabeth. Sir Francis Walsingham, the Queen's Puritan spymaster, approved the plan, too. As for Fenella, she liked the investment opportunity. She was clever with money.

"I'm writing Sir Humphrey to ask for a meeting," she said. "I have questions about where he's getting his provisions. And he's paying far too much for cordage."

Adam's mind had slid back to Robert. Absently, he stroked his dog Fleet's silky ear.

"Go," Fenella said softly. "Get it over with."

He did not move. "I dread it. Dread what I might hear."

"Don't. Trust Kate's account."

"But can I trust *Kate?*"

Fenella frowned. "You don't mean that." They had argued before about his daughter. Or rather, about Adam's antipathy to her marriage. Fenella always defended Kate.

"You're right, it's her husband I don't trust. He may have dragged her into his Catholic circle. Fenella, you cannot close your eyes to how he has corrupted her."

"Corrupted? Listen to yourself, you talk like a Puritan preacher. She is your daughter and you love her. You miss her, I *know* you do."

He looked down. The dogs looked up at him. "Yes," he confessed.

"So do I." There was blame in her voice.

They sat in silence. Kate's banishment from his house was a wound too raw to probe. Outside on Bishopsgate Street the morning clatter of carts and horses carried on. From the steps of the Merchant Taylors Hall across the street came the faint voices of traders and clerks coming and going.

"And for ten years," Fenella said quietly, "you've missed your son, too. Don't kill this chance to have him back. He's become a doctor, Kate says. He wants only to be home. That's all there is to it. Don't conjure demons where there are none."

"The demon is Frances. She's had him all this time. God knows what poison the boy has imbibed from her."

"Nonsense. Robert is a man now, with a mind of his own. Whatever hold his mother had on him, he has broken it. Why do you keep letting thoughts of her torment you?"

Because she's a Grenville and they never stop. "Her brother almost managed to kill Elizabeth," he said. "He did kill my father."

"But the brother is long dead. And the sister has not made a squeak in all these years. And in any case Her Majesty is supremely well guarded." The slightest smile played on her lips. "Adam, you do not have to protect the Queen and England all by yourself."

"We'll see," he answered grimly. No point in repeating his fears about Robert. Nor could he put off his departure any longer. "I must go." He leaned over and kissed her. "Rest. I'll see you at supper."

He got to his feet. The dogs stood up with him.

Fenella caught up his hand with sudden urgency. Her voice was low, serious now. "Do not cut your children adrift. Your son should be your heir. You may not have another."

Pity and love washed through him. And a surging admiration for her generous heart. He knew how much this statement cost her. He lifted her hand and kissed her palm. "We'll try again. When you're well."

The Queen's palace of Whitehall teemed with the activity of a town. Straddling the Strand, its precincts were a crowded jumble of houses, shops, barracks, stables, gardens, a brewery, a banqueting pavilion, a tennis court, a bowling alley, a pit for cockfights, and a tiltyard for jousting. The palace itself, a grand hodgepodge that was the result of almost a hundred years of additions and constant rebuilding, had over a thousand rooms.

Adam made his way along a corridor noisy with courtiers, foreign dignitaries, lawyers, place-seekers, clerks, and dogs. He reached a chamber at the rear of the clock tower courtyard and opened the door. The six men murmuring at the long table looked up as he came in. Two sitting at the far end were clerks. The other four were Adam's fellow members of Elizabeth's privy council, men he had known for years. Concern at his arrival creased the brows of the aged Sir Ralph Sadler and the spry-looking Sir Christopher Hatton. Veteran diplomat Sir Walter Mildmay busied himself with a document. A knot twisted in Adam's stomach. They had known he was coming, so why these troubling looks? Had they already found some damning evidence against Robert?

The fourth, Lord Burghley, got to his feet and came to him with a welcoming handshake. That dispelled the worst of Adam's anxiety. Burghley would not smile if they had already found Robert guilty. Sixty-two years old, Elizabeth's principal adviser, he was presiding.

"You do not have to be present, you know," Burghley said kindly. He nodded to the far wall. "Use Walsingham's peephole. He's at home in Barn Elms today."

Adam hated subterfuge. Whatever was coming he would face head-on. "I'll stay."

"As you wish. Have you seen your son yet?"

"No." He had not visited Robert where they were holding him. That would only muddy the waters, already so murky.

"Come, then. Join us." Starting back to his seat, Burghley indicated the empty chair to the right of his.

Adam sat down. Beside him Hatton murmured, "My lord," and offered an uncomfortable smile. Sadler shook his head and looked away, clearly concerned at having Adam present. Mildmay continued to pretend to read. Their disapproval made Adam grateful for Burghley's sympathy. They were old friends. Burghley had been a tireless campaigner for Elizabeth ever since her dark days in the Tower at the age of twenty, held captive by her half sister Queen Mary, dead these twenty-eight years. Plain Sir William Cecil back then, Burghley had asked Adam's family to help Princess Elizabeth when her sister had released her into house arrest. That had been Adam's first sight of Elizabeth and his introduction to Burghley, and the start of his lifelong friendship with both. He trusted Burghley's judgment in all things relating to Elizabeth and the realm.

"We had his room searched at the Lewes house," Burghley told him, all business now. "The entire house, in fact. Nothing incriminating was found. We also asked him to list every person he has had personal contact with in Brussels, both English and foreign." He handed Adam a paper. "Here is what he gave us."

Adam forced a dispassionate perusal of the names. There were dozens. He recognized only a few. A surprising sensation ambushed him as he recognized something else: the loops in the handwriting. He saw there the ghost of the child.

"Any of those names have significance for you?" Burghley asked.

"Beyond the Duchess of Feria, no." Adam had known for years, as did the others, that when Frances had fled England with their children she had found a haven with her old friend, Jane Dormer, the duchess. English herself, she was a supporter of the English community of exiles in Brussels.

Burghley grunted. "Small fry, really. Oxford scholars, minor nobles, priests. As for the Dutch and Spanish names, they're mostly merchants and shopkeepers."

Hatton pointed out like a warning, "Two of the priests are Jesuits." His hatred of priests was well-known.

"And we already keep a watch on them," Burghley assured him sternly. "All right, let's get started." He turned to the two clerks. "Henshaw, have them bring in Master Thornleigh."

Adam felt them all glance at him. He kept a stony face. Inside he was awash with dread.

As the clerk hurried out, Sadler addressed Adam. "My lord, may I suggest that you leave the questioning to us?"

"Might be best," Burghley agreed. "Keep it impersonal."

Adam had expected no other procedure. "Of course."

The others looked relieved. Waiting, they shuffled papers. Sweat prickled Adam's back. The windowless room was stuffy, hot. *Or is it just me?* His mouth was as dry as sailcloth.

Two guards brought Robert in. Warring sensations swept through Adam. First, astonishment at the man his son had grown to be. Wiry. Angular. Quick of movement. Hazel, alert eyes. *So like Frances.* Second, relief at seeing he had not been mistreated in detention. Then, pity at Robert's obvious fear . . . but then another surge of dread. *Men do not fear if they are innocent.*

Seeing his father, Robert's astonishment was plain. He opened his mouth to speak, and Adam was sure the word his lips began to form was "Father," but Robert choked it back, made no sound.

Burghley cleared his throat. "Let us begin." He launched into the formalities. Asked Robert to state his name, present abode, occupation, the date he had arrived in England, and at which port. Robert swallowed hard. When he spoke, his voice was tight but clear. Adam listened to the answers, his thoughts in turmoil. Burghley then asked Robert to explain his connection with four individuals he had listed.

Robert's voice took on an edge of fear. "They are friends of my mother, my lord."

The councillors looked unsurprised. They knew Robert had been brought up by his mother. Adam felt the presence of Frances hovering.

Sadler and Mildmay and Hatton each took a turn with the list, questioning Robert about names. His answers were short and brittle. Adam realized that his son's fear was that of anyone called to testify before men who had the power to cast him into prison or even order his death. It was not necessarily the fear of the guilty. It gave him an overpowering relief.

"And your mother," Burghley went on. "Where is she now?"

"The last I heard, my lord, she lives in Brussels still. I have not seen her in six years, though, so I cannot be sure."

"Yes, you spent five years studying at the University of Padua," Burghley said, scanning a paper. "You did not see her in all that time?"

"No, my lord."

"Nor hear from her?"

"She wrote to me. I answered. I owed her that much because she arranged my education. But since I came home I have not heard from her."

Home. Adam felt a catch in his chest.

"Nor written to her?" Mildmay probed.

"No, sir."

Burghley asked, "What is the source of your mother's revenue?"

Robert seemed perplexed. "Revenue, my lord? She has none."

"Come, come," Sadler said testily. "Does she not receive a pension from the pope? Or from Philip of Spain?"

Adam waited with excruciating curiosity. The pope and Philip paid handsome pensions to many of the English exiles, a reward for their loyalty to the Catholic church, and, Adam had no doubt, an inducement to act against England should the opportunity arise.

"No, my lord," Robert said. "She is poor. But her friend the Duchess of Feria has been generous to her. Her generosity extended to my education."

Sadler asked darkly, "And does your mother join the generous duchess in fomenting hatred of Her Majesty Queen Elizabeth?"

Robert looked pained. Adam held his breath. Sadler's words had been more snarl than question.

"My lords, I humbly submit to you that my mother is not the antagonist you seem to imagine." His voice turned bitter. "Of course, I am profoundly ashamed of her past crime. I lived with her for only four years, when I was a child, and as soon as I could leave for Padua, I did. But her crime is in the past. Now, she is merely a deluded old woman. She thinks she has the ear of men who serve King Philip's governor in Brussels, but in reality she has no influence, not even with the English exiles who grumble about Her Majesty. They do not listen to her. They find her pathetic. Many of the people she talks about do not even know her."

"The exiles," Burghley said, "tell us about them. What do you know about Sir Francis Englefield?"

"Nothing, my lord. I do not know who that gentleman is."

"Sir William Stanley?"

"I do not know him, either, my lord."

"Were you ever in the company of Lord Paget?"

"No."

"You do not know him?"

"I know of him. I never met him."

Hatton jumped in. "What about Father Joseph Creswell?"

"I know him by name only, sir. I have heard that he is a priest who begs for meetings at the court of King Philip."

Burghley resumed his attack. "How do you know Thomas Morgan?"

"How?" Robert looked taken aback. The knot in Adam's stomach twisted again. Morgan, who lived in Paris, was the chief gatherer of secret intelligence for Mary Stuart. "I am sorry, my lord, but I do not know this gentleman," Robert said. "Neither in person nor by name. Does he live in Brussels?"

They banged on, name after name. Jasper Heywood. William Crichton. Claudio Acquaviva, the Father General of the Jesuits. Robert assured them he knew none of these men.

Mildmay took over. "Were you ever in the company of the Earl of Westmorland?"

"The earl, my lord?" Robert looked amazed. "Goodness, my mother and I did not move in such high circles."

"And since you've come to England, have you been in contact with Anthony Brown?"

"No. I do not know the gentleman."

"Lord Montague of Cowdray?"

"No."

"The Earl of Arundel?"

"No." At this badgering, Robert looked distraught, as though struggling to dam up unmanly tears. "Good my lords, I know none of these men. I assume you consider them somehow dangerous to the security of Her Majesty and her realm, but I swear to you I neither know them nor know of them."

Adam caught the glint of tears in his son's eyes and a memory leapt: the fire in Brussels when he'd tried to get Robert away with Kate, but failed. He'd seen the boy crying, seen Frances and her henchman take him. The young, tear-stained face had haunted Adam all these years. Now, though duty demanded his skepticism, he longed to believe what Robert was claiming. He struggled to stay impartial.

The other councillors exchanged glances, a silent consultation over whether they had any more questions. "The witness?" Mildmay suggested quietly to Burghley.

Burghley nodded and motioned to the clerk.

A florid, well-dressed man was ushered in. Asked to state his name and occupation he gave clear replies, though tinged with nervousness. Gilbert Levett, merchant of Lewes in Sussex. He threw an anxious glance at Robert, who'd been told to stand to one side. Burghley asked him to explain how Robert came to live with him.

"Ten months ago I received a letter from my colleague John Hamilton in Padua, my lord. He said his son's friend, a young doctor, was coming to England and could I take him in. So when young Master Parry—"

"Thornleigh," Mildmay corrected him.

"Aye, Master Thornleigh, as I've now been told. When he arrived my wife and I gave him room and board as he set up to dispense his physic. He did not speak of his family beyond saying his parents were dead. I did not probe." As though afraid of censure for having been too trusting, he added defensively, "He's a well-behaved young fellow, my lord, well liked by all our neighbors. Always accompanies me and my family to church. He cured my daughter Judith of her asthma."

"Really? How?"

"Discovered the cause was feathers."

The councillors stared at him. "Feathers?" Sadler said.

"Aye, sir, turns out she can't be near them without losing her breath something terrible. We threw out all the feathers in the house and it has worked." He beamed. "She's suffered no more attacks."

The tale was oddly touching. Adam felt a tickle of admiration. And something akin to pride. *Clever Robert.*

They asked Levett about his business, his colleagues in Europe, his religious practices. His testimony revealed an exemplary loyal Englishman: a successful trader and pillar of his community who prayed to God every Sunday to keep Her Majesty in health and God's grace.

He was excused. Mildmay questioned Robert about his patients. He answered fulsomely about agues and fluxes, treatments and physic, his previous anxiety seeming to dissolve in his obvious love for his subject. With every answer Adam's admiration rose. Hope swelled in him. Could Robert be exactly what he claimed to be?

But Burghley and the others were not finished.

"Why did you steal into England under a false name?"

"To protect my family, my lord—my father and my sister. I understand why you mistrust me. I, too, would mistrust a man who foreswore his name. But, my lords, I had good reason. The taint of my mother's treason hangs over me. I had no wish for it to taint my lord father and my sister, too. That is why I wanted to stay hidden."

"Then why come to England at all?" Burghley demanded. "You have acquaintances and connections enough in Brussels and Padua. Why come here?"

The glint of tears sprang again in Robert's eyes. He took a deep breath to quell them. "I love England, my lord. It's as simple as that. No, 'simple' is not the right word. The craving for one's homeland is a tangle of yearning and misery and hope. Can you understand what it is to wake up every day longing for the sights of England? Her wildflowers and brooks. Her good, plain fare. Her honest, sturdy people. I fear that one day soon the King of Spain may wage war against Her Majesty." He held up his hands in a gesture of denial, adding, "No, my lords, I know no particulars. But I hear the talk in my patients' homes, and in church, and in alehouses, and the talk of Spain these days grows constant and fearful. If the terrible day comes when England is in danger, I want to be here, in the home of my birth, helping my fellow countrymen. I am no soldier, to be sure, but I am a good doctor. I want to be of use here, in my own land, not molder in the papist corruption of the Spanish-occupied Low Countries. And if England ever faces invasion I *will* turn soldier. I will fight for my country in her hour of need." He halted, as though to collect himself after this outburst. Then, quietly, he added, "I daresay I've been a fool to think I could go on pretending, hiding. But if I've been a fool, my lords, it is no underhanded motive that drove me to come home. Only love of my country."

Adam was so moved he found it hard to keep silent. *He's innocent!* He was so thrilled he could scarcely sit still. *Wait*, he told himself with difficulty. *Let Burghley and the others do their job.*

Burghley cleared his throat. *He's moved, too*, Adam thought with a fierce jolt of hope.

"Tell me this, Master Thornleigh," Burghley said very carefully. "Do you love your country enough to go back to Brussels and report to us?"

Robert blinked at him in astonishment. Adam felt equally surprised.

"Forgive me, my lord, but no. I am no spy."

"Yet you call yourself a patriot."

Robert looked tormented. "And so I am, my lord. But I will not inform on people with whom I have no quarrel. Some of them were good to me." His eyes swept them all, entreating. "I beg you, good my lords, I am a poor physician. I want only to be left alone."

"Lying in prison you would get your wish."

"Then cast me into prison! For I cannot do what you ask." He let out a shuddering breath. His shoulders heaved with the effort to hold back tears.

"Enough!" Adam said. He was on his feet. "Burghley, arrest him if you have evidence. If not, let him go."

Robert's mouth fell open. The councillors blinked at Adam in dismay. "My lord," Sadler said with quiet formality, "please take your seat."

"No. I've heard enough, Sadler. We've all heard enough. We are all careful in Her Majesty's business, of course. But admit it, there is no evidence to suggest my son is anything but what he says. Good God, if we hound and persecute loyal Englishmen, who will be left to defend the realm?"

He strode around the table toward Robert. His angry bluster was all show, a shield to deflect his colleagues' displeasure at his disregard of proper procedure. Inside he was giddy with gladness. Coming face-to-face with Robert, he looked into his astonished eyes. The nearness of him rocked Adam so deeply, he felt suddenly in danger of weeping. He clapped a hand on Robert's shoulder and forced steadiness into his voice. "Welcome home, my boy."

Robert shot an incredulous look at the councillors. "But . . . Lord Burghley . . . prison—"

"There will be no prison," Adam assured him. "Ha! Unless you call my house a prison." He laughed, too happy to care how paltry his jest sounded. On an impulse too strong to deny, he embraced his son. Robert stood unmoving in his arms as though too stunned to respond. Adam let him go, laughing again at their awkwardness with each other. But he kept a gentle hand on Robert's elbow, a signal that in his father Robert had a steadfast ally.

Adam looked at the councillors. "Well, Burghley?"

His old friend raised his hands in easy surrender. "I see no reason to detain the young gentleman."

"Then it's settled," Adam said, grinning. "You're coming with me, Robert. Coming home."

* * *

Kate crossed the clock tower courtyard of Whitehall Palace, keeping her face down and the hood of her cloak up to avoid being recognized. If anyone she knew hailed her she would say she was seeking an interview with Sir Philip Sydney to entreat a tutoring post for her husband. But it would be hard to speak calmly, so agitated were her thoughts. She had watched Robert's interrogation. Matthew Buckland had allowed her access to the room behind the interrogation chamber, a small space from which Sir Francis Walsingham or his agents like Matthew could observe the proceedings through a peephole. Kate had been alone, watching, listening. Doubts now swarmed, stinging her with painful questions. Robert had lied to the councillors. Why?

She reached the clerk's chamber, a cramped, windowless room on the third floor. He was waiting for her.

"You must be quick," he said, handing her a slim sheaf of papers. "This must be back on my lord's desk before he returns from dinner."

"I understand, Master Henshaw. This will take but a moment." She pressed a sovereign onto his palm. His fingers closed around the coin. "Thank you," she said.

She turned, opening the docket. Several pages of the councillors' questions and Robert's answers were rendered in Henshaw's neat handwriting. He waited by the door, ready to retrieve the docket and go as soon as she was done.

She leafed through the pages, scanning Robert's testimony. Her fingers felt cold on the vellum. Cold, though at the beginning of Robert's interrogation she had watched and listened with a glad heart, warmed by the satisfaction of having reunited her brother and her father. That had been her hope: Robert, welcomed home where he belonged . . . her guilt at seeing him left behind as a child, absolved.

Until this one statement. His words, though vague, had made her skin prickle.

Here it was. She had found it.

Sir Walter Mildmay: Were you ever in the company of the Earl of Westmorland?

Robert: The earl, my lord? Goodness, my mother and I did not move in such high circles.

She closed the docket, her heart beating painfully. The Earl of Westmorland. Thirteen years ago he had been a leader of the Northern Rebellion. Five thousand men had marched on Durham and taken the city, preparing to march on to London. But Elizabeth's forces had crushed the rebellion. Westmorland fled to the Netherlands, his property confiscated. Joining other English exiles, he now lived on a pension from the pope. All this was common knowledge.

What was not known was Kate's personal experience. The memory was still so clear. Her mother, all aflutter, curtsying to Westmorland at his house in Antwerp. The earl dabbing a napkin to his bushy moustache as he turned to her from his supper table with his guests. Kate and Robert curtsying and bowing as they were introduced to him, Kate ten, Robert eight. Robert mistakenly calling him, "Your Grace." Westmorland had ignored the childish error of address, but Mother had glared at Robert, making him red-faced with puzzlement. Once home, Mother had severely drilled him in the proper forms of address—for a knight, an earl, a duke—while Kate, behind Mother's back to make Robert smile, mimicked the earl dabbing his moustache, and Robert stifled a giggle. For days afterward the two of them had taken turns play-acting the moustachioed earl, making each other laugh. Despite the passing years, Robert would not have forgotten that.

Kate left the clerk's room, the question still stinging. *Why did Robert lie?*

❧ 10 ❧

The Countess

Arundel Castle, built in the eleventh century following the Norman conquest, overlooked the River Arun in West Sussex. The earldom of Arundel had descended to generations of d'Albinis and Fitzallans through female heiresses. By Elizabeth's reign it had passed to an ancient and powerful family: the Howards. Philip Howard, the twentieth earl of Arundel, was a friend of the Earl of Northumberland, whose Sussex stronghold, Petworth House, lay just sixty miles away.

The chapel of Arundel Castle had been a place of worship for centuries, but these days its windows were heavily curtained when the family gathered for mass, and access was guarded so that no hint of the Catholic rites within would come to the notice of the Queen's traveling officials, the pursuivants, who executed warrants drawn up by the royal council to investigate Catholic recusants throughout the realm.

Kneeling at mass, Owen Lyon glanced at the door to the sacristy. *That's where they lock up the pyx and chalice and the jeweled crucifix when mass is done,* he thought. He turned his attention back as the priest reached him, dispensing the host to the four supplicants. Owen took the wafer of bread on his tongue. *Where,* he wondered, *do they hide the priest?*

Northumberland didn't keep a secret priest at Petworth House as far as Owen had been able to tell. Though he'd had little time to investigate. He'd been kept in Northumberland's lockup overnight after they'd drowned the double-dealing porter, Rankin. The following day, though, Northumberland's interrogation had been perfunctory, as if he harbored no real mistrust, and he had then set Owen to work on his correspondence on a trial basis. "Be quiet and quick," he had ordered, "and maybe I'll keep you." Owen sensed he'd been kept in detention only to placate Northumberland's suspicious wife, the countess Catherine. That was a week ago. She was kneeling beside Owen now, in Arundel's chapel.

Kneeling with them were two other worshippers. To Owen's left was Arundel's wife, the countess Anne. Like Catherine, she vastly outranked him. To the right of Catherine was a guest, Captain Fortescue, a tall, black-bearded man of about thirty in dandy's clothing: a cherry-red satin doublet laced with silver and a red velvet hat with silver buttons. Owen had not yet discovered Fortescue's connection here. Something about the fellow seemed odd. For a military man his hands looked as soft as a lady's.

Countess Catherine slightly turned her head to Owen and he felt her scrutinizing gaze. He closed his eyes, pretending piety. Her watchful disapproval had kept him on his guard every day at Petworth. Whether at table with the household, or privately taking the earl's dictation in his study, where Catherine sometimes came to speak to her husband, Owen had caught her watching him with a frown, as though waiting for him to prove her right. Yesterday she had come to Arundel Castle to visit the countess Anne, bringing a train of servants, including Owen, who had been ordered by the earl to accompany her. Owen had groaned silently—his mission was to watch Northumberland, who'd remained at Petworth—but he was on probation and had to obey.

The priest moved on to Catherine. Owen opened his eyes, relieved to see her concentration turn to taking the host on her tongue. He kept his gaze straight ahead on the altar's jewel-crusted gold crucifix, and felt his frustration rising. He was at the castle because of the pale-faced Countess Anne, mumbling her prayers to his left. Though only twenty-five, the same age as her husband, she was as dour as a dowager. She fancied herself a poet, so Catherine had told Northumberland that Owen would be useful to her friend. Probably because Anne's Latin was deplorable, Owen thought. What foul luck to be brought here as a dancing dog.

He needed to get back to Petworth. The letters he had written so far for Northumberland had been innocent enough: instructions to his eldest son traveling in Italy, orders to his steward about a tenant vacancy, a dialogue with the Viscount Montague about a proposed marriage between their children. But Owen was keenly interested in a meeting the two peers had arranged. Montague, one of the wealthiest men in Sussex, lived in Midhurst just five miles from Petworth and Owen suspected that he and Northumberland meant to discuss more than the marriage of their children. They'd both had past dealings with the exiled Earl of Westmorland, and Owen was eager to observe as much as he could of the proposed meeting to catch any word that might pass between them about a planned invasion. These three old families' pasts, he knew, were webbed with conspiracy. Montague had been implicated in the northern uprising twelve years ago, though he had not been charged. Arundel's father, the Duke of Norfolk, had subsequently been executed for conspiring to marry the deposed queen of Scots, Mary Stuart. And now, the daughter of the exiled Westmorland, living in North Yorkshire, was suspected of intriguing with radical priests. Westmorland—that was whom Owen was most concerned about. All the rumors he had heard in prison about invasion swirled around Westmorland's links to Philip of Spain.

Owen watched the priest finish dispensing the host to Countess Catherine. A stocky middle-aged man in need of a shave, he had weary but alert eyes. He *had* to be alert living here, no doubt scurrying to hide in the priest hole in the attic or an outbuilding whenever a pursuivant came near. That took courage, Owen granted. If caught, the priest would land in prison, and if strident in his doctrine he could hang. Owen could not muster the Puritans' hatred of Catholics. He had nothing against them, or even against their faith. What mattered was when they threatened the liberty of England since the pope demanded their allegiance to him above the Queen. Their fervor, stoked by Mary Stuart's claim to the throne, was leading many of them closer to treason. That's what Owen was after: evidence about a planned insurrection or invasion, or a coordinated preparation for both.

But this weary, fugitive priest? Small fry, in Owen's opinion. He would duly inform Matthew Buckland about him in a message via the owner of the Angel Inn in Petworth, who would forward it to London, but Owen knew that Matthew's response would be to leave the priest in place. They were after men higher up. And the biggest prize of all: Mary Stuart herself.

Mass was over. Catherine and her two friends were leaving the chapel. Its treasures would be hidden away again behind locked doors. Owen followed his betters toward the exit.

Catherine stopped, letting the others go on. She turned to Owen. She was an attractive woman, but the near-scowl with which she always regarded him marred her smooth features. "The countess Anne wants to see you," she said brusquely. "She has penned some verse about her ancestor, the Duchess of Buckingham, and feels it requires your ear. Attend her in her solar after dinner."

Owen bowed, cutting off her beam of scrutiny. "With pleasure, your ladyship."

He spent the morning helping Arundel's butler in his pantry office write a long letter to the butler's brother in Hastings. It was better than pacing in angry frustration as he waited for his appointment to be Countess Anne's Latin dancing dog. He itched to be on the road back to Petworth House. Every hour he spent out of Northumberland's company was an hour in which he might miss some evidence of the man's treason. So far he had failed to coax any confidences out of Northumberland. None of his attempts, from flattery to grave comments about the state of the realm, had charmed a response in kind from the tight-lipped earl. His silence, of course, was partly the aristocrat's indifference to an inferior, but Owen sensed it also stemmed from the man's native caution, and he puzzled over how he might get Northumberland to lower that shield. Try he must. And he could not do so while stuck here at Arundel Castle. It was infuriating, all the more so because in his idle state he could not keep his thoughts from constantly turning to Kate. When busy, he could push his fears about her to the back of his mind, but with nothing to do he conjured torturing scenarios. Kate, discovered by Mary Stuart's people. Kate, cornered in a dark alley by murderers.

"That's the dinner gong," said the butler, folding the letter Owen had penned. "I'm much obliged for your help, Master Lyon."

"No trouble at all, Master Pym. I hope your brother soon recovers."

"Well, it's not the plague, so we thank God for small mercies."

After dinner with the household in the great hall Owen made his way upstairs to the solar, the family's favorite private room. He knocked. A female voice answered, "Come in."

He opened the door to find Countess Catherine sitting on a bench near a painting of a fierce-looking former earl of Arundel. The bench was wide enough for two to sit back-to-back to observe all the room's paintings. Owen saw that he had interrupted her reading a book. She appeared to be alone. No sign of Countess Anne.

"Perhaps I've come too early, your ladyship. I do not mean to disturb you. I'll come back later."

"No, no, Master Lyon, come in." She set the book down behind her. "Anne will not be joining us."

"I hope Her Ladyship is not ill?"

She shrugged. "Who can tell, with that sour face?"

Owen was taken aback. He had thought the two women were friends. "But, Her Ladyship's poetry—"

"Is abominable. Anne is a good soul, but a frightful poet. No, she has no part in why I asked you here."

Owen's guard sprang up. Was this to be an interrogation?

Catherine fixed her cool, green eyes on him. "I want to talk to you. Come closer. I am rather shortsighted."

He came and stood before her. Despite her slender body and the rich blond hair beneath her voile coif, she looked as forbidding as a judge.

"I have had a report about your wife."

Dread swarmed over him. *They've got Kate.*

"She was seen in London leaving a laundry frequented by the French ambassador. What was she doing there?"

His mouth was dry. He pretended bewilderment. "Having some clothes washed perhaps, my lady?"

"Don't insult me. She resides with Lady Thornleigh, who has servants aplenty. Tell the truth. Is your wife a spy?"

His mind tripped over itself scrambling for an answer.

She laughed lightly, smoothing the folds of her rose silk skirt. "Oh, don't worry, I'm only having fun. We need it in this dour house." She motioned to the spot on the bench beside her, patting its padded blue satin. "Sit down."

Her word flummoxed him. *Fun?*

"Sit down, man. I will not bite." A playful smile curved her lips. "Yet."

He trusted neither her reassurance nor her smile. But she had given an order. He sat down beside her.

"Now," she said, slipping off her coif and shaking loose her hair as though preparing to retire, "is your wife acquainted with Ambassador Castelnau?"

Tread carefully, Owen told himself. "Not to my knowledge, your ladyship."

"No? Perhaps through her father, Lord Thornleigh?"

"It is possible. But she no longer moves in such high circles. Because of me, I'm afraid."

"Yes, so you told my husband. Her father has banned her from his house. What a pity. You have not been married long, I understand?"

"Less than eight months, your ladyship. Six of those I spent in the Marshalsea."

"Poor girl." She touched his knee in sympathy. "To be so long deprived of your company." Her hand lingered on his knee. "My guess is that your wife is one of us. Am I right?"

"Us, my lady?" What in hell did she mean? What did she know? He answered carefully, "By birth she is closer to your ladyship than to me, but—"

"One of the *faithful*, I mean," she interrupted pointedly. "I know *you* are." She reached up and smoothed her hand over his head. He stiffened at the liberty. "This bristly hair," she murmured. "Was prison dreadful? I questioned Arthur about you and he told me how you helped him, shared your food with him. Arthur's an idiot, but he never lies." She slid her hand down his cheek, then his neck. Her fingers toyed with the edge of his collar. "Tell me about it."

Owen held his breath. *So that's what she wants.* It stunned him. He caught her hand to stop her, confusion somersaulting through him. "I thought—"

"Thought what?"

"That you hated me. The way you always glare at me."

She smiled, enjoying his amazement. "I told you, I'm short-sighted."

He couldn't think how to respond. Every instinct told him to beware—her interest in him spelled danger. But he had to find out how much she knew about Kate. Could he somehow turn this situation to his advantage? All he could think was: *Keep her talking.* If seduction was on her mind, he would feign delight. He looked into her eyes and squeezed her hand, a signal that he understood what she wanted.

She smiled, clearly pleased. She laid her fingertips on his mouth. He knew she was going to kiss him.

He spoke before her lips reached his. "Your ladyship, you speak truly. We, the faithful. It did my heart good to partake of mass this morning. The earl is brave to hide the priest. I did not catch his name."

"Father Gregory," she said, smoothing her hand along his chest.

"Has he come from Rheims?"

Her eyes met his with a hint of challenge. "You know about Rheims?"

"All the faithful do." He knew that Oxford graduate William Allen had established a seminary at the French university specifically to train English priests. Working with the Jesuits and financed by the pope, Allen was sending his newly minted priests home as missionaries. "I wanted to attend the seminary myself, but my father had not the funds. So I turned to the theater."

"A sound decision. Celibacy is not for a man like you."

He managed a smile at her implication. "Very true. Yet I am a loyal son of the church and long to serve her, which is why I am so proud to have your husband's trust. As for my wife, she is so ardent in her faith she can sometimes be impetuous. If she approached Ambassador Castelnau it may have been to assure him of our loyalty—hers and mine—to the one true Church. If so, she should not have acted so rashly. I will chastise her."

"Oh? Will you give her a tongue-lashing?" Excitement glimmered in her eyes and she leaned closer. Before Owen could react she flicked her tongue along his upper lip.

He let out a sharp breath, a pretense of being fired with desire for her. "You have me at a disadvantage, your ladyship," he said, as if held back only by the huge gap between them in rank. "You are so far above me."

She laughed at his discomposure. "Well, that can be overlooked."

"Your husband—"

"Oh, never mind him. I told him to let me have you to help Anne. He thinks you're here for your Latin."

"So I have you to thank for this Arundel diversion."

"You do. And it is customary to repay the ones we owe."

"I have . . . no words."

She let out a throaty laugh. "It's not your words I want." She cocked her head at him, her expression turning sober. "That's not quite true. Now that I know you are one of us there is some information I would have from you. Tell me about Lord Thornleigh."

He tried to think how best to use this. He had won her trust—that was good. Better still, it seemed she had no real interest in Kate, had accepted his claim that his wife was just impetuously pious. Best of all, it was dawning on him that he'd been blinkered in focusing his attention solely on Northumberland. Sitting beside him now was a possible great source of information. He had often seen her in intense private conversation with her husband. She might even know details about the invasion plan. "Gladly, if I can," he replied as smoothly as he could. "What do you want to know?"

"Is he really as stiff-necked a Protestant as the world believes?"

"He has always showed himself loyal to Her Majesty."

"So do many who are secretly loyal to the pope. Is Thornleigh?"

"What makes you think that?"

"His son is back in England."

Robert. He remembered Kate saying her brother wanted to keep his return quiet. Owen had wondered why, and suggested she keep clear of him. Had his return now become common knowledge—or did Catherine and her husband simply have spies everywhere? He asked cautiously, "Robert Thornleigh?"

"Yes. He was raised among our exile friends in Brussels. But I hear that Lord Thornleigh has welcomed him back to the bosom of his family. Why?"

This was news! "I know not," he said truthfully.

"Well, perhaps you can find out. In London. I daresay some of Lord Thornleigh's people at his house will blab to you. I will furnish you with enough silver to loosen their tongues." She took his hand. "Will you do me this service?"

Owen himself was now keen to find out about Robert. But his mission was to watch Northumberland. "Unfortunately His Lordship, your husband, requires my attendance at Petworth."

"Oh, he will give you leave. He wants this information."

Aha! "Then I am your servant, my lady."

"Good." Suddenly, she gathered her skirt up to her knees and shoved his hand underneath. "And, tell me," she said slyly, guiding his hand up between her legs, "will serving me suit you?"

With his wrist clamped in her grip, his fingers met her wet cunt. He was beyond astonishment now. She was as slick and yielding as summer butter. Her breaths quickened with desire. She closed her eyes, savoring his touch. Her mouth opened, her tongue pink and wet.

Owen made a quick decision to build her excitement. He withdrew his hand. "In London, of course, if that pleases your ladyship."

"But here first," she breathed, groping again for his wrist. "Now."

He held up both hands, a gesture of reluctant protest. "As I said, I would not presume. Your ladyship is so far above me. . . ."

Anger flashed in her eyes. "I am, indeed. So you will do as you are bid." Her breathing was still ragged. "If you do not, I shall tell my husband you molested me. Then he will have you killed."

He met her eyes, matching her steel with his own. "Threats, my lady, are not the surest way to harden a man's cock."

"I know other ways." She reached for his groin and pressed her palm on his member and rubbed. Owen could not pretend indifference at the sensation—nor conceal the result. She laughed in delight. "Aha! *This* will serve."

She unfastened his doublet, and he did not resist. Now was his chance to get details. "You and I trust each other, which is a great comfort," he said, "but what about the others in this place?"

"*Comfort?*" she parodied, her voice husky as she opened his doublet. She spread it wide, then hurriedly untied the lacings at the neck of his shirt. "I'll have no *comfort,* and nor will you, while you're still in your breeches." She reached again for his cock.

He caught her hand. "I'm serious, my lady. How far does the faith of our host take him?"

"Arundel? Don't worry, he is with us. So is Anne."

All the way to treason? he wanted to ask. Impossible to blurt that. "And his guest, this Captain Fortescue?"

"Black Fortescue, we call him. That dark skin of his, almost like a blackamoor." She resumed stroking his cock through his codpiece even as she slipped her hand inside his shirt and fondled the hair of his chest. "Like this lovely black hair of yours." She kissed his mouth, opening her own.

Owen flicked his tongue against hers. She trembled with desire. He broke off the kiss and asked, "Where is he from? How is he friends with Arundel?"

"What?" she breathed, too distracted to follow.

"Who is Fortescue?"

"That's not his real name. It's Ballard. John Ballard." She bent her head and licked his chest.

Owen drew back a little, leaving her with her tongue out. Then he rewarded her. He shoved her skirt higher and fingered her cunt. "Why the false name?"

Her head lolled back in ecstasy as he stroked her. She moaned. "He's come from . . . Paris." She gasped as his finger slid up into her. "Before that . . . Rheims."

By God, another priest sent by Allen and the Jesuits. "Paris?" he asked.

He itched to ask if Ballard was in contact there with Thomas Morgan, Mary Stuart's chief agent in France, but held back. She would ask how he knew about Morgan.

She grabbed his wrist to shove his finger farther up into her. He resisted, wanting more answers first, and withdrew his hand. She groaned in frustration.

But he was only starting. He licked his finger, wet from her. Watching, she almost swooned. He bit her earlobe. She gasped with pleasure.

He said, "I only want to be sure that everyone near you can be trusted. Is this Ballard known to my lord Northumberland?"

"So many questions," she said testily. "What an interrogation!" The word seemed to snap her out of her carnal trance. She blinked as her mind cleared. "Why do you want to know all this?" Suspicion lurked in her voice.

Owen realized he had gone too far. He dare not ask anything more about Ballard. Not yet. He saw she was about to speak. To stop her he kissed her—a shameless kiss, probing with his tongue to stoke her lust. And his own. She moaned, her excitement fired again.

Owen had a jolting thought of Kate. Before the day he met her he had not lived like a saint, but since that day—since falling so completely in love with her and making her his wife—he had never even imagined being unfaithful. But if Catherine had crucial information this was the only way he was going to get it. And, try as he might, he could not deny the throb of pleasure he felt at gaining mastery over this insistent, lush woman.

He pushed her onto her back, hard enough to push Kate from his mind. Catherine fell back with a gasp of pleasure, her legs flashing white in the swirl of rose silk skirt. He grabbed her ankles and spread her. She laughed in delight. He unfastened his codpiece to free his straining cock and came down on her, stopping her laugh with his mouth.

❧ 11 ❧

Confession

Kate sat at her dressing table at Thornleigh House struggling to decipher a letter in code. It was from Thomas Morgan, Mary Stuart's chief intelligencer in Paris, to a Captain Fortescue in Arundel, Sussex. Matthew's agent at Dover had intercepted it. The code's complexity was a brain-twisting challenge, and Kate had been at it since dawn. It was now almost noon; downstairs, her grandmother's kitchen would be preparing dinner. Looking for guidance, she flipped through pages of the *Stenographia* by the Abbot of Spandheim, then scanned the notes on it by John Dee, the Queen's mathematician friend who had adapted the book's concepts for English code breakers. Today, though, these well-thumbed sources yielded no answers. The *Stenographia* was decades old. This code was new. Frustrated, Kate slapped the book shut.

It was impossible to keep her mind off Robert. She was expecting him at any moment. She had told her grandmother he had returned to England, and last night she'd sent him a note at their father's house inviting him here. She needed to talk to him about his misleading testimony to the royal councillors. Owen's words came back to her: *He has been raised among England's enemies. You should stay away from him until he can be questioned.* Kate had scoffed. Robert was her *brother*, for heaven's sake. She would no more mistrust him than she would herself.

But now he had been questioned and had told a lie. About Westmorland. Why?

No doubt there was a simple explanation—that's what she told herself. Robert had naturally been nervous in front of their father and intimidated by Lord Burghley, so he had simply forgotten meeting Westmorland. Except, he hadn't sounded nervous. His reply—*Goodness, my mother and I did not move in such high circles*—had been too measured, too definite, to spring from panicky forgetfulness. So why hide Mother's acquaintance with Westmorland? She conjured murky scenarios that alarmed her. Innocent men did not lie. Yet what could Robert possibly be guilty of? He was a poor doctor. He had cut himself off from Mother years ago. And in any case Mother was no threat. Suspecting Robert of deception made no sense. Yet his words *were* a deception. Kate needed him to explain it.

Waiting for him, uneasy about how to question him, she again applied herself to the decoding task before her, the intercepted letter from Thomas Morgan in Paris to Captain Fortescue in Arundel. She now knew that Fortescue was the alias of John Ballard, a Cambridge graduate who'd become a priest at Rheims and was now back in England. Matthew had told her this; he had learned it from Owen's report sent from Petworth. She wished Matthew had also been able to reassure her that Owen was not in danger. His report said that Northumberland had had his spy drowned when he'd learned of the man's double-dealing. That made her shudder. "Be very careful, Owen," she whispered to herself.

Thomas Morgan was said to be a clever and determined man. His code was so challenging she had been able to decipher only a third of his one-page letter so far. Most codes were simple substitution ciphers in which a combination of numbers, letters, and symbols stood for names, places, and common words, so deciphering them was based on the frequency of use of letters of the alphabet. The letter *e* accounted for thirteen percent of all letters used in English, whereas *z* occurred only one percent of the time. Whatever letter, number, or symbol was used, it retained its original frequency of use, so the problem had to have a mathematical solution. By analyzing the frequency of the letters used in a code,

Kate could work out the consonant or vowel each substituted letter represented. In the most rudimentary substitution *a* was *z* and *b* was *y*, et cetera. *The last will be first and the first will be last*, as she'd told Owen, quoting the Bible. *Child's play.* But the code before her would require a child of freakish wit. Morgan had run words together with the breaks between them removed so as to avoid giving clues. And, to disguise his message further, he had included many nulls—letters that were fakes, representing nothing, and thus altering the rules of what must have been the original code.

Nevertheless, Kate had worked out some of his symbols. Two question marks together meant King Philip of Spain. A capital *X* followed by a backslash meant Mary Stuart. A backward *B* meant the Spanish ambassador, Don Bernardino de Mendoza. A zero with a diagonal stroke through it meant the French ambassador, Castelnau. The number five meant "ship." The number eight meant "packet"—a reference, Kate deduced, to the letters that Castelnau received from Mary's European correspondents. The references to Philip of Spain—"his wise decision"—and Mary—"she awaits word"—and Castelnau were tantalizing, but so far Kate had unearthed nothing that Elizabeth's government could take action on. Also, one symbol, repeated three times, was a complete mystery: an *L* inside a circle. What did it signify? What was Morgan telling Ballard?

Packet. She knew that Castelnau's embassy on Salisbury Court was the depot for letters to Mary from her European supporters. He bundled them into packets to be forwarded to Sheffield by a courier, and thence in to Mary at Sheffield Castle by some method still unknown to her English watchers. *That courier will be me*, she thought with a shiver. *If Castelnau ever gives me the signal.* It had been six days since her meeting with the ambassador in the humid laundry room. He had told her to watch for his signal: a flowerpot of carnations set out on the west, second-floor balcony of the embassy. Every day she had walked past the building, but no carnations had brightened the second-story balcony. This afternoon she would go again.

She puzzled again over that recurring symbol in Morgan's letter: the circled letter *L*. None of the suspect names on her list began

with *L,* and in any case the circle must surely give it added meaning. No combinations she had tried on her mathematical grid had
yielded a clue. The symbol refused to give up its secret identity.
Dipping her pen, she was sketching out a new grid when faint
voices reached her through her open window. A boat arriving?

She went to the window. Looking over the tree tops of the orchard she could see the riverside landing. Robert was climbing out
of a wherry onto the water stairs. How finely dressed he was! A
doublet of peacock-blue satin, fashionably slashed to reveal its
crimson lining, and a blue satin hat that glinted with gold piping.
He was fashionably attended, too, by a couple of servants wearing
the smart, Thornleigh livery. *He's been transformed,* she thought.
The modest, retiring doctor, now their father's proudly acknowledged heir. Emotions clashed inside her. She was glad for Robert,
of course—this status was his birthright. But the favor their father
showered on him made her feel even more cut off. Robert was living like a lord in Father's house while she was banished from its
doors.

She watched Robert jauntily go up the stairs and pass through
the garden of trellised roses that lay between the river and the
house. Reaching the building he disappeared from her view. She
steeled herself. *Don't let fantasies unsettle you. He'll have a simple explanation. Ask him.*

She gathered Morgan's letter and the *Stenographia* and her notes
and set them in the strongbox in which she kept these sensitive
materials. She locked it, then kneeled beside her bed and jostled
the box back into its hiding place between joists under a floorboard beneath the bed.

Downstairs in the great hall she found her grandmother with
four musicians she'd been conferring with, and Robert, making a
courtly bow to her. Kate put on a cheerful face as she joined them.

"Oh, I so wanted to be the one to introduce you two," she said.

"Introduce?" said Lady Thornleigh in high spirits. "Do you
think I would not know my own grandson?"

"Well," Kate said, "it's been ten years."

"Years that seem no more than a day, my lady," Robert said to
their grandmother, "for I see no change in you."

"Aha, Continental manners have made a courtier of you, Robert. I hope our blunt English ways do not dismay you."

"Everything English delights me, for England is the home of my heart."

His earnest declaration moved their grandmother, Kate could see. She could not help feeling the same. She so wanted to believe in him.

"As it should be," Lady Thornleigh told him warmly. "You're back with your father, where you belong. Welcome home, Robert." She opened her arms to beckon him. He came to her and she held him in a tender embrace. When he stepped away, Kate saw a film of tears in his eyes.

One of the musicians shuffled his feet. Lady Thornleigh turned to him. He looked apologetic for interrupting her conversation. "Master Wallace, forgive me," she said. "This is something of a family reunion, you see. You and I will resume our discussion later. And," she said to the others, "I thank you, good sirs, for coming so far." Kate noticed that sheets of music were spread out on one end of the long table. "Please, take your leisure here in the hall," her grandmother continued. She turned back to Robert and Kate. "Come, join me in my library, you two. I am eager to hear of your adventures, Robert. You must tell us everything."

"No," Kate said.

They both looked startled. "No?" said Lady Thornleigh.

"That is," Kate managed to say, "I assume you're discussing the music for your remembrance feast, my lady. Please, continue. Robert and I don't wish to disturb you. We'll take a stroll in the orchard."

"Feast?" Robert said with interest. "Tonight?"

"No, not tonight," Lady Thornleigh said. "And it's just a small supper."

"But a very important one," Kate told Robert. She took his elbow to guide him away. "Please, carry on with Master Wallace, my lady."

She led Robert out of the hall and down the screened passage. They stepped outside onto the broad terrace at the east of the house by the orchard. The sun shone and the air was apple scented with autumn's briskness. She guided him down the steps. "Let's walk," she said, indicating the graveled path through the apple trees.

"I'm so glad you asked me here," he said. "It's wonderful to see Grandmother looking so well. And this grand old house. What memories it holds."

His easy chatter unnerved her. "Come a little farther," she said, checking over her shoulder for anyone near. The knot garden with its late blooms of marigolds and salvia lay to the right. Kate could see no one there. To the left, near the far wall, two gardeners stood on ladders against a damson plum tree, pruning the boughs. A hedge of gooseberry and currant bushes ran between the gardeners and Kate and Robert. She tugged him farther along the path. Her skirt hem brushed the herb border of thyme and lavender, releasing their perfume. The autumnal peace—the herbs and sunshine and flitting birds—felt at odds with Kate's anxiety, all the more confusing because she could not name her fear. Evidence was forcing her to confront Robert, but her heart disbelieved the evidence. They reached the sun-splashed tunnel of apple trees and slowed their pace. Here they had privacy. The low-hanging foliage, tawny and russet and gold, surrounded them, masking them from the gardeners' view.

"Kate, there's so much to say. So much to thank you for. Indeed, I thank you with all my heart, for because of you I am reunited with Father. You don't know what it means to me to have you as my champion." He gave her a tender smile. "Just as you were when we were children." His smile turned sad as he added, "But who shall be *your* champion? I've learned from Father that your husband was recently in prison. For attending a mass, he says. Is it true?"

The question flustered her. Then she answered steadily, "Yes. Owen made an error. He has paid the price, six months in the Marshalsea. I trust that is the end of it, for I want no part in these religious wrangles."

"Yet you are loyal to him. Father told me. It grieves him."

"I took Owen for better or worse. I believe better days lie ahead."

"Where is he? He does not live with you here?"

"He has taken a position as secretary to the Earl of Northumberland."

Robert seemed surprised.

Kate looked away, uncomfortable. This was not what she wanted to talk about! She stopped walking.

"Why did you lie?"

He stopped, too, startled. "Pardon me?"

"Your interrogation at Whitehall. You told Lord Burghley and the others you had never met Westmorland. But you did. We both did. Why did you say you hadn't?"

Looking at her, he was still. His face, mottled by the leaves' shadows, was unreadable. He asked, "How do you know what I said?"

She was prepared for this. "I saw the transcript of your testimony. I paid the clerk to show me. So many people were ready to believe the worst about you, about Mother's influence on you, I simply had to know what happened when the council brought you in. So I found the clerk and paid him. Now, please answer me. That day at Westmorland's house when we were children, it meant so much to Mother she drilled you afterward on how to properly address him. We made sport of it for days, you and I. So why did you mislead Burghley?"

He stared at her for a long moment. "Mislead? I did no such thing. How could I, knowing Lord Burghley held my life in his hands?"

"I don't know *why* you did it, but you did. Everyone knows Westmorland is an enemy of England, so Mother's connection to him would hardly slip your mind."

"Perhaps I misspoke," he allowed. "The interrogation frightened the devil out of me."

His evasion unnerved her. "You will not explain your statement to me?"

"Kate, it was a slip of the tongue, no more." He offered a smile. "Come, have you never made that kind of innocent error?"

"Not when the fate of England may be at stake."

He stiffened. "I love England every bit as much as you do."

The face she was looking at seemed like a stranger's: obdurate. Where had her gentle, trusting brother gone? She swallowed hard before she spoke again. "If you will not explain yourself, I have no choice. I must report this to Lord Burghley." She turned, rocked by her own words. Sunshine splashed the leafy tunnel in a sea of brightness and shadows that was disorienting. She started back toward the house, gravel grinding under her feet.

"Wait." He caught up with her, grabbed her elbow. Her arrested footstep was unsteady, almost unbalancing her. "I'll tell you," he said.

His face had gone pale. His chin jutted in small jerks. His tic. He was suddenly nine years old again in her eyes, this twitch possessing him whenever he was nervous.

"I told the councillors I came back to England because I hungered to be home. That's not . . . untrue. But it wasn't the only reason. I was . . . sent."

Kate felt a streak of dread. Her throat tightened as if squeezed by a garrote. "Good God, Robert," she whispered. "Who sent you?"

His face crumpled. He twisted away from her as if in shame. He buried his face in his hands. His shoulders heaved and she knew he was fighting back tears.

Kate came around to face him. "Tell me."

He lowered his hands slowly as if it was agony to have her see him unmanned, unmasked. He closed his eyes, unable to look at her.

She slapped him. "Tell me!"

He gasped and his eyes flew open. His chin jutted in jerks. "Yes . . . Yes . . ." He gulped a swallow. "It was Mother. She has this obsession to . . . to free Mary Stuart. She's talked about it for years. It's like a sickness with her. She spins these wild, impossible schemes of raising an invasion army. Utter madness. But she's not alone. She has two foolish friends who whisper and scheme with her, hangers-on of the Countess of Westmorland. One's an old priest. The other is his cousin, a merchant's widow as bitter as Mother. No one listens to them and their harebrained ideas. But I did. At least, I pretended to." He gave her a pleading look. "Kate, you have to understand. I had no income. Mother depends on the

Duchess of Feria. The duchess paid for my education at Padua, but her largesse to me ended once I graduated. I had to make my own way. And that's when Mother's friends stepped in. They are not poor. They asked me to come to England to—" He faltered.

"To what?"

"It's so absurd. They asked me to reconnoiter the southern coast for places where an invasion force could land. I was to report back to them. Please understand—they offered to pay my way, cover my expenses. It was my chance to finally get back to England. So I persuaded my friend in Padua to have his father arrange my board with the Levetts." His voice cracked. "Home. Back where I belong, Grandmother said just now, and that's exactly how I felt, stepping ashore. When I rode to Sussex through the sweet, peaceful beauty of England I knew I would never go back. Kate, I did mislead Lord Burghley, but only to keep that day at Westmorland's house buried in the past where it belongs. If I have committed a crime it is only the crime of accepting passage money from Mother's friends under false pretenses. I have not contacted Mother since I arrived almost a year ago and I never shall again. She is dead to me." He let out a shuddering sigh. "The rest of the tale is as I've already told you. I settled down to make my way quietly by dispensing physic in Lewes. I had no wish to entangle you and Father in my shame. But then old Master Prowse *did* entangle you and—"

"Who are these friends of Mother's?"

"What?"

"The priest and the widow. Their names, Robert."

"Father Thomas . . . Thomas Crick. And Marion Forbes."

"Are they in contact with Westmorland?"

"Good heavens, no. They are nobodies. Like Mother."

"And you? Did you ever see Westmorland again?"

"Never. There was just that one time when you and I were both at his house, so really what I told Lord Burghley was true. Mother and I did *not* move in such circles."

"These schemes that she and her friends discussed. What were they?"

He groaned. "All mad nonsense. One was to hire a band of Scottish border raiders to attack Tutbury Castle, where Mary used to be held. Ha! Hire rogues and outlaws? Another idiotic plan was to poison all the people at Sheffield Castle, where Mary is now, and whisk her away. How, for God's sake?"

"Was the Duchess of Feria one of this cabal?"

He winced at the word. "Cabal?"

"Is she?"

"No, no, never. She gave Mother and us a home in Brussels because she pitied her old friend, you know that. But she would never involve herself with such beef-witted plotting. Mother knew that and kept it secret." He scoffed. "As if it mattered . . . as if anyone cared." Suddenly, he grabbed her hand. "Kate, please, don't tell Lord Burghley. It could mean prison for me."

She said nothing, her thoughts tumbling. The breeze sent a scatter of leaves, yellow and spotted, drifting down from the apple boughs.

"I see," Robert said bleakly. "You will do your duty as you see it. But oh, dear God, this will kill Father."

True, Kate thought with a pang. Father would rather fall on his sword like an ancient Roman than see his son convicted of conspiring with traitors. Robert's obvious distress moved her—that he would think of Father when his own life might be in jeopardy.

"Will you take pity, Kate, and let me at least tell Father myself? Let me explain so he'll understand?"

His pale, anxious face squeezed her heart. He had lied under oath, and it was her duty to tell Burghley, a deeper duty than Robert knew for she was an agent of Her Majesty. But Robert was her brother. And his explanation made perfect sense, for she well knew their mother's obsessive bitterness. And, after all, it was a small lie he'd told, an innocent lie to hide his shame. Really, would the realm be any safer by having her blameless brother in prison and her father shattered?

"Ah, there you are!" The voice was their grandmother's. They turned to see her beckoning them down the path. "Come in for dinner, you two. The musicians have the hall. We three can have a nice long private talk in the solar."

* * *

Robert stared at the food before him. Roast goose. Halibut with saffron sauce. Borage and fennel salad. Nutmeg custard tarts. He ate, but felt in such a rocky state each dish tasted alike. Kate's accusation had stunned him. And sent a flag of caution waving wildly in his mind. She had paid the clerk for a look at the transcript, she'd said. How had she known where to find it? And how did she know Lord Burghley well enough to threaten to take her concerns to him? How was she in a position to do that?

"More wine, Robert?" His grandmother's voice broke into his thoughts.

"Thank you, my lady," he said. "It is a fine Rhenish."

The three sat in Lady Thornleigh's solar, a small bright room adjacent to her library. Kate was being served a custard tart by a footman.

"A gift from Lady Mildmay," their grandmother said, beckoning another footman to fill Robert's glass. "In thanks for my gift of pears to her. Our orchard has produced a happy abundance."

He managed a smile. He drank some wine, watching Kate as she bit into the tart. *She has lived with Father these last ten years. He's likely on friendly terms with Burghley. That must explain it.* Still, her questions had been sharp, a field of thorns. He had barely slithered through.

At least he had convinced her, thank God. "You shall not tell Father, nor anyone," she had gently assured him when their grandmother had called them in. "And nor will I. It shall be our secret."

Yet Robert did not feel easy. Kate was not the naïve outsider he had thought.

The women's talk, as they ate, turned to Father. Lady Thornleigh was saying he had sent a note confirming that he and his wife would attend the private supper she was planning. "He is so delighted to have you home, Robert. And to think that Kate found you. It is so good to have the family whole again." She cast a reassuring look at Kate and added, "Your father will soften toward you, too, my dear. It is just a matter of time. He is a man who loves his children. Robert, you and I must work on him."

"Indeed, we shall, my lady," he said.

"Don't worry, Kate. We'll bring him round."

Kate smiled. "With such sturdy advocates, how could I despair?" Bravado on her part, Robert thought. She seemed less than certain.

Lady Thornleigh raised her glass. "To the family." They all drank.

Their grandmother, enjoying her wine, launched into tales of their father's seafaring exploits. She spoke of his sea battle off San Juan de Ulua in Mexico fourteen years ago when he'd captained the *Elizabeth,* one of seven ships in Sir John Hawkins's trading expedition. The Spaniards had attacked, sinking several vessels, and Father's had been one of the few to make it home. A few years later, she went on, he attacked one of Spain's pay ships in the Channel carrying gold to King Philip's troops in the Netherlands.

"Your father delivered the gold to Elizabeth and suggested that since Philip had borrowed it from the banker Spinola, Elizabeth should borrow it herself. Which she did. Spinola was happy to have his loan secured and the Spaniards, apoplectic though they were, could do nothing." She laughed. Kate did, too.

Robert pretended to join in their mirth. He had always been disgusted by his father's pirating crimes.

Lady Thornleigh's tone became serious, but still warm. "Your father is not my blood, but I have always loved him like a son." Robert caught Kate's nod. Their father was the son of their late grandfather's first wife. Lady Thornleigh went on, "He saved my life, you know."

Kate's eyes widened in surprise. Robert was curious, too.

"How so?" Kate asked.

"You were never told, of course, not while your parents were married. Then your mother and her brother committed treason and she stole you both away and Elizabeth granted Adam an annulment. Well, you are not children anymore, so I feel it's only right that you should know the extraordinary sacrifice your father made for my sake."

They both waited to hear, rapt.

"It happened twenty years ago," she went on. "I believe Frances was in love with Adam from the day she first saw him. He was kind to her, but did not share her feelings. This was during the reign of Elizabeth's half sister, Queen Mary, who ordered hundreds of Protestants burned at the stake. Years before, I had helped people persecuted by the church, smuggling them out of England on my husband's ships, but by the time Mary became queen that work was behind me and I lived quietly so as not to be noticed. Frances, however, knew about my past. Wanting Adam, she threatened that unless he married her she would denounce me as a heretic. I would be burned at the stake."

Kate looked astounded. Robert was equally amazed. They had known none of this! But he was sure his sister's reaction was very different than his. The vile slander against Mother made him burn with anger.

"Your father is my well-beloved friend," their grandmother went on, "for the sacrifice he made for me, and for the loyalty he has shown Elizabeth, who has also honored me with her friendship these many years. That is why Elizabeth and your father and his wife shall come here as my special guests, as they come each year on this special date, along with Lord and Lady Burghley, in remembrance of your grandfather. October twenty-fifth. St. Crispin's Day. The anniversary of the day we were wed."

Kate's hand went to her heart in awe. "Oh, my lady! I knew they would be your guests, but now I understand . . . about Father. What a tale!"

Robert could not speak. A bolt of excitement shot through him, so jarring he had to place his hands flat on the table to conceal their trembling. He had come to England to free Mary, his act to be coordinated with Westmorland's invasion fleet landing in the north and Northumberland's uprising in the south. The final hurdle would be the removal of Elizabeth by capture or death. That was Northumberland's mission, a perilous one because Elizabeth in her palace was well guarded. All of this complex planning would take some time longer, and Robert had been prepared to await orders.

But now, God had handed him a golden opportunity. Elizabeth

would be in this very house in less than three weeks. St. Crispin's Day. She would be supping in private with a mere handful of Grandmother's guests. Robert had access to this house. He was family.

His mind and body thrummed at the stunning realization. In the whole realm he was one of the few who could come near Elizabeth.

Near enough to kill her.

❧ 12 ❧

The Signal

"Lost your ponce, sweetheart?"

The question made Kate turn on the narrow London lane. The shop fronts, shadowy in the dusk, were veiled by wisps of fog, but she could make out the speaker. A runty fellow with crooked teeth, he was leaning against a doorjamb. At the window beside him a man with the weathered skin of a sailor leaned on the sill watching Kate. Leering. Both of them. For over an hour she had walked this circuit of Salisbury Court and Fleet Street alone looking for Ambassador Castelnau's signal—the flowerpot of carnations on his second-story balcony—and she now realized that these men took her for a prostitute.

"Her ponce don't know his business," said the sailor to the runt. Then to Kate: "No trade round here, chick, what with so many Bible men living near. Your fancy man should shift you over to Ludgate Hill."

Kate carried on smartly toward Fleet Street.

"Best catch your eel before curfew," the runt called after her. She heard them laughing. The other said, "She'd serve after a long sea voyage."

She melded with the heavier foot traffic on Fleet Street, glad to be anonymous among the crowd. The dusk was a foggy murk, and people trod carefully to avoid stepping in horse dung. Ahead a link boy holding his lantern high guided a couple of men down a lane toward the candlelit windows of a cookhouse.

Curfew soon, Kate thought anxiously. She could not keep making these circuits looking for Castelnau's signal. A full week had gone by since he had given her that instruction at the laundry. *Too long,* her fears told her. Had he abandoned their agreement? Had he found out about her? If so, every footstep behind her could be an agent he'd sent to get rid of her. It wouldn't be difficult. Drag her down one of these dark lanes and pull out a dagger and . . .

Stop it, she told herself. *A week isn't that long.* Castelnau had said he would need to wait until he'd received enough letters to Mary from abroad to make the courier's journey to Sheffield worth the risk. *The courier—me.*

An oily smell of fish clung to the fog. It was a chilly fog, too, with a hint of winter's bite. Changeable weather. Just yesterday when Robert had come to Lady Thornleigh's house the sunshine had made the orchard a blaze of autumn gold. Kate thought of her father with his seaman's knowledge of weather patterns. She remembered another orchard, at the house in Chelsea where she and Robert had been children. Remembered a day when she was about six, sitting atop Father's shoulders as he'd strolled under the springtime blossoms and pointed out clouds to her. The long, wispy clouds, he said, were called mares' tails. The pebbly ones, mackerel scales. He'd taught her the sailor's adage: *Mares' tails and mackerel scales tell tall ships to lower sails.* She had repeated it over and over in her child's singsong voice. Remembering, she could almost smell the cherry blossoms.

Only autumn leaves in the orchard yesterday with Robert. She'd been so relieved to learn that her fears about him were unfounded. He was an innocent, thank God. She wished she could say the same about their mother, plotting with her foolish friends. But she was just a bitter old woman no one listened to. Kate might have pitied her if she wasn't still rocked by the story Grandmother had told yesterday—that Mother had forced Father to marry her by threatening to inform on Grandmother. What an appalling foundation for a marriage! Kate now saw in a new light the tension between her parents when she was a child. Father's icy politeness.

Mother's tears. The angry looks and snarled words. Father's escape had always been to his ship and the sea. Mother had thrown herself into building a grand new wing onto their Chelsea house. But they had never lived in that wing. Before it was finished, Mother had abetted her brother Christopher's attempt to assassinate Queen Elizabeth in that very house. When Christopher was killed she had fled, taking Robert and Kate.

Kate now realized that her parents' marriage had been blighted from the day they took the vows. Unlike her grandmother's marriage: thirty-four happy years. Kate had been eight when her grandfather had died and all she remembered of his craggy face was his fascinating leather eye patch, but even at that age she'd sensed the loving bond between him and her grandmother. She thought: *One marriage blighted, the other one blessed.*

Her thoughts flew to Owen. *We are blessed.* Riches might never be theirs, but the love they shared was blessing enough. And as fellow agents of Her Majesty they also shared a deep and special trust. She thought of her grandmother's extraordinary revelation yesterday: *I helped persecuted people, smuggling them out of England.* Kate had always admired her grandmother and this new insight gave her a feeling of comradeship. Pride, too.

Walking south on Salisbury Court she was again approaching the embassy. She heard a faint splash and spotted a man urinating in a dark laneway. She smelled it, too. Hurrying on, she cursed the fog. All she could see of the embassy balcony was the balustrade, its rail wreathed by fog like rag shreds.

A shriek. She whipped around. A fat woman was shouting, pointing at a figure running toward Fleet Street. A cutpurse? A hubbub rose around the woman, people calling questions. Two young men dashed after the culprit. Kate was glad she'd hidden her own purse in a pocket of her underskirt. She turned back to the embassy and her breath caught at the sight. On the balcony, like a magic trick, a splash of pink.

Carnations.

The church of St. Bride's off Fleet Street was one of the most ancient churches in London. Kate opened its doors to the dim light of candles and the dank smell of old plaster. She kept her eyes down as she passed a scatter of people in the nave: a shuffling church warden, a scrivener at his desk writing a letter for a young man in fisherman's garb, an old woman with candles for sale, mumbling to herself.

Bells clanged faintly in the distance. Kate knew the sound—every Londoner did: the bells of St. Mary-le-Bow on Cheapside. Their ringing marked the end of the working day for the city's apprentices. It also signaled curfew. The city gates would close.

She went to the north aisle and stopped in front of a monument. Two stone figures, a man and a woman, lay side by side on their backs, their hands clasped in prayer. Faces smooth, they looked not much older than Kate. The inscription panel told they were Thomas Kimble, knight, and Dame Jane Kimble. Their stone garments were artfully chiseled, complete with pleated ruffs at their throats. The lady wore a stone cape round her shoulders; the knight, a stone half armor with his sword at his side. Their clothes were painted in gorgeous colors—pomegranate, popinjay blue, gold, spring green—and their heads rested on stone cushions. In the dim light the stained glass window of St. Brigit above them glowed duskily, like jewels under water.

Kate looked over her shoulder. The scrivener was still writing. His customer was doling out coins. The old woman was fidgeting with her candles, still mumbling. The church warden had disappeared. Kate turned back to the monument and reached into the narrow crevice between the stone cushion and its stone tassel. Her heart beat faster as her fingers met a soft wad of fabric. She tugged it out: plain brown cambric in a rectangle the size of a man's hand. Inside it she could feel the hard edges of tightly folded papers. Letters. Ambassador Castelnau's packet.

The walk from St. Bride's to Matthew Buckland's lodging on St. Peter's Hill would normally take less than ten minutes, but Kate took a roundabout route through lanes and alleys to shake off anyone who might be following her, so it wasn't until half an hour later that she reached Matthew's street. The fog had thickened, and her skin felt clammy, her nerves jumpy. The packet jammed into the lining of her cloak bumped against her thigh with every step. Could watchful eyes note the bulge?

Matthew lived near Paul's Wharf with its fishy reek of the Thames's mud banks. Voices on the water sounded ghostly, disembodied in the fog, yet the fog seemed to make every footstep behind Kate louder. Several times she hurried her pace. Once, sure that footsteps were gaining on her, she whirled around to face her pursuer only to find a dirty-faced boy engrossed in munching a carrot. He veered off on Carter Lane. She took a breath, telling herself: *Calm down.* She knocked on the door of Matthew's lodging. From an open attic window across the street came the sound of a woman singing a lullaby.

"A cold evening, Madame Lyon," said the stout French landlady as she peered past Kate into the gloom. She was a Huguenot émigré. All immigrants in London paid double taxes, but Matthew had finessed a reduction in his landlady's rate, a fair trade for her trust. She gave a slight shiver. "We call this time *l'heure entre chien et loup.*"

"Well said, Madame Mercier." The French saying—*the hour between dog and wolf*—was chillingly apt, Kate thought. She'd just had a taste of what it would feel like to be hunted.

The Frenchwoman lighted Kate's way with a candle up the bare wooden staircase to the second floor, then gestured for her to go on alone up the next flight. In the dimness, Kate knocked on Matthew's door.

"Ah," he said the moment he opened it and saw her. Even with that bent-head posture of his, Kate saw the eagerness in his eyes. He knew she would not have come unless she'd collected the packet. "Come in, come in." He closed the door behind her. "No trouble? No one followed you?"

"No. I was careful."

"Excellent." He beckoned her toward the hearth where two wooden chairs and a small table faced the glowing embers. A sooty kettle hung on a hook above. No carpet softened the wooden floorboards. Tallow candles on the table and mantel gave good light, but sent up oily tendrils of smoke. The two dormer windows were shuttered.

She looked around. They seemed to be alone. She was aware of Matthew taking the moment to hastily straighten his doublet and flick fingers through his trim, sandy beard as though to brush it of crumbs. She saw that she had interrupted his supper. On the table a half loaf of brown bread, a wine decanter and goblet, and a bowl of something oniony-smelling lay beside a sheaf of papers. Matthew had obviously been reading while supping. He seemed to be always at work.

"You have it with you?" he asked.

She nodded. Before pocketing the bundle she had unwrapped its loose cloth covering enough to check that it did indeed contain letters; no point in coming here otherwise. Unfastening her cloak now she pulled out the bundle and handed it to him. "Five letters. All from Paris."

Matthew discarded the fabric, setting it on the mantel. He shuffled the letters, examining the inscriptions. Kate had not broken the seals and neither would he. They would await his expert for that. But Kate had seen that the letters were addressed to commonplace names: Mistress Bainbridge, two letters. Henry Pitt, esquire, one. Dame Farquhar, also two. Kate and Matthew were familiar with these names: codes for Mary Stuart.

"I'll send for the others," Matthew said. "We must begin immediately. Can you stay?"

"Yes. I just need to send Lady Thornleigh a note to let her know."

"Caruthers will deliver it. And the Harts will cover for you." He nodded toward the adjoining room, gave Kate the letters, then opened the door to his bedchamber to summon his servant.

Kate took the letters to the adjoining room, one familiar to her. A windowless space, perhaps once used as a storeroom, it was now a communal workroom. Four desks, crammed together, were messy with papers, scrolls, inkwells, quills, and penknives, and the bookshelf was stacked with mathematical volumes and codebooks. Kate sat down and jotted a note to her grandmother, explaining that because of the fog she would spend the night with Alice and Roger Hart, the friends she had said she'd come to visit. Owen's friends, actually. Kate had met them only once, amusing gypsy-

like theater folk. Matthew paid them to vouch for his agents who
needed a cover story.

Matthew came in with his servant, Caruthers, who took Kate's
note for Lady Thornleigh and Matthew's instructions to first alert
the men they needed.

"Have you supped?" Matthew asked her when they were alone.
"I can have Madame Mercier bring you something."

Kate realized she was hungry. But felt too keyed up to eat. Her
eyes were on the letters. "No, I'm fine."

"How soon can you leave for Sheffield?"

"Right away, in the morning. But, Matthew, it may take days to
decode these."

"We haven't got days. Griffith usually set out with the packets
the same day he got them. Castelnau will expect you to be as
swift."

Griffith, the murdered courier. Kate understood. Any delay
could put her under suspicion.

"Tomorrow, then," Matthew said. "Can you still use the story
you'd planned for Lady Thornleigh?"

"Yes." They had agreed that she would tell her grandmother
she'd be riding north to visit her aunt, Lady Thornleigh's daughter. Isabel and Carlos Valverde lived north of Sheffield and Kate
had an open invitation. "She'll be pleased I'm going, actually.
She's always eager for news of Aunt Isabel and the children."

"Good." His eyes went back to the letters. So did Kate's. Ques-
tions rang in her head and, she was sure, in his. Who had written to
Mary? Had her correspondents revealed an invasion plan? Would
Mary endorse it, finally proving herself a traitor?

"Come back to the fire," Matthew said. "Gregory will be here
soon enough. Let me give you some wine at least. You must be
cold."

They returned to the main room, to the table by the hearth.
Kate sat, and Matthew fetched a second goblet from the sideboard
and poured her some wine, almost filling the goblet. He handed it
to her. "This will help."

She drank some, a rich mellow claret, and welcomed the
warmth that slid to her stomach. It relaxed her a little. Matthew

cut her a slice of bread. "Here, eat. We have a full night ahead of us."

She munched, glad in fact to eat something, though she scarcely tasted the bread.

He sat down opposite her. "You've done well, Kate." From under his brows he regarded her with such admiring intensity she could not help recalling Owen's words: *He's in love with you, poor fellow*. She had a deep respect for Matthew. His perseverance in working long hours over hills of paperwork was inspiring, and she was grateful for the care he took to safeguard his agents. She also felt a tug of pity. Would he ever find love? She doubted that many women looked past his afflicted posture, that constantly bent head, to see his fine qualities as she did.

"It will get harder from here, though, won't it?" she said. "In Sheffield, I mean."

He poured himself more claret. "You'll do fine."

"Will I? This is all new to me." She crumbled the bread, imagining a road on barren Yorkshire moorland and Mary's agents surrounding her.

"You've handled Castelnau beautifully. You'll do the same in Sheffield. You have his instructions about the meeting place. Harkness, isn't that the name he gave you?"

"Yes."

"So there's nothing to do but hand over the letters to this Harkness."

"And wait to be given Mary's replies," she pointed out. That was the crucial step. Bringing back evidence that could implicate Mary.

"Yes. You can either stay in Sheffield until they contact you again, or go to your aunt's, as long as you tell them to send word to you there."

"How long should I wait?"

"As long as it takes. But she's usually quick. Her replies always came to Griffith within a week. Don't worry, Kate. Remember, they have no reason to suspect you." He said again, soothingly, "You'll do fine."

She nodded, pretending agreement, but feeling frightened. "Have you had any more word from Owen?"

He seemed to hesitate. Then: "A note came from him this afternoon."

"Oh?"

"Very brief. No breakthrough. But he says he has developed a source of information."

"Northumberland is confiding in him? That's wonderful."

"No, not Northumberland."

"A kinsman? A servant?"

Matthew looked down, swirling the wine in his goblet. "I am not at liberty to say."

Kate had known this might happen. As just one cog in his machinery she could not be privy to all the information he collected, even from her own husband. Matthew himself was but a part of Sir Francis Walsingham's extensive spy network, one of several secretaries who handled agents. And there was probably much that Walsingham did not share with Matthew. They all had their own parts to play, sometimes in concert, but usually alone. Kate felt especially alone tonight. She missed Owen and was worried about him. "If anything should happen to him . . ."

Matthew reached across the table and touched her hand. "We'll always take care of you, Kate. Remember that."

It flustered her. She hadn't meant she was concerned about her *own* future, for heaven's sake. But clearly there was no point in asking him anything more about Owen. She and Owen, on separate missions, were segregated in Matthew's mind. She withdrew her hand.

He briskly changed the subject. "I have money for you. You'll need it for your journey."

"Thank you."

"I'm leaving tomorrow, too. For Bristol. Rumblings from the Irish. Again."

Kate knew little about the troubles in Ireland except that two years ago the King of Spain and the pope had financed a planned invasion of England led by Irishman James Fitzmaurice. Her

Majesty's forces had surrounded Fitzmaurice and his five hundred troops at Smerwick and crushed them.

The men Matthew had summoned arrived, six of them, coming up the stairs and walking in with looks of quiet excitement. They came singly, but all had lodgings nearby and they had hastened. Kate knew them all, having worked alongside them whenever a cache of information like this had to be copied quickly and, if possible, decoded quickly. Lately the decoding took longer and longer. Mary's agents and friends constantly changed their codes.

Of the arrivals, two were young law students under twenty. Two were in their thirties, men with some education, but few prospects. These four were copyists, in need of Matthew's pay. One was older, perhaps forty, a shy, sallow-skinned man with a slight cough. He was an artist fallen on hard times. The sixth, Thomas Phelippes, was an expert at deciphering, like Kate. Phelippes was thirty, slender, with dark yellow hair and a face pitted by smallpox. Educated at Cambridge, he was fluent in French, Italian, and Latin. Matthew had used him in Paris to intercept letters and decode them. These men could all be trusted, and not just because they needed the money. They knew a noose awaited anyone foolish enough to betray Walsingham. After exchanging brief greetings now, everyone made for the workroom. As the copyists set about sharpening quill pens and setting out paper at the desks, the artist arranged his pencils and his own paper. Phelippes set up a portable desk that Matthew brought out from a closet.

Without preamble, Matthew handed the artist the letters. "Get started, Muspratt."

The others chatted quietly as Muspratt sketched in minute detail the design of each letter's seal, reproducing them on his paper. This was in case the seals broke in the removal process. When he was done Matthew handed him his payment in coins. Muspratt left. He hadn't spoken a word.

Now, the rest sat waiting for the man they could not begin without, Arthur Gregory. He lived the farthest away, in Cripplegate Ward.

The five sealed letters to Mary lay on the desk waiting to give up their secrets.

"Apologies, Master Buckland," Gregory said, hurrying in ten minutes later with a forehead beaded from the fog. "It's dark as a Puritan's pleasure out there."

"Next time I'll arrange for a full moon," Matthew said dryly, gesturing for him to take a seat at a desk.

A bankrupt merchant's son, Gregory was about twenty. His fleshy, apple-cheeked face seemed at odds with his stringy frame. He was the expert at opening and resealing letters; his special skill was in forging seals. Kate had heard he'd been trained in engraving precious metals, a helpful background. He opened the kit he'd brought and set out its contents. Knobs of sealing wax the size of a baby's fist, in a variety of colors. Three small knives with fine-tipped blades. Tweezers. Engraving implements. A spoon. Two stubby candles. Everyone watched in silence as Gregory deftly prized off the seals. He lifted off each one in an unbroken disk. They all smiled at his skill. Muspratt's drawings would not be necessary.

Now it was the copyists' turn. Their quills scratched out careful copies, their fingers touching the originals as little as possible, for Mary must not know that the letters had been intercepted. As each man finished, Gregory went about his delicate job of resealing: heating wax in his spoon to match the original wax colors, then engraving on the soft wax a duplication of the original seal, referring to the original disks and to Muspratt's drawings.

Meanwhile, copies in hand, Kate and Phelippes set to work examining the words. In four of the letters it was soon clear that these were codes they were somewhat familiar with. Two of the letters were from Thomas Morgan, Mary's chief intelligencer in Paris. Within three hours Kate had decoded both, sent ten days apart. Morgan was informing Mary of meetings he had had with the Earl of Westmorland and William Allen, leader of the English seminary in Douai. He gave no details, however, saying only that his discussions confirmed information that Mary already had. A dead end.

Two other letters were from Archbishop Beaton, another of Mary's longtime supporters. Phelippes was working on those, and by midnight he had broken enough of the code to discover a reference to the Earl of Northumberland. Kate heard him tell Matthew this, and she instantly thought of Owen. What danger might he be in? But Phelippes had much more decoding to do before the Beaton letters were clear.

Kate wrenched her attention back to her own task, the fifth letter. It was written in a dizzying new code. She could not even decipher its author. But some of the symbols correlated to the Thomas Morgan letter she'd been working on at her grandmother's. She noted a repeated use of two question marks together, which she had earlier deduced to mean the King of Spain. The backward *B* meant the Spanish ambassador, Mendoza. The number 5 kept cropping up, and she knew this meant "ship." And, again, the symbol of an *L* inside a circle. In the letter at her grandmother's that symbol had appeared three times. Here, it occurred four times. But Kate still had no idea what it referred to.

However, one phrase in rudimentary code was clear: *the Netherlands*.

Whoever had written this seemed to be telling Mary that ships, perhaps paid for by the King of Spain, would sail from a port in the Spanish-occupied Netherlands.

What port? How many ships? Under whose command? Preparing to land where? What or who was the circle with an *L?*

By two in the morning Kate was so weary her eyes ached. The copyists and Gregory had long gone, though the stuffy room still smelled faintly of their sweat as she and Phelippes struggled on. Codebooks and mathematical diagrams and notes covered both their desks. Matthew had put the original letters safely inside a pouch for Kate to take to Sheffield. Earlier, Caruthers had stoked the fire in the main room's hearth and served them all hot spiced wine, but their cups were now empty.

Matthew said, "That's enough for tonight. Phelippes, you can carry on tomorrow."

Phelippes said good night and trudged down the stairs. Kate and Matthew remained alone. Frustrated, she scratched a line through a column on the mathematical grid she'd drawn. It had been no help. "I wish I could crack that circled *L*," she said. She hated that it eluded her.

"Phelippes will." Matthew gently took the quill from her hand. "You need to rest for your own mission."

She nodded, rubbing her itchy eyes with the heels of her hands. Come daylight she would take a wherry back to her grandmother's and pack for her journey north.

"You'll take my bedchamber, of course," Matthew said, a hint of embarrassed pink in his cheeks. "Madame Mercier put clean linen on the bed this morning."

Kate said good night. In his room she washed her ink-stained hands in the basin of water by the bed. She undressed down to her chemise and let down her hair and crawled between the sheets. Sounds seeped through the door, the scuffles of Matthew bedding down on a pallet that Caruthers had made up for him on the floor by the hearth. For a long time Kate lay awake, the code tormenting her.

A circled *L*. A place? A thing? A person? Names of suspected people on her lists tumbled through her mind. Scots: Archbishop Beaton . . . Bishop Ross. Spaniards: Ambassador Mendoza . . . Alava, their ambassador to Paris. English exiles: William Allen . . . Charles Paget . . . Sir Francis Englefield. English Catholics here at home: Philip Howard, Earl of Arundel . . . Henry Percy, Earl of Northumberland. Frenchmen: Ambassador Castelnau . . . the Duke of Guise.

Guise. She sat suddenly upright. Could it be that simple?

She pulled the blanket around her as a robe. Dressing would take too long. She hurried out to the main room.

"Matthew?" He was asleep. "Matthew!" she said more urgently.

He jerked awake, blinking up at her. "What is it? What's wrong? Kate, are you ill?"

She went down on her knees beside him. The fire's embers glowed orange. "No. I have a question. About the Duke of Guise."

"What?" Awkwardly, he propped himself up on his elbow, still looking confused. She saw his eyes flick over her loose hair, then over her bare left shoulder where the chemise had slipped. Again, his cheeks colored.

She tugged up the blanket to cover her shoulder. "The Duke of Guise. What are his titles?"

"Why?"

Henri de Guise was one of the most powerful men in France, head of one of its richest, most influential families. A daring military commander, he was a fierce defender of the Catholic faith. Ten years ago he had been among the leaders who had secretly planned and carried out the horrific St. Bartholomew's Day massacre of Protestants in Paris. Later he had instigated the Holy League. Mary Stuart was his cousin.

"His titles, Matthew. List them."

He cleared his throat, struggling to think, to focus. "Titles . . . yes. Prince of Joinville. Duke of Guise. Count of Eu. Grand Maître of France. Chevalier of—"

"But the original one. His birthright."

"Well, I suppose he's plain Henri of Lorraine."

"Exactly! It was the circle that threw me. Morgan added it as a half null to make it look like a symbol. But it's not, it's just a letter. A plain *L*. Lorraine. Matthew, I think he's another link in the chain. They're all connected. Westmorland. Philip of Spain. Guise."

He was very still as the implication sank in. "The English exiles. Spain. And now, if you're right, France, too."

They stared at each other. One thought loomed in Kate's mind and, she was sure, in his. The coalition so feared by England was taking shape. Catholic Europe, united, bent on invasion.

❦ 13 ❦

The Visitor

The countess, on hands and knees, shouted "More!" at her climax. Owen, behind her, inside her, clamped his hand over her mouth. Damn the woman! Her husband was just across the courtyard.

She bit his palm. Only a nip, but still he winced with a grunt. She laughed.

He pulled out of her and flopped onto his back on his narrow bed. Satisfying Catherine was an athletic endeavor. Finished, he lay naked, thankful for the breeze cooling his sweat. She had come to his room above the stable at daybreak and woken him with her tongue in his ear and her hand on his cock. Having roused him in both senses of the word she had hiked up her skirts and straddled his head, her cunt at his mouth. Christ, her boldness would make a dead man's prick salute. He'd responded with animal energy. Now, he lay spent, his lust a memory, mindless and meaningless. The air smelled rankly of their rutting.

She rolled onto her back, too. Fully clothed, she tugged her rucked-up skirts back in place. "Good morning," she purred.

He avoided her eyes. "Is it?" He felt caged. Rain spat at the rickety shutters on the unglazed window. Wet gusts had infiltrated the slats, dampening the floorboards beneath. His room was not much bigger than a horse stall.

"You should go back," he said. "He'll be awake."

"He's already up. He has a visitor."

"At this hour?"

"Last night, a late arrival. They went into his study before dawn."

Owen itched to ask who it was. Catherine appeared to trust him, but not with everything. She was almost as closemouthed as her husband about his activities. Was he plotting treason? Owen still didn't know. He had teased some information out of Catherine during their couplings, but he always had to be careful about how much he asked. That first time, at Arundel, he'd learned that the guest, Captain Fortescue, was actually a Cambridge-educated priest named John Ballard come from Paris, and yesterday, as he'd banged her against the wall in the wine cellar, he had found out that three men had sent Ballard. One was William Allen. No surprise there; he ran the English seminary in Douai. Another was the exiled Scottish Archbishop Beaton, also no surprise. But the third name Owen had not heard before in connection with the others: the French Duke of Guise. That was startling. And worrying. Guise was a power to be reckoned with. Was his involvement a new threat for England? And if so, what exactly was Ballard's mission?

This morning, waking to Catherine's groping hands and then tumbling with her, he'd had no chance to coax out further information, so he could not now let her leave without trying.

"I've been thinking about bravery," he said, arms crossed under his head.

"Oh?" she murmured, uninterested. Having settled on her side she ran her fingers through the hair of his chest.

"Wondering if I'd have the courage to suffer and die the way men like Campion have, for their faith."

"Father Campion is a saint." She kissed his nipple and added dryly, "I don't believe you'd qualify."

"Or even someone like this fellow Ballard. Spreading the word of God in England takes courage. I hope the people who sent him appreciate that. I mean, the Duke of Guise lives like a prince. Can he really imagine the fear of an ordinary man for the terrors of rack and rope?"

"What do you know of how a prince thinks?" She gave him a probing look. "Or care?"

Her look told him to push no further. His liaison with her was dangerous enough. Hard to forget that this very room had belonged to Rankin, the porter Northumberland had drowned. Owen dared not spark Catherine's suspicion.

He said lightly, "I'm a playwright, my lady. My mind plays in the minds of other men."

He swung his legs over the bed and got to his feet, taking his breeches from the hook. He pulled them on, then grabbed his shirt, glad to see Catherine sit up, too, and tidy herself. They were done.

"You should go," he said again, pulling on the shirt. "Before he leaves his study. You'll get wet going in through this rain and you don't want him to see you like that."

A thought of Kate ambushed him. In his mind he had walled off what he'd been doing with Catherine, had kept it separate from his life with Kate. His love for her stood apart, inviolate. But now he imagined her standing before him, looking at Catherine on the bed, stunned by what she'd just watched them do. Kate . . . her eyes filling with disgust . . . turning away from him.

He needed air. He went to the window and pushed open the shutters. The stable courtyard below was empty, the cobbles slick with mud. The air stank of horse shit. Rain misted his face and wet his chest where his shirt lay open. He welcomed it, a cleansing.

Across the courtyard the kitchen door opened and a man came out. Head down, he made for the stable, hunching his shoulders in the rain. He disappeared through the stable doors. Owen hadn't seen his face.

Catherine came up behind him and squeezed his buttocks. "Next time I'll ride *you*." She nibbled his ear.

He looked back at the house as the kitchen door opened again. Northumberland's retainer, Burkitt, the one with the mutilated ear, held the door ajar and looked toward the stable door. His ragged ear, as red as raw meat, was the only splash of color in the gray courtyard. He stepped back inside. Northumberland stepped out.

Owen lurched sideways, out of view, yanking Catherine with him. *Christ, is he coming for her?* She gave a small gasp as she caught sight of him.

Heart thumping, Owen said quietly, "Stick to what we agreed." She nodded. Their story was that she had come secretly to commission him to write a poem for Northumberland's birthday.

In tense silence they watched him cross the courtyard. He was making for the stable's main doors, not the side door that led up to Owen's room. Thank God. He had thrown on a cape against the rain and was nearing the stable when the stranger emerged on horseback, keeping his mount at a walk. Owen could see Northumberland's face, but not the other man's, only his back. The two halted as they met and exchanged words with evident earnestness, though the words were impossible to hear. Then the horseman turned his mount's head and kicked the animal into a trot, making for the open gates. Northumberland went back into the house with Burkitt.

Owen let out a breath of relief. So did Catherine.

"Who was that?" he asked, his eyes on the departing horseman.

"Are you jesting?"

He turned and caught her skeptical look. "No," he said. "Who is it?"

"You don't know your own brother-in-law?"

He could not hide his astonishment. *Robert Thornleigh?* He twisted back to look. The horseman had disappeared past Petworth's walls. Questions exploded in Owen's mind. Stunned, he said truthfully, "No, I've never met him." He added, stalling until he could think straight, "And I'm out of touch living here."

"Well, you'll soon be up to date," she said, turning away from the window. "You're going to London, as we discussed, to watch his house." She gathered her cloak from the chair and whirled it on. "Lord Thornleigh's son is a new acquaintance of my husband, who can sometimes be too trusting. In his interests I want to know more about this prodigal son's return, and where exactly his father stands. You'll leave immediately."

She turned back to him and said soberly, "You'll report only to me. For my husband's sake, I want to know what's going on between Robert Thornleigh and his father."

The rain did not let up all day. The roads were bogs of mud that caked Owen's horse's hocks and spattered his boots up to the knees. By late afternoon, when he approached Southwark across the river from the capital, he was soaked, cold, and bone-weary. His mind was a bog, too. Why had Robert Thornleigh been in secret conference with Northumberland? Every possible answer he'd considered was dark and slippery, linking Robert to treason. He was deeply sorry for Kate's sake. She would be devastated to hear how badly she had misjudged her brother. But Owen knew there was no option. He had to inform Matthew Buckland.

The rain finally let up as he trotted across busy London Bridge and turned onto Thames Street. He wished he could go to Kate before reporting to Matthew. He longed to see her, despite the unsettling news he was bringing. In fact, he wished for so much more—that they could step out of the shadows of their work and be together as man and wife, unburdened and independent. She was at her grandmother's and everything in him wanted to keep going westward through the city to its edge, past Charing Cross, and on to Lady Thornleigh's. But he resisted and grimly turned north at Paul's Wharf, heading for Matthew's lodging on St. Peter's Hill.

Matthew's landlady knew him, but she eyed his sodden garments and muddy boots as though wanting to send him around to the kitchen door.

"Dear Madame Mercier," he said, theatrically kissing her hand, "what a courageous woman you are to come and live among us despite our English downpours."

She snorted with a grudging smile and showed him in. Upstairs Matthew's earnest young clerk, Samuel Norton, opened the door, pale faced and black clad as ever. Owen had apparently interrupted him at work. A drift of dossiers lay on the table by the hearth where a low fire struggled to warm the room.

"Master Buckland was called away, sir. He's gone to Bristol."

"What's in Bristol?"

"Informers from Ireland. There's trouble anew in that barbarian land of papists."

Owen could not fathom the Puritans' special loathing for the Irish. Young ones like Norton seemed the most hardhearted. But Matthew trusted this cheerless fellow and occasionally installed him here in his absence to liaise with agents. "When do you expect him back?"

"Not for another week at least. Goodness, sir, it seems you've had a wet journey. Do come in. You're welcome to dry off by the fire."

"I'm fine. But I'll come in and write a message you can send him."

Five minutes later he came out into the street and untethered his horse. What now? Again, two claims on him were at odds: the job he had come to do for Catherine, and his desire to see Kate. Catherine had sent him to spy on Lord Thornleigh's house on Bishopsgate Street and he had his own reason for wanting to do so. Kate's brother, he'd learned, was living there now and he wanted to find out about Robert for himself. But there was no question of his knocking on his father-in-law's door—he would not be admitted. No, for his private investigation, and the report he would concoct for Catherine, he needed an informant inside Thornleigh's household. So he should go and observe the house to see who went in and out. Again, it was his duty.

But, again, everything inside him longed to see Kate. That went deeper.

He decided to go see her first.

He rode west through the city, then under Temple Bar and along the Strand. Past Charing Cross the fields and woods to his right stretched northward. To his left the setting sun crimsoned the rooftops of the riverside mansions. Swallows swept across Lady Thornleigh's roof slates, supping on gnats on the wing.

The closer he got to Kate, the more relieved he was to be away from Catherine. How his London theater mates would jeer if they knew. *Too much of a hardship?* they would taunt, having fun with the word "hard" amid much laughter. *I'll help out if she's too much for you!*

What a tangle he felt inside. He hungered to see Kate, but part of him squirmed. In spirit, God knew, he had not betrayed her, but he certainly had with his body. Just eight months married, and already a crude secret to hide. But hide it he must. Kate meant too much. He would not lose her over this.

"The blue wool, Susan, and the embroidered russet one," Kate told the maid, pointing out the gowns laid out on the bed along with chemises and stockings. "But the satin one can stay."

"Yes, mistress." The girl began folding the velvet bodice.

I won't need satin finery where I'm going, Kate thought with a twinge of nervousness as she went to her dressing table. Once Susan was gone she would take the packet of letters from their hiding place. Sitting down, she poured a cup of warm mulled wine from the earthenware pitcher Lady Thornleigh had thoughtfully sent to her bedchamber. She took a swallow. Its warmth was soothing. At supper she had told Kate, "Get a good rest, my dear. Your journey will be tiring."

But Kate didn't think she would get much sleep. She would be worrying about keeping the letters safely hidden among her packed underclothes when she set out in the morning for Sheffield. Despite her nerves, she was eager to be on the road. The day's torrent of rain had delayed her departure. Following her night at Matthew's the downpour had deluged London. But tomorrow morning she finally would leave.

"Oh!" Susan exclaimed.

Hearing the maid's surprise, Kate turned. Owen stood in the doorway. She jumped up, astonished. "Owen!"

"May I come in?"

"Of course! Thank you, Susan, I'll finish packing."

"Yes, mistress." The girl bobbed a curtsy and left.

Kate rushed to Owen. He took her in his arms. His kiss thrilled her. He held her so tightly she felt the tremor in his muscles, just like when they'd embraced outside the Marshalsea after his six months inside. It sent a wave of desire through her now and she returned his passion hungrily. It was as if they had been apart for months, not days.

She broke off the kiss as she realized he was soaking. "Oh, my love, you've come through all that rain!" she said, pulling away. His clothes were clammy, his face chilled.

"Yes, I'm afraid I left rather a puddle at Lady Thornleigh's feet. I promised her I'd be dry when we join her in the library." His smile was sheepish as he eyed the damp front of her bodice and skirt. "Sorry. Now I've got you wet, too."

"But, oh, so worth it," she said happily. "Here, let's get this off you." She unfastened his sodden cloak and pulled it off. It was heavy with its burden of water as she draped it over the chair at her dressing table. "What brings you to London?" He looked weary, as though he had not slept for days. An awful thought gripped her. Was he in need of a refuge? "Are you all right? Has Northumberland dismissed you?"

"No. I'm fine."

"You're sure? Nothing's wrong?"

He hesitated, but then said again, with a brief, reassuring smile, "I'm fine."

He sat on the end of the bed and tugged off his boots. Looking at the clothes laid out on the bed alongside half-filled satchels, he asked, "Packing? Where are you going?"

"Sheffield," she said with a spurt of pride. "I've got the packet for Mary."

He seemed startled. "From Castelnau?"

"Yes. Five letters."

He gave a low whistle of admiration, or perhaps alarm. "That was fast."

"Really? It felt like forever."

He looked concerned, and she was afraid he'd object again to her going. To forestall that she said brightly, "Dry clothes, that's what you need." She went to the chest that held some things he had left, and kneeled to dig out a shirt and hose and breeches. When she brought them to him he was on his feet and had unbuttoned his jerkin and was peeling it off. She said, "It's wonderful to see you, but what's brought you from Petworth?"

He slung the jerkin on the chair. "I've been sent on an errand."

"By Northumberland?"

He didn't look at her as he pulled off his damp shirt and slung it with the jerkin. "I came to report to Matthew. But it seems he's gone to Ireland."

"Yes, Sir Francis sent for him. Matthew told me when we were at work on the letters." Owen stood in just his breeches, his chest bare. She wanted his arms around her again. Wanted *him*. She caressed his shoulder. His skin felt so cold. "Oh, my love, you need to get warm. I'll go and fetch Anthony to lay a fire."

He caught her hand to stop her. "No, wait. I'm fine. And I need to talk to you."

"I don't want you catching a chill. I'll be right back."

She hurried downstairs. It took a few minutes to find the footman, and as he headed upstairs she carried on to the kitchen to get Owen a goblet. When she got back to her bedchamber she felt a twinge of disappointment at seeing him fully dressed, pulling on his boots. But they would have tonight. It was only polite to spend the evening with her grandmother, of course, but after that, she thought, they'd be alone. The footman was laying the fire. Kate poured mulled wine from the pitcher on her dressing table and handed the goblet to Owen. He took a long swallow. "This is good," he said. "I'm parched."

"Said the drenched man," she quipped.

They shared a smile, waiting as the footman finished.

"Thank you, Anthony," she said, closing the door after him.

"The letters you got from Castelnau," Owen said, wiping his mouth after draining the wine. "Whom are they from?"

"Thomas Morgan. And Archbishop Beaton. And someone we're still not sure about."

"Anything in them?"

"Enough to lead us to believe the invasion design is real and that Westmorland is involved. We think he may be procuring ships and will sail from the Netherlands. Also, the man financing it may be the Duke of Guise."

"Guise! By heaven, that fits."

"Does it?"

He looked as if he'd said too much. Her curiosity leapt. "Have you heard something about him?"

He turned and set down his goblet on the dressing table. "Did Castelnau tell you whom to contact in Sheffield?"

His evasion of her question jarred her. Had he heard something about Guise or not? "Yes, a man named Harkness. At a place called the Hall at the ponds. Owen, if you've heard any—"

"You must be planning to leave soon," he said, looking again at her satchels.

"At first light."

He looked at her finally, and she saw anxiety in his eyes. "Dear God, I wish this mission had fallen to anyone but you, Kate. I wish it were me going to Sheffield."

That moved her. He would not change her mind, but she was warmed by his love and concern. "Exchange missions?" she said ruefully. "No, Northumberland hired a secretary. I could not do what you're doing at Petworth."

Unease, like a shadow, crept over his face.

She took his hand. "I'll be fine." She drew him to the end of the bed and sat and indicated he should, too.

He sat down beside her, still uneasy. "Will you have protection?"

"Yes, I'm taking my grandmother's man, Soames."

He scowled. "Just one?"

"I won't hear an unkind word about Jasper Soames. He's a loyal fellow."

"But can he fight?"

"A fortnight ago he won a wrestling match with the neighbor's blacksmith. He'll do."

Owen opened his mouth to speak, still frowning. But then he seemed to concede the point with a tight sigh. "And what have you told Lady Thornleigh?"

"That I'm visiting Aunt Isabel at Roche Hall. Now, enough about that. I'll deal with tomorrow's problems tomorrow." She caressed his stubbled cheek. "Tonight, we have each other. My love, it's more than I had hoped." She kissed him softly.

He returned the kiss with a fierce intensity that surprised her, though she welcomed it. As they both caught their breath he looked into her eyes and whispered, "Ah, Kate. I've missed you."

"Has it been terrible at Petworth? The tension? I hear Northumberland's a brute. Owen, what's happening there? Matthew won't give me any details. Though he said you've at least developed a source."

He stiffened, glaring. "He told you that?"

"After I badgered him. He didn't say who, though. Who is it?"

He got to his feet. "I can't talk about my mission."

The rebuff cut her. "Why not? I've told you about mine." Why was he keeping things from her? He wouldn't even look at her. Staring at his back she felt a shiver. *Something's wrong.* "Owen, what's happened?"

When he turned to her, his face was grave. "I've come to tell you something very disturbing. At Petworth I saw your brother."

Her mouth fell open in amazement. "Robert?" It made no sense. "You met him?"

"No, just saw him."

"I don't . . . understand. You've never met, so how could you know it was him?"

"I was told it was him."

She stood. "Who told you?"

"The countess."

This was even more bewildering. "How does *she* know Robert?"

He looked irritated. "That's my point. Don't you see? I fear he's working with them."

Kate almost laughed. "Ridiculous. The countess was clearly mistaken. It was someone else, not Robert."

"It was Robert."

She bristled at his severe tone. "If it was—though I don't see how it possibly could have been—then I'm sure there's a simple explanation." She was about to say, *Like that small lie in his testimony. He explained it.* The words were on her lips, but she did not say them. If she told him that Robert had come to England at the deranged whim of their mother he would totally misconstrue the meaning. Robert had done a brave thing by cutting all ties to Mother once he got here, but she feared Owen would never accept that. Looking at him, she thought: *If you can hold back information, so can I.*

"I'm sorry, Kate, but you see I was right to caution you about him."

That fueled her resentment and she lashed out. "I see only this—that you've been bent on mistrusting my brother since the day I told you he'd come home."

"Nonsense. Kate, you cannot pretend this isn't cause for alarm. You cannot defend a possible traitor."

Traitor? He wielded the word like a weapon. Anger streaked through her. She hid it behind a scoff. "You've become as bad as the Puritans, seeing an enemy behind every bush."

"No, but when I see someone meet secretly with Northumberland I'd be a fool to close my eyes to it."

"So you're calling me a fool?"

"I'm saying we need to find out more about your brother."

"And I'm saying your suspicion is absurd. The countess was obviously mistaken."

He took a sharp breath as though to rein in his frustration. "What we need is facts. When did you last see him?"

Her own frustration was boiling. She grabbed one of her stockings that lay askew on the bed and balled it and threw it at the open satchel, then felt even more angry that he was making her act like a petulant child. "A few days ago. He visited Grandmother. I invited him. He is *kin*."

"Did you notice anything suspicious?"

"Of course not. I tell you, there is some explanation."

"No doubt. And I intend to find out what it is."

"If you are so mindlessly fixed on this I'll ask him myself. Will *that* satisfy you?"

"Don't. Don't speak to him, Kate. You'll be giving him warning."

"Warning? This is insane! The Queen's council interrogated him, for heaven's sake, Lord Burghley at their head. They found him blameless. But that's not good enough for you?"

"They may not have asked the right questions."

"And the fact that he lives now with my father? That alone should tell you how horribly wrong you are. You *know* how fiercely loyal Father is."

"Of course. What I *don't* know is what your brother is up to. But I'll find out. Or Matthew will."

"Matthew?"

"Yes. I sent him a message."

She felt as stunned as if he had struck her. "You told Matthew? Before I even have a chance to talk to Robert? How *could* you?"

"How can *you* be so blind? I can hardly believe what I'm hearing. You took an oath to protect the realm, yet you want to inform a possible traitor that he's being watched! Do you not realize how close to treason you're slipping *yourself?*"

She was trembling with outrage. "I know my oath very well. Just as I know my brother. It's *you* I don't know any longer."

"Oh, come! This is not about us."

"Is it not? Father warned me about you. You married him in haste, he told me. You did not know his true character, he said. I see now he was right. This marriage is no marriage if you trust me so little!"

"How *can* I trust you when you show such gross misjudgment?"

Fury held her like steel bands. Words crammed up in her throat. Blood pumped in her ears. "You said you intend to find out. What are you going to do?"

"Watch and wait."

"I see. Like a coward."

He stiffened, his face as pale as if drained of blood. She was glad to have struck back. "I would take this to my brother face-to-face," she said, "but you want to sneak and hide. How is that not cowardly?"

He snatched his cloak and turned to her with icy forbearance. "I see you are impervious to reason. And that my company is irksome to you. Please convey my respects to your lady grandmother."

"You're leaving?"

"I never said I could stay."

"Like a coward."

"I told you I was given an errand," he snapped. "To do it I must be in the city." He did not even look back as he made for the door. "God speed you on your journey."

She did not stop him. Humiliation and rage held her to the spot. Then, a stab of misery. How suddenly her marriage had been torn asunder!

∂ 14 ∂

The Banquet

"**A**sk her to dance, my boy."

Robert had to strain to hear his father's voice above the music and chatter and laughter around them. They stood watching guests dance to a lively galliard while others crowded the banquet tables, everyone enjoying themselves in the great hall of his father's house on Bishopsgate Street. Having maneuvered his way back into his father's good graces, Robert had been living here for three days and he found it strangely exciting to be back in the house he had left at the age of six. Tonight was quite thrilling. He was the guest of honor. His father was hosting the banquet to introduce him to his influential friends.

"Ask whom, sir?" Robert had to raise his voice, too. "Lord Burghley's daughter?"

His father laughed. "No, I'm afraid that's aiming too high. I meant Margaret Brooke. There." He nodded toward her, a slim girl, about eighteen, in demure gray satin. "She's the youngest daughter of Baron Cobham. Her mother has a prestigious position at court as the Queen's Lady of the Bedchamber. Cobham will settle a generous dowry on Margaret. And she's rather nice looking, don't you think?"

Robert did. He had noticed her earlier. "She is fair indeed, sir."

He watched her dance. Another unexpected bit of excitement.

Since coming to England he had been so focused on his mission to rescue Mary when the invasion came, and now on planning the more perilous goal of killing Elizabeth, he had not allowed himself any thought of the possibilities of life after victory. A settled home life. A pretty wife. How strange that his father should be pointing him in this direction. It was disconcerting to realize—his father cared about him.

Margaret Brooke turned away in the dance, smiling. She was partnered by the athletic, ginger-bearded Sir Christopher Hatton, whose wolfish grin at her snapped Robert's fantasy.

Sobered, he scanned the crowd for Captain Lundy, the captain of his father's guard. Robert was waiting for him to report. He had given Lundy a commission to procure him a pistol. No sign of him yet. Suddenly, at the thought of firing the pistol, he felt a clutch of anxiety. The bold idea of killing Elizabeth had sparked in him when he'd visited Kate at their grandmother's house. In twelve days Elizabeth would be dining there, in a house where he was a welcome visitor. Success was stunningly possible. Yet part of him cringed. Killing old Prowse had made him faintly sick. And now, to kill a queen! It was both thrilling and horrifying.

"Don't be shy, Robert. As my heir *you're* the catch," his father assured him. He clapped a hand on his shoulder. "A dowry is all well and good, but one day you shall be the third Baron Thornleigh."

His father's evident pride jumbled Robert's emotions even more. *You're proud of me now, but where were you during my hard years of exile?* Yet he could not help basking in the glow of his approval.

He turned to him with a smile. "Sir, would you introduce me to Mistress Brooke?"

His father beamed. "Gladly. Come, this dance is almost done and next there'll be a pavane. We'll get Hatton to surrender the field to you."

They crossed the crowded floor. The air was pungent with the perfumed sweat of ladies and gentlemen alike. Roasted meats on the banquet tables wafted succulent aromas. Candlelight from dozens of candelabra glittered off the soaring stained glass windows and the women's jewels. The boisterous music of the trumpets, viols, and shawms stopped at the close of the galliard, and the dancers' chatter rose in a crescendo as partners bowed and curtsied to mark its end. Robert was aware of how people watched him with clear curiosity. Several nodded greetings of respect. His finery of green and gold velvet matched that of any courtier present, as did the magnificent sword his father had gifted him. He found it exhilarating. He was in the company of the most powerful men in England.

The graybeards were Elizabeth's stalwarts—and Mary's enemies. Four of them had interrogated Robert at Whitehall Palace and he had not forgotten a moment of that harrowing experience. One was old Sir Ralph Sadler, Elizabeth's veteran diplomat, hobbling past the dancers with his cane. Thirty-three years ago, at Elizabeth's coronation, she had sent Sadler to Edinburgh to arrange an alliance with the Scottish Protestants who had deposed their queen, the celestial Mary. *Curse them*, Robert thought, *heretics all.* Beneath the musicians' gallery, laughing with Lady Burghley, was Sir Walter Mildmay, who had prepared the evidence that sent the Duke of Norfolk to his execution after the Earl of Westmorland took up arms against Elizabeth. Westmorland—exiled these thirteen years. There, eating strawberry pudding at the banquet table, was the great Lord Burghley himself, Elizabeth's closest adviser all her life. And over there, a late arrival, was the strutting Earl of Leicester with his wife, the beautiful Lettice. Leicester had once hoped to marry Elizabeth and become king of England. He still had Elizabeth's ear so constantly he might as well be king.

And, of course, there was Father, the most loyal to Elizabeth of all. Across the hall was his red-haired wife, still pale of face from her recent illness—a miscarriage, Robert understood—but statuesque in her blue brocade gown as she chatted with her guests. Fenella. Her name marked her as the poor Scot she was, Robert thought. Oh, she'd been friendly and gracious to him, had presented him with an exquisite pair of embroidered gauntlets of butter-soft calfskin to accompany his father's gift of the sword. He could not, in conscience, fault her. But every time he looked at her he saw a trollop who had usurped his mother's place and taken her title. Calling her Lady Thornleigh put his teeth on edge.

He and his father were now just paces away from Margaret Brooke, who was chatting with Hatton, unaware of them, when Robert spotted Captain Lundy. The swarthy soldier was coming in from the screened passage to the kitchens, slowing his walk, examining the crowd.

"Excuse me, Father," Robert said, "I just remembered, I promised to fetch Lady Sadler a glass of Madeira. She was feeling rather faint. I'll only be a moment."

Starting toward Lundy he heard his father protest that a footman could fetch the wine. Robert pretended not to hear.

Lundy saw him coming and jerked his chin to indicate the screened passage where they would have some privacy. They stepped behind the screen, keeping to one side to let servants pass in and out with platters and jugs. Lundy held up a shallow wooden box the size of a man's foot.

"This will serve, Master Thornleigh." He lifted the lid. Inside lay a wheel lock pistol. The steel barrel was engraved with a scrolling pattern. The stock was fine hardwood. The handle ended in an ivory bulb. A gentleman's weapon, but made for action. "Do you know how to use it?" he asked skeptically. Pistols were not common in England. "I can teach you."

"No need." Robert could load the ball and powder in half a minute. Westmorland had trained him. The snapped reply had sounded more harsh than he'd intended, and he saw that Lundy had taken it as a reprimand. His weathered face had gone pink.

"Pardon the liberty, sir. I'm just careful for your father's sake. I hope you understand."

"Of course, Captain," Robert said more gently. The story he had given Lundy was that he wanted the weapon to protect his father from lunatics like the gunman arrested on London Bridge after shooting at the Queen. Robert had heard the story from Lundy himself, who had been on the bridge leading his men alongside Robert's father. They'd had only swords against the man's pistol. "It was a bad moment when the villain aimed at Lord Thornleigh," Lundy had said, "but a skittish horse bumped his arm and that saved His Lordship. Then we nabbed the bastard. A close call, though." His tone was grim, as though he would rather be hanged than fail in his duty. "Glad I am that you'll be armed with this, sir," he said, handing Robert the box. "If anyone goes for Lord Thornleigh, you let him have it." He tapped the spot between his own eyes.

"I shall, Captain. Thank you. And remember, not a word to my father. He would only worry for my safety."

"Of course. And if I may be so bold, sir, welcome home." Bowing, Lundy took his leave.

Robert took the box upstairs to hide it in his bedchamber. As he went up the steps he saw his father watching him. The box was too big to cover; he couldn't help that. If his father questioned him about the pistol Robert would give him the same story he'd given Lundy: *a son's duty, gladly rendered.* Thankfully, his father turned away to greet a guest his wife was guiding toward him. Lutes sounded the opening strains of a stately pavane. The new dance began.

Excitement hummed through Robert as he went down the corridor to his bedchamber. Now that he had the weapon his squeamishness vanished. Possessing it made him feel stronger, calmer. He was a soldier in this war, doing his duty. It would be a dereliction of that duty to fail to take advantage of the extraordinary opportunity that had presented itself. He had said as much in his meeting with the Earl of Northumberland.

"We'll never get a more perfect chance, my lord," he had urged. He had reached Petworth late at night, and at daybreak had met with Northumberland in his study. "None of the faithful have access to the dowager Lady Thornleigh's house as I do. And I've carefully examined every facet of my plan. I can do it."

He saw how eagerly Northumberland wanted to believe it, but the man was cautious. He had not survived the watchful eye of Elizabeth's government for so many years by being reckless. And they both knew how many attempts against the Queen's life had failed. Mulling it, Northumberland chewed the end of his moustache, his eyes fixed on Robert. "Elizabeth will be guarded. The grounds, too—all guarded."

"I will be inside the house before she arrives. I will bring a gift for her. That will please my grandmother and she will welcome me in."

"And your father? You say he'll be there. He has risked his life before to save Elizabeth."

"But he won't suspect *me*. On the contrary, my lord, he is eager to introduce me to her. He has told me so. He will also arrive before Elizabeth—that's protocol—and when he sees me I daresay my presence will surprise him, but I will beg his indulgence, professing my eagerness to meet Her Majesty. He'll like that. As for the other guests, there will be only Lord Burghley and his wife. Burghley won't be an obstacle. He is old."

"And you're sure there will be no others?"

"None. Lady Thornleigh told me so herself. It is a private anniversary she shares every year with just Elizabeth, Burghley and his wife, and my father and his wife."

"How do you propose to do it? A dagger? Poison?"

"A pistol."

Northumberland allowed himself a cautious smile. "Good."

They discussed every detail, every possible eventuality, including Robert's escape. In the chaos around the Queen he would race for his horse in the courtyard and gallop west. Northumberland would have a man waiting at Kingston bridge with a fresh horse. Robert would race for the south coast, where another fresh horse would be ready for him at Guildford. At Portsmouth a waiting boat would take him to Ireland. The bold plan was coming together so fast, Robert scarcely let himself consider how nearly impossible it was for each piece to fall into place with so many people involved. But *nearly* impossible did not mean impossible. The first thing, the main thing, was killing Elizabeth. For that, he needed no one's help.

"I'll send word to Paris immediately," Northumberland said.

Robert almost jumped out of his skin with excitement. *Paris* meant the leaders of the invasion plan: Westmorland and the Duke of Guise. Influential English exiles would be part of the deliberations, too, including Mother. Westmorland was readying fifteen thousand Spanish troops to sail from The Hague in the

Netherlands and land in Yorkshire, while in the south Northumberland and the Earl of Arundel had seven thousand men ready to march on London.

"I am your servant, my lord," Robert said. "However, this means I'll be unable to carry out the rescue at Sheffield." Until this moment his mission had been to prepare his band of seven men to attack Sheffield Manor and free Mary when the invasion troops landed.

"As of now you're essential to the dispatch of Elizabeth. I'll have someone else take command for Sheffield. John Ballard can do it. He's at Arundel. He goes by the name Captain Fortescue. Can you go there to confer with him?"

"Willingly, my lord."

"It will mean more time away from your father's house. That won't be a problem?"

"I'll tell my father I have some business to conclude in Lewes. He knows I was practicing as a physician there."

"Good. Now, bring me up to date on the men you've organized for Sheffield."

They discussed how Elizabeth's assassination had to be perfectly coordinated with Mary's rescue. In the uproar of Elizabeth's death there must be no time for her faction, Robert's father among them, to send word to fortify the guard on Mary. Mary must be freed and immediately brought to London.

Daylight was breaking when Northumberland ended the meeting. "Go back to your father's house, Thornleigh. Unless you receive further instructions to the contrary, be ready to make good your plan."

Robert had ridden away from Petworth in a near fevered state of elation. He had scarcely noticed the deluge of rain. *Rejoice, Mother. Your faith in me is leading us to greatness.*

The following days at his father's house had tested his nerve. The warmth of his father's affection. The friendliness of his father's wife. The sense that stole over him in this house of being, truly, home. And then, tonight, the sight of pretty Margaret Brooke. These softening influences had beguiled him.

But now, with the pistol box in his hands, he felt strong again.

Elated again. And a breathtaking new thought stole over him. *My pistol shot might prevent civil war.* Once Mary swiftly took the throne at Elizabeth's death the vast majority of Englishmen would accept her coronation—after all, the two were cousins, sharing royal Tudor blood—so an invasion might be unnecessary. Northumberland would still need to use his forces to stabilize the realm, but bloodshed would be minimal compared to the havoc of an invading army. *With my shot the grand goal can be peacefully achieved!*

He opened the door of his bedchamber, the box cradled in his arm. The room was dark except for the candle he had left burning on the night table. He closed the door behind him and went to the bed to hide the box beneath it, and was about to go down on his knees.

"Enjoying the feast?"

He twisted around at the woman's voice. She stepped out of the shadows. Kate!

"Father certainly has made it a grand occasion," she said. "The street is clogged with waiting carriages and footmen."

"Kate, what a surprise!" He had thought she was banned from the house. "I didn't realize Father had invited you."

"He didn't. I came through the stable courtyard and the scullery. I can't stay long." She looked anxious, hollow-eyed. No wonder, Robert thought, with Father so set against her. So what was she doing here?

"What's that?" she asked, indicating the box.

His thoughts snagged. "This? A gift from Captain Lundy." He set the box down on the night table. "A pistol, purely ornamental."

"To welcome you home? That's kind of him." She sounded strangely sad.

Footsteps scuffed in the corridor. Robert saw Kate flinch.

"Just the servants," he said. "Kate, why have you come? Is something wrong?"

"I needed to see you. To ask you something."

She seemed nervous, standing stiffly, hands clasped in front of her. What was troubling her so much that she would come like this, sneaking into the house late at night? A thought chilled him. Had she heard something about old Prowse?

"Robert, why did you go to Petworth?"

The chill turned to ice in his veins. "Where did you hear that?"

"From my husband. I told you, he is Northumberland's secretary. He said he saw you at Petworth House. Saw you talking to Northumberland."

It took all his concentration to force a calm face. He picked up the pistol box. "I shouldn't leave this out in the open. It's rather valuable." He went down on one knee by the bed and shoved the box underneath the bed frame. He was furiously trying to think. How much did Kate know? How much did her husband know?

"Robert? Answer me."

Convince her. He stood up and looked her in the eye. "I'm not sure I'm at liberty to say."

She took a sharp breath. "Dear God. Don't tell me you've got yourself involved in something you shouldn't."

"Well, I *am* involved. Whether I should be or not you would have to ask Father."

She looked skeptical. "Father? What has he got to do with you being at Petworth?"

"Kate, can I trust you to keep this strictly between you and me?"

She did not soften. "Tell me!"

"All right. Father sent me. He'd heard a rumor that Northumberland might have some connection to a Spanish invasion plot. You know Father—nothing means more to him than defending Her Majesty. So he sent me to sound out Northumberland, surreptitiously of course, to see if I could detect any inkling of treason."

Kate looked baffled. "Sent you . . . under what pretext? What reason did you give Northumberland?"

"That I was conveying Father's invitation to a court festivity. Her Majesty is hosting a banquet for the Swedish ambassador next week to honor the birth of King Johan's son, and Father will host a hunt the following day for the visiting dignitaries. I was delivering his invitation to His Lordship."

Kate's face brightened as though the sun, breaking through clouds, now beamed on her. "Oh, Robin!" She rushed to him and threw her arms around his neck. "You don't know how happy I am to hear that."

"Why, what did you think I was doing there?"

"I don't know. Owen said . . . oh, it doesn't matter." She hugged him, laughing, but he felt the tension in her body and caught a stifled sob beneath the laugh. "All's well that ends well," she said.

Relief coursed through Robert. He had convinced her. But what had prompted her to ask? Why was she so obviously upset? He pulled her away and held her at arm's length. "What's this? Tears?"

"Tears of happiness." She smiled at him even as she wiped her wet cheeks.

"Kate, what's going on? You seem distraught."

"No . . . no, I'm just glad we had this chance to talk before I leave."

"Leave? Where are you going?"

She had pulled herself together. "To Roche Hall. I'm going to visit Aunt Isabel and Uncle Carlos." She stroked his cheek with a motherly caress. "I'll give them your love, shall I?"

"Yes, do. Good heavens, it's been so long since I've seen them. I probably wouldn't recognize our cousins."

"No, indeed. Nicolas is in Seville overseeing Uncle Carlos's Peruvian interests. Andrew is studying at Cambridge. Nell is betrothed to the son of a Yorkshire baron."

Robert shook his head in wonder. "I was six when I last saw Nicolas. He was twelve. He could leap onto his horse like a knight. I was in awe of him."

"I hear the young ladies are in awe of him now."

They laughed.

The door opened, startling them. Father walked in. He stopped in surprise. "Kate!"

She lurched a step back from Robert. "Father . . ."

"What are you doing here?"

Robert felt the tension between the two. Then Father's eyes widened in hope. "Kate, have you come home?"

She looked taken aback. "Home?"

"Have you left your husband?"

"No . . . of course not! I just came to see Robert."

There was a painful moment of silence. His father said awkwardly, "I see." He turned to Robert and said in a brusque tone, an attempt to sound businesslike, "Fenella said you were talking to Captain Lundy. No trouble, I hope? If so, Lundy should bring it to me."

"No, sir, there's no trouble." Robert managed to keep his voice calm, hiding how much he wanted his father to leave. This conversation could only lead to danger.

"And you?" his father said to Kate. "What's so urgent you had to see your brother at this hour?"

"Nothing urgent," she said. "Don't worry, Father, I won't disrupt your feast. I was just leaving." She gave Robert a peck on the cheek and whispered, "Good-bye."

"Where's your husband?" Father demanded. "He lets you come out late all alone?"

"He is in Sussex, sir," she said tightly. "As I think you know."

"Ah, yes. With Northumberland." His voice was dark with suspicion.

"He must take what employment he can," she snapped. "And if you are so eager for information about him you can send Robert again to spy."

"Spy?"

"Wasn't that his instruction from you? To spy on Northumberland under the guise of delivering an invitation?"

Robert's heart was pounding. "Kate, you promised!"

"I'm sorry, Robin," she said sadly. "I am not myself tonight. . . ."

"Quite right," their father said. "I *did* send Robert. He has shown himself both loyal and clever. When I mentioned my concern about Northumberland's allegiance he suggested that he sound the man out, and I heartily agreed. Thankfully for the peace of the realm, he detected no hint of treason." He added sternly, "I wish the same could be said for your husband."

Kate looked incensed at the insult, and Robert quickly showed her out before the animosity between her and their father could erupt. He returned to the banquet with a calm face, but his unease ran deep about Kate. What had prompted her suspicion?

❧ 15 ❧

Rendezvous

Four days of hard travel had brought Kate north to Sheffield. Four days of growing fear about this rendezvous to deliver the letters for Mary. Four days of torment about her ruptured marriage.

A cold gray fog cloaked the seven hills that shouldered the city as she and her grandmother's dour servant, Soames, rode in past gray stone houses, workshops, and warehouses. Not many people were out at this midday hour. They're supping in front of a warm fire, Kate thought. She felt chilled to the bone. Her weary mare clopped across the Lady's Bridge, whose five arches spanned the River Don. Cold mist hazed the river. Condensing moisture dripped from the bridge. It had once been called Our Lady's Bridge, named in a bygone Catholic reign for the nearby chapel dedicated to the Virgin Mary. Now the chapel was a wool warehouse.

A line from Chaucer's *Canterbury Tales* cut through Kate's troubled mind: *A Sheffeld thwitel baar he in his hose.* A "thwitel" was a long knife, and the brute character in the Reeve's Tale always carried one. For centuries Sheffield had been famed for its cutlery: knives, scissors, scythes, and shears. The city's seven hills were rich with iron ore.

Knives, Kate thought. Saddle-sore, she felt every step her mare took, as if a knife tip scraped her tailbone. Pins and needles prickled her right foot. Worst was the blade of fear cutting into her at the thought of the dangerous men she was about to meet. Ambassador Castelnau's instructions for making the rendezvous were clear. The place: a cutler's workshop at the ponds. Her contact: a man named Barnaby Harkness. What was terrifyingly *not* clear was how Harkness would receive her. Would he accept her as the follower of Mary Stuart she was pretending to be, or slit her throat as the agent of Elizabeth she actually was?

Yet just as painful was the cut in her heart from Owen. *A Sheffeld thwitel* . . . Chaucer's words seemed to mock her. She and Owen had quoted Chaucer to each other with smiles that night in her grandmother's library, had made love on the window seat in the moonlight. How long ago that sweet time seemed now. Their scathing argument about Robert had changed everything. Her own husband didn't trust her! He had virtually accused her of treason in standing up for her brother. He had written to Matthew about Robert behind her back, as though she was the enemy! The things he had said were so unforgivable, she wondered if she had ever really known him. They had spent most of their brief marriage apart, had lived together as man and wife for scarcely a month before he went to prison. Now, she felt she had seen the *real* Owen and it shocked her. What vile accusations—especially now that she had heard her brother's explanation.

She had passed along that explanation to Matthew, sending him a message to neutralize Owen's report. She had assured Matthew that Robert was blameless in visiting Northumberland. So blameless, he had in fact gone to test Northumberland's loyalty, visiting him under the guise of extending Father's invitation to a hunt.

Poor Robert—his inept attempt to sound out Northumberland was touching. He was so naïve about such things he had not caught a whiff of the treason Northumberland was actually plotting. *My brother would make a terrible spy,* she thought wryly. She wished she could tell Owen that, throw in his face how utterly wrong he was about Robert. But he was so blindly obsessed by suspicion he would probably still fight her about it. In any case, God knew when she would see him again. Nothing was certain, including the rocky state of her marriage. She felt adrift. It had been hard enough to bear her father's antagonism for standing by her husband, and now Owen had set himself against her, too, for standing by her brother! It seemed that the only one of her male kin she could rely on was Robert. That bond, forged in childhood when they'd had only each other, felt like her lifeline.

"Turn east here, mistress," said Soames.

They had stopped on the south side of the bridge, keeping to one side to let a carter with a load of firewood rumble past. "Are you sure?" Kate asked. Mist shrouded the way ahead. She didn't know the city. She had told Soames she had come to buy a gift of knives to take to her aunt.

He pointed down the street. "The barkeep said the ponds are just down this hill." The landlord of the inn last night had been a Sheffield man.

"Very well." She jigged the reins and turned her mare.

Their horses plodded down the muddy, sloping street. The houses thinned, looked poorer. A dirty little boy sat on a door stoop plucking a chicken. Two housewives harangued each other over a pail of fish. Then there were no more houses, just scrubland.

The ponds. Kate heard the water before she saw it: gurgles and a dull splash. She smelled it, too: the rankness of rotting vegetation. The ponds lay in the marshy area where the Porter Brook met the River Sheaf, the city's boundary. She heard the change in terrain as her mare's hooves sounded soft thuds on the spongy earth. No more knife-tip jabs at her tailbone. Yet the soft surroundings of marshland and mist felt somehow more foreboding, as though she was being swallowed up by an amorphous sink, a murky no-man's-land.

They turned onto a narrow track that skirted a pond. Bushes straggled close on one side. On the other, bulrushes crowded the shore. A frog leapt, escaping the horse's hoof. Kate heard a muffled thumping, a repeating rhythm. A mill, she realized. She could see its outline ahead in the distance, a vague block in the mist. Knives were not the city's only trade; another was wool cloth. Once woven, the cloth was fulled, pounded in a mixture of clay and water to clean and thicken it. Wooden hammers worked by watermills pounded the wool. *Thump . . . thump . . . thump.*

Kate heard it like a warning drum, for the cutler's workshop had to be near. Never had she felt so alone. *I'm not trained for this,* she thought with a pulse of panic. How could Matthew believe she could manage it? She was good at decoding, that's all. Card games—he had found her clever with numbers and had recruited her. But this was different, this was no game! The closer she got to the rendezvous the more frightened she was that she would let something slip and betray herself. And die for it.

"I reckon that's the earl's hall, mistress," Soames said, pointing.

She looked to the spot he indicated across the pond. On top of the far slope rose a handsome timber-framed building, its white-washed checkerboard façade oddly bright in the vapory haze. The innkeeper had told them about the hall. It belonged to the Earl of Shrewsbury, part of his estate. He used it as a banqueting hall for his parties hunting wildfowl in the ponds. That meant Sheffield Manor, his grand home, lay less than two miles away. That's where Mary Stuart was. During her fourteen-year confinement in England she had been moved between Shrewsbury's various castles and manor homes, his entire household moving periodically so the premises could be cleaned. Though Mary was a captive she enjoyed comfortable private accommodations and was served by a small personal retinue. She owed this kind treatment to Elizabeth, who insisted that her cousin be treated in accordance with her rank as a former queen. She was lucky. Many men on Elizabeth's council had called for Mary's head.

Seeing the hall, this tangible evidence of Mary's proximity, Kate felt freshly alert. Mary was so near, not two miles away across that mist-shrouded plain. At this very moment she might be dictating a letter to her secretary to be sent in secret to Philip of Spain, urging him to send his armies to invade England under Westmorland's command. Philip craved to conquer England, and Mary craved to be England's queen. So far she had been careful to keep her correspondence free of an outright call for Elizabeth's death, but many Englishmen, secret Catholics, were in her thrall and she encouraged their treason by not discouraging it. Elizabeth would never be safe as long as Mary promoted her downfall. Kate thought: *If only she would put it in writing. Then we'd catch her.*

That was her task here. Get Mary's letters. She straightened in the saddle, braced by new energy. Her mission was crucial. Frightened she might be, and inexperienced compared to Mary's veteran agents, but the danger she faced was nothing compared to the danger England faced. Her wounded marriage and the loss of her father's love—these were pinprick problems compared to the bloodshed and misery that invasion and civil war would bring. The thought sent a ripple of resolve through her. It gave her courage. She was on the side of Elizabeth and England. If she had to risk her life for them, she was ready. Untrained? No, her four years of exile had prepared her, because no one could love England more. One day Owen would realize that. One day, so would Father.

The path dwindled into a copse of spindly trees and rust-colored bracken. In its midst lay a squat building of rough stone. The cutler's workshop?

"This must be it," Kate told Soames. Though she was not sure. There was no one in sight. The windows, three that she could see on this side, were filmed with dirt, obscuring what lay inside. Moss slimed the pond-side wall like a fungus. Water dripped from the thatched roof, making a muck of the earth beneath.

Kate told Soames to tether the horses and stay with them. She left Castelnau's packet in her saddlebag. The letters had to stay hidden until she could be sure.

She knocked on the door. Silence. Taking a steadying breath, she lifted the latch. The door creaked as she opened it. "Is anyone here?"

It was definitely a workshop. In this front room a whetstone on a wheel stood beside the broad fireplace. Spread on the hearth were the tools of a smith: blackened tongs, bellows, hammers, a barrel of water. A long dusty table was littered with scraps of metal and leather. A wall of shelves held blades of all kinds and sizes, from eating knives to shears and awls. An arch opened onto another workroom, but its interior was so dim Kate could make out nothing but the outline of a worktable. The building seemed deserted. She felt a deflating shudder of disappointment. Had she puffed up her courage for nothing? Should she come back tomorrow? But today was the appointed day. Was this not the right place after all? She regarded the shelves of knives, some filmed with dust. *A Sheffeld thwitel . . .*

"Looking to buy?" a deep voice asked.

Kate whirled around. A man stood in the archway. He was large and flabby and wore a smith's scarred leather apron. Even paces away Kate could smell the charcoal smoke that permeated his homespun clothing. His forehead was furrowed, his head bald, and his cheeks had the spidery red threads of the drinker. His sharp eyes narrowed as he looked her over. Kate was glad Soames was nearby.

"No trade today," he growled. "Been puking my insides out with a flux. Come back next week." He turned to lumber back the way he'd come.

"Wait, please. I've come about another matter." He turned, scowling. She paused to clear her throat, then spoke the password Castelnau had given her: "The sea is calm, the wind fair."

His scowl deepened. He sucked his teeth, looking annoyed at trying to make sense of her words. "We're a long bloody way from the sea."

Kate bristled under his scrutiny. She was becoming impatient. "Are you Master Barnaby Harkness?"

"Harkness?" he said warily.

"Never mind." Clearly, she had come to the wrong place. "Forgive me for disturbing you. Good day." She turned to leave.

"I'm Harkness." A different voice.

Kate turned back. Another man had come through the arch. "Please, mistress, don't go. What was that you were saying about the sea?"

She hesitated. She had been told Harkness was a cutler and the big man fit that description, as did his workshop, but this new man was no laborer. He was slim and erect, and he spoke like a lord. Dressed like one, too, in fine wool and expensive riding boots. The sleeves of his marigold doublet were fashionably embroidered with blue silk. His velvet cap sported a blue feather. His blond moustache was neatly trimmed and his fair hair, curling under the cap, was so blond it shone.

"The sea?" he prompted her again. He looked keenly curious. "Perhaps you are on your way to the coast?"

"No, sir." She felt unnerved, unready. But Harkness was her

contact—she had to take the next step. "However, I have been told that the sea is calm, the wind fair."

The faintest smile curved his thin lips. "Ah, that is good news. The stars will shine and the moon will light the way."

A nervous thrill rippled through her. He had answered the password correctly.

"Thank you, sir." She raised her hand to show him the ring on her finger. Its signet was a fleur-de-lis crowning a vine, the symbol of Castelnau's family from Touraine.

He looked at the ring, then intensely at her, as though fascinated the courier was a woman. "You are most welcome," he said, and cocked his head with a look of expectation. "Mistress . . . ?"

"Agnes Durant," she answered. This was the alias Castelnau had given her. The less anyone at Sheffield knew about her the better. She noticed that the big man was still frowning at her.

"It's all right," Harkness told him, his eyes still on Kate, "this is the friend from London we've been expecting." Then, to Kate: "You must forgive Timms, he didn't know the password." Harkness had not broken his intense appraisal of her. "I must commend our London friend for sending such a lovely new messenger. Definitely an improvement over the last wretch."

Kate felt a warning prickle. The last courier had been Griffith. Had Harkness been a party to his murder? She could not let him see how much the thought frightened her. She said with feigned zeal, "Wretch, indeed. He met the end he deserved."

"That he did! And may the same end come to any who endanger God's work." He glanced at the door, still open. "You came alone, I trust?"

"I brought a manservant."

"Naturally, there are highwaymen." He added with a gallant bow of the head, "And I would hate any interference to befall such a fair messenger." When he raised his eyes to hers his renewed intensity sent a heat of apprehension to Kate's cheeks.

"Well now," he said, "to business, mistress. You have the packet?"

"I do, sir."

She excused herself to fetch the letters from her horse. When she returned she found the two men deep in conversation, Timms's voice quiet but forceful, Harkness's eyes lowered as he listened. Were they talking about her? Noticing her, Harkness waved his hand dismissively at Timms. The big man, looking unsatisfied, lumbered away toward the shelves of knives. Kate tried to hide her alarm. Had she underestimated Timms? Did he have a higher standing in this nest of traitors than she had believed? Ignoring her, he scanned the blades as though looking for a particular one.

"Here, sir," she said, handing Harkness the leather pouch.

"Ah! Thank you." Eagerly, he tugged the drawstring and pulled out the packet, five letters bound with a green ribbon. He tossed the pouch and ribbon onto the worktable. Kate's heart thumped as she watched him shuffle the letters, carefully checking each seal. *He's no fool*, she thought. *He must suspect the letters might have been intercepted before reaching Castelnau.* She knew that Matthew and Walsingham expected that fate for some of their own letters to the Continent. It was why both sides in this spying war used codes. She held her breath as Harkness closely examined one of the seals, maroon wax on paper the color of onion skin. At Matthew's lodging Kate had watched Arthur Gregory open this very letter for the copyist. It was one he had not been able to open without marring the seal, so to reseal he had dribbled melted wax from his spoon and then engraved a facsimile of the original signet stamp.

Harkness shuffled the letter, moving on to the next one for the same inspection. Kate breathed again. But it was terrifying to have come so close to detection: Harkness was thorough. What was his background? Whom did he report to? Northumberland? Or did he deal directly with Paris, with Thomas Morgan and Westmorland? Or even the Duke of Guise?

"How will you do it?" she asked.

His eyes snapped to hers. "Do what?"

"Get the letters inside Sheffield Manor."

Timms turned and growled, "That's no concern of yours!"

Kate flinched inside. But she answered stoutly, "In fact, it is. Our friend in London requested my report. He said he needs assurance that the flow of correspondence for which we are all risking our necks will reach its destination. In both directions."

They both stared at her for her boldness. Timms's scowl deepened. Harkness's intensity was intimidating. Kate had surprised even herself by asking. Castelnau had given her no such order. But it was information Matthew would want and need.

"Tell him he can rest easy," Harkness finally said.

She could push the issue no further. Besides, she needed to find out what mattered most. "May I ask, will there be a reply?"

"Almost certainly. I trust you can return to collect it?"

"Yes. I have arranged to visit relatives nearby. When you need me, send word to the Bull's Head Inn in Rotherham."

He nodded. "Well then, I believe our present business is concluded. I would offer you refreshment, but Timms keeps a meager larder. And, in fact"—he glanced at the big man—"it's best if you do not tarry."

She had no wish to! Relief washed over her that the meeting was over and she could go. Yet she felt a small swell of pride. She had managed this well. Really, the thing had been simple! She felt almost foolish at having been so frightened.

She was almost at the door when Timms stomped toward her. "Stop!"

Kate froze. He was coming at her with a long knife! In an impulse of terror she reached out for Harkness. "Sir!"

Timms lurched between them. "Take it!" he growled.

She gaped at him.

Harkness heaved an irritated sigh. "Forgive his rough ways, Mistress Durant. He thinks it is wrong for London to have sent a woman. He wants you to take this weapon as protection henceforth."

Kate almost laughed in tickled relief. Timms—the gallant ogre!

Roche Hall was three stories of honey-hued stone rising into the blue Yorkshire sky. Lying near Rotherham on gently rolling terrain eight miles northwest of Sheffield, it belonged to Kate's uncle and aunt, her father's sister. They had bought the manor recently and this was Kate's first visit. The morning after her rendezvous in Sheffield she woke up in lavender-scented sheets to the liquid warbling of a wood thrush.

As a child she had loved visiting the family at their residence farther north, Yeavering Hall. That place had seemed immense to her then, an entire world of its own with acres of gardens and orchards and its busy outbuildings of bakery, brewery, dairy house, and barns. Later, at thirteen, she had been fascinated by the obvious conjugal bond between her lovely, cultured Aunt Isabel and Isabel's rugged, base-born Spanish husband, Carlos Valverde, who had once made his living as a mercenary cavalryman on the battlefields of Europe. Though theirs was an unlikely match, anyone could see the deep affection they shared. Kate had seen looks pass between them hinting at a carnal intimacy that had made her adolescent self blush with curiosity. Having spent her early years in the tense gloom of her own parents' marriage, she was enthralled by her aunt and uncle's happy union. It shone in her imagination as the ideal marriage.

Uncle Carlos had served Elizabeth with distinction, had even once saved her life, so Kate's aunt had told her with pride. Yet Her Majesty had not rewarded him with a knighthood, a slight that everyone in the family, even Kate's father, regarded with suppressed indignation. Elizabeth would never raise up a man of Carlos's unfortunate Spanish origins. Nevertheless, he had prospered, chiefly from his landholdings in the New World, that vast and mysterious swathe of the globe owned by Spain. At the beginning of their marriage the couple had spent five years in Peru, where Carlos had served the governor as captain of the guard, and thanks to his connections there his family now enjoyed the fruits of his rich Peruvian holdings, including a silver mine in the fabled city of Potosí.

Kate remembered Yeavering Hall ringing with the giggling voices, running feet, and high spirits of their boisterous children. Roche Hall was smaller and quieter. The three eldest children were grown and both sons lived elsewhere, Nicolas overseeing his father's Peruvian business interests in Seville and Andrew studying at Cambridge. Eighteen-year-old Nell would soon be marrying a Yorkshire baron's son and would leave the nest, too. Then, only nine-year-old Anne would remain.

Arriving from Sheffield, Kate had been disappointed to find that her uncle was away.

"He's been with Nicolas in Seville since August," Isabel had said, hooking her arm in Kate's to lead her in from the front doorway. "We are a house of women. I hope you won't find us dull, my dear."

Kate didn't mind in the least. The men she had been thrust among in the last months had demanded much of her and the turmoil had left her feeling tender as a bruise. Gentle female company seemed a godsend.

"They're on their way home, though," chirped Anne, skipping alongside and holding Kate's hand. "So you'll see them!"

"Good, I'd like that."

"They're coming by the Irish Sea," Isabel said. "We expect them in a few days."

"How long can you stay?" asked Anne.

"Long enough to chide cousin Nicolas for his scanty letters," Kate teased her little cousin, tousling the girl's springy dark curls.

Anne's eyes went wide at such bold banter about her eldest brother, for she held him, a man of twenty-six, in as high esteem as her father.

"Kate!" cried Nell, scurrying down the staircase to greet her. "We've been looking out for you since yesterday. Oh, it's wonderful to see you."

They embraced, and Kate smiled with almost a mother's pride at the pretty young woman her cousin had become.

"How is Lady Thornleigh?" Nell asked.

"Hale as ever. And mightily engrossed in building her library."

"As ever," Isabel echoed. "Which reminds me, I have found an antiquarian volume on botany she has been seeking. I'll send it back with you."

The four of them chatted over a supper of game pie, plums, and custard, then spent the evening in the parlor, where Isabel plied her embroidery while conducting Anne's French lesson, a casual set of questions about what clothing a lady would don in dressing for the day. The child answered from her stool by the hearth. Kate and Nell played backgammon, quietly studying the board. A ginger cat padded past them, aloof.

"And what would the lady put on her feet?" was Isabel's next question in French.

"*Chasseurs,*" Anne answered. The others laughed at this, the French word for "hunters."

"*Chasseurs,*" her mother gently corrected her.

Anne dutifully repeated it. Nell moved her backgammon piece with aggressive glee. Kate felt a tickle at her foot. The cat was weaving loving circles around her ankle. Isabel murmured on in French to Anne while tugging her needle and yarn. Kate smiled, enjoying the homey gathering. She had almost forgotten how restful an evening like this could be. She felt her tension about the Sheffield rendezvous drain away. The hardest part of her mission was over. She had succeeded. All that remained was to pick up Mary's letters of reply and take them back to London, first to Matthew for his copyists and then to Castelnau.

But her tranquil mood did not last long. About an hour after Anne was sent to bed yawning, Isabel put aside her embroidery hoop and began winding the silk yarn around its parent ball, finished for the night. Taking her cue the two young women also rose to retire. Nell left the parlor and Kate was about to follow her upstairs, but Isabel motioned her to stay, saying, "I would speak with you." Kate stood before her, waiting, as Isabel wound yarn until Nell's footsteps could no longer be heard.

"You put on a brave face," Isabel said finally. "But I know it is a struggle. You have said nothing about your husband."

The statement startled Kate. Then she chided herself. Naturally, the family news had reached Roche Hall. "There is nothing to say, Aunt."

"Is there not?" She set down the yarn in her lap. "Why did you not accompany him to Sussex when he went to serve the Earl of Northumberland?"

"My grandmother wrote you, I see."

"So did your father. He is mightily troubled, Kate."

"He need not be on my account. I am perfectly content."

"Do not play false with me. I know he has barred you from his house. It grieves me. I know it must grieve you. So, please, I am trying to understand." She let out a sigh. Concern softened her face. "I know you married for love. I cannot fault you for that—I did the same. Love is a fine thing when it nurtures. When two work as one to build a life together. But if one partner undermines the union, puts you in jeopardy—"

"Pardon me, but you have heard only Father's tales."

"I have heard facts. Was your husband not in prison?"

"Yes, but—"

"Was he not convicted for attending an illegal gathering?"

"He made an error. Who can say they have not done that?"

"Oh, be careful, Kate. These are dangerous times. In London you may not feel the danger, raucous as the place is with over-confident Puritans. But here in the north people cling hard to the old ways. They are a multitude, each as stubbornly righteous as any Puritan, and bold withal. At Preston they will not take the sacrament in their hands, but only the old way, in their mouths. They hide priests and have them christen their children. Old women tell their beads at Communion. I confess I pity these people."

Kate had listened with pretended innocence, well aware of the north's underground Catholic strength, but her aunt's last words surprised her. "Pity them?"

"Theirs is a lethal dilemma. If they hold to their faith they are punished by the state as traitors. If they conform they disobey their church and are cast out. A great many have chosen their church, and they protect one another, especially the gentry. When the Jesuit Campion came into Lancashire he was sheltered by long-landed families, traveling between them—the Houghtons, the Talbots, the Westbys. In Yorkshire, the Watertons and the Lilburnes are high-ranking recusants. They pay the recusant fines rather than attend Communion. So, too, the Inglebys of Ripley. In the vale of York, the Markenfields."

Kate knew of these, and thought of the men in the cutler's workshop. Harkness. Timms. And how many unknown others in their cabal?

Isabel shook her head. "They are strong hereabouts. Even magistrates are in their ranks. In the last quarter sessions not one recusant was presented. Oh, Her Majesty's government sent the pursuivants to try to search them out. Sir John Southworth was sent to prison. They say he disinherited his son for conforming. Sir Henry Towneley paid four thousand pounds in recusancy fines, an enormous sum. He is very rich. But many poor folk, too, are hazarding all for their religion. Their numbers grow every day. And the situation could turn deadly if the rumors are true."

Kate asked with new keenness, "Rumors?"

"About their ties to the English exiles and Spain. About schemes for an invasion."

"Who told you that?"

"No one," Isabel scoffed, "and everyone. Voices in the wind. The recusants whisper it with glee. Loyalists whisper it in fear."

So, no evidence, Kate thought. Rumors were not news. She said, again pretending innocence, "But, dear Aunt, these things have nothing to do with me."

"They *do*. Because of your marriage. That taints you and leaves you suspect. You know it does. Unless . . ."

"Unless what?"

"I ask again, why did you not accompany your husband to Sussex?"

"There were matters to see to in London. I am searching out a house for us." She knew how thin her fabrication sounded.

But it seemed to spark hope in her aunt. "If you have abandoned your marriage, Kate, it is no more than wisdom."

Kate's thoughts were a dark web. *Had* she forsaken Owen over Robert? No, Owen had forsaken *her!*

Isabel rose. They stood face-to-face. "You love him. I see that. You want to be loyal to him. But allow me, as someone who has had your welfare at heart since the day you were born, to warn you before it is too late. Sometimes we have to make hard choices. Choices that go beyond ourselves and what we want. Sometimes a higher loyalty is necessary, Kate. For the good of all. For England."

She had to bite back words of self-defense. She needed no sermon about loyalty! How like Father her aunt sounded. And how alone she felt against their drumming demands.

* * *

Kate did not get to see her Uncle Carlos and cousin Nicolas. Harkness's summons from Sheffield came two days later. She pretended the note was a message from Owen calling her home. Her aunt looked anxious. Her cousins were surprised and disappointed that the visit had been so short. Kate gave no further explanation, even in the face of Isabel's clear concern. They saw her off, waving good-bye from the courtyard as she and Soames rode out. There were tears from Anne.

Kate was sorry to leave them, but glad this meant her mission would soon be over. She quickly covered the eight miles to Sheffield, feeling none of the fear of her first approach to the city. In fact, she was eager to get there. Get it over with. Even the weather seemed to urge her on. Sunshine from a blue sky warmed her as she crossed the Lady's Bridge. She considered what the letters she was on her way to collect might contain, and a quiet excitement stirred in her. If Mary had written to her friends in Paris encouraging invasion, Elizabeth's councillors could proclaim that, make public her deadly scheming. That would turn many once sympathetic hearts against her. The breakthrough could devastate Mary's support at home and thus force Elizabeth's enemies abroad to abort an invasion. It could bring peace and stability back to England—*and to me.*

The ponds shone in the sunshine. Bulrushes nodded in the breeze. Kate watched a heron rise from the shore, its broad wings beating, lifting it into the blue on a journey no human being could take. Filling her lungs with the cool autumn air, Kate realized she was looking forward to her own journey south. She was fulfilling her duty to Elizabeth, to England. In the welter of her personal worries, that felt good.

"Mistress Durant, you travel swiftly," said Harkness. "We did not expect you for hours." The cutler's front room was again deserted, no sign even of Timms.

Kate heard men's voices in the far workroom. "We, my lord?" Could it be his accomplices? If so, she wished she could see their faces. More information for Matthew.

"Our friends," he said cryptically.

Her curiosity leapt. Mary Stuart was less than two miles away, and Matthew knew—everyone knew—that her followers, especially the youngbloods among them, itched to free her. Attempts in the past had been either discovered early or repulsed by Shrewsbury's men. Might they now be going to try again? Who were they? She had to know. It might be the only chance she would get.

"Excellent," she said, "I shall extend to them our London friend's good wishes." And before he could stop her she went through the arch into the smaller workroom.

"Wait," he demanded. "We are not ready for you."

She ignored him.

"Wait!"

The workroom was deserted, but the voices led her to a closed door. A storeroom? She opened it. The voices fell silent as she walked in. Four men seated in a circle turned to her. Three were strangers. The fourth was not. He gaped at her.

Kate's breath stopped.

The fourth was Robert.

❧ 16 ❧

Castle of Grain

When Kate was fourteen she'd seen a man killed in a brawl, stabbed through the throat with a sword. When the assailant pulled out the blade, blood gushed from the gash in the victim's throat and bubbled over his lips, but he remained on his feet, rigid, in shock. An onlooker said in a hushed voice, "Dead man standing." Only when he was kicked did he fall, dead.

That was how Kate felt, seeing Robert. Stabbed. In shock. Still standing.

Robert looked just as stunned. They stared at each other. Kate's mind had frozen. It was as if a blade, rammed through her, pinioned her.

She had interrupted four men talking. All looked up at her now from their stools. One, black-bearded, gaudily dressed in a crimson doublet, scowled at her. "Who's this?"

"The courier," Harkness said, coming in behind her. "She brought the London delivery. She's come back for the return pouch."

"Ah," said Blackbeard, appraising her with new interest.

Harkness said testily to Kate, "I told you, we are not ready for you. Our contact at the manor cannot bring the pouch until this evening."

Kate heard him as though clods of earth clogged her ears. She struggled to understand what was happening.

"You'll stay the night," he went on, "and leave first thing in the morning."

They looked at her, expecting acknowledgment. But Kate's mind had seized.

Blackbeard said to the others, as though losing patience with her, "All right, let's carry on. Timms, show her where she can stay."

Timms, the big cutler, rose from his stool. "Storeroom, mistress. This way."

"I'll show her," Robert blurted.

Kate flinched. If part of her fantasized he was some imposter, hearing his voice snapped that thread of illusion. It was Robert's voice, though tight, choked. The other men looked at him, mildly startled by his tone.

"Very well," Blackbeard told him brusquely. "Go." He motioned to Timms to sit, then turned his attention to a map spread out on a barrelhead.

"We'll see you at dinner, mistress," said Harkness, pulling up a stool to the map.

She made herself speak. "Thank you." The words hurt, like splinters in her throat.

She followed Robert out, her limbs as numb as a sleepwalker's. Her thoughts thrashed in this wide-awake nightmare. *He's one of them.* . . .

She walked sightlessly behind him across the workroom. He glanced back, agitated, and laid a finger to his lips to tell her not to speak. The warning was unnecessary. Kate was so shattered she could not have uttered a single word. *Owen was right.* . . .

At the far side of the room Robert opened a door. The storeroom was small. Its single window, high up, was glazed with rough glass so thick the sunshine was weak as moonlight. There was no furniture. Bulging burlap sacks stacked haphazardly to waist height lined the walls. They gave off a dusty, earthy smell.

Robert closed the door. They were alone.

"Kate . . ." His voice was a hoarse whisper of wonderment. "Dear God, is it true? You're the courier for Castelnau?"

She swallowed. He could not know about Castelnau unless he was in Mary's camp. That was the final kick. *Dead man, falling.*

"Yes," she managed, though her tongue felt encased in clay. "And you"—she had to swallow again—"you're with us?"

"Yes."

They stared at each other. Kate was looking at a stranger. His face was as pale as a midday moon. *Does he suspect me?*

He let out a strangled laugh. "Now I understand! All those sharp questions you put to me. Why did I mislead the councillors? you asked. Why did I go to Petworth? you asked. Now it all makes sense. You were probing me, trying to see if I was on the same side as you—the *right* side!" Clumsily, he embraced her. "Oh, Kate!"

She felt him tremble. She was trembling, too, overwhelmed with relief that he had accepted her . . . and a swamp of horror running below her relief. He had lied to her. Gulled her. *He is the enemy.* Enduring his embrace, she stood as still as a post.

He let her go, gazing at her again in amazement. "Kate . . . I praise God. It's incredible! You and I, soldiers in the same righteous cause!"

A fierce light shone in his eyes. A look of profound affection. Kate felt queasy. She forced a smile, feeling it must look like the grin of a corpse.

Her legs felt suddenly weak. She feared they might give way. Give *her* away. "I . . . need to sit." She looked around. Nothing but heaped sacks.

"Ha, so do I!" With a burst of energy he heaved sacks off a pile, reducing the pile to just two. "Here, before you fall." Taking her elbow, he guided her to sit down on the makeshift seat, the sacks rising on either side.

She hesitated. "What's in these?"

"Grain."

She sat stiffly. He flopped down, too, grinning. "I daresay I'm as much of a shock to you as you are to me!"

They sat side by side, snug in this notch between the walls of grain. *Like children playing soldiers in a castle,* she thought—a thought so distressing it reamed her heart.

"How long . . . ?" she began, but had to swallow again, force down her queasiness. "How long have you been part of this?"

"Oh, forever," he said joyfully. "Mother is wise."

Mother? That shook her so deeply it took a moment before she could speak. "So . . . that story you told me in the clerk's room . . . that you came home to get away from Mother. I should have known you didn't mean it."

He smiled, and in his self-satisfaction she saw a trace of the boy he once was, preening at how he'd fooled old Master Prowse at their lessons.

"And your physic work in Lewes?" she asked. "That was all a cover?"

He nodded, then said eagerly, as though to reassure her, "But I'm a good doctor. I like helping people."

The warmth in his voice rocked her. This was the brother she had protected as a child! The brother she had loved!

He took her hand and squeezed it. "Now, together, we're going to help all of England. Dear sister. How long have *you* been involved?"

Tell your cover story. Don't let him see the truth. "I'm rather new to it, I'm afraid," she managed. "I could do nothing while I lived with Father."

"Of course. Poor Kate. That must have been hard. What changed, then?"

"I married Owen Lyon."

He gave a small gasp, as though realizing that this fact should have been obvious. "Of course! You have been in disgrace with Father because of your husband. He went to prison for his faith. Yet it never occurred to me that he had brought you to our cause."

"Yes . . ." she stammered. "Owen's courage gave me courage."

"How wonderful. I would like to meet him."

Kate smoothed her skirt to avoid his eyes. Tears scratched her throat. *If only I had listened to Owen!*

She felt Robert's eyes on her, felt his curious wonder. "How did Castelnau recruit you?"

He didn't. I went to him. "Through his wife, Marie. We're friends."

"Ah!"

Her mind felt split by an axe. Yet she knew she had to make the most of this moment. Had to find out what she could about Robert's cabal. What were they planning? Who was their leader? "Robert, Castelnau told me to be absolutely sure about my contacts. Do you really trust those men?"

"Oh yes. On my life."

"But why are there so many? It can't have taken five men to smuggle one packet of letters in to Her Majesty." She used this title for Mary as Matthew had tutored her. Mary's followers did not acknowledge her deposed status.

"Their mission goes beyond that."

Does it, by God? "Who are they? That man with the black beard—"

"That's Captain Fortescue."

Kate stifled a gasp. Fortescue—the name she had decrypted in the letter from Morgan. A Cambridge-educated priest now returned from Paris. Owen had told Matthew he'd seen Fortescue at Arundel Castle . . . and the Earl of Arundel was a close friend of the Earl of Northumberland! Kate hardly knew how she managed to keep a calm face. She coughed to cover her turmoil. "Dust," she explained, waving absently at the air.

"It's barley," he said with a nod at the sacks. He patted the one they were sitting on. "I'll pull down a few to make you a bed. It's hardly one of Grandmother's feather mattresses, but I daresay you'll find it soft enough for one night. I'll bring you a blanket."

"Robert, what is the group's mission?"

He looked eager to speak, but checked himself. "Sorry, I'm sworn to secrecy. But don't worry, they're all good men, proven men."

"Is Fortescue your leader?"

"Actually, he's just taken over from *me*."

This was *Robert's* conspiracy? The horror swarmed over her again. *Owen was right!* "Taken over? Why? Are you leaving?"

He smiled slyly. "Just to London. I have a new mission." She waited, hoping for more. But it was clear he had said all he would about it. "As for Lord Henry," he added brightly, "he runs the letter delivery into Sheffield Manor."

"Lord who?"

"Harkness. That's his alias. He's Lord Henry Alward, from up north. His father is the Marquis of Craddock."

This was even more surprising. The Marquis of Craddock was not a known Catholic recusant. Quite the opposite—Kate recalled Matthew mentioning that Craddock had spoken in support of Queen Elizabeth's religious settlement. He was a committed Protestant.

Robert, seeing her confusion, said with contempt, "His father found it politic to conform."

"But Lord Henry obviously does not."

"He pretends to, for our purposes. His bloodline gives him the privilege of access to Sheffield Manor, you see. His father has long enjoyed a friendship with the Earl of Shrewsbury, who has the keeping of Her Majesty, so Lord Henry is a welcome visitor."

Clever, she thought. "And once he is inside they actually let him see Her Majesty?"

"No, that is too much to hope for. But there is a loyal maid in her retinue whose acquaintance he has cultivated. That's how the letters you brought made their way to Her Majesty."

Kate could not help being impressed. "Goodness, this is all still so new to me. Hidden loyalties. Secret missions. Alias names. My head is spinning."

He grinned. "Indeed, *Mistress Durant.*"

She managed a smile, almost genuine. But then a new thought made her wary. "Do they know who *you* are?"

"They do now, since I moved into Father's house. We knew I could best serve Her Majesty as the trusted son of Baron Thornleigh."

Moved in . . . thanks to me! Misery roiled in her. She had enabled Robert's return into Father's affection. *Infiltration by the enemy . . .*

"Oh, Kate, it's so good to have you with us." His voice was warm, intimate. "All those years without you. I missed you so much." He smiled. "But that's all changed now. Wonderfully changed!" With his longer legs, and the seat so low, he had drawn up his knees and settled his forearms across them, relaxed in her presence. "I'll tell you something," he said quietly. "It's been strange being back with Father. I had thought I hated him. Abandoned, never hearing a word from him all those years. But now that I've been back, it's . . . well, different somehow. He's been so happy having me home. That banquet he threw for me. He's not a bad man, really. I think you feel the same, in spite of how he's treated you. He's just been caught up in Elizabeth's evil policies. But once things change in England, once the true faith is restored and proper order established, I think we can bring Father round. In any case, when that great day comes I mean to do my best to protect him from retribution. You can help, too. They'll listen to two of us."

Kate was holding her breath. *The true faith restored? Retribution?*

He looked deeply into her eyes, his expression fervent. "I dream of that day, Kate. Dream about the future—a lasting, peaceful future for us all." His cheeks went pink and he added shyly, "I might even marry."

His trust in her rocked Kate. His unshakable affection. She could not manage her somersaulting emotions. Being her brother's confidante was too much.

"Goodness," she said, feigning a sudden thought. She got to her feet. "I'd forgotten about Soames."

"Who?"

"Grandmother's servant. He's waiting outside. I'd better tell him we're staying the night."

"Good, have him bring in your things." Robert got up, too. "And I'll go and tell my friends who you really are."

Her heart kicked. *He knows?* A heartbeat later, at his delighted smile, she realized what he meant: telling his fellow conspirators that she was his sister. She would much prefer to maintain her anonymity, but she saw that he had made up his mind. Besides, this group's superiors, whoever they were, probably knew already, since Castelnau had no doubt got their approval for his choice of courier. They would have accepted her exactly as she and Matthew and Owen had wanted, as the wife of a Catholic sympathizer disgraced in the eyes of her father.

Leaving Robert, she crossed the front room in a daze of distress. She stepped outside into the dazzle of sunshine. Everything looked disorientingly normal. The dry bracken rustled in the breeze. A heron swooped across the pond and alighted on the far shore. Soames sat on a tree stump beside the tethered horses, his eyes closed, arms crossed, enjoying the sunshine.

She roused him and told him they were staying. When he went inside with their satchels Kate tried to bend her distracted mind to the crisis.

What were these men plotting? The leader, Captain Fortescue, had ties to Morgan. Morgan was Mary's agent in Paris with ties to Westmorland. And Westmorland, Kate believed from Morgan's decoded letter, was planning an invasion. And Mary? How did she fit into an invasion plan? She was less than two miles away from this very spot. Delivering letters to her did not require the five men here . . . but organizing her rescue would. Were they coordinating the two operations: invasion and rescue?

Yet, there seemed to be *three* operations. Harkness—Lord Henry—smuggled letters from Mary's correspondents in to her and her replies out to Castelnau. That was the only mission that was clear. The second was whatever Fortescue was planning, perhaps Mary's rescue—in any case some scheme that Robert said he had originally led himself. But now he said he had a *new* mission. What was it?

Three words he had said swarmed her like hornets: *Mother is wise.* He had lied to the councillors in claiming Mother had no connection to Westmorland and later Kate had accepted his explanation. She had thought then: *Westmorland was once kind to Mother, that's all.* But was there more to it, something Robert was hiding? Had Mother maintained her connection with Westmorland all these years? *Is Mother, too, implicated in this plot?*

Father, she thought with a pang. *Robert gulled him just as he gulled me.* The horror and humiliation cut so deep, she could have wept. Robert had even persuaded Father to let him visit Northumberland under the guise of delivering an invitation and thus sounding out the peer's loyalty. A boldly clever ploy by Robert. What had he and Northumberland discussed? Her brother's web of deceit was staggering!

Robert. Mother. Northumberland. Westmorland. Mary. The names, each one more ominous, sounded in her head like death knells.

She had to get word to Matthew. Immediately. The fate of England could depend on stopping this cabal.

Tell Matthew . . . and then what? These men would be arrested. Taken to London. Interrogated to divulge their plot and reveal who gave them orders. Would Robert talk? Kate had seen his fierce determination. If he refused to talk he would be tortured. His thumbs crushed. Joints ripped on the rack. His body cramped to paralysis in the Tower's terrifying chamber known as Little Ease. His suffering would be horrible. Kate imagined his screams. Worse, whether he revealed information or not he could still be tried and hanged.

She shuddered. Standing in the warm sunshine, she had never felt so cold. How could she send her own brother to his death? Despite her shock and disgust at what he was doing, despite her fury at him, she felt in the deepest part of herself that he did not deserve to die. She knew him. He was not evil. As a child he had been turned onto an evil path by the people who had raised him, indoctrinating him with their poison. Mother. It was she who had perverted the boy's gentle nature. She had made her son a traitor.

And deeper still, so deep it had eaten into Kate's heart, was her guilt from the night she had left him, a child of nine, crying outside the burning house in Brussels. Had abandoned him. Left him behind. Rational it might not be, she knew that, but strong within her was the terrible sense that Robert had become what he had become of her. *I didn't do everything I could to get him out. I grew up here, happy with Father, while he was left to Mother.*

She looked up at the sky. *What am I to do?* Clouds scudded overhead like abandoned ships. Watching them, she felt it was *she* who was moving, flung into the vastness, adrift. Her aunt's voice sounded in her head. *Sometimes we have to make hard choices. Sometimes a higher loyalty is necessary. For the good of all. For England.*

She had meant that Kate should distance herself from Owen for his faith, unaware that her warning on that score was unnecessary. How benign that choice seemed compared to the horrifying one Kate faced now. Her country . . . or her brother's life?

She felt a lash of panic. There was no time for vacillating. She had to choose.

❧ 17 ❧

Matthew

Kate reached London after four days of muddy roads through snow-speckled shires and bad food at roadside inns, and arrived with saddle sores and a stiff back. Her physical aches were nothing compared to her mental distress. She was no closer to a decision about Robert than she had been the morning she had left him at Sheffield.

Riding in through Bishopsgate she sent Soames on to her grandmother's house while she continued south to Matthew's lodging. Londoners bustled around her engrossed in their day-to-day lives: buying, selling, carting, carrying, gossiping, arguing. Kate felt sadly cut off from them. Never would they have to make the terrible choice she faced. To denounce her brother meant abandoning him to torture, perhaps death. To keep silent might endanger England.

But there was no avoiding Matthew Buckland. He was back in London and she had to deliver Mary's letters to him. Harkness—Lord Henry—had visited Sheffield Manor, where Mary's maid had secretly passed the letters to him, and he had brought them back to the cutler's workshop in a black leather pouch. Robert himself had packed the pouch in Kate's saddlebag as she had mounted her horse. Looking up at her in the saddle he had squeezed her knee and wished her a safe journey.

"God keep you, Kate," he had said, affection shining in his eyes.

She turned onto Cornhill and passed the London Exchange, bustling with merchants and lawyers coming and going, then carried on along Cheapside, thronged as usual with people and wagons, donkey carts and dogs. Outside the Mermaid Tavern two scruffy men and a haggard-faced woman were locked in the pillories, people ignoring them as they passed by. Precious wares gleamed in the windows of the goldsmiths' shops. She remembered a winter morning when she was seven, holding Robert's hand, both of them excited at visiting Chastelain's shop on Goldsmith Row with Father. He had brought them along on his excursion to order a Christmas gift for their mother, one of his attempts to make peace at home. With a child's scant understanding of her parents' relationship, Kate had sensed only the truce between them and was giddily happy about it. Five-year-old Robert had picked up her mood and they'd stood giggling while Father gave the goldsmith his specifications for a brooch set with rubies.

"Roodies," Robert whispered to Kate, stifling a giggle, and they had both burst out laughing.

Kate winced, remembering. The following summer Mother had committed treason and fled with her and Robert.

She put these memories behind her as she reached Matthew's lodging on St. Peter's Hill. Clear thinking, not tangled emotions—that's what she needed now.

"He came in late last night," said Madame Mercier, puffing as she mounted the stairs with Kate behind her. "What a fuss in the darkness, *quel bruit*, him and his clerks tramping in with their coffers of papers." She indicated the third floor with a disinterested wave as she carried on down a hallway. "Go on up, madam. He is there."

Matthew answered the knock at his door, an ink-stained handkerchief in his hand. "Ah, Kate! Glad I am to see you. Welcome home."

She thought he looked tired after his own journeying, his face drawn as he eyed her from his familiar head-bent posture.

"You must be glad to be home yourself," she said. "Irish troubles are never easy."

"You speak truly." His look was grim as he stuffed the handkerchief into his sleeve. "Her Majesty is beset by danger on all sides. Spain and the pope are not content to threaten her from the east so they stir up the wild Irish to menace her from the west. Come in, come in." He motioned to the chairs in front of the cold hearth. Kate saw that the table there was strewn with papers, and two open coffers of documents lay beneath the table. "What news from Sheffield?" he asked. "Have you just returned?"

"Yes. Just now."

He looked at her so closely, she was sure he must see the anxiety tormenting her. "Good heavens, you came straight to me? No rest at all?"

"I wanted to report to you right away."

"Well, I commend you for that, though I am sorry for your pains. I trust you made the delivery?"

"I did. And have brought back Mary's replies." She withdrew the pouch from the inside pocket of her cloak. "Here."

His eyes gleamed as he took it from her. "My God, Kate, you have done well." Untying the pouch's drawstring, he called to his servant in the bedchamber, "Caruthers!" Then, to Kate, "I'll send him to fetch Gregory and the copyists. We'll get to it right away."

"Yes, good." It wouldn't take long for them to get here. They all lived nearby.

"While we wait you can give me a full report," he added.

Kate glanced away to hide her agitation.

"Is the man deaf?" Matthew muttered when no response came from his servant. Impatient to see the pouch's contents, he thrust his hand inside it and pulled out the packet of letters. They were wrapped in white linen and tied with twine. Kate wasn't sure how many letters there were—Matthew's instructions had been to keep the packet intact, wrappings and all—but from the size and weight of it she thought there were perhaps four or five. Matthew took scissors from the mantel and snipped the twine. He tossed it and the linen wrapping on the table. Letters in hand, he scowled at his bedchamber door and called impatiently again, "Caruthers!" No response. Shaking his head, Matthew shoved the letters back into the pouch and handed it to Kate. "Please, take it in," he said with a nod toward the workroom. He headed for the bedchamber.

Kate went into the workroom and set the pouch on one of the desks. She unfastened her cloak and hung it on a hook. Within moments Matthew would expect her report. How much should she tell him? Never had she felt such agonizing indecision.

She heard Caruthers rush out and slam the door. Matthew came to the workroom doorway. "Kate, come back and sit down. Have some wine and tell me all. Did you have any difficulty in Sheffield?"

She followed him to the chairs by the hearth. "No." She sat. "It all went smoothly."

He poured a goblet of wine and handed it to her. "You made the rendezvous with the contact, this man Harkness?"

"Yes." She took a swallow. Sweet malmsey. She swallowed more, trying to order her thoughts. "And some other men with him."

"Ah. Who?"

"One they call Captain Fortescue."

His eyes widened. "Morgan's man!"

"Yes."

He sat in the chair beside her and pulled it close so they were knee to knee. "You spoke to him?"

"Briefly."

"What's he doing in Sheffield?"

"I don't know. I asked as many questions as I dared, but I could not find out. I did see, though, that they were studying a map."

"Of what?"

"I could not make it out." She decided to venture her opinion. "I wonder if they might be planning an attack on Sheffield Manor to free Mary."

He mulled this, his eyes still on her, but made no reply. She knew that previous attempts by Mary's supporters to free her had been uncovered and prevented.

"Who else was there?" he asked.

Avoiding that answer, she said, "Harkness is the one who takes the letters in to Mary at the Manor and brings out her replies."

"How? How does he circumvent Shrewsbury's people?"

"He doesn't. Shrewsbury welcomes him as a guest. Harkness is not his real name. He is Henry Alward, son of the Marquis of Crad-dock."

Matthew listened keenly as she explained how the son was be-traying his loyal father's position behind his back. "Well, well," he said, digesting it. "This is good to know. How did you find out?"

She swirled the wine in her goblet, pretending detachment. "They told me. They trust me." She looked up. "I explained who I am, you see. I thought it worth the risk, and it was. They think it's wonderful to have Lord Thornleigh's daughter on their side."

Even as she told the lie she knew it was still possible to follow it with the truth: that it was Robert who had told her about Alward, Robert who had confided in her. But she could not pry that truth from her heart. It had taken refuge there like a criminal claiming the sanctuary of a church. If only she knew which was worse, truth or lies! Which duty bound her the most—family or country?

"Did you get any other names?" Matthew asked.

"One they called Timms. A cutler. It was his workshop we met in. Another is a young man they call Townsend. Of course, those may be aliases."

He shook his head, pondering. "They're not names I've heard before."

"No. Nor I."

"That's four. How many more were there?"

Here was the crisis. *One more. My brother.* She looked at Matthew, struggling for an answer. Aunt Isabel's words again swept through her mind: *Sometimes we have to make hard choices that go beyond our-selves. For the good of all.*

"Forgive me, Kate," he said, his voice suddenly gentle. "I can see it's been an ordeal for you. And you're weary from the road. And like an oaf I've barraged you with questions." His smile was apologetic. "That's no way to treat my valuable agent. Drink up now, and rest a bit. Then, as soon as the copyists get to work, you and I can continue."

"Thank you." She swallowed the last of her wine, avoiding his eyes.

He leaned forward in his chair, his eyes shining with admiration.

"I'll admit, I was worried about you. I wondered if I'd been wrong to send you there, into danger. But, by God, you've done well. You're magnificent."

She felt far from it! "Tell me, did you hear from Owen at Petworth while I was away?"

He leaned back. Looked down. "I've had two reports, yes."

"Anything significant?"

He shook his head. Kate knew he would not give her details, but she longed for even a scrap of news about Owen. "Is the source he developed still cooperating?"

He got to his feet. "He confirms that is the case. More wine?"

She shook her head. They fell silent, waiting for the others to arrive. Matthew busied himself, looking through papers. Kate sat thinking of Robert. Of that night in Brussels, the fire, the cries of men around her, her father carrying her outside to safety. She remembered seeing, through the smoke, her mother pushing Robert up to a soldier on horseback, the soldier grabbing the weeping boy, then turning his mount and disappearing into the smoky night. *I escaped. Left Robert behind.*

Footsteps sounded beyond the door. Matthew opened it and the first copyist tramped in. Matthew sent him to the workroom. Within fifteen minutes the others had arrived: four more copyists and Arthur Gregory, carrying his box of tools with which he would remove the letters' seals and, after the contents had been copied, close them again with engraved counterfeit seals. Last to arrive was Thomas Phelippes, Kate's fellow decoder. One by one they greeted her and she returned the greeting and they all carried on into the workroom. Matthew stayed behind in the main room, giving Caruthers instructions about procuring food and drink. It was going to be another long session.

Kate picked up the leather pouch of letters as the copyists got settled at their desks and quietly chatted with each other, arranging their pens and penknives, their ink pots and paper.

"Been riding, Mistress Lyon?" Phelippes asked Kate pleasantly.

She followed his gaze to her shoes and noticed the soles were rimmed with mud. The hem of her skirt, too, was spattered with dried mud flaking off. "Through a bog, it must look like, Master Phelippes," she acknowledged wryly.

They watched Gregory set out his wares: the small knives with fine blades, the tweezers, the engraving implements, the knobs of sealing wax in various colors, the spoon and stubby candle.

Knowing that Matthew would want to begin without delay, Kate withdrew the letters from the pouch. Five in all. She shuffled them, scanning the inscriptions: Thomas Morgan . . . Cardinal Beaton . . . Sir Francis Englefield . . . another for Morgan . . . one for Marion Forbes. The last name sounded new to Kate. The others were all known agents of Mary's abroad, but Marion Forbes was not. And yet, as she moved forward to hand Gregory the letters, something about the name quivered a string of memory. Where had she heard it before? The recollection was vague, elusive, like a clutch of notes in a forgotten song.

"Master Gregory, are you ready?" she asked.

"One moment." He was meticulously laying out the last of his small knives.

The copyists went on chatting, arranging their papers. Phelippes took a seat, relaxing until his services at decoding would be required. He leaned back, watching Gregory.

Kate watched, too, waiting, and that's when the memory jolted into sudden clarity. Robert's voice. In the clerk's office when she had confronted him with his lie. He was sent, he had confessed— sent by Mother and her two friends. "Hangers-on of the Countess of Westmorland," he had said. "One's an old priest. The other is his cousin, a merchant's widow."

"Their names, Robert."

"Thomas Crick. And Marion Forbes."

Kate stared at the inscription—Marion Forbes—transfixed by the handwriting. Her heart thumped. She recognized that flourish in the *F.* Recognized the unclosed tops of the *O*s. Recognized the very pressure that made the looping letters so bold.

Robert wrote this.

Her right hand moved quickly, lowering the letter, hiding it in the folds of her skirt. She had done it without thinking, a reflex too swift for thought. No one had noticed. The copyists were chuckling over a jest. Phelippes picked a speck of something off his sleeve. Gregory had laid out all his tools. He looked up at Kate. "Ready, Mistress Lyon."

She handed him the letters in her left hand. Four letters only.

Gregory set to examining the first seal. The others watched him, silent, fresh energy rippling through the group now that their work could begin.

No one looked at Kate as she turned to her cloak and slipped the fifth letter into the pocket.

"Everything all right?" Matthew stood in the doorway, watching her.

❧18❧

The Letter

Kate entered Lady Thornleigh's great hall and was jarred by the sound of laughter. She found her grandmother and two guests—Lord Burghley and his wife—standing at the oriel window enjoying a private jest. They all turned to her, still chuckling. Kate's tense hands balled into fists at her sides. Burghley, her grandmother's longtime friend, was the Queen's closest adviser, the most powerful man in England. He was the last person Kate wanted to speak to now. The letter she had stolen from Matthew's lodging lay in the pocket of her cloak. In her troubled imagination it felt as conspicuous as a dagger dripping blood.

"Kate, my dear!" her grandmother exclaimed in surprise. "I didn't expect you back so soon. That was a brief visit."

"There was talk of coming snow," Kate said. "The roads were already bad so I thought it best to leave early." She curtsied to Burghley and his wife. "My lord. My lady."

Burghley gave her a nod and muttered a barely polite, "Mistress Lyon." Kate was used to the cool tone, and not just from him. She was the wife of a felon.

"And how are they all at Roche Hall?" Lady Thornleigh asked eagerly.

"They are very well, your ladyship."

"Glad I am to hear it." She turned to her guests. "Kate has been north to visit Isabel and the girls." Then, to Kate: "That is, I don't suppose Carlos and Nicolas are home yet from Spain?"

"Not yet. Aunt Isabel said they were on their way. Oh, and she sent you a botany book for your library. It's in my luggage."

"Ah! The Otto Brunfels volume? The *Herbarum Vivae Icones*?"

"I believe so." Kate was finding it hard to act normally. Nothing would settle her distraught mind until she could read the letter. Matthew, thank God, had not seen her pocket it. She had waited in a fever of anxiety until a copyist had completed one of the letters to Morgan, and then she had turned to Matthew, pleading exhaustion from her journey, and asked his permission to take the copy to her grandmother's house to work on decoding it there.

"Of course," he had said, looking concerned. "Kate, are you sure you're all right?"

"I'll be fine. Just need some sleep."

Both letters—the one addressed to Marion Forbes and the copy of the one to Morgan—now lay pressed together in her cloak pocket.

"Come join us, my dear," said her grandmother. "I was just offering Lord and Lady Burghley some refreshment. They have brought a beautiful gift of venison for my anniversary supper. It is Her Majesty's favorite meat at this time of year." She smiled at her guests, well pleased. "Most kind of you, Mildred."

"As selfish as kind," Lady Burghley said pleasantly, "since William and I shall enjoy it just as much as Her Majesty will."

"Indeed, so shall we all," Lady Thornleigh agreed. "We happy few."

Kate tried to show interest. She knew the supper was to be a small, private affair with just the old friends who had held her late grandfather in the highest esteem. There would be Her Majesty— her presence a great honor, of course—plus Lord and Lady Burghley and Father and his wife. Her grandmother had marked the occasion this way annually since her husband's death fourteen years ago. Kate herself had attended last year, the year she had turned twenty-one. "It's next week, isn't it?" she asked.

"No, no," her grandmother corrected with eager precision. "The day after tomorrow."

But Kate could no longer feign attention. "Would you excuse me, my lady? I'm rather tired from the journey."

"Yes, of course, my dear. I understand. Go and rest." As Kate left the hall her grandmother called after her, "The musicians are going to rehearse their program. I hope they won't disturb you."

On her way upstairs Kate asked the footman to light a fire in her bedchamber. He went to fetch a taper and she carried on up the steps. In her room she whirled off her cloak and took out the two letters: the copy to Morgan, neatly folded by the copyist, and the original to Marion Forbes, still sealed. Tossing her cloak on the bed, she took the letters to her dressing table at the window, where late afternoon sun bathed the room in golden light. The window looked out on the Thames. No one could see in, but a primeval need for privacy made Kate close the curtains. She left just a crack of light.

She sat down, her reflection in the looking glass skimming past her vision as she moved. Examining the letter's seal, she saw that it was rudimentary—a blob of brown wax pressed by what looked like a thumbprint. The seals on Mary's other letters were far more elegant. Her secretary used a silky red wax, and the image, whether a stamp pressed by Mary's own hand or simply approved by her, was of a crucifix. The crudeness of this brown seal was evidence that the letter had been sealed by someone other than Mary. It gave Kate a sickening mixture of relief and dread. Relief, because the seal would be easy to duplicate if she had to; she had watched Gregory do so often enough. Dread because the evidence confirmed her belief that the handwriting of the inscription was Robert's. And why would he have inscribed it unless he had also written the contents?

"Mistress?" said the young footman, coming in with a lit taper. "Shall I light the fire now?"

"Yes. Thank you." Waiting, she pretended to fuss with the vase of flowers the maids had left beside the looking glass. Yellow roses, Michaelmas daisies, late purple asters. Gardening was her grandmother's passion, and a fresh bouquet in every room was the rule.

Once the fire in the grate was flickering the footman asked, "Anything else, mistress?"

"No. That will be all."

When he had gone she locked the door. She lit a candle from the fire and took it to the dressing table and sat. She picked up the slim silver letter knife beside the vase of flowers. Holding the blade above the flame, she warmed the metal. Then, gently, she slid the knife tip under the seal, careful to protect the paper from showing any sign of tampering. If she was wrong about the handwriting and the seal—if her fears were just the work of her overanxious imagination—she could reseal the letter and return it to Matthew with a story of having forgotten it in her saddlebag in her weary state.

Gradually, the warmed seal gave up its grip. She lifted the paper edge, then unfolded the paper. It was blank. But another letter slipped out onto the table. Tightly folded, it was more worn than the enclosing paper. It bore the same crude seal: brown wax impressed with a thumbprint. Kate picked it up and turned it over to read the inscription.

F. Grenville.

Her heart shot up her throat. *F* for Frances. Grenville, her maiden name. *Mother.*

With chilled fingers she warmed the blade again over the flame. She slid it under this second seal and gently pried it off.

A half page of writing. Robert's handwriting. In code.

She felt suddenly sick. She dropped the paper on the table. Sweat prickled her forehead, slicked her palms. Her heart felt like it was thrashing in her chest. Even as she struggled for control she realized what Robert had done. Knowing that Mary's letters were going to Castelnau to be distributed abroad, he had slipped this letter to Mother inside the packet. The evidence was clear proof of Kate's suspicion: Mother was part of the cabal of Mary's supporters.

She laid her hands flat on the table, fighting to subdue her panic. She had seen this code before. A glance told her that. It was the same one Morgan had used in his letter to Fortescue, the one she had decoded two weeks ago at this very table. It had contained the symbol of an *L* inside a circle, signifying the Duke of Guise.

Lurching to her feet, she took one more moment to get control of herself. Short though the letter was, she needed her decrypting notes. She went to her bedside and went down on hands and knees. She lifted the loose floorboard under the bed and lifted out the metal box and unlocked it with the key she kept on a long ribbon around her neck. The box held the *Stenographia* volume and her notes. Leaving the book, she took the notes to the dressing table, got a pencil and paper from the drawer, and set to work.

> *My dear Mother*
> *By the time you read this our world will be remade.*
> *I am about—*

Music jolted Kate. A wheezing sound of rebecs, flutes, and sackbuts tuning. The musicians' rehearsal. She bent again to her task.

> *My dear Mother*
> *By the time you read this our world will be remade.*
> *I am about to bring our enterprise to its sublime*
> *fulfilment. Look for joyful news the day after St.*
> *Crispin's Day. It will reach you as sweet music. I want*
> *nothing more than the knowledge that you will hear the*
> *news with pride.*
> *But, Mother, with the joyful account may come*
> *another with no joy, reporting my death. For the*
> *tyrant's followers may cut me down. Or they may*
> *capture me. I fear I lack the strength to withstand their*
> *methods to tear names from my broken body. Therefore,*
> *I will not let myself be taken. By my medical training I*
> *have furnished myself with the means to a quick end.*
> *God will forgive the sin. This truth I have learned from*
> *you, that righteousness is never sin.*
> *If I return to you, we shall rejoice together. If I do*
> *not, pray for my soul. Be proud of your son. He will be*
> *with God, waiting for you to join him.*
> *Until then, may He keep you and protect you.*
> *R*

Kate stared at the words. Her pulse thrummed in her ears. Her hand was cramped. The decrypting had taken over an hour. The candle had burned down an inch. She set down her pencil and looked sightlessly into the flame. *I am about to bring our enterprise to its sublime fulfilment.* What enterprise? She remembered his words when they had talked among the walls of sacks, their castle of grain, in Sheffield.

"Are you leaving?" she had asked.

He'd smiled. "Just to London. I have a new mission."

St. Crispin's Day. October twenty-fifth. Today was the twenty-third. Kate gasped. Grandmother's supper! The Queen would be here, in this house. Could Robert's mission be . . . assassination?

It's madness. He's completely mad.

She locked the papers in the box, the key slippery in her damp palm, and replaced the box under the floorboard. She went downstairs, trying not to run. She crossed the great hall, passing under the gallery, where the musicians sawed noisily at their tune. At the hall's far end she reached the library, where she found her grandmother alone, seated at her desk, writing in her ledger.

"Have Lord and Lady Burghley gone?" Kate blurted.

Her grandmother looked up. "Yes. They are expecting guests. Why?"

"My lady," Kate began, her mouth dry, "your anniversary supper, is it—"

"I wanted you to be there," her grandmother interrupted. She set down her pen and regarded Kate sadly. "This remembrance of Richard should be for all his family. All in London, at any rate. Isabel is too far. But I wanted you." A cross look tugged her eyebrows. "But Burghley will not have it. He says your presence would be an irritant to Elizabeth. I'm sorry."

"I understand," Kate said. The insult to her was the last thing on her mind. "So, Her Majesty will definitely attend?"

"Of course. She has for fourteen years. And I think Burghley underestimates her. I have known Elizabeth since she was a princess and I know her clear-eyed ways. She would not be troubled by your presence." She stood up with a weary sigh. "But I want no discord, and so I have deferred to Burghley. He and Elizabeth have troubles enough steering the ship of state in these dangerous days."

She came to Kate. Her voice was earnest. "Understand me, Kate. Your husband is no enemy of mine. I have stood all my life for rationality. This warring to the death over faith—worship with a mass, worship without a mass—it makes me despair of mankind. I dream of the day when we move beyond such lunacy, though I am sure it will not come in my lifetime. Meanwhile, we all must live in this world. You made your bed, Kate, and must lie in it."

"I understand, my lady, truly. Tell me, will Her Majesty arrive with her usual guard?"

The question clearly surprised her. "Usual? No, rather *more*, I should say. There have been too many attempts against her life." She turned back to her desk and moved papers as though looking for something. "Elizabeth shows a brave calmness about her safety, but the latest attempt frightened even her. That gunman your father cornered on the bridge. No, Burghley will not let Elizabeth stir from the palace without a doubling of her guard."

Music swelled. Kate glanced through the open door to the great hall and across to the musicians' gallery, her thoughts tumbling. She looked back at her grandmother.

A doubled guard, she thought. *Robert would be utterly mad to try.* He would never get past them. Even if he made it inside the house they would capture him. His fate would be sealed. Prison. Torture. Execution. And not a simple hanging as Kate had thought his end would be for mere connection with conspirators. For personally threatening the monarch he would suffer the full agony of a traitor's death decreed by law. He would hang with a short rope that would not mercifully snap the neck, but instead slowly strangle the victim. He would be cut down still living. Then castrated, screaming. Disemboweled while still breathing. His body butchered, hacked into quarters. His head speared on a pike to gape in death atop London Bridge.

Stop, she told herself. There was not a scrap of evidence that Robert was planning such an insane endeavor. Only a vague letter to Mother and a date. No proof at all. *Perhaps I am the brainsick one.*

"Ah, here it is." Her grandmother held up a paper. "This was delivered while you were upstairs resting. It's from your brother. He asks to attend the remembrance supper. He says"—she scanned the page and read from it—" 'To do the family justice, I request the great honor of an introduction to Her Majesty so that I may abjectly apologize for my mother's treason fourteen years ago. Please, your ladyship, allow me to come early to deliver a gift.' " She put down the letter. "I must say, the sentiment does him credit. I have dispatched a note to him at your father's house giving my consent." She added dryly, "Of *his* attendance I am sure Burghley will approve."

Kate was appalled.

Her grandmother's voice became gentle. "I wanted to let you know, my dear. You might wish to visit friends that night."

"Yes . . ." she mumbled. "Thank you." She left the library. She crossed the great hall, crossed under the musicians' gallery, their tune a grating noise in her ears, and went up the stairs to her bedchamber.

Who would believe her? Not her grandmother. No evidence. Not Lord Burghley, who thought her a pariah.

Father? He would not believe her, either. He trusted Robert, not her.

Matthew. That was where her duty lay. Matthew *would* believe her.

But to explain her brother's mad plot would be to abandon him—again. She had so desperately been avoiding that. Robert had done nothing wrong yet, but Matthew would arrest him nonetheless. His fate would be taken out of her control, would become state business. If he was found guilty of plotting to kill the Queen he would die a traitor's death. No one could stop that.

And stop it Kate felt she must.

She reached her bedchamber. Her hand stilled on the doorknob. There was only one person she could go to. One man who might help her do what had to be done.

❧ 19 ❧

Decision at Petworth

The next day Kate rode out of London alone.

Before leaving she had gone to Matthew's lodging in the early morning, pretending to him that all was normal, and collected from him the four letters that had been in the Sheffield pouch, Mary's correspondence to her agents in Paris. The fifth letter—Robert's dispatch to Mother—was locked in the strongbox beneath her bed at her grandmother's house. She went to St. Bride's church off Fleet Street and tucked the packet of four letters behind the stone monument of the knight and his dame recumbent under the stained glass window of St. Brigit. Ambassador Castelnau's agent would collect it. Castelnau would then distribute the letters abroad, unaware that Matthew had copies. Thomas Phelippes was at work decrypting them now.

She reached the village of Petworth in the late afternoon. Her destination was Petworth House, the Earl of Northumberland's Sussex home. She had finally decided what to do about Robert. She was going to see Owen—and was praying she could smooth over the rough feelings of their last parting.

The roads were dry, the chill air ripe with the smells of scythed grain fields and harvested orchards. Leaving the village, Kate passed a field where starlings pecked at fallen kernels. The birds rose abruptly into the sky and her startled horse jittered. Kate watched the starlings sail away, undulating in a dense mass like a shaken blanket. Her spirits were charged with cautious hope. Her plan had its risks, and she hated her lies of omission to Matthew, to Lady Thornleigh and, soon, to Owen. But she truly believed this action would bring a resolution that everyone could live with. She was going to stop Robert—and save his life, too.

If she could persuade Owen to help her.

She felt a quiver in her stomach at the thought of seeing him, that familiar spark in her blood, her body wanting his. But beneath it ran a tremor of doubt. Would he forgive her? In the three weeks he had been living at Petworth they had seen each other only once, and in that time had wrangled so bitterly about Robert. The memory fired her cheeks with shame. She had brazenly defended her brother against Owen's warnings. They had rowed so rancorously she had feared she had married a hard man she scarcely knew.

But he had been right. She knew that now. Robert *was* involved with traitors. She regretted every harsh word she had hurled at her husband. He loved her, and his suspicions about her brother had been born as much from concern for her safety as for the realm. And how had she answered his concern? With foul-tempered insults and vile accusations. She longed to make it up to him. Longed to apologize and let him know how deeply she loved him.

And needed him—needed his nimble mind and his daring if she was going to save her brother. Her request would surely astonish him, but if she could convince him to help her she vowed she would never wrangle with him again. She would show him how much he meant to her, and do everything in her power to make him happy.

A peddler was coming her way on the road, a shaggy old man trudging beside an equally shaggy old dog that pulled his cart. Hanging from the cart sides the man's tin wares—ladles, cups, pots—jangled over the ruts.

"Is this the way to Petworth House?" Kate asked.

"Aye, mistress." He squinted up at her, the sun in his eyes. His walnut-colored face was puckered like a dried apple. Wound around one shabby sleeve were bright-colored ribbons, and around

the other lace trim and gold cord, advertisements of his dainty of-
ferings. "Keep on as you are," he said, pointing, "and turn right
after Hoby's Wood. You'll be at Petworth in a trice."

"Thank you." She gave way to an impulse. "Have you any ribbon in blue?" A memory tingled: Owen coming upon her naked
after her bath and untying the blue ribbon in her hair to let it
tumble.

"That I have, mistress." The peddler raised the lid on his cart,
revealing its many-drawered interior. There was a surprisingly var-
ied selection of ribbons, including a bouquet of blues: peacock,
turquoise, cornflower, azure, and a cobalt like the summer sea at
dusk. Kate chose the cornflower shade. She had worn cornflowers
in her hair on the day she and Owen were wed. The peddler
thanked her for the farthing she paid him. She tucked the ribbon
inside her cloak, thinking: *Tonight. When I undress.*

She passed a wood brocaded with autumn's colors—Hoby's
Wood, surely—and a few hundred yards ahead the earl's medieval
manor house came into view. It looked more castle than house. A
moat. High stone walls enclosing a jumble of steeply peaked
rooftops and a square stone tower. A timber-framed gatehouse, its
toothed portcullis raised. Behind all this stretched the earl's forests.

Her horse clopped across the worn wooden drawbridge. The
moat's water level was low and gave off an odor of slime. She
passed a fat woman waddling out of the precincts with a brace of
live geese trussed to a yoke across her shoulders. Ahead, a boy
sauntered in balancing a basket of cabbages on his head with one
hand. Two men on horseback came riding out together at a fast
trot, hoofbeats clanging through the passage under the gatehouse.
Kate nudged her horse to one side to let them pass. They were
well dressed, and there was arrogance in their uninterested glances
at her and the people on foot. Kinsmen of Northumberland? The
horses' hoofbeats sped up to a canter as they gained the road, then
faded in the distance behind Kate.

She carried on. Looking up at the portcullis suspended above
her she saw that one tooth of its black wooden grid was splintered
with age. Darkness enveloped her as she rode through the tunnel-
like entrance beneath the gatehouse. Perhaps it was the cutting of

the light—she felt a stab of fear for Owen's safety. He had taken a great risk in infiltrating Northumberland's household.

She emerged into a courtyard where servants ambled to their chores. A freckled young woman swept the doorstep of the main entrance, where the door stood open for two men unloading firewood from a wagon. A little girl scuffed past with a wheel of cheese almost too big for her to carry. Coming from the dairy house, no doubt. The child smiled up at Kate. She smiled back, shrugging off her fear. She would have heard if anything had happened to Owen. He was sending regular reports to Matthew. He knew how to take care of himself.

She passed a low stone block of living quarters, then came to an alley that, judging from the sight of a groom leading a gray stallion that way, and the whiff of manure, led to the stables. She followed the alley and dismounted at the stable, where she asked a groom where she might find His Lordship's chamberlain. "Great hall, mistress," said the groom as he took her horse. "He's reckoning with the bailiff."

At the front entrance Kate received an idly curious glance from the girl sweeping. She entered and reached the great hall, a gloomy vaulted space that smelled of damp wool. Two men were seated at the far end of a long table, ledger books before them. The household administrators, she decided. "Master Chamberlain?" she asked the one who looked up at her.

"Aye, mistress, I'm Sutton." A portly fellow, he eyed her figure with undisguised appraisal. "What can I do for you?"

She introduced herself as Owen's wife and asked where she might find him.

"Haven't seen Lyon since dinner."

"Perhaps he's attending His Lordship?" she suggested.

He shrugged. "Usually is." He directed her outside. "His Lordship's at the butts. By the pond."

Archery did not seem a likely activity for Owen, but Kate decided to check. Where Northumberland went, Owen probably followed.

Once back in the courtyard she asked the men at the wagon for directions and they sent her down a passage that squeezed between the rear of the house and the brewhouse. It led through the compound wall and came out into a field. The open ground sloped down to a pond. On this side of the water a throng of men stood at archery practice. There were thirty or forty, and all looked intent, disciplined. Ten were lined up with bows raised, strings pulled taut. The others watched, waiting their turn. The drillmaster's voice boomed and arrows flew, thudding into the straw butts. Kate knew that a nobleman training his retainers and tenants was a common sight. England had no standing army, so all peers were required to supply musters to fight for Her Majesty should an enemy threaten the realm. But the focused, martial air here gave her a sting of suspicion. Was Northumberland training his men to fight *against* his queen?

There was no sign of Owen.

She saw two men in private conversation near the drillmaster. One was stocky, wearing a battered leather jerkin, his cropped gray hair and weathered face the marks of a veteran soldier. The other was taller, lean, with sharp cheekbones and bony hands. Listening to the soldier, he scratched absently at his beard, russet-colored like his moustache that curved like two drooping wings. He wore a doublet of good green wool, though plain and unadorned. In the scabbard at his hip glinted the jeweled hilt of a sword, a very expensive weapon. He watched the drill with hooded eyes, like a judge, as though these men belonged to him. Kate felt this had to be Northumberland. She was curious to see him up close.

She made her way to the pair and curtsied. They both turned to her, frowning at the interruption. "Pardon me, sirs. Your lordship, I presume?" she asked the bearded one.

"Yes?" he acknowledged gruffly.

"My lord, I have just arrived from London. I seek my husband, Master Owen Lyon."

Northumberland's frown cleared and a look of keen interest took its place. "Ah, Mistress Lyon! He said nothing about you coming."

"He does not expect me, your lordship."

"Well, you are welcome at Petworth." The soldier, uninterested in her, had turned back to watch the archery drill, and Northumberland added quietly to Kate, as though sharing a secret, "Very welcome."

A shiver ran through her. *He's heard I was at Sheffield. He thinks I'm one of them.* She imagined the trail: Fortescue sending word about her with his update about the Sheffield cabal. Had Northumberland confided to Owen about her? About Robert? She prayed that he had not.

"Looking for him, are you?"

"Yes, my lord."

He pointed a bony finger at the house. "Library. Writing a letter for me. He's good at that foppish language of court. It's to go with a gift for Her Majesty, a prize goshawk." He added smoothly, "We must keep our friends close, eh, Mistress Lyon?"

Kate knew the rest of the saying: *And our enemies closer.* Was he inferring that Her Majesty was his enemy? Kate could not tell. Though blunt-spoken, he was certainly too wise to bluster his thoughts aloud to her.

"Go on in," he said. "Find Sutton, my chamberlain. He'll show you." He turned back to the soldier, saying over his shoulder to Kate, "Supper soon. You're welcome at table, of course."

Back into the great hall she went and asked Sutton the way to the library. This time he barely glanced up from his ledger, merely waved a hand toward a corridor. "That way." *Rude man,* she thought as she thanked him.

The corridor was short and ended at a door. Kate's heartbeat quickened as she reached it. In a moment she would be in Owen's arms asking him to forgive her.

She opened the door. And froze. A woman stood at the desk, bent over it, her naked buttocks facing the door. Owen stood beside her, his hands on his half-unfastened breeches. His head jerked to Kate. His mouth fell open.

She lurched back. Shut the door. Turned down the corridor. Her heart crashed against her ribs.

The door slammed behind her. Running footsteps. "Kate!" he called.

She kept walking. She could not look at him. Knives of shock flayed her.

"Kate!" He caught up to her and snatched her elbow. "Stop, please!" he said in a fierce whisper. She yanked her arm to free it, but he held tight. He glanced toward the great hall at the corridor's end, then pushed her against the wall so they could not be seen.

Fury flared through her. "Let me go!"

Gripping her shoulders, he pinned her to the wall. He looked distraught. "Please, listen to me. You—"

"For God's sake," she spat, "what is there to say?"

"It's not what you think."

"Oh? I did not see you with a trollop?"

"She's not—" He gritted his teeth. Glanced again at the hall, then at the closed library door. "Not that."

Sutton suddenly loomed at the end of the corridor. "Everything all right, Lyon?"

Owen let Kate go. She sprang forward, itching to get away from him. But he caught her hand, stopping her. His grip almost crushed her fingers. "Yes, all's well, Master Sutton. My wife is giving me news of home." He shot her a pleading look of warning, then carried on loudly to Sutton, "It's been a while since we've seen each other." With a theatrical smile he kissed Kate to show his meaning.

"Ah," said the chamberlain with a smirk in his voice. "Then I won't keep you from getting your *news*." He plodded off.

Kate pushed Owen away. Trembling with rage, she kept her voice low lest anyone else hear her and witness her mortification. "Who is she, then? A scullery maid?"

He gritted his teeth again. "No, damn it." His voice was a whisper, tight, urgent. "The countess."

She gaped at him. This was too much. "Ha! It's not enough to humiliate me? Do not insult me, too!" She started for the hall.

He grabbed her arm again and spun her around. "It's true. Listen—"

"Let me go!"

"Kate, she is my *source!*"

The word was ice water dashed in her face. Amazement rushed over her. She looked at the library door, astounded.

He seemed to sense the change in her, sensed that she understood. He ran a hand distractedly over his bristled head. "Come. We can't talk here."

She walked with him through the great hall, then outside and down the alley to the stables. She forced herself to dam up the questions that thrashed inside her. Forced herself to quash the image of the woman's white buttocks . . . white thighs above white stockings gartered with yellow at her knees. Owen took her to the side of the stable block and up an outside staircase. At the top he opened the door to a small chamber and ushered her in. A narrow bed. A scuffed table with an earthenware jug. A spindly stool. Smells of horse and dank straw.

He closed the door. They were alone.

Kate turned to him. "So," she said stiffly. "The countess."

"Yes." He watched her like a man facing a wounded lioness, gauging if she was subdued enough for him to approach.

Kate didn't know *what* she felt. Not subdued, no! Still angry. Wounded and smarting. But also, grudgingly, impressed. The countess could have invaluable private knowledge of her husband.

Still, it hurt to look at Owen. She glanced around at the cramped, fetid quarters. "This is where you live?"

He nodded.

Mortification pierced her again. She thought of the blue ribbon inside her cloak. Tears sprang to her eyes. "Has *she* been here?"

"Kate, I swear to you, she is only—"

"No!" She held up her hands to stop him. "Swear nothing." She would not cry! She took a breath to steady herself and forced a calm tone. "Just tell me this. What have you learned from her?"

He let out a tight sigh, and she knew it was his relief at having pacified her. "Much," he said. Words rushed from him as though to prove his point to her. "That Northumberland and Arundel are stockpiling arms at Arundel Castle. That Fortescue has received messages here from Thomas Morgan in Paris. That Morgan meets regularly with the Earl of Westmorland, and Westmorland was recently the guest of the Duke of Guise. And that Fortescue has now gone north to Sheffield."

Much indeed! "I just came back from Sheffield," she said.

His eyes went wide. "Castelnau gave you letters? You delivered them?"

"Yes."

"To whom?"

She hesitated. She dare not tell the whole truth about Robert. "The rendezvous was complicated. But the passwords worked. And I was given Mary's letters in reply. I brought them back to Matthew. He had them copied, and this morning I delivered the originals to Castelnau."

Owen gave a low whistle of admiration. "Good work, Kate."

She bristled at his patronizing tone. "*Dangerous* work. I've put myself at risk while you've been—" She bit back the words. Bit back her anger. She turned away and moved to the window and looked out in misery at the stable courtyard. Matthew had told her Owen had a source. Did Matthew know it was the countess? Humiliation roiled through Kate. She loathed being forced into this tawdry role of the wronged woman, like in some tired comedy by one of Owen's hack playwright friends.

He came to her. Worry strained his voice. "That's what I meant. The danger. Kate, all I care about is that you're all right. I hate that Matthew sent you there."

His sincerity rocked her. "I'm fine," she said.

He laid his hands on her shoulders, gently this time, and turned her to face him. "Your coming here could be dangerous, too. If Northumberland finds out that you work for Matthew—" He stopped, his face creased with concern. "Why *have* you come?"

She did not know what to answer. Her carefully planned phrases deserted her. And yet, her reason for coming had not changed. Robert's fate lay in her hands. Whatever her own hurt feelings, her brother's situation was far more urgent. His *life* was at stake. To save him, she needed Owen's help. Her thought of a moment ago about playing a role came back to mock her. She needed to playact now. Needed to get his help while hiding her worst suspicions about Robert.

"I came to ask you something," she said.

She moved to the bed—it was a mere two steps away—and sat

down stiffly on the edge. The thin mattress of straw rustled as she sat. She stared at it, touching it with her fingertips as cautiously as if it were dusted with poison. She saw again the woman's white thighs. How often he had bedded her? Catherine, that was her name.

"Kate—" he stammered, coming to her.

She looked up at him in confusion. This much was not play-acting. The disorder in her mind was real.

He sat down, too. Beside her, but not close. She held herself rigid. They stared ahead like strangers. She sensed the tension in his every muscle.

Begin, she told herself.

"What are your orders from Matthew?" she said. "Must you stay to find out more?"

He shrugged. "She only talks when I—" He caught himself, did not finish.

"I see."

He slumped forward, his body loosening like a man weary of a fight. He laid his forearms on his knees. He clasped his hands and stared at them. "You're cut out for this work, Kate. You know that? You care about it, care about what happens to the stubborn people of this island. You love England. It's in your blood. Me? I got into this work for just one reason. To get you."

She looked at him. She had never heard him talk like this. No self-assurance. No swagger.

He went on staring at his hands. "I had nothing. And I wanted everything. Wanted it so that I could get you and keep you. I carried out every assignment Matthew gave me, and did them well, made myself invaluable to him, and to Walsingham. Did it so that one day they would reward me with a rich post and then I could give everything to you. Give you the life your father gave you. The life you deserve." He looked sideways at her with a sad smile. "Strange, isn't it? You didn't want to get involved in this work beyond decoding, but now you fly with it as easily as a thrush through forest. I pitched into it to get rich, but I'm really just a journeyman. And now . . ." His head slumped lower. His voice was raw. "Now the job has brought me to this place, and what I've done here is turning you from me. Walsingham could pour the rubies of the Indies into my hands and it would be sand through my fingers if I lose you."

She could not speak. Tears scalded her eyes. Her rage was spent, but in its place was a morass of confusion, resentment, and, in spite of everything, most bewilderingly, love.

"Fly with it?" she echoed. "No. I've botched some things. My brother for one. You were right and I was wrong. I came to tell you so. To apologize."

He looked up at her, startled.

"Owen, Robert is not who he said he was."

He straightened, alert. "What's happened?"

Her apology was from her heart. If she had listened to Owen earlier she might have turned Robert from his path. But now, having apologized, artfulness was needed. She could not tell him she had seen Robert in Sheffield. And she absolutely could not share her fear that he planned to kill the Queen. Of that she had no proof. She could be wrong. She prayed she was. But Owen, if he heard of it, would certainly tell Matthew and this time Matthew would have Robert arrested.

"He told a lie," she began. "At his interrogation by Lord Burghley and the councillors. I observed it. Matthew gave me leave to watch through the peephole in the next room. Robert told the councillors that our mother did not know the Earl of Westmorland. The fact is, she did. She met Westmorland once, when we first arrived in Brussels. Robert and I were there. Just children, but we were there. His testimony disturbed me. So afterward I confronted him about it. And he made an extraordinary confession."

She turned, leaned closer to Owen. He was listening, rapt.

She kept her voice low, as quiet as a conspirator. "He told me Mother sent him to England." She repeated the story that Robert had told her in their grandmother's orchard. That Mother had for years spun a fantasy of helping powerful exiles like Westmorland plan an invasion to dethrone Elizabeth. That she, along with two wayward friends as foolish as herself, had sent Robert to England under the cover of his medical profession. His task was to reconnoiter the Sussex coast for landing places for invasion ships.

"Mother," Kate sighed with derision. "Her twisted dream. Robert said that as soon as he stepped back on his native soil he realized how wrong and pitiful Mother was. She and her two friends played at intrigue with no more effect than Bedlam inmates planning escape. He swore to me that he had cut himself off from Mother. And I believed him. Why would I not? Mother may be bitter, but she is powerless. And it seemed to me that Robert had done no harm. Besides, Father welcomed him back with joy. How could I object to my brother's return to his rightful home?"

She looked down, mortified indeed at remembering. "Then you told me you'd seen him here at Petworth and we argued, you and I. I defended Robert. But that night I confronted him again, this time at our father's house. He was offended by my suspicion. Father sent him, he protested. Sent him as his emissary to invite Northumberland to a hunting party. And Father corroborated this in my presence. So, once again, I accepted Robert's innocence. But now . . ." She looked away as though overwhelmed. "Now I have learned otherwise."

Owen sat motionless but alert. Kate felt it, felt his eyes on her, waiting. She had carefully led him to this point. She suffered a squirm of shame at manipulating him, and at the sin of the lie she was about to commit, but she quickly banished that weakness. She owed this to her brother. And, as she thought of the countess's white thighs, she felt that her husband owed *her.*

She turned back to him. "This morning I delivered Mary's letters to a secret place known only to Castelnau and whatever underlings he trusts. It is in a church. I waited so I could observe whom he sent. Waited over an hour, hidden, on a bench behind a pillar. Someone finally came and retrieved the letters. It was Robert."

Owen let out a soft groan. "So."

There, she had told the lie. Now there was no going back.

"Yes. You suspected Robert and you were right. He is involved with the Queen's enemies. It seems they use him as a go-between. Like the scores of shiftless men that Matthew and Walsingham themselves hire from time to time. Listeners. Informants. Message carriers."

Owen added grimly, challenging her, "And full-blown agents."

"No. I know my brother. He has become involved with treacherous men, but he is not evil. He may be a fool, but he's harmless."

"That's not for you to decide."

"I *have* decided."

"My God," he said, a sudden realization. "You haven't told Matthew, have you." It was a statement, not a question. And with it, a look of dismay. "Kate, don't be ridiculous. We have to report this."

"No. That's exactly what I want to avoid."

"Impossible."

"He'll be arrested. He could hang."

"He made that choice."

"*Mother* made that choice."

"He's a grown man. And you have no idea whom he may be working for."

"For Castelnau. A tiny cog in greater men's wheels. He is young, Owen. His whole life has been Mother and medical studies and now a taste of minor intrigue. He is nothing compared to the men we need to fear. You said I love England. I do. You know I would never do anything that might bring harm to Her Majesty's realm."

He frowned, unconvinced.

"Your brothers live happily in Wales," she said. "But what if one of them made the terrible mistake my brother has and you held his life in your hands. Could you send him to die? Could you set the noose around your own brother's neck?"

She saw the tiniest crack in his armor, a glint of sympathy in his eyes. Yet still, suspicion darkened his face.

Kate had no more arguments to offer. Only the truth. "He is my brother, Owen. I love him."

"You love the boy he was. Not the man he has become."

"I cannot separate the two. It would be like separating my arm from my body. You were right to mistrust him, but I am right about his soul. He's gotten mixed up in something he shouldn't and if he hangs for that it would kill me. I want to save him."

He looked astounded. "Save him? How?"

"I want to send him away. Someplace foreign, where he'll be far away from Mother."

"How? You can't make him go."

"No. But you can."

"I?"

"Please, hear me out. You know people that I don't. Ship's captains who can be bought. A captain who will take a passenger, no questions asked, and slip out of England with a night-time tide. I have thought this through. I will tell Robert he's been betrayed and must flee on the ship we've arranged. If he balks, you have the strength to force him. There is no time to lose, Owen. It must be done tomorrow." St. Crispin's Day. Grandmother's remembrance supper.

He looked pained. "I don't like it. I'm sorry, Kate, but we have to tell Matthew. It's our duty."

"And what of my duty to my kin? I left Robert behind ten years ago in Brussels. If I had been able to bring him home he would never have become what he is. *He* is my duty. I cannot abandon him again."

"You cannot blame yourself. He chose his way. And there you cannot follow."

His intransigence rocked her. This was not what she had expected. But she could not give up. She could not forsake Robert—nor leave him free to kill the Queen.

She got up from the bed. "I am going to get my brother out of England. Tomorrow. I want your help. But if you refuse I will find someone else. Prisons make hard men, and any let out recently would jump at the purse I will offer." She held his gaze, and found the courage to go on. "Don't make me resort to that, Owen. Help me, and I promise you we shall never wrangle again. If you will not, I swear I will never return to you. So choose. Right now. Your duty to Matthew, or me."

20

The Rescue

Snowflakes scurried like fugitives over London's rooftops and scampered down streets and alleys. Frost slicked the cobbles under Kate's shoes as she reached the gates of her father's house at twilight. Across busy Bishopsgate Street, at the intersection with Threadneedle Street, the sun had slipped down behind the Merchant Taylors Hall, where clothiers and their clerks tramped in and out, finishing the day's business. The snowflakes, winter's advance infiltrators, were barely visible in the dying light.

Kate had not a moment to lose. Her grandmother's remembrance supper was tonight. Within hours the Queen would step onto her barge at the water stairs of Whitehall Palace and her oarsmen would carry her around the bend of the river to Lady Thornleigh's house. If Kate was right about Robert, he would soon set out from their father's house for the same destination.

She passed through her father's open gates into the courtyard where a few servants were going about their chores. She kept to the shadows of the big gates, her eyes on a maid carrying a basket of turnips on her hip. "Susan!" she called softly.

The young woman turned, startled. "Mistress Lyon!"

"Come here, please." When the maid approached, Kate asked, "Is my brother inside?"

"Master Robert? Aye, he is."

"You're sure? You saw him?"

"Oh yes, just now in the long gallery. He was asking John the footman about the snow."

Thank God. That had been Kate's worst fear, that he might already have left. "Take him this." She handed the girl a folded paper. "And hurry. It's urgent."

Surprised, the girl gestured to the house. "Won't you come in, mistress?"

"I cannot. Now go. Quickly!"

She watched the maid disappear into the house. Walking out again through the gates she looked up at the sky. Dusk was stealing over the city, but enough twilight remained to illumine gray clouds pregnant with snow. A memory ambushed her of Robert beside her on the terrace of their father's old house in Chelsea, the two of them catching snowflakes on their tongues. They had run out to see the year's first snowfall. She was seven, he was five.

"Tastes like nails," she had said.

"How do you know? You don't eat nails."

"I'll eat *you*," she had said with an ogre's crazed grin, and chased him back inside, Robert squealing with glee.

She banished the memory. The sweet time with her little brother was long past, its bright enchantment turned to ashes.

Would her message flush him out? She crossed Bishopsgate Street, her nerves as taut as a bow string. A scruffy beggar sat slumped at the foot of the steps of the Merchant Taylors Hall and he eyed her intently as she passed. Something about his hard-eyed stare made her even more nervous. She chided herself. *I'm in a sorry state when beggars start looking like enemies.*

She reached the alley that ran between St. Helen's churchyard wall and the walled garden of the Leathersellers Hall. There, under a leafless mulberry tree where he had tethered the horses, Owen stood waiting.

"He's there?"

"Yes. Susan took my note."

"And you're sure he'll come?"

"He'll come." Her bravado sprang from having Owen with her.

She loved him so much for standing by her. It buoyed her with hope that her plan was going to work.

As they watched the alley mouth, waiting, he took her hand and gave it a squeeze to calm her nerves. She looked at him and smiled her thanks. Snow speckled the shoulders of his black wool jerkin and instantly melted at his body's warmth. Kate felt that warmth in his hand—and in the memory of their lovemaking last night.

Her passion had surprised her. When he had agreed to help her save Robert the anger she had felt at that awful scene of him with the countess was swept away in a grateful tide of love. She could not wait to have him. His passion matched hers, and they had pulled off each other's clothes and fallen on his narrow bed of straw with a hunger born of days of separation in body and spirit. Then, without words, they had slowed, savoring long kisses and caresses, giving and taking, loving each other silently with lips, tongues, fingertips, with sighs, moans, gasps. They had shared the inexpressible, exhilarating communion of being reunited, being man and wife again. Being one.

They were one now as they stood waiting for Robert.

The day, though, had been one of excruciating suspense. First, Owen had had to ask Northumberland for leave to go to London. He'd done it cleverly, requesting the honor of delivering North-umberland's gift of a falcon to Whitehall Palace for the Queen. Kate had heard with relief that his request was approved. As soon as they reached London Bridge Owen hired a porter to deliver the falcon to Whitehall Palace while he and Kate went down to Galley Wharf. At the Black Whale, a fetid seaman's haunt in the shadow of the bridge, Owen sought out a ship's captain, a gap-toothed, greedy rogue named Halter, and bargained with him. Kate watched their talk, well aware that she could never have managed the shifty transaction herself. All this, while the hours until her grandmother's supper marched closer. Excruciating hours. But now, with Robert just across the street, she allowed her hope to surge. Success was so near!

And yet, holding hands with Owen in the alley, waiting, she felt a twinge of shame. She had not told him her awful suspicion about

Robert, that he was planning to kill the Queen this very night. After all, her fear might be nothing more than her fevered imagination. She had no evidence, only Robert's vague letter to Mother. But if she was right, she would stop him now by sending him away, far from Mother's evil influence. No one would ever know of his mad scheme. The perfection of the plan made Kate almost giddy again with hope. With this one act she would save Her Majesty's life and save Robert from a traitor's death—all without destroying her own cover or Owen's.

A shouted order and the tramp of feet sounded. Kate and Owen tensed. The alley mouth was dark in the gathering dusk, making the snowflakes darting past it look like eddying cinders. They moved closer to investigate. A troop of men was marching toward them down Bishopsgate Street. Their lines were ragged, undisciplined, but even in the fading light Kate saw that the faces were sober with concentration, like boys imitating soldiers.

"A company muster," Owen said. "Coming from Moorfields, I warrant."

"The Leathersellers?" Kate suggested. The captain was heading for their hall. The city's livery companies and trade associations all had to train a troop of their men, ready to serve the monarch in time of war. The Leathersellers Company hall was next to St. Helen's, by whose churchyard wall they stood.

"Looks like," Owen agreed. "They're shabby enough. And green as girls."

He sounded amused and Kate saw that he was right. The Leathersellers were not a rich company and many of the men were armed with only pitchforks or clubs. Unlike their wealthy colleagues the Mercers, the Grocers, the Drapers, and the Goldsmiths, they could not afford experienced captains or smart uniforms and weapons. She could not help being touched by the patriotic effort of these amateur soldiers. "They'll do Her Majesty well enough in a fight."

Owen cracked a smile. "That they will. I've seen them knock heads at football. They're bulldogs."

"Like England," she said with a rush of pride. That was how

she saw her small country facing the threat from abroad—like a bulldog protecting itself from a ravening bear. She looked at Owen, her heart full. "We're doing our part in the fight, too, you and I."

He grinned. "God help any foe who meets *you* in a dark alley."

She laughed. It felt good to laugh with him. She kissed him. "No, my love, it's mettle like *yours* that makes England strong." She had never felt the truth of it so powerfully. Though the image of him with the countess still held a sting, she knew he had lain with the woman only to get valuable information to protect the realm. Like the Leathersellers, Owen stood up for England, and not from a lust to invade and conquer, but from a need to protect what mattered most: hearth and home. She would never forget how he had opened his heart to her, confessing that he had become a spy to win her. For all his intellectual quickness and vigor he was not so different than the company men plodding into their hall after a hard day of training. It warmed her in the deepest part of herself. A people who fought for these things would always prevail over tyranny.

He pulled her into his arms and growled with mock lechery, "I'll show you my mettle when I get you alone." She laughed. Turning serious, he murmured, "Kate, my Kate. My heart's desire." He held her and kissed her. She gave herself to the kiss, letting its promise thrill her.

Owen let her go, his eyes flicking past the top of her head to the street. "Here he comes."

Kate's heart kicked. *Robert.* She turned to see him hurrying across the street toward the alley, his clothes flapping in his haste. He looked distraught.

Owen looked at her. "Ready?"

"Ready."

Robert jerked to a halt at the alley mouth. Seeing his sister, his eyes went wide. "Kate!" he cried. He held up her note. "What's the meaning of this? You say my life is in danger?"

"Hush!" she hissed. "Follow me!" She turned and hurried toward the horses.

"Follow?" he said in bewilderment. "Where? Why? What's—"

Owen grabbed his arm before Robert could get out another word. "Come!" he said darkly, and shoved him after Kate.

Robert staggered a few steps from the shove, then angrily dug in his heels and shrugged off Owen's grip. "Who's this?"

Kate was untying her horse's reins. "My husband. Owen Lyon."

"Good God." Robert gaped at Owen.

"That's right, he's on our side," Kate said, and added sternly, "and he is risking his life to save yours."

"Greetings, Master Thornleigh," Owen said with mock courtliness. He had untied one of the other two horses. "Forgive me if I don't wax eloquent about the pleasure of meeting you. We'll enjoy that chat later, you and I, when our necks are not in jeopardy." He thrust the reins into Robert's hands.

"Kate," Robert demanded, "what has happened? Why—"

"They've found out about you!" she shot back. "The Queen's men. They *know*. Now come! You have to get away."

"What?" Wild-eyed, he looked from her to Owen and back at her. "Found out? How?"

"To horse!" Owen ordered him, pushing him toward the saddle. "Talk later." He cupped his hands for Kate to mount her horse.

"Do it, Robert," she said, settling onto the saddle. "You have to get away! Now!"

"Get away?" he said, resisting, distraught. He threw a desperate look back toward the street. The tramping of the Leathersellers echoed hollowly down the alley. He dropped the reins. "No, I . . . I can't go anywhere! I have an important—"

"They're *coming* for you!" Kate cried. "Don't you understand? You have to come with us now, this very moment!"

"But . . . how did you hear?"

"At Grandmother's house. Lord Burghley came to inspect the security for the supper with Her Majesty. It's tonight. Sir Francis Walsingham rode in not two hours ago. I heard him tell Burghley they have discovered a cabal—that's what he called it. He named Captain Fortescue and others. And *you!* He issued orders for your arrest. Now, to horse! We're taking you away."

He gaped at her. "Away . . . where?"

Owen said, "Galley Wharf. There's a ship. I've paid the captain." He had untied his own horse and again thrust the reins of Robert's horse at him. "Mount, man!"

Robert looked distractedly at the reins in his hand. He took an unsteady step toward the horse, then halted. "No. My mission . . . tonight . . . cannot abandon my mission . . ."

Kate leaned over her pommel and hissed at him, "Listen to me, Robert. They're coming for you right now and if we tarry a moment longer we'll *all* go to prison. And then to the scaffold. I don't want to die. And I won't let you die, either." She nodded to Owen.

Owen snatched the back of Robert's collar. He had drawn a dagger and he held it at Robert's chin. "I'll carve you some new whiskers before I let your sister be taken. So how about you save your fine-looking face and save all our lives?" He gave him another shove.

"Yes . . . yes," Robert stammered. He gave a last agonized glance in the direction of the house. He let out a strangled curse at his fate, his face contorted with a last flash of fury. Then, resigned, he slid his foot into the stirrup.

As soon as Robert was mounted Owen swung up into his own saddle. "Follow me."

They left the alley single file, entering Bishopsgate Street, Owen at the head, Robert next, Kate at the rear. The trudging Leathersellers' troop crowded the street, forcing them to keep to one side and keep their horses at a walk. From the company's hall Kate caught a whiff of roasting meat and heard laughter. She imagined them, tired from their day of training and glad to be at table.

She did not know if she wanted to laugh, too, or cry. Laugh with relief, because soon her brother would be on a ship bound for Portugal. Cry, because she was horribly sure now that she was right. He *had* meant to make an attempt on Her Majesty's life. *"My mission . . . tonight . . . cannot abandon my mission."* It rocked her. She held tight to her horse's pommel, glad to have to concentrate on riding. Darkness was claiming the streets. A linkboy holding his lantern high led a gentleman down a lane toward a cookhouse where candlelight glowed in the windows.

Once past the straggling troop she and Owen and Robert

spurred their horses into a fast trot. Robert fell back just enough to ride alongside her and he threw her a look of misery. "Thank you," he said, his voice raw with furious frustration, but his thanks sincere.

Kate said nothing. She wanted no more words with him. By his abominable "mission" he had cut himself off from her. He had severed the bonds of the childhood love she had once thought were unbreakable, had befouled that love with his monstrous intent. Well, she had thwarted his intent. And once he was sailing to Portugal her debt to him—her guilt at having once abandoned him—would be discharged.

She was done with her brother forever.

The beggar sitting slumped on the steps of the Merchant Taylors Hall looked up as the three of them approached. Kate caught his eye. She saw that his right ear was mutilated, a red-raw, shriveled thing. Pity for him flashed through her. She slipped a sixpence from her purse and tossed it to him as she rode past. For luck. She felt a twinge at the childish practice. *Old habits die hard.*

The beggar watched her go, ignoring the coin that rolled by his boot.

❧ 21 ❧

Tower Hill

Kate and Robert and Owen rode fast in the deepening dusk and turned east off Bishopsgate Street onto Fenchurch Street. Their horses' pounding hooves matched the pounding of Kate's heart as she kept up with the men. Owen had set this headlong pace and zigzagging route to keep Robert believing their fiction that the Queen's men were after him. Robert was riding for his life.

With buildings rising on either side of her Kate felt she was riding down a dark canyon. Obstacles squeezed the way: a wagon, pedestrians, an oxcart, a water conduit, a plodding donkey. She dodged them narrowly as the three of them cantered down Mark Lane. Owen glanced back to make sure she was keeping up and she thought she saw him smile, though the darkness made it hard to see his face clearly. East again they turned and cantered along Hart Street. In a gap between houses Kate glimpsed the tower of All Hallows Barking church at Tower Street. Birds flying over it were black specks against the rising full moon. Just ten minutes more of this punishing pace, she told herself, and they would reach the river. At Galley Wharf a wherry would take Robert to the flotilla of merchant ships lying at anchor off the Tower of London. The *Nancy Willoughby*, bound for Portugal, would carry him away.

And then, finally, this long day would be over.

They were approaching Seething Lane, about to turn south, when they came up behind a lumbering carriage and had to draw rein. The sedate vehicle painted blue and gold rattled along at a leisurely pace, its progress causing congestion. Carriages were a rarity in England so people stopped to look. Apprentices rolling beer barrels down a wagon's ramp, housewives carrying supper home from cookhouses, boys and beggars, gentlemen and servant girls—all paused to peer at the vehicle as though it might contain the Queen herself. Torches flanked the liveried coachman. Dogs barked at the flames.

Kate watched Owen turn his mount toward the gutter to skirt the congestion. Robert followed, kicking his horse, desperately eager to get on. Kate coaxed her mare after them and edged past the rear of the carriage. She was an arm's length from it when it came to a halt and the door swung open in front of her. A man stepped out, his back to her. He handed out a woman who lifted her hood against the snowflakes as she turned to Kate.

Kate flinched. It was Marie de Castelnau, the ambassador's wife.

"Mistress Lyon!" she said, beaming. "I *told* Michel it was you."

The man turned. The ambassador! He looked equally startled to see Kate, but quickly guarded himself. "Mistress Lyon," he murmured in greeting.

Kate stammered, "Madame . . . Monsieur . . ."

"What a delightful surprise," said the lady. "Are you joining us for supper?"

"Supper?" Distracted, Kate was watching Owen, who had halted, observing her with a questioning look that said: *What's happening?* Robert looked horrified, as though he feared this was an ambush.

The French couple did not notice them. "Yes, with the Lumleys." Marie gestured to an imposing house behind a stone wall.

"Oh. No, I'm not." Kate was trying to think. She could not let Castelnau see that she was with Robert and Owen!

"Ah, too bad," said Marie. "It has been so long since I've seen you."

Castelnau turned to the coachman and said, "Bring in the wine, Henri." His wife glanced at him and Kate snatched the moment to gesture frantically to Owen to move on, mouthing: *Go!* Owen did not know who these people were, but he could not miss her urgency in that one unspoken word. He nodded, turned his horse's head, and broke into a trot. Robert quickly followed, clearly anxious to be out of here.

"Do you know Baron Lumley?" Marie was asking.

Kate collected herself. "No," she answered as pleasantly as she could. "Is this his house?"

"His London house, yes. He is from the north. The greatest coal owner among the English aristocracy, I am told."

From the corner of her eye Kate watched Owen and Robert canter on. She would catch up with them.

Marie was looking at her, faintly anxious. "Where are you going at this time of night, my dear, all alone?"

Castelnau eyed Kate soberly, waiting for the answer.

"South here!" Owen pointed down Seething Lane and he and Robert cantered into the turn. He had to raise his voice above the pounding of their horses' hooves.

Robert threw a nervous look back over his shoulder. "But why did she stop? Who was that?"

Was he anxious about his sister? Owen wondered. No, more likely about his own skin. "Not sure," he said. "Someone she could not ignore."

But Owen *was* anxious about her. He didn't like leaving her alone with night closing in. Londoners locked their doors against the thieves and felons who would be slinking out from their daytime haunts. Business men heading home in the dark often had their sturdy apprentices accompany them armed with clubs.

Felons, he thought with a glance at Kate's brother riding beside him. Robert Thornleigh was working for the enemy. It would be easy to rid the world of him. *Turn him off*, as Owen's underworld acquaintances would put it. Any of the night-dark alleys they were riding past would do. Matthew would commend him, might even reward him. But Owen knew he could not do it. Kate had asked him to get her brother safely away, and her trust was a thing more precious than gold.

They were almost at Tower Street, a wider thoroughfare. The tower of All Hallows Barking church rose dead ahead. The Thames was so near Owen could smell the fishy reek of river mud. To his left stretched the dark wasteland of Tower Hill. Beyond it rose the massive precincts of the Tower of London. The moon skulking behind it was bright enough to etch the bare trees and bramble thickets of Tower Hill and the gallows that stood upon the mound. Snowflakes eddied around the gibbet.

Hoofbeats rumbled behind them. Owen glanced back in surprise. Horsemen, perhaps a half-dozen, were galloping down Seething Lane toward them.

"Oh God!" Robert gasped. "They're after me!" He whipped his mount in panic and galloped for Tower Hill.

"No, not that way!" Owen called after him. The fool! The horsemen were likely a pack of the night watch chasing a thief, or maybe a merchant's guards riding to join his ship. But Robert was too panicked to stop. Cursing him, Owen cantered after him along Barking Lane.

The horsemen turned onto Barking Lane, too. Owen glanced back, startled to see them coming, and gaining on him. He caught up with Robert at the base of Tower Hill. They had to slow at the edge of a black hollow fretted with brambles. Robert savagely yanked his horse's reins to turn it south, but the frightened animal whinnied and shied and staggered toward Owen.

"Thornleigh!" A shout from the horsemen.

Confusion raced through Owen. He turned his horse to face the oncoming men. Five of them. Moonlight lit up their grim faces. Owen's heart thumped. He knew the ginger-bearded leader, one of Northumberland's armed retainers. Hooper was his name. He and the four men with him reached Owen and Robert in a rumble of hooves and jangle of harness, and surrounded them.

The scruffy man beside Hooper turned his head. It was the beggar from the steps of the Merchant Taylors Hall. Owen saw the mutilated ear and his stomach lurched. *Burkitt* . . . Dressed so raggedly, his face down as they'd passed him, his identity had not registered with Owen. The truth now flared over him like a flash of Kate's coin. Northumberland must have posted Burkitt to spy on Kate's father's house. Seeing Robert ride away with her and Owen, he must have hustled off with the information to Hooper.

"Hooper!" Robert cried in amazed relief. "Thank God it's you! But what the devil, man, you turned my blood cold! Why—" He didn't finish, casting a frightened look back the way they'd come. "Never mind. No time. Let me through! We cannot stop!"

He made to break through the circle, but Hooper snatched his horse's bridle, halting him. "Question is, Thornleigh, what are *you* doing? It's east you should be heading. We've got everything ready. A fast horse waiting for you at Kingston."

"No, no! I had to abandon the plan. Now let me go! They're after me!"

"Who is?" Hooper scowled in puzzlement, but held firm to Robert's bridle. "And what about you, Lyon? You're supposed to be at Whitehall delivering His Lordship's gift. What are you doing here with Thornleigh?"

"He's saving my life, you idiot!" Robert snapped. "They're coming! Walsingham's men!"

Alarm flitted over Hooper's face. "Who told you that?"

"Lyon did. And my sister. They heard!"

Hooper frowned, looking at Owen. "Whom did you hear, Lyon?"

Owen had to think fast. He would stick to what Kate had said. No other lie was possible. "Walsingham himself. At Lady Thornleigh's house. Lord Burghley was there. Walsingham came and told him they were about to make arrests and he named names. Thornleigh was one." He was talking quickly. His best bet was bluster. "Now let us pass! There's a ship at Galley Wharf that'll take him to safety. Come on, Thornleigh."

Robert ordered Hooper, "Yes, *move*, you blockhead!"

Hooper ignored Robert and kicked his horse a bold step forward to block Owen's escape. "Not so fast."

Owen looked him in the eye. "Do you want Thornleigh's arrest on your head? Don't risk it. His Lordship would carve out your liver and eat it."

Hooper's eyes narrowed in suspicion. "You heard Walsingham say this? Today?"

Robert cursed in frustration. "Are you deaf, man? Of course today!"

Hooper's gaze had not left Owen. "Walsingham's in Canterbury. Rode there yesterday. And Lord Burghley fell sick with a flux last night at his home in Cheshunt. Hasn't left his bed all day."

There was silence. Owen heard his own pulse throbbing at his temples.

Robert was staring at him, his face blank with bewilderment. "Lyon? What does this mean? Kate heard something . . . didn't she?"

Owen's tongue felt thick in his throat. He would not implicate Kate. It would do no good in any case. Her story lay in shreds.

Burkitt, the beggar-spy, spoke up from the encircling pack, his tone full of suspicion. "Lyon's the one that turned over Rankin last month. In His Lordship's hall, remember?"

Rankin, the porter, Owen realized. Matthew's double-dealing agent. The one Northumberland had drowned.

Hooper looked irritated at the interruption. "What's Rankin got to do with it?"

"His Lordship had his things searched, remember?" said Burkitt. "'Cause Lyon said to look. They found a purse of coins and a letter, and that's what sealed his death." He glared at Owen. "I always wondered why Lyon said to search his things."

They were all watching him, all suspicious now. "So he did," said Hooper. "How did you know Rankin would have that letter, Lyon?"

"An educated guess," Owen answered steadily. "I look out for His Lordship's interests with vigilance."

"Or maybe with a reward in mind. Walsingham's gold. Is that whom you're working for?"

"I serve His Lordship the Earl of Northumberland, same as you. And," he added, making it a threat, "you know he values me. If you value your own hide you won't interfere in matters you don't understand."

"I know this much. You're a lying bastard."

Owen knew that glint in the man's eyes. Like a dog that smells blood. He looked for a way to bolt. But now they were all alert for any move from him.

"Lies!" Robert cried. His eyes bored into Owen's in fury. His face darkened, the darkness of hatred. "All lies—" The words seemed to choke him. "No one is coming after me. You lured me. You and Kate. I can't believe it . . . my own *sister*—" His voice broke.

"No, I made her say all that. I knew you'd listen to her. I convinced her we had to get you out of the country for all our sakes. For His Lordship, for all of us." He looked at the other men, hoping to coax them to his side. "I wanted Thornleigh out because he's not up to the job. He's a fool, a hothead. He's going to make a slip and get us all arrested."

"What was your plan?" Robert's voice was strangled, his face white with rage. "Get me into the shadows of the wharf and cut my throat?"

"No. There *is* a ship." Owen appealed to the others. "That's the truth, my friends, so help me God. Captain Halter of the *Nancy Willoughby*. He's expecting Thornleigh. His ship's bound for Funchal. Portugal. Thornleigh will be out of the way there. Safer for us all."

He looked from face to face, into the eyes of men he had lived with for almost a month, willing them to believe him.

❧ 22 ❧

Red Moon

Kate steadied herself against a yew tree on Tower Hill. Breaths sawed her throat, raw from her haste, her fear. Her legs felt spongy from shock. Robert . . . with five other men on horseback! They had taken Owen. Marched him into a stand of trees. Moonlight whitened the grass to a frost, but did not penetrate the huddle of trees. It was a shaggy darkness spiked by a tangle of brambles.

Who were they? Why was Robert with them? Her mind was a roaring blank. All she knew was that Owen was in trouble. *My fault . . . my fault! I made him come!*

She relived the events of the last few minutes, as if by halting them in her mind she could change the terrible thing that was happening.

"Where are you going at this time of night, my dear, all alone?" Marie de Castelnau had asked.

Kate had forced a pleasant smile. "Oh, I am not alone. My husband is with me. He's just ahead, but didn't see me stop. Please excuse me, I must make haste to join him."

And she had carried on along Hart Street to catch up with him and Robert riding south on Seething Lane. Five horsemen had galloped past her. She saw them turn down Seething Lane. Nervously alert, she followed them. When she reached Tower Hill she saw with a lash of dread that they had surrounded Owen, an aggressive encirclement. And Robert had joined them! Stunned, she had held back. They had not seen her. They took Owen in among the trees, all of them still mounted except him. When they disappeared into that darkness she slid off her horse and tethered it to a bush, her hands trembling. She crept to the yew. Now, pressed against its knotted bark she strained to hear the men. Low words, like animal growls—too faint to tell what they were saying. Then a louder voice. Robert's.

"Whom do you report to?"

Silence.

"Tell me! Who? Who knows about me?"

Low words from Owen. She could not hear!

Robert's voice rose. "Speak now, you double-dealing heretic, or never speak again."

A faint curse from Owen. A rising confusion of voices. "Pull out his tongue," Robert ordered. "You won't need it, Lyon, if you won't speak. So tell me. Now!"

A cry from Owen. It ripped Kate's heart. She thudded her forehead against the tree to keep herself from rushing to him. She wanted to run in screaming her fury. But against six men? She would not get past the first.

She twisted around, looked toward Tower Street. Houses there. People. Run—get help! She pushed off from the yew tree, about to race to the nearest house, when a horse bolted out from behind her. She froze. The horseman pounded past, bent over the animal, oblivious to everything in his headlong dash.

Kate's heart sprang into her throat in joy. *It's Owen! Escaping!*

But . . . *was* it him? Moonlight washed the figure white as a ghost. She could not tell. No one followed him.

An explosion of hoofbeats. Horses crashing through the wood. But not toward her—the opposite direction. The rumble of hooves broke out past the trees, became muffled, then faint. The men were riding north.

She held her breath. Had they *all* gone? Silence. In the distance a dog barked. From the houses on Tower Street came a faint trill of music. A flute. A spirited tune.

Wait, she told herself. *Be sure.*

But she could not wait. She had to know.

She moved into the trees. The naked branches cut the moon-light into a jagged netherworld of light and dark. Hard to see. She stumbled on a tree root. Brambles snagged her skirt, her sleeve. A horse snuffled. Kate twisted around. The animal was a silver chestnut, a white blaze down its nose. Owen's horse. Kate's heart plunged. The rider who had dashed past her was not him.

She softly called his name. "Owen?"

No answer. *Did he get out on foot? He's so clever, he surely found a way out.* "Owen?" The silence crowded into her ears. *Yes, he got away! That's why they all rode off—he escaped them!*

Ahead something glinted on the ground. A rivulet, black as night. It snaked out at the base of a tree. Kate approached. A cold-ness squeezed her heart.

She rounded the tree. Her heart stopped.

Owen lay on his side, hands trussed behind his back. Blood blackened his open mouth. His tongue . . . hacked off. Blood blackened his throat . . . slashed.

Later, she would remember the savage colors. Silver blades of moonlight in his open eyes. Gold bubbles of moonlight in his blood. Blood-red vapor behind her eyes when she cast a wild, sightless glance at the moon. Blue-black pain in her chest where her heart thrashed like a caged beast.

She would not remember thudding to her knees. Pressing her sleeve against his throat as if it might seal up that obscene gash. Gasping for breath between the sobs that choked her. Grief and rage warring inside her like molten steel, shooting hot vomit up her throat. Heaving on all fours . . .

All she would remember was her stick-pale fingers shaking as she closed his eyes . . . fingers cold against his still-warm skin. And her words to Marie ricocheting in her skull: *I am not alone. My hus-band is with me. I must make haste to join him.* Words that would tor-ture her until her dying day.

The notes of the flute on Tower Street flitted like bats across the barren waste ground and looped through the brambles.

Music. Robert's letter scythed through her battered mind. *Look for joyful news the day after St. Crispin's Day. It will reach you as sweet music. . . .*

She dragged herself to her feet, swaying as the truth cut into her. The man who had galloped past her was her brother. Owen's murderer. On his way to make another kill.

❧ 23 ❧

To Kill a Queen

The snow had stopped, but a cold wind had risen. It kicked up choppy waves that hacked at the bow of the wherry. Kate sat shivering in the stern, one hand gripping the gunwale, her knuckles as white as the moonlight. She had abandoned her horse on Tower Hill. Riding through the city would take too long. She was not a skilled horsewoman; Robert was. Riding fast, he would soon reach their grandmother's house. Kate's best hope was the river.

She had walked west on Thames Street, then down to the water to hail a wherry at the first landing past the bridge, the Old Swan Stairs. She had moved in a daze, her limbs stiff, her mind narrowed to a tunnel. *Think of what has to be done, nothing else.* If she let herself think, let herself see again Owen's gashed body lying in the darkness, the earth soaking up his blood, she would sink to her knees and wail like a soul deranged. She fought back scalding tears, a struggle that squeezed her breath like a hand at her throat. She would not weep. Not yet.

The wherryman, plying his oars, anxiously eyed her disheveled hair, her bloodied sleeve. Owen's blood . . . still damp from her wild effort to stanch his blood. She stared back at the wherryman and made no move to cover the stain with her cloak. What did it matter. Nothing mattered now except the mission. She was not acting for England now or even for the Queen. She was doing this for Owen. She would stop his killer.

She did not know how she would do it. Not yet. Robert was on his own murderous mission and had become such a monster he might kill her, too. She knew only that Owen lay dead because of her. It was a weight so crushing she could not imagine living with it. She would welcome death. Her words to Marie de Castelnau pulsed in her head: *My husband . . . I must make haste to join him.* But first she had to stop her brother. If she was not already too late.

"Hurry!" she ordered the wherryman. She yanked the purse from her cloak pocket and tossed it at his feet. "Row faster and it's yours. All of it."

His eyes went wide at the windfall. "Aye, mistress!" He doubled his effort at the oars.

With her hair streaming in the wind, she looked ahead at the highway of black water. The waves punched the craft head-on as if to thwart her, but the flood tide was more powerful and it was with her. She felt as though the sea, with its last gasp, was pushing her toward her grandmother's house.

The city's landing stairs slid past. Cold Harbour. The Steelyard. Three Cranes. Queenhithe. Paul's Wharf. Blackfriars. Temple. Behind the deserted wharfs the lights of London flickered. The wherry passed a poor fisherman's smack struggling against the current, then passed a tilt boat making for Southwark, the male passengers under its canopy laughing drunkenly, off for a night's carouse. Moonlight glinted off the writhing river and grief slashed through Kate as she saw again the blades of moonlight glinting in her dead husband's eyes. In moonlight she saw only death. She would hate and abhor moonlight forever. As much as she hated her brother.

The jumbled lights of London were behind her now. The stately riverside mansions loomed on the shore. Leicester House. Arundel House. Somerset House. The Savoy.

There, at her grandmother's landing! The Queen's barge!

"Faster!" she cried to the wherryman.

He hauled on the oars, wheezing at his labor. Kate saw soldiers of the Palace Guard on her grandmother's landing. She counted fifteen, standing stolidly at their posts. The royal barge bobbed alongside, resplendent with golden prow, glassed cabin, and fluttering red silk banners. Aboard it the Queen's oarsmen lounged on their benches, and their voices carried by the wind, though faint, were relaxed. Kate's worst fear lifted. If the Queen had been killed the landing would be in a frenzied uproar. She was not too late.

Torches on posts lined the water stairs, the flames flaring in the wind, and also lined the path leading up through the sloping gardens. The light glinted off the steel helmets of soldiers posted along the terrace. Kate scanned the grim martial phalanx. They would not let her in. Her grandmother had told her she was not welcome tonight, and the captain of the guards would not let anyone through whose name he had not been given.

Should she land and inform the captain of the danger? But what could she say? That an assassin might be near? *Might* be—how foolish that would sound. He would detain her, question her, and precious minutes would slip by. And what evidence did she have? None. *She* would be the one who looked suspicious.

"Carry on!" she told the wherryman.

"But this be Lady Thornleigh's home. You said—"

"Carry *on!*"

He grunted and rowed on. She looked ahead to the next great waterfront residences: the Savoy, Russell House, Durham House, York House, then the river's scything curve that led to Whitehall Palace. She scanned the property adjoining her grandmother's, the Savoy. A derelict hulk, it lay dark. Unlike the neighboring mansions whose gardens sloped gently to the river, the Savoy stood with its feet in the water, which lapped the walls now at high tide. Once a grand palace, the Savoy had burned centuries ago and been rebuilt as a hospital, but that had been dissolved and the place had fallen into decay. Vagrants were known to camp within its barren rooms.

"There!" Kate told the wherryman, pointing. "Put in at the Savoy."

He shot her a look that said he thought she was mad, but he

obeyed and hauled for the Savoy landing. The moment the bow nudged the stone water stairs Kate scrambled out. "Keep the purse."

The lower stairs were awash with cold water that soaked her shoes. The upper stairs, long disused, were filmed with river slime. She almost slipped as she reached the top and hurried along the landing. The wherryman's oars splashed as he turned back toward the city.

Kate looked up at the black bulk of the onetime palace. The arched river entrance was barred, and rising above it the wall loomed like a cliff face. The naked windows above were dark, but through one on the ground level a dim glow flickered. A dog inside barked. Kate flinched. The barking, aggressive, threatening, rumbled as though from a cave.

At the eastern end of the landing a flagstone walkway led around the side of the building. Kate passed it, hastening toward the adjacent property, her grandmother's. She stepped off the stone landing onto spongy ground. It was overgrown with weeds and low brambles, the spillover from the abandoned garden whose gray stone walls had crumbled to uneven levels like rotted teeth. It was not difficult to squeeze through a gap in the ruined wall. Above it she could see the night-dark roof and chimneys of her grandmother's house. She crossed the tangled garden, passing a collapsed garden shed. Its gray boards were splayed among the weeds and she had to slow down to pick her way over the planks slick with a film of melted snow. She reached the garden's far wall, thankful to find that it, too, had half crumbled. She clambered through a gap, then pushed through a swathe of brambles that pricked her hands and snagged her skirt. Before her rose her grandmother's garden wall of trim red brick.

The wall was higher than her head. She looked to the top where the black sky met a faint glow from the torches of the soldiers on the riverside terrace. Behind her, the dog's barking had stopped. Music, soft as summer wavelets, washed over the wall. Kate imagined the people inside blithely enjoying the remembrance supper. Her grandmother. Her father and stepmother. The Queen. And

Robert? Had he arrived? He had an invitation so the soldiers would let him in. Their grandmother would welcome him. Would introduce him to Her Majesty. And then . . .

Frantically, she felt the wall for a way to climb over: a chink in the bricks, or a thick climbing ivy—some way to purchase a foothold. But in both directions as far as she could see the brickwork was bare and smooth, bleached by moonlight to the color of dried blood.

A ramp? She hurried back to the collapsed shed. Gripping a board, she wrestled it from the clutch of weeds. Splinters gouged her palms. The dog inside began barking again, making her skin crawl. She half expected the creature to bound from the building, snarling, and snatch her ankle in its jaws. She dragged the plank across the waste garden, hauled it up through the gap, then through the brambles. She was breathing hard by the time she got it to her grandmother's wall. Positioning it to make a ramp, she let go the top end and it clattered against the brickwork. She held her breath. Had the soldiers heard? The barking had abruptly stopped as though the animal was straining to hear the noise. An owl hooted in the distance. The dog set to barking again, more urgently than before.

Kate scrambled up the ramp. The board, half-rotted, creaked and bowed under her. Would it hold? She reached the end with a grunt of relief and stepped onto the top of the wall. It was so narrow she had to balance herself with arms akimbo like a tightrope acrobat she had seen as a child. Then, quickly, she crouched lest a soldier see her.

Her grandmother's grounds spread out before her, still and quiet except for the faint music from the house. The rose garden and its treed alley, the knot garden and its pathways—all were dark. To her right the soldiers on the riverfront terrace were lit by the flaring torches. To her left soldiers stood guard in the courtyard that fronted the Strand, the cobbled yard lit by more torches. In between lay the house. A scatter of soldiers were posted along its side, but, as she had expected, far fewer than those posted at the entrances on the river and at the street.

She looked straight down. She had no ramp on this side to ease her descent. The rose garden's perimeter path lay directly beneath her, a walkway of chipped stone. The gardener had left a wheelbarrow. Straightening, she moved a step sideways to avoid it, took a deep breath, and jumped.

She landed hard on the flinty path, pain flaring up her shinbones. Her bunched skirts hobbled her and she almost lost her balance. She crouched again, terrified that she'd been seen or heard.

Silence. Even the Savoy dog had stopped barking.

She hurried into the treed alley that led from the rose garden, making her way to the house. The trees formed a dark, leafless tunnel, their trunks close together, hiding her from view. In a flash of horror she saw again the dark trees that hid Owen's body . . . the ground soaking up his blood . . .

Don't think! Just walk!

She reached the end of the alley and stopped to gauge the way ahead. The perimeter path ran parallel directly in front of her and beyond it rose the house, just a long stone's throw away. The ground-level window to her right was her target. It opened onto the wine cellar. She saw no soldiers along this section of the house.

She darted diagonally across the path and reached the wall. Pressing her back against it, catching her breath, she glanced both ways. No one. She turned and kneeled at the window. Unglazed, it was barred only by wooden shutters. How well she remembered this window from her childhood. When the wine merchant's men delivered the barrels they rolled them down a fixed ramp and she and her little brother would use it as a slide, careering down with whoops like bloodthirsty pirates boarding a prize vessel.

She pushed in the shutters. The stone wall was four feet thick. Through it the cellar lay in darkness. Kate sat and swung her legs over the casement, stretching them to feel for the ramp. When she felt it beneath her feet she pushed off. She slid down into the blackness. Her body was heavier than in those carefree childhood days, her slide now a slow descent. When she reached the bottom and got to her feet a sick feeling shuddered through her. Robert used to stand here with his boyish grin, poised to attack her with a hickory-stick sword. Was he here tonight, upstairs? Ready to attack her with cold steel?

She had no weapon. She had only her hate.

It took a few moments for her eyes to adjust to the blackness. The window was a pale square of moonlight. She wished she could close the shutters, but she needed the light to see her way. She could only hope no soldier would patrol along the house and notice the shutters were open.

She looked around. The cellar was a stone-ribbed, brick-vaulted undercroft. At the far end was a small, dim glow. The air was as cold as outside and tanged with the sweet-acidic smell of wine. The stronger odor was of damp masonry, cold and musty as a grave.

The music sounded louder here. Muffled by the floor, but more pronounced.

Kate made her way past the stacked barrels, making for the dim glow. When she turned the corner she came to its source: a candle on the table of the small room that was the domain of Her Ladyship's cellar man. She had taken a gamble that he would not be here. The wines for tonight's supper would have been decanted earlier. The cellar man, his work all but done, was likely relaxing with a pot of ale in the butler's pantry, on hand in case any change was requested.

Up the stairs she went. As she opened the door at the top the music instantly swelled. She was in the corridor between the kitchens and the great hall. Two servant girls bustling with platters disappeared into the screened passage that led to the hall. They hadn't noticed Kate. She heard the voices of the guests and their soft laughter.

Following the servants along the screened passage, she emerged at the foot of the hall. She stopped. The far end blazed with hanging candelabra above the four diners, who sat at a table covered with a white damask cloth spread with aromatic dishes. Her Majesty glittered in a black velvet gown embroidered all over with silver stars, and pearls glowed in her hair. She was laughing. Kate's father, beside her, was making gestures like a painter's brushstrokes as he regaled her with some tale. The others were laughing, too: Lady Thornleigh at the Queen's other side, and, beside Kate's father, her stepmother, elegant in green satin. Footmen and servant girls moved about, serving food on platters, removing plates, pouring wine. Behind the table, on either side, two guards stood like statues with upright pikes.

No sign of Robert.

Kate stood still, tense and bewildered. Had she arrived here before her brother? Directly over her head was the gallery where the musicians played on, the music so loud she found it hard to think. Robert was coming, of that she was sure. She had to warn her grandmother. Warn Her Majesty.

"Kate!"

She flinched. Her stepmother had spotted her and called to her, smiling in amazement.

Her father cut short his tale and stared at Kate with equal amazement. "Kate!"

"Goodness, Lord Thornleigh," said the Queen in surprise, still smiling from his tale, "is this who I think it is? Your daughter?"

He glanced at the Queen with a look of alarm, then back at Kate, a scowl of mistrust darkening his face. "It is, Your Grace."

Her Majesty's smile turned wry as she regarded the new arrival. "An interesting costume."

Kate was aware of her wild hair, her ripped skirt, her bloodstained sleeve. The look of a madwoman. She stood frozen, in awe of the queen suddenly so near, resplendent. Yet so vulnerable. So human. The focus on stealth that had possessed Kate up to this moment burst. Nothing mattered now except protecting Her Majesty. "Is he here?" she cried, rushing across the hall toward them.

"Who?" Her grandmother was on her feet, angry, mortified. "What is the meaning of this, Kate?" she demanded. "Have you no sense?"

"Has he come through here?" She barged past servants, making a maid holding plates stumble backward. The plates hit the floor, smashing. All the diners rose in consternation, even the Queen. Kate ignored them and made for the two guards. "Has he passed you?"

They grimly lowered their pikes, blocking her way.

"Enough!" her father shouted. He strode around the table, coming for her.

"What's amiss?" the Queen asked her hostess, anxious now.

"Kate, are you ill?" her stepmother asked in concern.

"Brainsick!" her father growled, taking hold of Kate's elbow. "Have you indeed lost your mind?"

"Let me go!" She tried to shrug out of his grip. "Let go! I will find him!"

He held her fast. They were all staring at her. The music dwindled. Maids struggled to clean up the smashed crockery and mess of food. Her grandmother started toward her, fuming. "Out. I will have her out."

That's when Kate saw the movement across the hall. A man with his back to her, quietly opening a door beside the gallery. He wore the tabard of a musician with her grandmother's colors, rose and green. The sight of the back of his head sent a shock through her.

Robert.

He closed the door behind him and disappeared.

Kate threw off her father's hand. She dashed across the hall.

"Guards!" called her father. "Follow me!"

Running, Kate heard him pounding after her and the guards clattering forward. She reached the door and threw it open. A staircase rose to her left. She looked up it, one flight to the musicians' gallery. She bolted up the steps and burst out onto the gallery. The musicians stared in bewilderment at her and at the confusion in the hall below.

She looked behind them, up the three steps that led to the back of the gallery. Robert stood in the shadows at the top, lifting something from a box. Kate's heart kicked. A pistol. The musicians at the back saw it, too. They jumped up and scrambled out of the way, making for the door. Kate heard her pursuers pounding up the steps.

She twisted around at the hip-high railing. The Queen, on her feet at the table, was turning to speak to Kate's stepmother. A clear shot.

Her father burst into the gallery. The fleeing musicians jammed his way forward as they scrambled to get to the stairs. He fought to get past them, the guards behind him. "Robert!" he cried in surprise.

Robert pointed down the three steps at Kate and shouted, "Stop her! She's come to kill the Queen!"

Their father, aghast, broke through the musicians. He reached Kate and snatched her arm. She clawed his face. He flinched as her nails drew blood and she wrenched out of his grip. The last musicians scrambled past him, knocking him back a step.

She twisted around to see Robert. He was taking aim at the hall. With his shot the Queen would die.

Kate lurched forward, her body between him and his target, as he fired.

The bullet slammed into her shoulder, throwing her back against the railing. She was pinioned against it, disoriented by shock. Hip high, it barely kept her from falling. Pain seared her side. She felt the hot wetness of blood.

There was screaming. "Stop her!"

Robert was coming down the steps, reloading his pistol. Their father gaped at Kate, stunned. The guards were still engulfed by the escaping musicians.

Robert reached Kate at the railing. Ignoring her, he raised the pistol and aimed at his target below.

She struggled past the pain. She knew what she had to do. Justice. Death for Robert. And for her. *My husband . . . I must make haste to join him.*

Kate heaved herself toward Robert. She flung her arms around him, an embrace that would carry them both to death. With a sudden, savage wrench she lurched with him, pulling him over the railing.

He screamed as they fell. She saw the wild terror in his eyes. His pistol smashed on the hall floor.

She did not release her brother. She held him tight. Justice.

Owen . . . Owen . . . Owen . . .

❧ 24 ❧

After the Storm

The night's snowstorm had battered London, a December gale that had snapped tree boughs, ripped thatch off poor folks' roofs, and buried churchyard tombstones under snow. Having done its worst, the storm then rampaged east. Londoners awoke to an eerie morning calm.

The stable courtyard of Adam Thornleigh's house lay muffled under its thick, white burden. No breeze clattered the winter-bare branches of trees that had survived the onslaught. All was silent but for the scrape of shovels on the cobbles as servants cleared snow off the walkway from the house, and the quiet talk of other servants picking up strewn branches.

Snow crunched under Adam's boots as he surveyed the damage on his way to the stable, his two greyhounds trotting behind him, sniffing the path. Snow drifts white as stormy sea foam obscured the stable wall almost to its roof where icicles hung like spear tips. Across the courtyard a beech bough had crashed onto the dovecote. In sliding to the ground it had ripped off some roof slates, and the shattered pieces pocked the snow. One of the dogs bounded toward the debris. Adam saw why—a dead dove lay there, its soft body bloodied by the jagged shards. A shudder ran through him. *Kate.* He saw again the horror of her and Robert falling, joined in an embrace, hitting the stone floor. Heard again that nightmare *thud.* Several weeks had passed, but Adam relived that terrible moment every day. The image of them falling was branded on his mind. His children. *One dead . . . one living.*

He looked up at the cloudless blue sky. Sunshine, bright and strong, was already melting the icicles with a gentle *drip, drip, drip.* The calm was so complete, the sun so blithe, it was as though the world had no memory of the night's storm. *Is that how life is supposed to go on?* he thought bleakly. *Are we supposed to just forget?*

The dog had the dead bird in its jaws. "Fleet, leave it!" Adam commanded. But his voice didn't come out as he'd expected. He sounded hoarse. Watching Fleet obey and trot back to him, he thought: *Three weeks, yet I still don't sound like myself.*

He met Lundy, the captain of his troop, inside the stable. Lundy was brushing his chestnut stallion and the strokes sent dust motes dancing in the filtered light. He was expecting Adam and jerked his head in his customary token bow. "My lord."

Adam handed him a purse heavy with silver coins. "This will cover expenses for the ride to Portsmouth. Leave with the men as soon as you muster them. We sail for Cork on Friday." Adam's new orders from Elizabeth were taking him to Ireland. His commission was to hunt down the rebellious Earl of Desmond, who had sacked Kinsale and devastated the countryside and was now hiding out with his fighters in the mountains of Kerry. Bringing him in would be a challenge, but Adam was not sorry to have a job that would tear his mind off his children. *How could I have been so wrong about Kate? So wrong about Robert?* "I'll ride from Whitehall tomorrow after my meeting with Her Majesty. I'll join you in Portsmouth."

"Very good, my lord." They had already planned this. Lundy needed only the silver.

Adam glanced through the gloom toward the open door. The bright square of cheery blue sky seemed counterfeit, like a showy painted backdrop in a play. "At the ships have Phillips manage loading the horses."

"Aye. He's best."

"And give that new man, Harcourt, some responsibility." A good fighter, Harcourt. Adam could use ten more like him. As if ambushed, his thoughts leaped to Kate. *She always was a fighter.*

Lundy cleared his throat. "Harcourt is laid up, your lordship. Broke his leg in the exercises Saturday, if you recall."

Adam looked at him, chastised. "Pardon me, I'm getting forgetful."

"Understandable, my lord. Grief can do that to a man."

Adam caught the sympathy in Lundy's eyes. It pained him and he turned away. "I'll see you in Portsmouth."

The dogs romped up the stairs to the bedchambers. Adam climbed the steps after them. He needed to talk to Fenella. There was one last thing to arrange.

The dogs bounded down the corridor, always eager to see her. He heard her greet them with a laugh. He came in and found her on her knees, packing his clothes into a trunk with the help of her maid.

"Pack your own clothes, too, my love," Adam said. "I want you to come with me."

Fenella stood, surprised. "To Portsmouth?"

"To Ireland."

"What?"

"You'll be comfortable in Cork."

"While you're out ranging the mountains of Kerry?"

"We'll be together while I'm in the city. The rest of the time you'll be near, at least. Come, please."

"Oh, Adam, you know I'd love to, but we agreed about Kate."

"I've changed my mind about that." He turned to the maid, who was pretending not to listen. "That will be all, Susan."

"Yes, your lordship." The girl curtsied and pattered out. The dogs flopped down beside the hearth where a low fire warmed the room.

"Adam," Fenella said, "what prompted this? We decided I should stay, for Kate, and it really is the right decision." Her eyes softened in sympathy. She caressed his cheek. "This action in Ireland will be good for you. I have watched you these past weeks. You grieve your son too deeply."

He took her hand to halt her caress. "It is not grief." Robert, the son he had welcomed home, had played him foul. Had come close to killing Elizabeth! These wounds were too raw for Adam. He would not speak of Robert. "It is not grief," he said again. "It's horror at how close we came to losing Kate."

"But we did not lose her. She lives."

"Yes. Thank God." She was still at her grandmother's house, recovering from the bullet wound in her shoulder. Fired by Robert. It made Adam almost sick to remember that gunshot. And what Kate had done in the next moment still astounded him. Her sacrifice. When she had seen Robert aim again at Elizabeth she had pulled him over the railing with her, knowing they both almost certainly would die. Falling with him, she had held him tight. He had hit the ground on his back, snapping his neck. His body had saved Kate's. The one good thing he'd done, Adam thought with the biting ache of bitterness and sorrow that never left him these days.

Later, when Kate was well enough to speak, he had learned the extraordinary truth about her husband. Lyon had been a spy in Elizabeth's service! It pained him to remember his antipathy to Lyon and his threat of disinheriting Kate unless she abandoned him, while all the while Lyon had only been pretending disloyalty in order to get close to Northumberland. Kate had known that, and protected his secret. But Northumberland's men had found it out. In Robert's company. So Robert murdered Lyon. And would have murdered Elizabeth, too, if Kate had not stopped him. The monstrous evil of his son's actions nauseated Adam. And Kate's loyalty and bravery had brought tears to his eyes more than once these past weeks. How he had misjudged her!

"So, my love," Fenella said, "go and do your duty and I'll do mine. Mine is a happy one. I shall go today, as we agreed, and ask her to come back to live with us. She is still weak and once here she will need care."

They had indeed agreed to invite Kate home. But that was in the first days after the horror, when he was so overwhelmed with gratitude that she had survived and so racked by Robert's treachery and death he could hardly think straight. Since then, though, he had been thinking hard. He took Fenella's hand. This is what he'd come to say. "I have decided we should not ask her."

"What? Why not?"

"She may not be able to come."

"But she is much better, according to Lady Thornleigh. Well enough to make the short journey here. And once she is here, I promise I shall take good care of her."

"I know that." Just as he knew that he could trust Fenella with anything. But if the conclusion he had reached about Kate was right, it was best for everyone that even Fenella remain innocent of the truth. So he held it back. "I have abused her with my mistrust," he said, "and it may be a long time before she can forgive me. So, for now, let her remain where she is. She is in good hands with her grandmother. There will be time for healing the breach when I return from Ireland. Let her be. And come with me to Cork."

The girl reminded Kate of herself at that age. Thirteen, no longer a child but not quite a woman, and slyly curious. Jane Fowler was her name. She was the daughter of her grandmother's chamberlain and Kate had been giving her lessons from her bed at her grandmother's house. Today, the morning after the snowstorm, they sat at the desk in the library. This was the first time she had felt strong enough to come downstairs. It was a relief to be out of the sickroom where her thoughts had free play to torture her. Nevertheless, she sat gingerly, her wounded arm in a sling and her bruises still tender. She would not defy her grandmother's command that she spend no more than three hours out of bed.

Kate watched the girl read. Over the past two weeks she had set her lessons from the library's volumes: mathematics, geography, Erasmus's *Praise of Folly*. Kate had always admired Erasmus's gentle wisdom. Broadening Jane's education had been her grandmother's idea as a way to keep Kate occupied, keep her mind off her loss. *My loss.* Strange word. As if it were a bracelet or a hat she had mislaid. Not the hole in her heart where winter wind blasted through.

Owen. I killed you. By bringing you to Robert, I killed you. . . .

Reading, Jane giggled. She darted a shamefaced look at Kate. "I'm sorry, Mistress Lyon, but it's so funny!"

Kate managed a small smile. The reading lesson she had assigned was from the second chapter of *The Canterbury Tales*, and who would not delight in Chaucer's wit? "No apology is necessary. Your enthusiasm is a tribute to the author."

Given this license, Jane beamed. "What a lark!" She eagerly flipped back a few pages. "First, Nicholas tells old John there's going to be a huge flood that will swamp the world and he gets him busy building a boat, just so he can get John's wife, Alison, alone!"

Kate remembered her own glee the first time she had read the tale of the crafty young lovers, right here in her grandmother's house. "And does he?"

Jane's cheeks went pink. "Yes!"

"As for that boat, who is famous for building one for a flood?"

"Noah."

"Have you seen the carpenter's guild here in London present their play about Noah?"

"No."

"They portray him as a plain fellow, mocked by his neighbors for neglecting his fields and wasting his time building a silly boat."

"Ah, but Noah knew better!" Jane's eyes then went bright with a discovery. Shyly, she tested it. "Is that the carpenters' theme?"

"It is. Do you think it a shrewd device?"

Jane considered this. "I do."

"Why?"

"Because people watching may think that they, too, have sometimes been mocked, but feel they are right. Like Noah."

"Clever girl." She reached out to point to a passage, but pain flared through her back from her stitched shoulder. She sat back, trying not to wince. "Go on. Tell me what happens next."

Jane launched into the tale's development about the fastidious young neighbor, Absalom. "He's in love with Alison, too, and he comes to her window and begs a kiss. But she wants nothing to do with him, she loves Nicholas. So to get rid of Absalom she agrees to kiss him and she comes to the window, but instead of bringing her lips to his she sticks out her bare behind!" Red-faced, she sputtered a laugh. "And he *kisses* it!"

Kate let the girl laugh and chatter on. It was good to hear laughter. She saw enough sad faces these days. Her grandmother's anxious solicitude, though kindly meant, was sometimes trying. Matthew Buckland had visited several times, but always stiffly formal, standing at a respectful distance from her bed, his face grave, and his affliction, that perpetual bent-head posture, marking him like a mourner. As for Father's visits, he was shattered by Robert's treachery, and his sorrowful looks dragged her spirits down. It was some comfort that at least he now knew the truth about Owen. Matthew had allowed her to confide to him and her grandmother that Owen had been acting in the service of the Queen. But none of her kin knew about *her* involvement. Matthew had been clear in instructing her to maintain silence on that matter.

Jane's voice chirped on, and Kate's eyes drifted to the window seat. There, she and Owen, smiling about Chaucer, had made love. There, the moon had slipped past the casement as though to give them privacy. No moonlight now. Bright sunshine sparkled off the snowdrift that rose to the window ledge, the legacy of last night's storm. Jane's laughter . . . the sunshine. It almost made Kate believe that a day might come when grief, finally, was drained. When nightmares about Robert falling with her would no longer leave her writhing, his eyes wild, his cry in a child's voice, *Kate! Help me!* A day when she didn't wake every morning and remember Owen's blood, black in the moonlight. *I killed my brother. And I killed my husband.* Both were with her every hour, waking and sleeping. On the surface, bewilderingly, life smiled at her. The Queen had handsomely rewarded her for saving her life. A heap of gold delivered in a golden casket. The deed to a rich manor in Kent. A personal letter with Her Majesty's heartfelt thanks. *I have all the wealth Owen wanted to give me,* she thought in misery, *and would drop it in the Thames and beg in the street if it would bring him back.*

"And then . . . oh, Mistress Lyon, it's too funny!" Jane clapped her hand over her mouth to bottle up her mirth, but she could not hold it back. "Absalom decides to get even with Alison for her prank, so he comes back to her window with a red-hot poker to burn her and calls to her, saying he has brought her a golden ring and he'll give it to her for one more kiss. But then Nicholas decides to make Alison's prank even funnier and he puts *his* bare behind out of the window, right in Absalom's face . . . and lets fly a fart!" She let out a snort of laughter that sent mucus flying, speckling a swathe of the desk. "Oh!" she said, mortified. "I beg your pardon, mistress!"

Again, Kate had to smile. "Wipe that up with your handkerchief, Jane, but do not rue your pleasure. 'The Miller's Tale' has made folk laugh for a hundred years and I daresay it may for a hundred years to come."

Voices sounded at the front entrance of the house. The library door was open and through it Kate saw Matthew crossing the great hall, coming this way, batting snow off his shin.

She closed the volume. "That's all for today, Jane. Tomorrow, shall we begin 'The Reeve's Tale'?"

"Oh yes, please, Mistress Lyon! Thank you!" Passing Matthew on her way out, she bobbed him a shy curtsy.

He scarcely glanced at the girl, making his way straight to Kate. He had brought a rose-colored muslin bag the size of his hand and deposited it on the desk before her. It was tied with a yellow silk ribbon. "Sweetmeats," he said. "Candied apricots, I believe."

His grave look in speaking of sweets amused her. Practical, businesslike Matthew. "You believe?"

"So I was told. By my sister. She makes them."

His little gift touched Kate. She hadn't even known he had a sister. That gave her a pang. *Brothers . . . sisters.* That drift of thought was painful, and to halt it she focused intently on Matthew's face. His trim, sandy beard. His keen gray eyes. She realized that from her position on the chair, looking up at him, the oddness of his perpetually head-bent posture vanished. Looking down at her, his gaze was like that of any man. Except that today he seemed somehow different. More alert.

"Chaucer?" he asked, his eyes flicking to the volume.

"Yes. I have an apt young pupil. She is much amused."

He gave her a look that was both probing and gentle. But his tone when he spoke again announced that he was back to business. "It is good to see you up and about." He glanced at the window as though expecting to see something there. "How are you?"

"Better. Better every day." A lie. Her body was mending, but her soul, she felt sure, never would. Both were beyond her control.

"Good. It's time for you to leave."

"Leave?" His statement, out of the blue, surprised her. "Why?"

He went to the door and closed it. Coming back, he looked more serious than ever. "It's not safe for you here. They know about you."

Now she understood. "Northumberland's men, you mean." She had already thought about the problem. Robert would have told them, that night on Tower Hill, that she had enticed him to flee with the lie that the Queen's men were after him, so they likely now considered her a spy. When they'd discovered Owen was a spy they had killed him.

"And Mary's," Matthew said pointedly. "We have to assume that word has reached them. So you cannot stay here. It's too dangerous."

Kate shook her head. "It's been several weeks. If they wanted to kill me, they would have sent someone to do it by now."

"We cannot know if that is true."

"Goodness, Matthew, I live and breathe. What more proof do you need?"

"That is not proof that they did not come. I took measures."

"What are you talking about?"

"I have had this house surrounded, watched night and day."

She stared at him, amazed. She'd had no idea.

"Twice," he said, "my people turned men away, strangers who could not account for themselves."

"Strangers? You mean . . . assassins?"

"I believe so. I had both men followed. They melted into the tenements of Blackfriars. We are watching them still."

She felt a fool. And very lucky. "You . . . saved my life. Twice."

His earnest eyes held hers. "I told you, Kate. I will always take care of you."

The warmth in his voice tugged a memory of Owen. His voice. His swagger. His love. Tears threatened, hot pins at the back of her throat. She looked away, unwilling to weep in front of Matthew. If she did she might lose control.

"You mourn Lyon," he said quietly. "Believe me, so do I."

She could not hold back the grief. "I killed him, Matthew! He warned you about my brother, sent you word that he'd seen him visit Northumberland. Owen told me. But I didn't listen to him. I sent you that hasty message that Robert was loyal, had been sent by my father to report on Northumberland." She groped for his arm and shook his sleeve, impotent with anguish and self-fury, as if by shaking him she could erase her sin. "If I hadn't done that you would have stopped him and Owen would still be alive!"

"No, Kate. You are not at fault for that message." He lifted her hand from his sleeve and his fingers closed around hers to still her. "Listen to me. I may not always be free to tell you everything, but what I do tell you will always be the truth. And the truth is, I paid no heed to your message. I was already watching your brother. I had decided to leave him where he was."

"What? Leave him . . . ?"

"I hoped he would lead us to Northumberland. Or even all the way to Mary. But I misjudged how dangerous he was. *You* found that out. And *you* stopped him. Good God, you were ready to *die* to stop him." He squeezed her hand. "Truly, you are a wonder."

She stiffened. She deserved no such praise. And she realized that his judgment to leave Robert in place was a tactic she should have foreseen. Yet it did not change anything—his decision did not absolve *her*. She had killed Owen, and that was a wound that would bleed forever. But the earnest light in Matthew's eyes was genuine and she was grateful for his kindness. It occurred to her that he was the only person she had been completely honest with. During his previous visits she had told him everything: her appalling, blind faith in Robert, and her fatal decision to withhold from Owen her suspicion of Robert's murderous design on the Queen. Matthew should despise her. That he didn't—that he seemed, in fact, to understand—gave her a bleak touch of comfort.

Voices sounded in the hall. Matthew looked sharply at the door.

"The servants," she reassured him. "Preparing for dinner."

He turned back to her. "Two strangers coming near you is two too many. I could not move you when you were so ill. But now, you must leave."

She nodded. "Yes. You need to employ your men more productively than in watching this house. I'll go." She looked up at him, feeling suddenly at a loss. "But where? I cannot go to my father's house. Or even my aunt's. Those are the first places Northumberland would look. Besides, it could put my kinfolk in danger."

He frowned. "Do you imagine me so unprepared? I have arranged a safe house."

"Ah. Where?"

"A remote hamlet in the highlands of Scotland."

Scotland! She tried to conceal her dismay. This was banishment! But she made no protest. She had brought this on herself. In justice, she deserved far worse, deserved a prison cell. She swallowed and told herself to accept her lot. "Very good. I promise I shall live so quietly no one will notice I'm there. In truth I shall be glad to do so, and to give you no more trouble."

He smiled and shook his head as though indulging a backward pupil. "You really do not know yourself." He glanced at the volume of Chaucer as though it might be a witness for his argument. *The Canterbury Tales.* He laid his hand flat on the book. "Is there anything more English than Chaucer's folk? You have much in common with the author, Kate. Like him, you love England. I know you. And I—"

He seemed to catch himself, as if anxious he had said too much. When he spoke again it was calmly and deliberately, to give instructions. "You sail tomorrow night. The ship is Danish, its captain English. It will call in Hull and Newcastle, then Dundee, Scotland, where you will disembark. You will be met by my agent, who will take you inland. The safe house is the home of a crofter and his wife. He is a cousin of my sister's husband. You will join his modest household as a widowed relation. You will maintain that identity and live quietly indeed, going nowhere, seeing no one, until I send you word."

She felt a tingle at the back of her neck. "Send word? To what purpose?"

"That it is time for you to slip back into England and resume doing your job."

Her thoughts tumbled, eddied, would not cohere. "I . . . do not think I am able. I have misjudged things so badly. Besides, my shoulder—"

"Will heal. And we have all made mistakes. Kate, I know you have been laid low, both in body and in spirit. But it is time for you to rally. England is in danger. Your brother was not the only one of his faction I left in place. Fortescue has been in contact with a young Catholic named Babington who has ties to Thomas Morgan. My lord Walsingham has kept a watch on Babington and we suspect the foulest of plans."

She felt a prickle of dismay, but was not surprised. "Their target is Her Majesty?"

"Yes. If they succeed in murdering her you know what will follow. The Catholic gentry will be emboldened to arm their tenants to rise up. The royal council will prepare the realm for war. Orders will go to the governors of the Welsh borders and Ireland to prepare for insurrection. Here in London the city militias will muster, unprepared as they are. There will be panic. The realm, rudderless without our monarch, will see government cease as we face riot, rebellion, civil war, and invasion. Because that moment when we are at our most vulnerable is when Philip of Spain will strike. His troop ships, swollen with battle-hard German mercenaries, will march through Kent. Our countrymen will skirmish with them and be cut down. The invaders will march on to London. Within a week the city will fall. England will belong to the King of Spain. Kate, we must do our all to prevent that catastrophe. We are the bulwark against it, you and I and all who love our country. I need you back. England needs you."

He fell silent, waiting for her response. Still, she could not order her thoughts, her feelings. She felt so unready!

Voices sounded beyond the door. Women's voices. "My lady grandmother," Kate said distractedly. "She may ask you to stay to dinner."

He frowned, annoyed. "Dinner? I cannot think of dinner. Come, give me your answer. What say you?"

She had never seen him so keyed up, though still deliberate, resolute. Just like the first time she had met him, at her father's house over an evening game of cards. He had recruited her almost before she knew it.

She knew more now. Knew the dangers, and the stakes. And knew, beyond her troubled thoughts, what that faint tingle at the back of her neck was. A longing to be active. A longing for justice. For Owen's sake.

She had to smile. Matthew had recruited her again.

She rose from the chair, forcing herself not to flinch at the pain in her shoulder. Matthew was taller, and even with his bent-head posture they stood eye to eye. She felt the bond between them. Honesty. Solidarity. Purpose.

It was enough.

"What is this Danish ship's name?"

The Custom House quay looked ghostly in the moonless dead of night, but the seamen loading cargo aboard the merchant ship *Katten* were loud and lively. Under lanterns hung in the rigging they hefted crates and rolled barrels and slung sacks, lowering them through open hatches into the holds.

Kate stood by the mainmast, obscured in the shadows of stacked crates, and gazed out at the flickering lights of London. Matthew's instructions had been to get belowdecks immediately and stay there until the ship was out in the estuary, but she felt she had to have this last look at the city she loved. Soon she would be heading into an unknown world of Scottish strangers. She did not understand the language of the Danish seamen tramping past her, intensifying her isolation. The English captain had spoken only a few gruff words to her before stomping away, cursing the pilot who had not yet come on board. The ship could not leave without the pilot.

Kate shivered in the night wind edged with December's steel. Christmas was coming, her first Christmas without kin, without friends. She had told her grandmother the story she and Matthew had agreed on: she was going to France to visit a friend in Toulouse, to recover from her wound and her grief. Her message to her father and stepmother had told the same tale. That had been hard, leaving them without saying good-bye. *Stealing away like a thief in the night,* she thought. Like the last time she had left London, dragged away by Mother. With Robert.

No, she told herself sternly. *This is different, this time I go willingly. There is important work to do. I will heal in Scotland and be ready for Matthew's summons.* This last look at home gave her a pang, but in that pang was something bracing. *I am leaving England so I can come back and* help *England.*

Yet her inner sermon did little to cheer her bleak spirits. The wind keened in the rigging above her, making the lanterns sway. She hugged herself for warmth. Come dawn it would be warm in the bakehouses along Thames Street, she thought, gazing at the winking lights of the city. On London Bridge to her left, so near she could see the torches at the northern arch waver in the wind, there would be the banter of traders as the sun rose. At the Tower looming to her right the guard would change, and the night watchmen, cold and weary, would head home for a warm bowl of porridge. The taverns and shops, the breweries and the companies' halls would be warm with the season's good cheer.

A seaman was coming up the gangway from the quay. Her eye was drawn to him because of his slow pace, head down, so different than the briskly moving crew. He wore heavy sea boots, a scarred leather jerkin, homespun breeches the color of mud, and a floppy hat that covered his forehead and eyes. He seemed older, a veteran, independent, taking his time. Was this the tardy pilot the captain was waiting for? If so, they would soon be underway. She turned to look for the captain. Last time she saw him he was berating a crewman on the quarterdeck. Not there now.

When she turned back the veteran seaman stood right in front of her. She gasped. "Father!"

"Shh!" he warned, a finger to his lips. He jerked his chin toward a recess among the stacked crates.

She was stunned, but took his lead and stepped farther back into the shadows. He came with her.

"Kate." His voice was warm, urgent. "I could not let you go without saying good-bye."

Her heart leapt. She had never been so glad to see anyone! "But
. . . how did you know I was here?"

"I am an old hand. I know these quays." He glanced around.
The crew tramped past, oblivious. He turned back to her. "They
tell me this ship sails for Scotland."

Caught in her lie, she could not think what to say.

He held up his hand as if to forestall her reply. "I don't know
why you are going there. I know it's best that I do *not* know. Best
for you, for everyone. I only want to tell you how proud I am of
you. Because I know . . . well, I suspect . . . the thing you cannot
tell me."

Her breath caught. *He knows.*

Shouts came from the foredeck.

Her father stiffened. "They're readying to cast off. I must go."

No! There was so much to say! "Father—"

Before she could speak another word he grabbed her hand,
placing on her palm a small metal object. In the gloom she could
not make out what it was. She took a step out into the feeble light
of the lantern.

"A captain's whistle," he said, coming to her side. "Pure gold.
Her Majesty gave it to me years ago. It replaced mine of staghorn,
which she had taken from me with these words: 'I shall treasure it
always, to remember what you risked for my sake.' I give you this
now, Kate, deeply mindful of what you are risking for *all* our
sakes."

Tears shot to her eyes. She threw her arm around his neck. "Father."

He held her. "God be with you," he murmured.

More shouts. Boots stomped behind Kate. She turned.

"No passengers on deck, mistress." It was the captain, coming
toward her. "We're getting under way."

"In a moment," she insisted. "You have not your pilot yet."

"Aye, he's just come aboard. Stewed, but aboard. So get yourself
below now, if you please."

"Wait, I . . . I have orders for my serving man here before he
goes."

He frowned, looking about. "What man?"

She turned. Her father was gone.

She scanned the gangway for him, and the quay. No sign of him. She was alone. She raised her eyes to the city, its flickering lights, its dark roofs and towers. The black sky above.

But the night no longer felt cold. She turned to go below. Smiling inside, hoarding her father's words, she held the golden whistle tight, warmed by the small flame of happiness he had kindled in her heart.

Q&A WITH BARBARA KYLE

The Thornleigh series focuses on the Tudor era. What drew you to this time period?

One of the most intriguing characteristics of the Tudor period is its predominance of women rulers—from Mary I, known as "Bloody Mary" in her own time, to her half sister Elizabeth I, who ruled so cleverly for forty-three years, to their cousin Mary, Queen of Scots, whose life was as dramatic as an opera. My Thornleigh books have featured all three.

Also, the Tudor era fascinates me, and so many readers, because the actions of these larger-than-life personalities like Elizabeth and her father, Henry VIII, had a tremendous impact on the people of England and the world. One example is Henry's extraordinary creation of a national church just so he could divorce his first wife and marry Anne Boleyn. Another is Elizabeth's famous rivalry with Mary, Queen of Scots, keeping her under house arrest for nineteen years and eventually executing her. And then, of course, there was Elizabeth's brave stand against the mighty Spanish Armada, and England's amazing victory.

I call crucial events like these the "hinges of history" and I set my Thornleigh books during these times to test my characters' mettle as they're forced to make hard choices about loyalty, duty, family, and love.

Your books are unusual in the world of historical fiction, in that you created fictional characters to take center stage alongside the historical figures. How did this affect your research?

I'm meticulous about being faithful to the historical record whenever my fictional Thornleigh family members interact with real people of the day. From my research I'll know, say, what Queen Elizabeth did in 1554 and where she did it, and around that I weave the activities of my created characters. For example, *The*

Queen's Captive begins with twenty-year-old Princess Elizabeth's captivity in the Tower of London at the command of her half sister, Queen Mary, and Elizabeth's terror that she would be executed—all true—and into that crisis I bring Honor and Richard Thornleigh and their seafaring son, Adam, in their mission to save her.

What traits do you feel women from the Tudor era displayed that helped them? And what hindered them?

Education, in both cases. The royal women in Tudor times were exceptionally well-educated. Queen Elizabeth, for example, had studied Greek, theology, philosophy, mathematics, geometry, history, and literature, and could converse fluently with foreign ambassadors in French, Italian, and Latin. Her writings are elegant and erudite. She was also an accomplished musician. But the vast majority of ordinary women were ill-educated. And all women, even of the aristocracy, were barred from universities and, of course, from all posts of official power: government, the church, and the military.

You have mentioned in interviews how you find parallels between the intrigue of the Tudor/Elizabethan period and our own time. What did you mean?

Tudor England was a time of extraordinary energy that burst out in bold voyages of exploration and a brilliant flowering of literature. But it was also a time when the English people were gripped by fear of invasion by France or Spain, the two great powers of the day. Religious paranoia fed a lot of the fear, since Elizabeth's England was Protestant while most of Europe was Catholic. So alongside the extraordinary positive energy ran a deep mistrust about foreigners, an atmosphere in which networks of spies infiltrated suspect groups, and authorities imprisoned and tortured suspected enemies of the state. Sounds to me a lot like our own time.

Do you find that your background as an actress gives you a different perspective on the writing process?

Yes, definitely. My writing style is cinematic. More important, my twenty years of acting in theater, film, and television gave me a bone-deep sense of dramatic structure, and a focus on getting deeply inside my characters' motivations: their deepest desires and fears. Historians and academics may examine the actions of historical players from a detached viewpoint, whereas actors work from the inside out: the motives that *drive* people to take the actions they do.

What has been your greatest pleasure in writing the Thornleigh books?

Hearing from readers. I cherish every email that readers send, and I reply to every one. It means a lot to me when people take the time to let me know that they've enjoyed the books and how the Thornleigh family's challenges, sufferings, and triumphs have moved them. That interaction—connecting with the readers I write for—makes my work a joy. I invite readers to get in touch through my Web site, www.BarbaraKyle.com, or to follow me on Twitter @BKyleAuthor. I'll happily reply.